F   Carroll, James,
Carroll   1943-

          Secret father.

DATE			

Secret Father

Books by James Carroll

MADONNA RED

MORTAL FRIENDS

FAULT LINES

FAMILY TRADE

PRINCE OF PEACE

SUPPLY OF HEROES

FIREBIRD

MEMORIAL BRIDGE

THE CITY BELOW

AN AMERICAN REQUIEM

CONSTANTINE'S SWORD

TOWARD A NEW CATHOLIC CHURCH

SECRET FATHER

Secret Father

James Carroll

Houghton Mifflin Company
BOSTON · NEW YORK
2003

For information about permission to reproduce selections from
this book, write to Permissions, Houghton Mifflin Company,
215 Park Avenue South, New York, New York 10003.

Visit our Web site: www.houghtonmifflinbooks.com.

Library of Congress Cataloging-in-Publication Data
Carroll, James, 1943–
Secret father / James Carroll.
p.   cm.
ISBN 0-618-15284-9
1. Americans — Germany — Fiction.   2. Runaway teenagers — Fiction.
3. Fathers and sons — Fiction.   4. Berlin (Germany) — Fiction.
5. Male friendship — Fiction.   6. Teenage boys — Fiction.   7. Cold
War — Fiction.   8. Widowers — Fiction.   I. Title.
PS3553.A764S43 2003
813'.54 — dc21   2003041725

Printed in the United States of America

Book design by Robert Overholtzer

QUM 10 9 8 7 6 5 4 3

AUTHOR'S ACKNOWLEDGMENTS

I am grateful to Robert Bly for permission to reprint lines from *Selected Poems
of Rainer Maria Rilke* (Harper & Row). Copyright © 1981 by Robert Bly.

Among works consulted for historical background to this novel, particularly useful
were *The History of the German Resistance, 1933–1945* by Peter Hoffman (translated
by Richard Barry); *Stasi: The Untold Story of the East German Secret Police* by John O.
Koehler; *Berliners: Both Sides of the Wall* by Anne Armstrong; *Cold War* by Jeremy
Isaacs and Taylor Downing; *Wiesbaden* by Wolfgang Eckhardt; *The Fourth and Richest
Reich* by Edwin Hartrich; and *Battle Ground Berlin* by David E. Murphy, Sergei A.
Kondrashev, and George Bailey. In writing this book, I had invaluable support, again,
from my editors, Wendy Strothman and Larry Cooper, and from my agent, Donald
Cutler. Thank you all. And I particularly acknowledge my family — Elizabeth and
Patrick, who inspire me, and Alexandra Marshall, my wife, who sustains me.
I dedicate this novel to her, in love.

For Lexa

Real love, compared to fantasy, is a harsh and dreadful thing.

—FYODOR DOSTOYEVSKY

Part One

1

For Isaiah Neuhaus

I F ONE DAY can mark a person forever, what of two days? Those two days, when I knew your father, when he was young, have marked me since. I can tell you what I know of his story only by telling you the marked part of mine. Your father. His mother. My son. Each life altered, or ended, by events that for you can be a source of indelible pride, your patrimony, a legacy from which to take the measure of all that honors the memory of your father. But these are events that had a different meaning for me, the measure of which, I tell you at the start, is the sadness you may already sense in the space between these words. I have never told this story to anyone. Because your father asked me to, I am telling it to you.

People of my generation, ahead of his, saw so little as it actually was then, as if the Manichean division of the world into East and West, bad and good, gave shape also to our most intimate relationships. An iron curtain ran not just, as Churchill put it, from the Balkans to Trieste, but between those of us who claimed to be grown and in charge and those, like your father and my son, who seemed still so unfinished and, as I thought of them, vulnerable. When Michael was away from me, I often feared that he would get lost, which was my way of fearing, I suppose, that I would lose him. It was a fear I could not acknowledge as being more for myself than for him, because I had yet to reckon with what I had already lost.

What characterized our personal East-West division — broadly dubbed in America a few years later as the generation gap — was that Michael was the wounded one. That was presumptively a function of his longtime status as a handicapped child, but then it also became a matter of my efficient pretense that the loss we'd undergone together the year before was more his than mine, as if what I did was for him, never for myself. Thus, if the world we'd inherited was to be a jungle, I would be Michael's brush cutter, leading the way through impassable thickets with my machete, hacking out a path for him, calling over my shoulder, "This way, son. This way." Not noticing until too late that he had stopped following. That he had disappeared.

This story, which I've told myself a thousand times, always begins with the sixth stroke of the clock, the grandfather clock with the elaborately carved oaken case that I hear ticking now, not far from where I sit writing in my old house in New York City. In our German days, the clock was in the sitting room of the big house the bank had leased — not for me, since five nights out of seven I was there alone, but for the holders of my position. I'd found the clock in a warehouse near the Rhine: all Europe could still seem a flea market in those years, with the fine things of a lost world for sale cheap. I bought the clock, I think, to stake a claim to the timbered mansion assigned to me, and the sonorous Westminster gong wafted through those lonely rooms like the regular greeting of a friendly ghost.

If any house had the right to be haunted, it was that one. It was built after the First World War in Dahlberg, a near suburb on the opposite side of Frankfurt from the factory and rail yard district, which was why it had not been bombed in the Second. After those two wars, Germany was a nation of ghosts, an infelicitous place for a man and a boy yoked together by blood and affection, of course, but also by that knot of loss. We never asked it of each other, but our question was, If she can vanish from our lives, why then can't you from mine?

Five, beat, six. I remember looking up from that day's *Frankfurter Neue Presse,* a newspaper I felt obliged to look at as a way of improving my German. "Improving" overstates it perhaps. In my months in the country, I had come up against a linguistic mental block, and German had so far remained impenetrable to me, a blow more to my pride than my professional performance, since everyone in banking spoke English. All that week, however, I had been especially motivated to decipher the local news. As I lumpishly tracked through the text of a particular story, the clock had struck six. Without being

4

aware of it, I had kept the count, and it was exactly then that the question first rang in my head: *Where is Michael?*

It was late in April 1961, a Friday evening. I looked up from the paper fully expecting to see Michael's shyly grinning face in the archway that marked the entrance foyer off from the sitting room. I saw the tall green ceramic-tiled brazier on the near side of the arch, and through the arch, the mahogany bench onto which Michael would have dropped his bag and his stick. In a trick of a mind ready to worry, his absence supplied a vivid sensation: an image in the vacant air of his lanky, thin frame at a slouching angle, the loose posture of a young man with leg braces.

"Hey, Dad."

Is he grinning? Has he left behind his anger at me? Our first awful fight.

"Hay is for horses," I would have said, a daring echo of what had been his mother's good-humored correction. Humor as a ladder out of the pit of hurt.

But where is he?

April 1961. The newspapers had been full of what came to be called the Bay of Pigs fiasco, the first shocking failure of the young Kennedy administration. There is no way to convey now the palpable sense of danger with which we all lived in those years. Kennedy and Khrushchev were like the cowboy gunfighters then dominating movies and television, men forever on the verge of drawing weapons, but weapons that would kill us all. Political fear was entirely personal, but personal fear, for that reason, could seem nuclear, too. Worry that something had happened to my son, or, if I was lucky, that he was only angry at me, was as deeply unsettling as my fear of what I read in our awful newspapers.

But the news story I had been trying to follow that week was about an event that had taken place right in front of me, as if to warn that even a life like mine could be dangerous. On the previous Monday, I had attended a conference of Germany's major steel producers at Rhine-Main Hall, a new convention center in the reborn heart of Frankfurt. The meeting had been called by the Bonn Ministry for Economic Cooperation. Gathered in a function room were about two hundred dark-suited men, mostly German but also including

European Coal and Steel Community delegates and a smattering of financiers from various countries, of whom I was one. At meetings like this, the language spoken was always English, which was a main reason my German never improved. The purpose was to lay the groundwork for the creation of an ECSC consortium to develop iron imports from Africa.

The third of a number of speakers in the afternoon session approached the podium, a distinguished-looking man who — thin, tall, well tailored, and bald — reminded me of Britain's Prince Philip. I had actually been thinking of slipping out, but the agenda notes identified him as having lived in Moravia for a decade as the representative of Rheinstahl, one of the great German steel companies. He had no doubt been acquiring options on Liberia's inland iron mines, and his on-the-ground experience in Africa set him apart from the other speakers, and I decided to hear what he had to say. At the podium, he opened the folder that held his notes, took a sip of water, and was about to speak when a man appeared from behind a curtain at the edge of the stage. He crossed quickly to the speaker, approaching from the rear, and before the speaker noticed him, the man extended his arm, seeming to touch the speaker in the back of the neck. Then the shot, the first such sound I had heard since the war. It was a tinny noise I did not recognize, since my experience of gunfire had always been outdoors. Then the man fell forward, and an image of the crimson spray had remained with me all week.

Michael, where are you? I am sure it was a Friday, and I am sure of the time, because on Fridays Michael always caught the 4:07 from Wiesbaden to Frankfurt, then the 5:20 from the *Hauptbahnhof* to the Dahlberg station, and then it was a ten-minute walk to our house, even for Michael, whose gait was awkward but steady. This distance he insisted on covering by foot, a point of valiant stubbornness to which I relented because I knew how he hated being taken for disabled when, as he put it once, he was only slow. I knew also that his doctors in New York had encouraged him to walk as much as he could. On that one day of the week, I made it a habit to be home by 5:30 so that I would be there when he came through the door with his *sack und pack* and stick at 5:50.

But quickly I remembered that this Friday was to be different. Michael was to be home at the usual hour, but he was coming back to Frankfurt not by train but by car, my car, which he was driving. That realization made me sit up, the trite reaction of every parent who'd ever overcome a qualm to let a teenager take the car. At the end of the previous weekend, he had made a rare request, asking if he could drive back to school instead of taking the train. He knew I didn't need the car during the week, since my job brought with it a car and driver. And he knew, I think, how pleased I was that he had taken so naturally to driving, despite his handicap. It was the beauty of the then new automatic gearshift — in truth, he'd have had trouble with a clutch — and I'd bought the snappy Fairlane convertible the summer before thinking of him as its eventual driver. The pleasure I'd seen him taking at the wheel since obtaining his license was my pleasure, too. All of this went into his clear assumption that I would say yes.

"But boarders are forbidden to have cars," I said.

"Just to and from Wiesbaden," he offered. "I'll leave it parked for the week. The dorm director will never know."

I saw how he had allowed himself to count on it, which, perversely, may be what prompted my initial no, as if the boy needed a lesson against presumption. Michael was seventeen years old, a senior at the American high school in the charming spa city near the Rhine, fifty miles away. Eisenhower had made Wiesbaden his headquarters after crossing the Rhine, and by our time it served as headquarters for the U.S. Air Force in Europe — "U-Safe," in the argot. The sons and daughters of NCOs and officers who lived in Wiesbaden's several American enclaves attended the school, but not only them. A three-story dormitory also accommodated the teenage children of U.S. servicemen stationed across Europe. And some additional students, like Michael, were children of American civilians with Defense Department connections — NATO-attached tech reps for Lockheed or Martin-Marietta, say, or cigarette wholesalers charged with supplying the vast PX system of the occupation army.

My own DoD connection was thin, and ran through New York, not Washington. I was chief of the Frankfurt office of the Chase International Investment Corporation, a spinoff of Chase Manhattan Bank, which had begun a decade before as a main funnel for Marshall

Plan funds when American investment shifted from governments to businesses. The war had left the Continent starved for consumer goods, and German manufacturers, with the advantage of needing to retool from scratch, had pounced on the market. Those of us at Chase — investing not in the state bureaucracies but in individual entrepreneurs and private companies — embodied the beau ideal of American democracy, what would later come to be called free-market capitalism. So we were frontliners in the Cold War, too, and it did not hurt that returns on our investments were running at thirty or forty percent, which set off a second-stage boom in finance as the industrial recovery of the Bundesrepublik began to fuel itself. We called it the bottom-line blitzkrieg.

People like me, in our recognizably American Brooks Brothers tailor-mades, prided ourselves on having nothing to do with the omnipresent but culturally isolated U.S. military, who, out of uniform, favored Ban-Lons and double-knits. We did not shop in their commissaries, and we did not work out in their gyms. Our chauffeurs drove us in Taunus sedans or Mercedeses, decidedly not Oldsmobiles. And we spoke German — or, as in my case, felt guilty if we did not.

If we had school-age children, they boarded at English public schools, Swiss convent schools, or back home at New England prep schools. Rarely would the child of someone in my position have been a candidate for General H. H. Arnold High School at Wiesbaden Air Base, a putative reproduction of a small-town American secondary school. But it seemed the right place for Michael that year, and as for me, I wanted him close.

When he was little, Michael was a boy who loved movement above all — if possible, on wheels, so his love of driving was no surprise. The first real change in his life came with his tricycle, a Christmas present when he was four or five. It was a machine on which he could demonstrate his true character — his daring, his restlessness, his bright assumption that the earth was flat so that he could go fast. When I would come home in the evening, nothing would do but that I take him down to the basement of the apartment building where storage cages lined a labyrinthine passageway that Michael regarded as his personal racecourse. I recall chicken wire stretched onto lumber frames, naked light bulbs on the ceiling every twenty feet or so, a succession of right-angle turns. His circuit was quick and, with all that cushiony chicken wire, I thought, safe. But near the doorway to the stairwell, one sharp cinderblock corner jutted into his path, a hazard I had never noticed because he always cut by it easily. Once, however, I made a pretense of giving chase, which made Michael laugh and pour it on. As he barreled through the maze now, pulling away, he tossed triumphant looks back over his shoulder at me. He disappeared around a last turn, I heard his crash, and knew at once he'd hit the cinderblock angle. He took the sharp edge on his face, breaking his nose and opening a gash in his forehead from which blood was gushing, as from a pump, by the time I got to him. The sight of his wrecked face filled me with panic and guilt, but he remained calm. Stunned into calm, I thought, but that wasn't so. Michael was in pain, awash in blood — crimson spray — but he wasn't afraid because he was certain that nothing bad would happen to him if I was there.

But I wasn't there some years later, the day he came home early from school — he was ten years old, it was April of 1954. He was a student at the Cathedral School of St. John the Divine, in Morningside Heights. Edie was a volunteer docent — a sort of guide — at the Metropolitan Museum of Art, and she was there when the school nurse called to say she was sending Michael home in a taxi because he had a fever. I was in Washington, preparing to leave for Paris as part of a government delegation. Edie called me that night and described fever, headache, loss of appetite, vomiting. I would have come home, but she said the doctor had labeled it flu and was confident the symptoms would abate in a day or two, and they did. Soon Michael was back to normal and returned to school, and I boarded a plane to Paris. Two days later, Michael's symptoms came raging back, accompanied by the general muscular weakness known as paralysis. I was in a meeting with finance ministers, in a room with extremely high ceilings and Palladian windows overlooking the Tuileries, when an officious clerk interrupted to hand me a telegram: "Come home now. M. has poliomyelitis. E."

I remember being struck by the fact that Edie, not spelling out Michael's name or her own, had spelled out the full Latin name of the disease, preferring it no doubt to the blatantly descriptive "infantile paralysis." I remember also feeling a blast of anger at the injustice of it, since that was the spring of Jonas Salk, and the broad assumption was that the scourge of polio had been defeated. Indeed, Michael would be one of the last American children to succumb.

When I saw him next, it was in a large room at St. Luke's Hospital, also in Morningside Heights. The room contained about a dozen iron lungs, the airtight metal cylinders that encased patients up to their necks, helping the more severely affected children to breathe. By the time I walked into that room, I had done my homework and knew that the virus attacks the motor nerve cells in the spinal cord, an interruption of communication from brain to muscles. Most cases of infection did not rise to the level of diagnosis even, and the virus was shaken off without lasting damage, without ever being identified. Most of those whose symptoms were recognized did not become paralyzed. Most suffered muscle impairment from which the body recovered. Few polio victims were left crippled, and my desperate hope, as I followed the nurse to my son sealed in iron, was that he not be one of those. Let the other children in this room fill out the odds, I prayed with exquisite selfishness. I loved my son with a ferocity that would have exchanged the world for him, to the point of killing it. My son was all there was.

It was nearly midnight, and the room was dark. I had just come from the airport. The hum of mechanized respiration, a dozen unsynchronized motors, filled the room, but the sound registered as a kind of quiet. The children lay sleeping in their cylinders with their heads protruding like knobs, like magicians' assistants waiting to be sawed in half. Michael, too, was sleeping when we came to him, and the sight of his eyes benignly closed filled me with grief. I only then realized what I had been most dreading, the statement in his blank look as it met mine: "If you had been here, Dad, this would not have happened."

"I'm here now," I meant my eyes to say, but Michael, asleep, had no need to rebuke me. Awake, later, he never did. I bent to kiss his forehead and saw the salty residue of a tear track running from his eye down across his temple to his ear. Dried tracks like that marked each side of his face. A stoic child who goes to sleep weeping, unable to wipe the tears from his eyes. So, naturally, I supplied my own rebuke, and it would be as permanent as his condition.

Michael would not walk at all for a year. And without, first, crutches, then leg braces and a cane, he would never walk again. How could we not assume that this illness would forever mark the defining moment of his life, and we did. But only for six years, when the absolute line dividing before from after — mine as much as his — was drawn.

As the nurse in the polio ward said I would, I found Edie that night in the darkened cathedral a short walk down Amsterdam Avenue from St. Luke's. The nurse told me that Edie had been at Michael's side nearly all the time. Only after he was firmly asleep would she go over to the hulking church, leaving the nurse with the impression that she needed to pray. "Your son will need you, Mr. Montgomery," the nurse presumed to say to me, "but so will your wife."

Edie was a confirmed Episcopalian, but she had never been devout, and I could not imagine her on her knees. She loved the cathedral, but in the way American patricians love Gothic spaces. We had been married there, and her father had been a benefactor and longtime vestryman. One or two Sundays a month, she had found her way to St. John the Divine, but for vespers; she preferred the evening service of chanted psalms to the more showy morning communion. We presumed Michael inherited his religious indifference from me, but what Edie really preferred, I knew, were the soaring shadows of night — the feeling of being in Chartres, in the heart of human genius more than in the presence of some divinity. It was no surprise to me that she would seek rest and refuge there.

But prayer? I found her at a side altar, sitting in front of a shrouded statue of what I took to be the sorrowful mother of God. Approaching from behind, not wanting to startle her, I whispered her name tentatively. In truth, I half expected a rebuke from Edie, too. She could be angry and unforgiving, and in our twelve years of marriage I had had my moments of both resenting her reactions and fearing them. *Why the hell were you in Paris when our son got sick?*

But when she realized I was there, she stood and turned to me, her hands clutching at her mouth. She fell into my arms with a desperation I could not have imagined. "Oh, Monty!" she said.

"Monty" was her teasing endearment for me — teasing because she knew that from anyone else I hated it. We were not nickname people — her name was Edie, not Edith — which is why we called our son Michael, and only that. Edie was trying to speak to me, but her sobbing made it impossible. "Monty," she said again, and the only other word that made it through her lips was "Michael." The two names prompted in me the sweet thought that her love for her son and her love for her husband had become the same thing, and I had the further thought, holding her as she shuddered against me, that that was how I felt. What to her was a moment only of unspeakable anguish was to me a revelation of this most basic fact of our condition: one love bound the three of us.

For me, our son's illness, evoking that love, would be an axis around which our otherwise separate lives turned as one life. But for Edie, it would be something else entirely. She abruptly pulled back from me, as if offended by my physical resoluteness. Her eyes were wrecked, bloodshot, foolishly stained with mascara, crazy looking.

"I can't," she said.

"Can't what?" I asked.

"Cope," she said. "Cope with this. I can't."

"Yes you can." I pulled her back into my embrace — not to console her but to avoid having to look into her terrified eyes.

I was right, of course. Edie coped magnificently from then on. She was at Michael's service morning, noon, and night, as his masseuse, his physical therapist, his coach, his tutor enabling him to stay at class level in school. She was his motivation, the soul, ultimately, of his success. Everyone who knew us would admire Edie's stalwart love, and Michael would worship her for it, which he showed by getting steadily better. All of which was more than enough for me.

But in the one thing with which heroic Edie needed help — the thing that nurse had sensed — I was useless. In the cathedral that night she had shown me her terror, and I could not look at it. I could not stand it. Left alone, she coped with it by means of a savage act of will, which left her feeling, I see now, like a woman going through the motions of love instead of loving. She reproached herself for dutifulness, for the rigid discipline of her care, for doing what she could for Michael because she should. All of which, of course, defines love at its truest. But for Edie the former ease of spirited affection and maternal fondness had suffocated in the fumes of rubbing alcohol and the stink of soiled bandages and pus-stained plaster casts and the dead skin of our son's inert legs, as she worked all the while to bring them back to life.

Something inside Edie, it seemed, had turned to stone. The one acute feeling she would allow herself from then on was that of self-loathing, which I beheld clear as day every time she exploded in anger — never at Michael or in his presence; always, apparently, at me, in mine; but, I realized later, really at herself. Unconsciously, she was recruiting me to punish her, and I was capable of exploding back, alas. But even when, as was mostly true, I maintained a relative equanimity, she took it as a signal of my detachment. She angrily charged me with detachment, not from Michael but from her, which was how little she had come to know of me. This was the emotional impasse at which we had found ourselves when the question arose of my transfer to Germany.

As events unfolded, I started the job in Frankfurt at the end of the summer without Edie. The assignment, not a major promotion but the prerequisite to one, had been in the works for months. On the surface, Edie, Michael, and I had all been looking forward to it — the transatlantic passage on the USS *America,* a month's travel across the Continent before settling into the privileged life of postwar American supremacy. But below the surface, our family was in turmoil, stirred by every decision involving Michael. After six arduous years of corrective operations and physical therapy, all organized around his ongoing schoolwork, he was doing well — far better than we'd dared to hope. Walking confidently with his leg braces and elbow cane, working hard to think of himself as other than crippled, our son was, in effect, recovered from polio, and had learned to manage what it had left him with. Edie and I, in our separate ways, had arranged our lives around what he needed from us, but what he needed from us had changed. Edie and I came more slowly to knowing that than he did.

Taking a large clue from him, we had finally settled on a plan that called for Michael's return from Germany to New York in September, so that he could complete his senior year at St. Dunstan's, his prep school in Riverdale, but now as a boarding student. Polio had tempered Michael's exuberant personality, but we were able in the end to see that what others took for shy insecurity was in fact the quiet resolve that had seen him through. We knew that he was ready for life apart from us — knowledge that Edie and I separately resisted.

But now he was a senior at Wiesbaden High School, an hour away from me. We had decided together, in the end, that I would take the job in Germany after all and that he would go too. As it turned out, the jovial atmosphere of a self-consciously American high school — cheerleaders! pep rallies! — was far better for him than the faux cloister of an all-male prep school. His boarding five days a week at Wiesbaden seemed about right, and his coming to be with me in Frankfurt on most weekends did move us to a new, if unarticulated, intimacy. Beginning in the fall, we had formed a habit of taking long Saturday drives in our new blue Ford convertible. We explored the winding roads, hillside vineyards, and hock towns of the Rhineland wine country. We visited half-reconstructed river cities from Mainz to Koblenz to Cologne. We went several times to the Roman ruins at Trier, a small city that had been home to the emperor Constantine and, even more remarkable to us, to Karl Marx.

In November, Michael turned seventeen, the permit age in Germany, and after that he took the wheel more often than I did. The pleasure I took in riding beside him in the passenger seat was, I see now, an unconscious return to the games of wheels that had been such a bond years before. I don't recall ever giving him driving lessons as such, and in Germany there was no question of driving school. Even with those leg braces, his body seemed naturally to know what to do, and his right leg on the pedals was his better leg. At the wheel of a car, Michael's physical grace returned. That Michael was relaxed as a driver relieved me, and the routine of those jaunts soothed us. In the car, especially with the top down, we felt no need to force conversation, and a certain self-isolating silence came to seem all right. It was our silence together. By the spring of that year, in other words, we had each found reasons to regard our weekends as the matter of a mutual compact, not something either of us would violate lightly.

Ironically, it was also then that we began, for the first time, to differ about things, first small things, then larger ones. I knew enough to anticipate mundane teenage moodiness, but the weight on Michael was heavier than that, which I understood. But there were things I didn't understand. The gulf that opened between us came as a disheartening surprise. The silence of our rides, I began to sense, carried an undertone of my son's resentment, which mystified me.

Driving through Trier one day, he said offhandedly that Marx had been misunderstood, and that the only trouble with his ideas was they hadn't really been tried. "That's ridiculous," I snapped, and he shot back, "What would a banker know about the real meaning of Karl Marx?" His direct challenge, offered with the pristine self-righteousness of a committed leftist, so shocked me that at first I could not reply.

"*Deutsche* marks," I then deflected, as Edie would have, "not Karl." But I wondered where the hell this was coming from. Soon enough I would know.

In fact, at the beginning of that week we'd had what you'd have to call an outright argument, sparked by his resentment at my first saying no, he could not take the car if it violated school rules. "Don't treat me like a cripple!" he had blurted, as if my mere enforcement of a rule did any such thing. But the statement stunned us both, and, as he hoped, I suppose, his rare open expression of anger forced me to back off. I let him take the car despite myself, but he had still gone off angry, leaving me to fume even more. I recalled that with horror now, because that was how Edie had gone off.

Michael, where are you?

Friday afternoons at Wiesbaden were marked, as I imagined it, by an explosion of pent-up all-American energy — boys heading out to the ball field, girls in the gym putting up crepe-paper streamers for the sock hop, kids in dungarees and pedal pushers going over to the teen club to feed the jukebox and the Coke machine. I pictured it all from my place at the large bowfront window looking across the garden toward Mosbacher Strasse, and the happy images of young people at play undid me. I took in the teeth a blast of new self-reproach. So Michael wanted to stay over in Wiesbaden and what, go to the big game the next day? Or take a date to the American movie theater at the base exchange? Or — hell — go to that sock hop, even if he didn't dance? And why not with a car? Why had I let that become an issue? And what was it about me that sparked anger in those I loved? Did his failure to show up now mean he was still angry? Was this my punishment for the real offense, which he had dared to name, that I *did* treat him like a cripple?

Michael, where are you?

The clock was striking again, and to my surprise, the half-conscious count I kept brought me to seven. Seven o'clock. It was nearly dark outside. He wasn't here, and he hadn't called. If there'd been a wreck, would the German police have a way of knowing to call here?

The thought of the German police brought me back to the scene in Rhine-Main Hall on the previous Monday, what I had been reading about, what I had witnessed. I replayed it — the intruder coming up behind the tall German, seeming to touch the back of his neck; the hollow crack, the speaker slumping forward on the podium, that red spray. The gunman disappeared through the curtain as quickly as he had come. In short order, the green-uniformed police arrived, the meeting was adjourned, and I returned to my office, where, almost at once, I began to wonder if I had imagined it all.

The dead man had been identified in the program as Markus von Siedelheim, a name that meant nothing to me at the time. The killer had escaped. I gathered from several days' deciphering of the *Neue Presse* and from talk at the office that the police's assumption was that von Siedelheim had been murdered by crackpot revolutionary elements who saw new economic ties between Germany and Liberia as a renewal of imperialist adventurism — or perhaps by rightists who opposed German participation in the recently chartered Common Market, of which the ECSC was a forerunner. The theories made no sense to me at the time, although such acts of political violence would become common in a few years, with the arrival of the Red Brigade and the Bader-Meinhof Gang on the left and various neo-Nazi groups on the right. What jolted me instead was the rank senselessness of the act — it was von Siedelheim's first return to Germany in seven years. In an odd way, the murder epitomized the feeling we all had then of living on the edge of an abyss. That was literally true in Germany, with divisions of Soviet tanks poised to strike at any moment, igniting Armageddon. But the feared violence of the Cold War could be defined by nothing so rational as the later political radicalism, for a kind of moral anarchy had come to undergird the East-West standoff, even if we could not openly see it as such.

If there was a car wreck, I realized, the police would call the school. I went to the foyer, to the telephone, and checking the list that Mandy, my secretary, had typed and taped into cellophane nearly nine months before, I found the number of the hall phone in Michael's dormitory. When the operator came on, I recited it for her in my unornamented German. Numbers I could handle.

The odd, blasting rings went on and on. Finally someone answered, a boy whose accent dropped me back to Mobile, Alabama, where I'd done Navy boot camp as a twenty-year-old, more than twenty years before. I asked for Michael Montgomery. The boy grunted and the phone clattered down. I could picture the handset dropping, slapping the wall at the end of its cord. Bright noises in the echo chamber of the corridor made me see a rough game of keepaway. At last yet another boy — New Jersey? — came on the line to say that Montgomery was a "fiver," as if that explained everything. I knew that about half of the dormitory students — who were themselves a minority in the school — were five-day boarders, routinely going home on Fridays to American posts, bases, and stations within a couple of hours of Wiesbaden. I asked the boy if he was sure Michael Montgomery was not there. He said yes, and was about to hang up. I declared myself a parent, which made him say "sir." He went to check again, leaving the phone to bang against the wall. After another few minutes, he returned to say that Michael was nowhere around, that if he'd stayed over, they would have seen him in the caf at dinner, but nobody had. I asked if there was a dance that night or a big game the next day, and took what I needed from his answer that he didn't know. I hung up before he did. *Where are you?*

Once, at our place in the Adirondacks, Michael and I stayed up late into the night, sitting on the deck of the boathouse with our feet dangling in the lake. He was around eight years old, two years or so before his polio. What kept us up was a sequence of shooting stars. At irregular intervals they crossed the black sky beyond the even blacker silhouette of Mount Marcy. What made the sight doubly thrilling was the way the night sky was reflected in the cobalt sheen of the water stretched out before us, so we could see the stars by looking down as well as up. Every falling star had its twin — until one or the other of us raised a foot to break the glass of the lake surface, an impulse coming, perhaps, from a need to remember which of the realms before us was real. In the rippling water, the stars danced. "Will we ever do this again, Dad?" Michael asked at one point. His profile emphasized the delicacy of his features, the sharp nose he had from Edie, the small knob of his chin that she always swore was mine. The slight upturn of his upper lip could make it seem at times ready to tremble, and it did now.

"Sure," I said. "It's only a matter of knowing when to look." I joined my gaze to his, facing up. Just then another bright dot of light carved its swift arc in the speckled darkness.

Michael jumped. "Eleven!" he announced. He was gunning for an even dozen. Soon he was leaning into me, half asleep. "That's not what I meant. Not about the shooting stars. I meant about doing this with you."

"Sure," I answered too quickly. "Every August."

"Will I still love it?"

"Yes." I pulled him closer.

When, later, the twelfth star fell, I thought of waking him, but then it was too late, and I let him sleep on against me.

I went to the kitchen for more ice. Nicolaus, my white-haired, solemn steward, was sitting on his stool in the corner. He looked up from that week's *Der Stern,* which had Fidel Castro on the cover, with upraised fist.

"I'm sorry, Nicolaus," I said, with a nod toward the oven, where by now the roast would be dried out. "Something kept Michael at school. There's no point in your waiting dinner any longer."

"And you, sir?"

"Why not just prepare a couple of plates and keep them covered. I'll wait to eat with the boy."

"Yes, sir."

"And you can go. No need for you to wait."

"I do not object."

18

Nicolaus never referred to me by name. To others, as when he answered the phone, I was Herr Direktor, and the point had been quickly made that he and I were strictly ex officio. He had come with the house. He and Frau Marpingen, the *Putzfrau,* and Gerhard, my driver, had been taking care of Chase executives for a decade. A thick scar crossed Nicolaus's right cheek and, rising, disappeared in his hair. He suffered the wound, he'd told me, on the eastern front. Once he spoke of Stalingrad, but vaguely. Every time he turned that side of his face toward me, I felt him making a claim. If what Germans told the occupying Americans — investment bankers included — was true, then every Wehrmacht soldier who'd fought in the West was dead, just as no surviving German had ever really admired Adolf Hitler.

I had no trouble picturing Nicolaus's right arm upraised at the infamous angle. If he and his kind hated Hitler now, it was for having lost the war. But Nicolaus kept his resentment passive. He was efficient, talented in the kitchen, and, for my purposes, thoroughly reliable. His only open show of disapproval toward me was tied to my pouring my own whiskey, which I did out of a habit tracing to my father, who used to say it was a way to remind the servants whose house it was.

He was watching me at the ice tray. I realized he was taking the measure of my concern.

"*Die Jugend,*" he said.

My impulse to deceive him surprised me, as if there were secrets to protect. "Just something at school," I said, and all at once the images I was fending off were, first, of a tangled blue highway wreck, and second, of Michael in his iron lung. Then I saw him falling forward, as if he'd been shot from behind.

Nicolaus was staring at me. I turned to leave the kitchen, aware that as I did so, he turned to the oven, to do as he was told before going home.

I went back to my chair in the sitting room, and in the silence, which was total but for the hum of the brazier's fire and the tick of the clock, I sipped my drink. When it was drained, I thought of going for another. Instead, I began a mindless set of rounds, going from vacant room to vacant room, snapping on lights, as if a family lived there and not a man with — what, a missing son?

Missing son. By now I was alternating between open worry and anger, and it was anger that I preferred. *Goddammit, where are you?*

I could not pass a front-facing window without stopping to look out, eyeing the moving forms of Mosbacher Strasse, the flow of cars. I remember lighting cigarettes at those windows, watching the flare of the match illuminate my face in the black glass. That your father was a heavy smoker came to define him, but in those days we all were.

I climbed the stairs. Michael and I could each be in the house without the other knowing, it was so large. When my predecessor had proudly showed me around, I demurred at first because of the size, but then he led me into the walnut-paneled game room on the third floor. A stout mahogany pool table was enshrined below a hanging green lamp. On one wall, the cue rack held a dozen elaborately carved sticks, ash and ebony. Along another wall stretched the scoring string, and in the center of the third was a large fireplace. The tan felt of the table's playing surface shimmered under the cone of light. I took the house to have that pool table, because I knew Michael would love it — a game to be played without strong legs. Was that treating him like a cripple?

Now I racked up as if he were here. I chalked, broke, shot, chalked, shot — running the table once, then again. The noise of the ceramic spheres, one against the others, with the faintly erotic punctuation of the pocket thunks, defied the stone silence of the empty house. The stick gliding through my fingers and the kick in my right elbow at each stroke kept my mind tethered to physical sensation.

Nicolaus had set the fire roaring in the ornate hearth before he'd departed for the evening, as he always did on the Fridays we expected Michael, but it was down to embers before I noticed. I remember consciously deciding not to add a log. *Where are you?*

But by then the question had moved away from Michael. The raw particularity of eight-ball solitaire had failed me. My mind had cut loose from one snapping sequence of sounds to drift, with no leave from me, back to that other: the slamming of the screen door that took her from the summer kitchen out into the breezeway, then into the garage, and another slam. My God, she could get angry! And then into the car — slam! — the rev of which I heard so clearly because I'd followed her for once, this time to apologize.

That memory brought me back to the fight that had taken Michael away on Sunday — "You can't treat me like this!" — and my knees became weak. Have I done it again? The very question made me tack.

I saw her across a narrow gap of the churning water of Long Island Sound. With her hair hidden by her long-billed cap, she was skipper of her father's Lightning, bearing down on mine as we both drove in on the last mark in the last heat of the Manhasset Memorial Day Regatta, a class race that drew boats from all over the Northeast. I took her for a boy as she was shrilly screaming, "Starboard tack! Right of way! Right of way! Starboard! Starboard!"

I refused to head up, exactly as she later charged. At the last second, she fell off, and I took the mark ahead of her, to come in sixth out of more than fifty. She came in eighth, and lodged a protest with the race committee. Her protest was promptly overruled. Where was the collision?

Only at the hearing did I discover that my deadly rival was a girl. I went up to her and apologized, saying that had I known, I would certainly have given way — and she nearly spit at me. Later, at the commodore's ball, I asked her to dance. After blatantly looking me over and tossing the raven hair I had not seen before, she accepted. When she came down to the beach with me, after the band had packed its instruments, I teased her that she clearly wanted to be with a man to whom she could yield, but while feeling superior. She did not find my remark funny in the least, because to her, she said, the inability to rightfully ram another boat broadside was no virtue. She regretted falling off. So where was superiority? It was a point I conceded in all sincerity, realizing that this girl was something new.

We talked for hours, sitting on the sand, staring at the stars. When I said good night, we kissed, and kissed again. Much later, she told me that I knew nothing of a woman's readiness to yield, since she had already chosen to be with me for life, and would have made love right then on the beach had I only pressed. How she took delight, after that, in teasing that I was more timid on sand than on water. All I knew was that with this fierce girl I felt complete for the first time in my life, and I was not about to risk losing that.

Although we had made our home together in the apartment on

Central Park West, and though we continued to spend weekends at her family compound on the North Shore of Long Island, most of my memories are of our place at the lake. Not the lake as it is, a deep blue finger pointing through the north woods toward Canada, but the lake in my mind, which broke free of the good times — Michael and me sitting on the dock at night; taking the cliff walk hand in hand with Edie after the boy was in bed — to become the hazy emblem of what went wrong.

Even the clacking of billiard balls, evoking slams, could take me there. Now the date was May 31, 1960, nearly twenty years after Edie and I met, and nearly one year before the start of this story. We had gone up to the lake for the Memorial Day weekend — me, Edie, Michael, and one of his chums from St. Dunstan's. It was Monday, and the boys had gone out in one of the boats. Michael was a crack sailor, another sport for which one does not need legs. Edie had intended to finish laying out her summer garden, but instead we fell to arguing over God knows what. And the next thing I knew she was hurling at me my having admitted the day before that I dreaded Michael's being an ocean away once we moved to Germany in the fall.

Edie had had her own trouble in coming to terms with that, I knew, but now, with perverse unfairness, she accused me of needing our son too much; "an unnatural dependency," she said, speaking of perverse. I fired back that perhaps now that he was whole, she needed him too little, as if only his infirmity could interest her. It was an unforgivable retort, and I regretted it before the words had cleared my tongue, but it must have plucked the nerve of her self-loathing because it was then that she stormed out of the room and beyond, slamming doors along the way.

Bang! I thought of that sound in Rhine-Main Hall, then put the thought away.

I usually let Edie go when she flipped out like that, but recognizing my own cruelty for once, I went after her — a mistake, because to get away from me, she left the house in her rage, which she had never done before.

By the time I reached the threshold of the garage, Edie had already backed her car out and was swinging it around, kicking up pebbles and gunning away, leaving me staring at the road long after she had disappeared.

I stood there until at last I realized she wasn't coming back. I didn't know yet what would happen, but I already knew for sure it would be my fault.

In the Frankfurt version of that awful scene, Michael did not slam doors at me, but, while driving off, he refused to look back, to return my regretful wave.

Where are you?

2

A T ELEVEN O'CLOCK, from my study, I called the dormitory again, and when a student answered, I asked for the number of Mr. Jones, the residence hall director, a man I had never met but whose name was on the previous fall's welcome letter that I found in my desk. The student did not know the private number, nor if there was one. He said he'd find out, and once again the phone dropped into the oceanic limbo of sounds — harsh laughter, throbbing music, a shout. At last a rough voice grunted its hello, a brusque impatience that made me realize both that this was Mr. Jones and that he had just been woken from sleep.

"I am the father of one of your students, Mr. Jones, and I am looking for him."

"Who is that?"

"Michael Montgomery."

At once the stark silence of his nonreply registered in the knob at the base of my spine. I knew somehow to take his hesitation as the main revelation.

"Michael Montgomery," I repeated, only now with the inflection of demand.

"And you are?"

"Paul Montgomery. His father. I am calling you from Frankfurt."

"Michael is a five-day boarder, Mr. Montgomery. It *is* Mister, isn't it?"

Most Wiesbaden fathers would have been addressed by rank, and I sensed Jones's relief to be up against another mere civilian.

"I expected my son home tonight, and he did not come."

"Well, as a five-day boarder, sir . . ." Jones hesitated, I realized, to summon his nerve. ". . . he wouldn't actually be our responsibility after 1700 hours of a Friday. Not actually."

It was easy to picture him as a short, bespectacled physics teacher, one whose utter lack of physical assurance would prompt such curial devotion to the rubrics of the actual. Rules as a barrier to hide behind.

"I am not concerned with actual responsibility, Mr. Jones. Not at this point. I am concerned with the whereabouts of my son."

Again his silence was a declaration, but of what?

"Mr. Jones?"

"Yes?"

"I am asking for your help here. I expected my son home at six o'clock this evening — 1800 hours, if you prefer. He did not come. He did not call. My son would never not come home without calling me."

"Your son is a high school senior, Mr. Montgomery. They do these things."

"What things?"

"Not come. Not call."

"I get the distinct impression you are not telling me something."

"No, sir. That's not it."

"What is it, then?"

Again his silence.

"Mr. Jones."

"Maybe you'd better talk to someone else. I'd like to help you, Mr. Montgomery, but I'm not —"

I forced myself to wait. Now my mind went to the sound of a bulkhead slamming. I heard it through the bones of my feet, a sound from well below decks. A sensation from sixteen years before, just after our bucket, the *Stephen Case,* took a hit well below the waterline. As exec on the bridge, my job was to keep the glasses at my face, scanning for the telltale trails of more torpedoes, but what I was most aware of were the bulkhead hatches banging shut below against the inrushing sea, as now I worked to seal off the flood of feeling this strange bastard had opened in me. And then *bang!* A gunshot.

"Not what?" I asked.

"Supposed to."

"You're not supposed to? Let me understand. You are not supposed to discuss what you know of a student's whereabouts with the student's father?"

"That is right."

"Look, Jones, I can be over there in an hour. Do I have to come over there so that you can explain to me what is going on?"

"You'd better talk to General Healy."

"What?"

"General Healy. That's all I am going to say. I've said too much already."

"Who is General Healy?"

"National security, Mr. Montgomery. They said it is a matter of national security." Jones's inflection as he uttered that phrase was its exclamation point.

By now, at the dawn of the century's last decade, as I am writing this, the words "national security" seem to have been reduced to weightless souvenirs from another time, like small bits of the Berlin Wall that hawkers have been selling around the world. In the era of the amiable and feckless Mikhail Gorbachev, it is impossible to use the phrase with anything like the punch it carried when Joseph Stalin had emerged in the American nightmare as Adolf Hitler with the bomb, or when Nikita Khrushchev then arrived as a kind of Mussolini, only madder. "National security" had, in fact, been brought into the lexicon by a man named James Forrestal, whom my father knew well from their time together at Princeton. Forrestal was famous as the first American secretary of defense in the late 1940s, although he had been secretary of the Navy during the war, near the top of my own chain of command when I was in uniform. Before that, he had been head of Dillon, Read, a Wall Street investment firm. But Forrestal's own fate — he jumped from a sixteenth-floor window of the Bethesda Naval Hospital in 1949 — reveals "national security" as code for a state of mind that is anything but secure. I believed in it as much as anyone at the time, but now see how it was always invoked, whether by the greatest statesmen of the era or by bureaucratic nobodies like Jones, for the same ends, which were to silence, to hide, and to intimidate.

26

Apparently, my silence could intimidate, too. Jones's voice shook as he added, "They said it was their responsibility to deal with you and Sergeant Carson, not mine."

"Who is Sergeant Carson?"

"I've said too much already. Talk to the general. He's handling the whole thing. He's the one who told me."

"General Healy?"

"Major General David Healy, here in Wiesbaden. I don't think you should worry, because it involves his son, too."

I was unable to get General Healy's home telephone number, which spiked my irritation but soon forced me to stop and think. Instead of caroming like a billiard ball from room to room in the empty house in Dahlberg, I went downtown to my office in Frankfurt's Bundesbank building, a glittering new skyscraper that was a monument to the German boom. Even at that hour of the night, it seemed half the offices of the forty-story tower were lit, with restless German bankers doing business across time zones to the east.

I was there, thinking west, to place phone calls to the States. In those pre-touch-tone days, most transatlantic calls involved two or three operators, often requiring multiple prearranged appointments at both ends, a cumbersome process compared to that made possible by the direct trunk lines that had been put in place for the Pentagon, and that companies like Chase were happy to buy into.

My office was on the twenty-seventh or twenty-eighth floor, I don't remember which. It was furnished in Bauhaus chrome and leather, with the austerely elegant furniture set off by a vast Bijari carpet. At my desk I placed a call to Earl Gifford, expecting he would be just arriving at his Park Avenue apartment, home from a day's work. Gifford was number two at Dillon, Read by then. Perhaps that fleeting thought of Forrestal had put me in mind of him — or was that fleeting thought from now, not then? Either way, the old firm was still a player in Washington. C. Douglas Dillon himself, son of the founder, was Kennedy's secretary of the treasury in 1961, and had the kind of first-order clout that Gifford would not actually have to invoke to wield.

We had served together on the *Stephen Case* in the Pacific. It was Gifford who'd brought me into Chase Manhattan in 1950, before he'd decamped to the Treasury Department in '52. Although he'd come back to Wall Street after Eisenhower's first term — to Dillon, Read, not Chase, because there were no Rockefellers blocking the way to the top — Gifford's Midas touch in New York depended on the gold threads tying him to the alchemists in the Federal Triangle, the chiefs of whom would return his calls themselves. When he answered the phone, all I had to say was "Earl, it's Paul. I need some information."

For the next couple of hours, I sat in the corner of the long sofa staring out the floor-to-ceiling window, the dark sky a screen onto which were projected unbidden images of what I'd lost and what I feared to lose yet. Random scenes of auto accidents and assassinations punctuated my free association, but my mind was tied, as always in such brooding rumination, to the lake; to Michael with his feet dangling; to Edie in her sheer peignoir, lounging under that starry sky in a hammock strung between the pair of giant white pines behind the house. Edie could make that hammock softly sway without any perceptible exertion, her right arm drifting in the air below the perfect curve of her hip. That hammock holding her would swing even without a breeze, even when she was asleep, as if just the earthward pressure of her willowy body were enough to set things moving, which I knew from my own experience to be the case.

When Michael was an infant, I would be the one to go to him when he cried, but only to bring him back to our bed, to Edie. He was the size of a meatloaf, but since he fit in the crook of my arm, I carried him like a football. Edie was always up against the headboard and ready, baring her breast as I handed him over. He took to her hungrily. I would slide back into bed next to them and dreamily watch. Happiness, someone said, is the wish to be what you are. I wished, exactly, to be his father and her husband. When Michael was sated, his face would fall away from Edie's breast, and he would already be asleep. I would take him back to his crib and then return to bed deeply consoled. Edie would dreamily receive me back, transported by love, and we would fall asleep with our heads together. I would sleep as contentedly as if I were the one who had drained my sweet wife of her precious milk.

But more than once, that bliss was changed instantly into horror, with Edie screeching at the top of her voice while pounding me awake, tearing at the blankets. "You're lying on the baby!" she screamed. "Get up! Get up! You've suffocated the baby!" This happened six, maybe ten times in that half year. And every time, I believed it to be true — I had killed our son by falling asleep on him. "Goddammit, Paul, get up!" she would scream, having been transformed into rage itself. *Right of way! Starboard!* It was a rage I'd learned to dread like nothing I had ever dreaded before. "You've killed him!"

And I would leap back, tearing at the blankets and sheets with her, looking for Michael's body, prepared to hate myself as much as my son's mother clearly hated me now. More than once, between us in our frenzy, we stripped the bed naked of its linen. Another time, I continued the search on my hands and knees, looking for him between the headboard and the wall. Always I was first to realize that it wasn't true, that Edie had simply conscripted me into the dark center of her nightmare. I never once fell asleep without having returned Michael safely to his crib. I never once fell asleep with his body under mine. I never once failed my son in that way, never betrayed that part of my wife's trust. In order to convince her that that was so, I would lead Edie into the alcove where the crib stood, so that she could see for herself, although sometimes our frenzied commotion awakened him and he howled majestically, as if some beloved one of his were dead as well; as if he, too, had been thought capable of some heinous deed.

Of course, the words I dreaded hearing, once my relationship with Michael grew tense that year, were "You killed Mom." He had not quite said it, but I heard the accusation in the rough edge of his voice. It was a charge I could not deny, and now I wondered if, after all, Edie's charge that I killed Michael had come true as well.

When I heard the teletype machine begin to whir in my secretary's adjoining office, I turned away from the window, the jagged nightscape of a half-recovered city. I watched as the pink paper rolled out of the machine, and I quickly saw it as an innocuous military personnel file. Then Earl called back to help me read, as he said, what was written between the lines. General David Healy was "Commander of the Joint Intelligence Group — Europe," based at Lindsay Air Station in Wiesbaden, the headquarters of what was called in the argot "J-2." Healy's previous assignments would not seem to have prepared him for such a position. For more than a decade, he had rotated through a series of Air Force operations jobs, most recently as commander of the 3rd Weather Reconnaissance Wing (Provisional) at Wiesbaden Air Base. Gifford told me that when Gary Powers's U-2 was shot down over the Ural Mountains the year before, Healy's phony NASA weather wing had given the glider-like CIA spy plane its cover. Once the weather-plane story collapsed, the NASA wing in Wiesbaden was quietly disbanded — provisional indeed — and Healy had come out of the mundane operations rotation in which he'd buried his intelligence function since not long after the war. Thus, Healy presided over all U.S. military espionage in Europe — everything from photo reconnaissance by air to the dark brutality of secret agents on both sides of the Iron Curtain.

I stopped Gifford in his recitation, alarmed that he was referring to such things over the telephone, but he laughed. "This is from a staffer on the Armed Services Committee, Paul. Senator Javits put in the call for me. If there are classifieds here, they're already out of the corral. Healy was a 'Man in the News' in the *Times* last year, after the U-2 affair." Gifford read on, a summary of a career. London for two years right after the war. Then Berlin for three, Washington for two, Paris for three, and Wiesbaden for nearly five. As theater chief now of military intelligence, reporting to the Joint Chiefs in the Pentagon, he was openly the man in charge of tracking the Soviet battle order in Eastern Europe, even if the "wet" side of his job would never be referred to. At forty-seven years old, he was five years my senior. He was married, with a grown daughter stateside and an eighteen-year-old son, a senior at the American high school in Wiesbaden.

I was in Wiesbaden the next morning by eight o'clock, approaching the main gate of Lindsay Air Station, a satellite military post on the opposite side of the city from the sprawling American air base with its twin runways flanked by dozens of fighter aircraft and midrange bombers. Lindsay, by contrast, was a walled compound of office buildings and residences dating to before the war, when it was a Gestapo headquarters. My driver slowed, approaching the gate. Lindsay was identified in Healy's file as a records processing depot, but Gifford said its main function as a nerve center of U.S. military intelligence was no particular secret. Various buildings housed offices devoted to signals interception, communications security, cryptanalysis, and the management of human intelligence resources — "'humint,' in the jargon," Gifford had said. "What the rest of us call spooks."

"Jesus Christ, Earl. What could my son have to do with spooks?"

"The son of a spook, Paul. Not a spook. It's not the same thing."

I looked over my driver's shoulder to see the compound's buildings looming in the morning drizzle, four and five stories high with steeply pitched roofs and chimneys, all painted the gray-green color one forever associates with the Wehrmacht. The road veered, taking us parallel to a ten-foot wall made of cement blocks painted the same color. Along its top ran a gyre of rusted barbed wire — a wartime vestige, I assumed. The road turned again, bringing us to the gate with its arched entranceway on which was spelled out "H. Lindsay Air Station, the United States Air Force." A flagpole rose above a small guardhouse, the Stars and Stripes drooping in the rain. A figure in an olive poncho stepped out of the guardhouse to halt us with the thrust of a white-gloved hand.

Something in the way the stout black Mercedes slowed to a crawl drew my attention to my driver. Gerhard was a dour German with a deformed right hand, its fingers frozen in a kind of claw that hooked just enough to give him purchase on a steering wheel. A war injury? I never asked. He'd told me once that he had worked as a truck driver for the American military before landing his job as a chauffeur for Chase executives. Thinking of that, I had asked him as we left Frankfurt if he'd ever been to Lindsay. He had said no, but even in the haze of a wet morning, it seemed he'd driven here as if he had, and now he stopped the car on the sentry's dime.

He stared impassively ahead with his window up, so that the American would have no choice but to turn to me in the rear. I was seated on the right side. Gerhard discreetly lowered the left rear window, and the air policeman leaned over to peer in at me. He had an unsmiling black face, but when I saw how young he was, he looked less a sentry than a lost tourist. I reached across to hand him my passport through the window. "I am here to see General Healy."

From under his poncho he pulled a clipboard and matched my

passport to it, a futile check for my name. "I am not expected. I assume you'll let him know I am here." I waited for the guard to look at me. "Tell him I'm Michael Montgomery's father."

He turned away, entered his booth, and put a phone to his face. He soon returned and handed me the passport. He began to recite directions to the general's quarters.

"Tell the driver, please," I said.

Only then did Gerhard lower his window.

Moments later, because of the rain, I left the car at a clip, hunched over as I made my way up the neatly bordered chipped-stone path toward Healy's house. As I raised my fist to knock, the door opened ahead of me. An Asian steward — Filipino? His white coat was uniform enough — stood beside the door, ushering me in. I correct myself: not "steward," a Navy word, but "orderly." And probably not Filipino, either. That, too, was Navy.

Without a greeting, he led me across a polished foyer and into a large dining room. Its most striking feature was a gleaming ebony banquet table at which a man in a light blue shirt and dark blue tie was seated, alone, at one end. Coffee, triangles of toast, and a plate of eggs were spread before him, along with a sheaf of loose pages on which I glimpsed, in addition to text, columns of numbers and, on one sheet, a map. Several beats passed between my arrival at the threshold and the moment he looked up at me.

General Healy was a startlingly handsome man. Tyrone Power, I thought, but with a mustache. His dark hair was slickly parted at the crown of his scalp. The fine line of a jaw culminated in a strong chin, which he aimed at me now, quizzically. Instantly, I disliked him.

"Good morning, General. I am Michael Montgomery's father. I am under the impression you can tell me where he is."

General Healy touched the corner of a linen napkin to his mouth with one hand while closing the cover of the file he had been reading with the other. I saw that the jacket was marked "Class II." He rose half out of his chair, indicating a place at the table. "Please join me, Mr. Montgomery." His grace was at the service more of deflection than courtesy. "Will you join me in some breakfast?"

Until that moment, I had not admitted to myself how agitated I'd become through the night, but all at once, faced with his convincing calm, I felt the tension fully — even to note its partly draining away. Whatever else was happening, this man's son was all right. So, therefore, was mine.

I sat in the chair he indicated, recalling from my own time in the service the grave aura the brass seemed always to carry. Admirals and generals say what they want, then wait to get it. We call it giving orders. I had been one of that legion whose job was to obey. But what about when the general is a father confronted by a fellow father? I disliked him, I realized, only because he had somehow taken Michael from me.

"Coffee would be welcome, General," I said coldly, reining in my feelings. "Coffee would be quite enough. Thank you."

The orderly appeared with a place mat, a napkin, and silver, all of which he spread before me with expert flourish. To my right, at the foot of the table, was an untouched place setting, a glass of orange juice already poured. Directly across from me was another setting, a plate with a half-eaten piece of toast, a cup half full of milky coffee. In an ashtray there, a cigarette, half stubbed out, was still emitting its ribbon of smoke.

The general picked up a pack of Camels, popped a cigarette out, and offered the pack to me. We had to reach toward each other for me to take one. The orderly was there with a flaring wooden match — first the general, then me. As I took the light, I saw half-moons in the cuticles of the man's fingernails. I glanced at his face to nod my thanks and thought, Not Filipino but Korean. He left the room.

Smoke billowed in the silence. Finally Healy said, "The boys sprang this on us yesterday. I am sorry you weren't informed. I assumed your son told you. I should have insisted on it."

"Where are they?"

Instead of answering, he put the cigarette to his mouth and slowly drew on it. He exhaled with pursed lips, a thin vapor trail. Only then he answered. "Apparently there's some kind of club trip. That club they have."

"I'm sorry. Club?"

"The sports car business. The Formula One circuit. Juan Fangio. Sterling Moss. Ferraris. Porsche Spyders. They're off on a lark. They've gone to Nürburgring to watch the Grand Prix. I gave Rick

33

permission. It never occurred to me your son hadn't spoken to you if he was supposed to. He's the one with the car. You let him take the car." The general paused, as if underscoring my violation of a rule. But then he shrugged; no violation to him. "It never occurred to me there might be some issue with the dormitory. Chalk it up to mixed signals." Healy tapped the ashtray with his cigarette. "Anyway, they'll be home tomorrow. Nothing to worry about."

My first thought went to the mystery of what defines a father, how different one man can be from another. A club. My son in a club, and I don't know it? Of course, it is the business of adolescents to have lives apart from their parents. There was no reason for me to know it. Mixed signals indeed. My son off on a perfectly normal youthful adventure. Even at worst, I had a son who had deceived me about the car, asking for it with rank premeditation, planning this escapade. Maybe Michael's fight with me — "You treat me like a cripple!" — had also been staged, a ploy to get me to agree. But if so, so what? It would be a shock to be deceived like that, but such manipulation, too, fell within the range of normal when it came to kids. Why do I react as if something terrible is coming? Why does the shock of my ignorance open a wound? And why, when this other boy's father . . . And then it hit me: the general is not ignorant, and he's not telling the truth.

"Issue with the dormitory, General? What do you mean?"

"Well, who exactly was giving your son permission?"

"Permission?" I heard myself pronounce the word as if there were an insult in it. "Is permission the issue here?"

"What else would be the issue, Mr. Montgomery?" The general asked his question with a steely edge. I heard the dare in it, and I saw his cold intelligence clear. A formidable man. "If I may ask," he added. "Father to father."

"Simply that my son does not take off for the weekend without telling me."

"Well." He paused, but not from uncertainty. The pause was a display of rhetorical authority. "He did this time, didn't he?"

At that moment, as if this delay, too, were controlled by the general, the orderly came through a swinging door behind me. He slid a cup of coffee onto my place mat. I waved away his offer of cream and sugar, yet then I put the spoon into my cup and stirred the black liquid, stalling. How had the general and I become adversaries so soon? Then I realized: he was writing this scene, but I was off the script.

"And who is Sergeant Carson?" I asked.

He shrugged a bit too quickly. "The father of another student. I told you. They have a club."

"So this is an organized trip? Chaperones and so forth? The school involved?"

General Healy pushed back from the table, turning the folder over as he did so, hiding that designation, "Class II." He smiled at me thinly. "I think you know it is not a school-sponsored trip, Mr. Montgomery. I gather you have spoken to Mr. Jones."

"He called you last night, after I called him."

"As a matter of fact, he did."

"As you had instructed him to do. Is Mr. Jones one of your agents?"

"My agents?" The scornful incredulity in his voice — why? The very idea of the physics teacher as an intelligence officer? Or, more simply, that I would be so crass as to make such an open reference?

I pressed him. "A lark, you said. What makes a high school lark a matter of national security?"

Instead of answering me, he let his gaze drift up and to my right. Just as I realized someone was standing in the doorway beyond my line of sight, perfume registered in my nostrils, a subtle but pungent scent.

"Come in, dear," Healy said. "This is Mr. Montgomery, Rick's friend's father."

I started to get up but Healy raised a hand, a gesture that said, Not necessary. I turned nevertheless, half out of my chair. She was tall, very slim — as slim and tall as Edie, whose image ambushed me for an instant. Then I realized why. Mrs. Healy was dressed for riding, in tan jodhpurs and boots that came to her knees. The flair of fabric at her hips emphasized a narrow waist. Her white long-sleeved shirt, like a man's dress shirt, had a column of ruffles to hide its buttons, the top two or three of which were unfastened. Edie, too, had been the sort of rider not to be deterred by a morning's rain.

But Mrs. Healy's translucent white face was very much her own, made all the paler against a downpour of rich auburn hair that rode lightly on her shoulders, still damp from the shower. Was that why she hesitated, a woman unready to be seen by a man not her husband?

But no. Hesitation had nothing to do with her. She had made the doorway into a frame merely by pausing in it. The woman had a lifetime's habit of knowing how to impress. It was unconscious, natural. Once my eyes caught hers for a second, she seemed released to move, as if my being drawn to her was the key to her entrance. She crossed to her chair just ahead of the orderly, who pulled it out for her. They exchanged the barest of nods, a woman accustomed to servants.

"Good morning, darling," General Healy said. The chill in his tone was familiar as one I had struck myself at another breakfast table. The intimate aftermath of lovemaking was not so different, in its complications, from the awkwardness following a particularly painful argument. In my life with Edie, I had become a connoisseur of hurt in the air. Since Edie, I had arranged my life to avoid it, but now, with Michael, had it come back?

"This is Mr. Montgomery," he said again.

But she cut him off, addressing me. "I am very fond of Michael. He is a good boy."

Her simple statement put several things on display. Her accent, most strikingly, a telltale slant in the word "good" toward "goot," the *v* of "very" alliterating with the *f* of "fond." Fewer than a dozen words, yet it was clear that she was German, which in that setting seemed an offense against nature. An American general with a German wife? It seemed impossible. A grown daughter in the States and a son of eighteen. Marriage, therefore, early in the war. Impossible.

Also manifest was my mistake in attributing hurt to her, an assumption of vulnerability at odds with the quick authority she had just claimed. Unlike the general, she knew Michael's name. She had a relationship with him. She asserted the right to judge him and find him good. So why would that cut me?

A more mundane revelation: her timbre carried the gravelly dryness of too many cigarettes. Indeed, she just then opened a silver box on the table in front of her and took one out. The orderly was in the kitchen. Aware of Healy's impassivity, I nevertheless stood and took the two steps toward her, flicking my lighter as she leaned to the flame. Her hair fell onto my wrist. The shower.

That the woman took my gesture for granted, as if I, too, were her servant, made me dislike her as well. How quickly I'd come to be at odds with these strangers. "How do you know Michael?" I asked, back at my place.

"He comes here to dinner with Rick. A special pleasure for us, Mr. Montgomery."

I did not know her son, and it jolted me to realize that I knew none of Michael's friends. What kind of parent never wonders at his son's coming home forever alone? Wonder at it? I welcomed it. Yet now I saw that these friends he'd kept away from me were part of what had gone wrong between us. Karl Marx, misunderstood? What puerile fool had put such a thought in Michael's head? Surely not a general's son.

Mrs. Healy was saying, "Michael seems quite — what is the word — deep."

"Michael is quiet." I let a beat fall, then said, more formally, "He didn't come home last night, Mrs. Healy. He didn't call. That is entirely unlike him. I learned from the dormitory director" — here I shifted to face her husband — "that you know what's going on, General. Your explanation doesn't match what I was told last night. You were about to explain to me what my son could possibly have to do with national security."

"Did I say that? National security?"

"Yes. To Mr. Jones."

The orderly came in again, now with a single egg in its cup and a rack of toast. In the silence that settled over the table, I sensed General Healy's relief to have yet another interruption. The orderly placed the food on the mat before the general's wife, who said, "What will have you, Mr. Montgomery?"

"Nothing, thank you," I answered, although her small mistake in word order made me wonder if these two were putting me on. The orderly left. As he went through the swinging door, I sensed that someone else was in the kitchen, listening. I said, "I simply need to know where Michael is, and then I will leave."

"I told you," General Healy said. "They went to the race, the sports car race." As he said this, he stared at his wife, who had no trouble meeting and holding his eyes, a fierce field of energy between them.

"At Nuremberg, you said."

"No, Nürburgring. A different place."

"But a racetrack."

"Yes."

At that, Mrs. Healy looked down. She picked up a spoon, but only to stare at it.

"And they will be home tomorrow?"

"Tomorrow night at the latest," he answered easily. "Our son is fluent in German, an experienced *Jugendherberger.*"

"What?"

"Youth-hosteler. They're having a blast." He smashed his cigarette in the ashtray.

I turned to Mrs. Healy. "Is that your sense of it as well?"

She continued to stare at her spoon, which was as unmoving as she.

"Of course it is," the general answered. "Isn't it, dear?"

There was command in him now, and she looked up sharply. "Yes," she said quietly. "I suppose it is."

With a concluding air, the general said, "These young people are adults, Mr. Montgomery. I have airmen under my command who are their age. Airmen with real responsibility. Your son is fine. I think you're a little . . . overconcerned perhaps?"

Mrs. Healy chose that moment to strike her spoon against the shell of her egg — a punctuating click. The general dropped his napkin onto the table and pushed away. "The kids will be fine," he told me with dismissive condescension. He stood, and to his wife said, "Excuse my not waiting, darling. If I'm going to get on the golf course this afternoon, I have to get to the office now."

Mrs. Healy nodded. Her one hand was tapping the shell of her egg, the other still holding a cigarette. Her hands, I noticed, were chapped, rough-skinned, her fingers blunted.

The general collected the folder from its place on the table, then made a show of waiting for me to stand. "Can I arrange a car for you, Mr. Montgomery?"

"My driver is outside."

"Then I'll show you to the door."

There was no question of my remaining behind, to be alone with his wife. I glanced at her as she wearily put the cigarette to her mouth.

38

I stood and, following the general's gesture, led the way out of the dining room without a word to Mrs. Healy, who was not going to look at me in any case.

Along the short hallway was a door, slightly ajar. The room behind the door was invisible, but a sharp odor came from it, and I was past before I realized what the odor was — developing fluid. A darkroom. A household with an amateur photographer.

In the broad foyer, sunlight angled through the fanlight above the wide wooden double door, leaving a wash of illumination on the dark parquet floor. Where had the thick weather gone? The buoyant morning light defied the grim weight of what had brought me here without lifting it.

Beside an oval entranceway table — telephone, a woman's kid gloves, a small blue vase with a spray of edelweiss — the orderly was standing with the general's blue tunic ready, holding it open as if it were armor.

Healy turned, and as he did I leaned ever so slightly toward the telephone, the disk with its set of digits.

When I faced the general again, he was slipping his arms into the tunic's sleeves, deftly transferring the file folder from one hand to the other. As he did this, he was watching me closely, working to measure my height and bearing. Physically, we were a match.

A pair of silver stars rode on each of his shoulders, insignia guaranteed to snag the gaze of a man of my time. And as any veteran's would have, my eyes then went to the four rows of banded ribbons on the general's blouse, automatically deciphering. Nestled among theater ribbons were battle honors, including the purple and white of the Purple Heart and the blue of the Distinguished Flying Cross. Despite my visceral dislike, I could not look at General Healy's decorations without admiring him. Whatever else accounted for his marriage to a self-possessed German woman, it was clear, at least, that this man, surviving the chaos of battle, had known how to offer survival to others.

Above the ribbons were the silver wings of a command pilot, featuring a star and a laurel wreath. I indicated his wings with a nod. "I gather, as J-2, your flying days are over, General."

He ignored my thrust. "I log my time, Mr. Montgomery. To keep the rating up, for old times' sake." And then he parried, "You served?"

"Yes," I answered, without saying "sir." "Navy. Destroyers. The Pacific."

"And now?"

"Banking."

"Ah, yes. The new Germany."

"With any luck."

As the general looked me over in my gray flannel suit, I wonder now, what did he see? Not, I presume, what Americans think they see in that emblem of faceless conformity. Aware of each other as veterans of the war, Healy and I could assume the same winding of the mind around an absolute past: him at the stick, say, of a B-29 homing in on Düsseldorf, his wingman on fire, his concentration fixed on the cone of target, outside of which all was chaos; me on the pilothouse bridge of the *Stephen Case,* glasses to my face, desperately searching the blue surface for the telltale streak of the second torpedo that had to be coming. We knew it was coming, the skipper waiting for me to tell him where, where, before ordering the rudder over, shifting course to present a shrunken target. I never saw the bloody thing.

The USS *Stephen Case.* Her specifications as permanently imprinted as the address of the house I grew up in. Displacement: 2,200 tons. Length: 376 feet, 6 inches. Beam: 40 feet, 10 inches. Draught: 19 feet, somewhere in the midst of which the unseen second torpedo struck. Crew: 251 men, 23 officers, of whom 197 men and 12 officers died that day when the *Stephen Case* sank in 150 fathoms, 12 miles south-southwest of Vangunu, one of the smaller of the Solomon Islands, northeast of Australia. It was February 4, 1943, more than three months, the naval historians say, after Admiral Halsey had secured the waters around Guadalcanal. Most of my shipmates were dead, but two weeks later I was on leave in Honolulu, in a hotel room overlooking the beach at Waikiki, sometimes thinking that I, too, had drowned, which alone explained how I could be in bed with Edie, in bed for days. It was the only time in my life when the main sensation, during sex, was of watching myself, as if there were mirrors on the ceiling. I was endlessly fascinated by the sight of my own writhing, naked body, bubbles streaming from my nose as I clawed up, up, up toward the surface of the sea, which, from below, *is* a mirror. I could never reach that surface. A drowning man is his own voyeur.

"What?" Edie had asked, and asked again. "Tell me," she said. "Tell me." When I couldn't, she let me see her disappointment. When we parted at week's end, it seemed we had accomplished nothing, but that was not so. I was assigned to another destroyer in the same battle group, but I never stopped thinking of the *Stephen Case,* never stopped feeling that I had lost her. Edie went back to San Diego, where she worked in the Blood Donor Service. A month later, she wrote to say she was pregnant and heading home to New York, but under Halsey we had pushed all the way through the Solomons to New Guinea. I didn't receive her letter until summer. Michael was born in November.

3

S omewhere behind us a screen door slammed. Someone leaving
the house ahead of us?

With a brusque nod, General Healy turned toward the door,
donning his hat. The folder was under his arm.

He led me out into the newly glistening sunshine. His sky-blue
limousine, a Lincoln, was at the curb now, nose to tail with my black
Mercedes. My driver was at his passenger door, waiting. Healy's,
a blue-uniformed airman, was coming around his car, having just
closed the far door for someone else, a passenger already in the rear
seat. As Healy and I approached the curb, the airman saluted.

I sensed the tension in Gerhard, the positive energy it took not to
raise his arm at the infamous angle, like the positive energy it had
taken me, moments before, not to say "sir."

Healy called his farewell to me: "The kids will be fine." Then, with
a wave of the folder, he ducked into his car. He said something to the
passenger who was already there, another man in uniform whose
profile I glimpsed. He was blond.

Stooping to my own car, I knew that the general was right, provided all that he said was true — knowing equally that all that he said
was not.

A mile or two from Lindsay Air Station was the center of Wiesbaden, as defined by the barrel-vaulted *Hauptbahnhof.* Above the
red-brick railroad station was a sentry-like clock tower, its spiked
dome evoking the helmet of a kaiser's cavalier. Before the station
stood a three-tiered Roman fountain around which the light auto-

mobile traffic of a Saturday morning flowed. Opposite the station a broad park was spread, acres of grass, trim as a bowling green. Clusters of spring flowers in every color wore the beads of the recent rain like a dust of glass.

Wiesbaden, a hospital town in the war, had not been badly bombed, and so it alone of Rhineland cities retained its prewar beauty. Running along one side of the park were the Baroque nine-teenth-century buildings of the municipality, and along the other, the colonnades of the *Kurhaus,* site of the ancient hot-spring baths. Next to the *Kurhaus* was the elegant casino, the *Spielbank*. One client of mine, bringing me here in the winter, had joked, at Chase's expense, that *Spielbank* means "play bank," while another client had let drop that Dostoyevsky's *The Gambler* had been set there.

As my car approached the three-tiered fountain, sliding into the traffic rotary immediately in front of the station, I impulsively instructed Gerhard to pull over. I told him to keep the motor running, then left the car for the station, thinking of that gambler. In the ticket hall, I found a pair of telephone booths, chose one, and put a ten-pfennig piece into its slot, my slot machine. I dialed the number I had memorized in the general's foyer.

"General Healy's quarters." I assumed it was the orderly who answered, although I had not heard his voice during my visit. He spoke so flatly it was as if those three were the only words in his vocabulary.

"I would like to speak with Mrs. Healy, please. Kindly tell her this is Michael Montgomery's father."

A long time passed.

Then the one sharply articulated word, "Hello?"

"Mrs. Healy, forgive this interruption. I had the feeling that with General Healy having to rush off, you and I hadn't quite completed our conversation."

Again a long silence.

Then, so quietly I wasn't sure I'd heard, "Had we begun it?"

"I'm sorry?"

"Our conversation. Had we begun it?"

"I am only trying to understand what's going on with my son."

"I really . . . have . . . nothing to add to what my husband told you."

"You said you know Michael. You said you like him."

"I do. Yes."

"Can you imagine how I feel? How unlike him it is to have done this?"

"Done what?"

"Not come home. Not tell me."

"Oh."

"What do you think he has done?" I waited a long time for her answer. Finally I said, "I know you are worried, as I am. Why are you worried, Mrs. Healy? Your husband says there is nothing to worry about, but he is worried, too. I can tell. We're all worried parents. That's why I called you."

"Not worried about the same things."

"What?"

"I cannot talk to you, Mr. Montgomery."

"Mrs. Healy, Michael is —" I checked myself — stopped myself from blurting, "Michael is all I have." That I shamefully depended on my child for emotional equilibrium had not been true when Edie had made the charge, but it was true now. I had almost just said so. Such was the forbidden line I was already being dragged across, as if I knew what lay ahead.

I veered, saying, "Michael has had his problems, Mrs. Healy. And I would just be far more at ease knowing what is going on."

"I wish to be able to help you. I do not know myself, as you say, what is going on. I do not know where Ulrich is — your son, or Katharine."

"Ulrich? Katharine?"

"Rick. He is also called Rick. I call him Rick. They call Katharine Kit. With Americans always the *Spitzname*."

"Not always. My son is —" But I stopped. If he had a nickname, would I know it? This woman would.

She finished my sentence. "Your son is Michael. It is true. A good full name for him. Michael the archangel."

"You don't know where they are, Mrs. Healy? I gathered from what your husband said that you did know. Nürburgring. The Grand Prix race. The sports car club."

"There is a club," she said. "And the race was what Rick told his father and me. But it is not true. Rick lied to us. They are not at races.

44

They are not at Nürburg. My husband concluded that yesterday afternoon."

"And so called Mr. Jones at the dormitory."

"Yes."

"So your son, my son, this girl — they simply disappeared?"

"For them it *is* an adventure, the *Lerche,* lark. I am satisfied that my husband is right about that. The young people have no sense of danger."

"What danger?" I heard the involuntary escalation in the pitch of my voice. "Your husband is tracking them now? And he is doing it surreptitiously?"

There was a loud noise behind her, in the background, a door banging, a carton falling, something. The sudden hollowness in my ear told me that she had cupped the mouthpiece of her phone. She spoke to someone, a crisp order in German I could not make out. Then to me, with an edge, she declared, "I have nothing to say to you more. It is impossible that you and I should talk together in this way."

"Not impossible at all, Mrs. Healy, since we are doing it. We have something important in common, you and I."

"What is that?"

"I don't know. You tell me."

When she did not answer, I thought, crazily enough, Spook! The wife of a spook. The exotic, mysterious German wife of a man whose wife should have been anything but.

She had just admitted that her son had lied, that her husband had lied, too. Lied to me. She had allowed it.

I expected her to hang up, but I waited. A full minute passed and she still had not disconnected, and I thought, She is considering the question — what we have in common. And now I knew. "You are serious about your son," I said.

"Absolutely."

"So am I about mine."

"Where are you?" she asked abruptly. The change in her tone, I understood, meant a new decision.

"The *Hauptbahnhof,*" I answered. "A pay phone."

"Where is your car?"

"Outside. My driver's waiting."

"Do not return to your car," she said. Authority came easily to her, and for the first time since the evening before, I found it possible to suspend what had made me suspicious. "You must do exactly as I tell you. Your car is being followed. Leave the station by a side door. Take an auto-taxi to Hainerberg. Browse in the base exchange. Become lost in it. Then walk up the hill to the clinic, where there will be more taxis. Be sure you are not followed. Take a second taxi to the Russian Chapel. The driver will know. Wait there."

The disconnecting click came so quickly I knew she did it with her finger.

The Russian Chapel was visible from everywhere in the Rhine River valley. A sepulchral shrine with three golden onion domes, it sat on top of a small mountain on the eastern edge of the city. A local duke had it built a hundred years before, in memory of his wife, a niece of the czar, after she died giving birth to her first child. I had seen the chapel only from a distance, but I needed no taxi driver to tell me where it was. I'd had it pointed out on practically every visit to Wiesbaden. None of my hosts ever seemed to know if the child, whether boy or girl, had lived or died.

The surprise in actually visiting the chapel was to find that it stood with its back to the view. In the valley I had been admiring it from behind. A small Orthodox church, the entrance faced a gravel circle that was ringed, in turn, by an oval grove of birch trees, the tops of which fell short of the troika domes. The life-size veiled head of a woman, carved in stone, stared blankly out from the meter-wide medallion above the portal. More than inert, she seemed vividly dead.

I pulled the heavy door open and stepped inside. While my sense of sight failed at once, my sense of smell came alive. The pungent odors of stale incense, candle wax, dust, and perhaps the leavings of small animals all combined to evoke the airless musk of religion. What I took to be a sanctuary lamp burned above me, but then I realized the red glow was from the glass of a rose window strategically placed to illuminate the otherwise dark reaches of a very high ceiling.

As my eyes adjusted, I saw what a cramped space it was: an altar, a grilled screen before it, a half-dozen pews, and on the wall to the right, below the rose window, a gilt-framed icon whose face I could not make out.

46

A rack of squat, mostly burned-out candle stubs stood before the icon. Altogether, the shrine might not have been entered in the century since its princess died, and suddenly it seemed more mausoleum than church. I backed out, feeling like a profaning interloper.

Aware of the crunch of my shoes on gravel, I circled around the building to the small fenced plaza behind. I took in the vista of the city spread below, the needle spires of Wiesbaden's Lutheran churches, the brick tower of the *Rathaus,* the town hall. A line of haze hung over the Rhine, an otherwise invisible river perhaps five miles distant. From that direction — ultimately, from the North Atlantic — storm clouds marched steadily overhead, having overrun the sun again. I took the driving wind squarely in my face, the way a deck officer does.

I studied the view as a way to avoid looking at my watch. The taxi had dropped me at the bottom of a curving gravel road that marked the limit of the secluded site. Odd that the chapel should be so visible across the province yet so isolated. A Saturday morning, but there were no other visitors. Then it hit me that Mrs. Healy would have known that.

Not for the first time, I wondered what Gerhard would be making of my having vanished. A decade or two later, expatriate American executives holding positions like mine would be at risk for kidnapping, even in Europe, but not then, when we Yanks were still unvanquished. I knew that before calling the police at my disappearance, Gerhard would call Butterfield, my assistant, back in Frankfurt. So from Hainerberg, I had called Butterfield first, and told him to have Gerhard wait for me at the station.

And I, precisely what was I making of the melodrama into which I had been conscripted? I had never been a man for mystery novels or spy thrillers, and if you had told me that I would take seriously a warning of being followed, whispered by a woman with an accent, I would have laughed at you. But that was before mystery had come to define my life, the mystery of what Michael was becoming, the mystery of what Edie's absence had done to both of us.

Soon I was no longer seeing Wiesbaden; my mind's eye drifted back to that other grove of birch trees, in the far corner of the Holy Trinity churchyard in Oyster Bay. Those trees marked the Elgin burial plot, where Edie's family members had been laid to rest since the middle of the nineteenth century. We mourners were not actually to witness the interment, so custom dictated. But as the others were ushered by undertakers away from the casket and its mound of flowers, I stonily refused to move. The minister approached to touch my elbow. Edie's father looked at me with disapproval.

I had not seen her die. It had never occurred to me I would not see her remains entrusted to the earth. How many times could I be missing from this woman's side when she needed me? Near the mahogany box that held her crushed body, I stood with no comprehension of anything but her absence. Edie's absence was what required my presence.

Her parents' concentration had already been transported from the churchyard to the country club, where the caterers would have spread the collation. When Edie's mother took my arm, I was aware of it, but I must have shaken her off, because then she was gone, and so were the others. For some moments there, because Edie had ceased to exist, so had everything else — including Michael, which, when I realized it later, seemed a betrayal of him. I do not know with whom my bereft son drifted from the graveside back to the cars, or if he walked off alone. That my state was one of pure anguish does not change what else it was, a feeling in grief, which later seemed another betrayal, of being more intensely alive than ever.

"Hello, Mr. Montgomery."

She was standing behind me.

I turned. "Hello," I said awkwardly, unclear for the instant what I was doing here, or who she was.

She looked different, for one thing. Her hair was up from her neck, showing the long line that curved up from her shoulders to her face. She had changed from riding clothes and now wore a dress of some kind beneath a trench coat, with the coat's belt tightly cinched. She wore tan linen gloves, an item of style, not warmth, and she wore heeled sandals, which drew my attention to her shapely ankles.

The odd thing to strike me was that she shaved her legs, which of course every American woman did. I had grown up assuming hair grew no more on female legs than faces, and though by then I knew better, nothing had cracked my self-presumed sophistication like the discovery that year that most German women did not shave their legs, not even some of the most fashionably coifed of those I'd met in Frankfurt. But Mrs. Healy did. Shaven legs, and the relatively compulsive hygiene they represented, would have been just one self-reinvention following her marriage to a well-placed American. Then the exotic aroma of her perfume hit me again. I deflected the sensation. She was the mother of Michael's friend, that's all.

"I apologize, Mrs. Healy, for putting you in a difficult position."

"Not difficult. Impossible."

"I understand."

"No, you do not understand, because you could not understand. When you came to our quarters this morning, you — what is the word — trespassed on a different realm."

"Trespassed? And so one must be aware of being followed?"

She shrugged. "If you are seen doing business with my husband, you become of interest."

"To whom?"

"Shadows who watch from shadows."

"But there are no shadows on an American air base. Unless American. Who would have seen me coming and going except people under your husband's control?"

She glanced at me, a quick dismissal. Shadows, she had said. Shadows in shadows. Spooks. "They watch you?" I asked.

She snapped her head to the side, no. "I am taken for granted. I am the clock, the chair, the domestic pet, the *Frau*. Nothing to notice if I maintain my routine, which normally I do without thinking. Today I must think about it. That is why I made you wait. I had to take my horse out. The day must be like any other. It is why my husband goes to the office this morning, the golf course this afternoon. A Saturday like any other."

"And your visit here?"

She cast her eyes toward the golden domes. "My *kleine Kapelle*. An ordinary visit. I come often here. I say a prayer. I light a candle. I am alone. The place has the advantage of being too obvious to be observed." Without moving from where she stood, she thrust her gloved hands into the pockets of her coat, a definitive gesture.

She let her gaze come surely to mine. Nothing uncertain in her, yet her eyes skittered away, the domestic pet made to scat. An ambushing qualm, I felt it, too. Strangers, yet from the moments in the dining room of her refusal to second her husband, and of my instinctive memorizing of a telephone number, we had taken a plunge into the surreptitious.

Nothing to do against a climate of deceit but openly declare whatever comes to mind. "I went into the chapel, Mrs. Healy. Candles, you said. No one lights candles in there, not in ages."

With that, she took her hand out of her coat to display a small white candle about two inches thick, four inches high. Stubs of such candles were what I'd glimpsed in the vigil rack before the icon, wrongly taking them for an ancient vestige of devotion. Was it also my mistake to have assumed her readiness, like her husband's, to lie?

As if reading me, she looked away. This rendezvous, all at once, could seem to be aiming at anything. I became more conscious still of her exceptional attractiveness, how life had ushered her, whether gently or not, out of the round lightness of youth into the far edgier gravity of a woman who knows what time it is, knowing what time is doing. It was a trajectory I had tracked once before in watching Edie across twenty years. For a brief while the previous summer every woman had reminded me of Edie. Then none had.

"My husband is afraid that our son has stumbled, how to say, into his arena. That is why my husband is not telling you. He cannot."

"But you can."

"But I know less than he."

"A clock, you said. A chair. Furniture is witness to everything. Your husband confides in you."

"Not as you mean it. But in front of me he takes calls. For meetings in the middle of the night, people come to our house."

"Last night."

"Yes."

"This morning. Someone was at the table just ahead of me at breakfast."

"Yes."

"And you listen?"

She did not answer, but I sensed that this was what she had come to speak of. "You listen," I said quietly. "Because this time it's not the U-2. It's your son."

She gave me a look. "How do you know about my husband and the U-2?"

"General Healy's weather reconnaissance wing? Is that still secret?"

She laughed. "Not from the Russians."

"How long was it secret from you?"

"You should perhaps understand something, Mr. Montgomery. My husband tells me nothing. And I need to know nothing."

"How does that work, if you don't mind my asking? Your husband suddenly is a weather forecaster, and you don't wonder?"

"To the U-2 I never gave a thought. But this is different."

I saw that this was what I'd walked into that morning, the fierce electric air between them. This *was* different, because Rick could not have stumbled into his father's arena without bringing in his mother. To which the general had said, practically in front of me, no.

And then I saw something else, a simple matter of arithmetic that all but an oaf would have calculated at once. An eighteen-year-old boy would have been born in 1943, of an American father or a German mother — not both. "Rick is *your* son, and not the general's."

She shook her head, denying not my point but its unhappy implication. "That has nothing to do with this. In all ways that matter, my husband is Rick's father."

The crisp certitude of her statement reminded me once again of Edie: the antidote to doubt is assertion. If Edie, in her anger at me, took a curve on that mountain road at sixty miles an hour, it was because she knew there would be nothing coming at her from the other side. Surely not a ratty pickup truck being driven by a kid who'd been at his father's moonshine.

"So 'Rick' is short for — ?"

"Ulrich. I told you that."

"And his biological father — ?"

"Killed in the war," she said with exquisite abstraction.

"And you and General Healy — ?"

Now she looked at me sharply, as if my concern had become interrogation. Nevertheless she said, "We met in 1947 and married in 1949."

"In Berlin."

"You know that?" Surprise transformed her face into something youthful, innocent almost.

"I know from having read the general's official file that he was stationed in Berlin in 1949."

She stared at me for a long moment, and I found it possible to meet her hard look. Finally she said, "I did not come here for discussing my husband or my life."

"I understand that, Mrs. Healy. You told me to meet you here because you want me to know what you think is happening to our children."

She nodded.

"So why not tell me?"

She slowly removed her gloves, then stuffed them in her pocket. When she brought her hand out, she held a nearly new pack of cigarettes, blue in color, French — not what she'd smoked in her dining room. While she readied one, I went for my lighter, but by then she had hers out. It was gold, slim, monogrammed. I took it from her, as men did in those days, and offered its flame. The cigarette drew my attention to her fingers and hands, which, I saw now, were more than chapped. They were vaguely twisted, misshapen. The nails were manicured, but there was a thickness in her knuckles, a hide-like quality to the skin that was completely unlike the rest of her. She had the hands of an overworked peasant.

When she'd exhaled, she cast her eyes about, then led me to a bench in the shadowy lee of the chapel.

We sat side by side, out of the wind. I became aware of being cold. My raincoat was in the car with Gerhard, who was — what, resentfully cooling his heels at the station? With my left hand, I stroked my right arm to warm myself, waiting for her to speak.

"Thursday night, Rick and my husband fought." Her rough voice was eerily devoid of affect. "The plan had been for Rick and his friends — although not including Michael, as far as I knew — to leave for Nürburg at the end of school on Friday. Rick suddenly wanted to, you say, skip?"

I nodded.

"Skip his classes, to leave Wiesbaden in the morning. *Friday* morning. A day of school. I had told him no, impossible, which he seemed to accept. But when my husband came home — the general was very late that night, having been away — he said that missing a day of school was forbidden. This is what I had said, what I had thought Rick accepted. But now Rick defied my husband. At times they are very angry with each other, and they were then. My son is very much needing to be —" She stopped, more full of feeling than she had, until then, made evident.

"Himself?" I suggested.

She nodded. "He is a German boy living as an American. Until this year, he was in schools in England. And it is very confusing for him. Ulrich is his name, but everyone calls him Rick. Even I do. And he says that now seems wrong."

"Why England?" I asked.

She ignored the question, which I would remember later.

"On Thursday night he said the name 'Rick' seems wrong to him, but he said it angrily. My husband hardly heard him, and answered that such feelings are irrelevant, but I think not. My husband will not be contradicted in an argument. Meanwhile, Rick — Ulrich — will no longer be commanded into obedience. As if a child."

As she spoke, it was Michael's face I was seeing — *his* mouth twisted with resentment. So this kid Ulrich was the source of Michael's new rebelliousness. I felt the rush of *my* resentment again, happy to have this other family to blame.

"My husband," she was saying, "told Rick that the Nürburg trip was off, and that instead he was confined. *Confined*. As if the boy had been brought before a military court. Confined for the weekend. As soon as school was out on Friday, yesterday, Rick was to be home and in his room. Ridiculous idea. Do you confine your son?"

I shook my head. I couldn't even say no to him about the car this week, when I should have.

"Rick banged into his room, the slam of his door sounded like a gunshot."

"I heard a gunshot recently," I said, not knowing why I brought that up. Deflecting the memory of a slamming door?

She didn't hear me anyway. She went on, "Then I told my husband I thought they had both behaved like children. I went to bed, and by the time David came into our room, I was asleep."

She had finally referred to her husband by name — an unconscious expression, perhaps, of the moment's intimacy, a thwarted intimacy, to be sure. But I knew from life with Edie that the heat of argument was still heat. Mrs. Healy stared at the red tip of her cigarette. Aware of myself as an uninvited witness to this family's complexities, I knew better than to prompt her, but I also knew that the story had just begun. *Where the hell is Michael in this?*

"The next morning — yesterday — we woke to find that Rick was gone. He left a note on the kitchen table, addressed to me, in German, saying only that he could no longer go on living like a *Heuchler,* a hypocrite. The purity of youth. He signed it formally, 'Ulrich.'"

"Rejecting his American name," I said.

"Yes. More completely than you think. He signed it 'Ulrich von Neuhaus,' as if he is no longer one of us as Healy. And then he is leaving the note in the kitchen where my husband, too, would read it. Von Neuhaus is Ulrich's name before my husband adopted him as a boy of six, my husband who loves him as I do, but who cannot understand his impossible position."

"Von Neuhaus," I said softly, sensing the blow it would be to Healy. "His biological father's name."

"No," she said a bit too emphatically. "My family name."

"But you said —"

"Von Neuhaus was Ulrich's original name because his father and I never married. His father was the war. That is all."

"I see," I said. But of course I saw so little. The aristocratic "von" would explain her self-assured bearing, although now she seemed ready to forfeit that under the weight of sadness. The barest alteration in color had come over her throat and neck, a pinkish flush that rose from the chute of two slender bones just visible inside the collar of her coat. As she drew on her cigarette, her cheekbones seemed to press out against her skin. Impossible position, she had said. The wave of feeling I saw in her seemed one of simple regret, as if her choices, long made, more than her husband's or her son's, were the ones that had been wrong.

"Rick was gone," she said slowly. "And" — she paused, flagging what she was about to say — "so was my husband's flight bag."

"What?"

"His flight bag. An overnight bag. A government-issue canvas bag with zipper pockets. It was gone. Apparently Rick took it. That seems to be the main problem, Mr. Montgomery. My husband's problem — his flight bag. He had brought it the night before home with him, after being away, supposedly in Brussels, but I do not know. Such things he does not confide in me, as I said to you — nor should he. I know what I know only because I saw his irritation at Rick become a matter of gross alarm when he realized the bag was gone."

"National security."

"I believe so. Yes."

"Why would Rick take his father's bag?"

"He needs a bag. He sees a bag. He takes it." She shrugged, shaking her head. "An expression of anger, perhaps." She smiled wanly. "But also maybe the Air Force bag had its own appeal. This could be near to funny. Our rebellious son who works to be free of his father's shadow, who wants to reclaim a pure German spirit — still, he loves to be the American general's son. In his British school, until last year, it was the nationality. In the American school this year, it is the rank. He hates it. He loves it. If he took my husband's bag, it is, I think, also because of the letters printed on the blue canvas: USAF. Because of the silver stars on the tag, making it a general's bag."

"So what does your husband carry in such a bag? What would alarm him?"

Mrs. Healy shrugged again, definitively this time. She dropped her cigarette distractedly, an indifferent bombardier. Her foot went quickly to snuff it, a firm movement that took me into a vivid memory of Edie's shoes, shoes with heels, straps, buckles, shoes on her feet or sideways on the floor, kicked off in the bored aftermath of an evening, or in eagerness, kicked-off shoes beside satin underwear.

She said, "So both of us went to the high school. There was no question, since this was Rick, of my not going. It was not yet nine in the morning. We learned soon enough, waiting until the attendance roll was taken, that two other students were also absent."

"Michael."

"And Kit."

"The girl."

"Katharine. A friend of Rick's, and, I suppose, of Michael's."

"Rick's girlfriend?"

She rotated her hand in a way that said, On and off. "She lives in the dormitory. Her parents are at a base in Turkey. It was her roommate who said they had gone on ahead of the car club to the race at Nürburgring, to see the qualifying heats that began yesterday. Apparently Michael had a car?"

"Yes. I let him take the car to Wiesbaden this week."

"They went in Michael's car," she said without accusation. Still, I heard the implication: Michael's car was the source of the trouble. My allowing a violation of a rule.

"Why didn't you call me?"

"My husband had his reasons. As for me, I honestly thought, as with Kit's parents, that you would not know, or need to."

"And you heard the general tell Mr. Jones not to call me. So you didn't."

"My husband is a man of authority."

"Except where your son is concerned."

"Is that what you propose to do? Calculate a score? One team of parents against the other?"

My silence was not deliberate, yet it served, apparently, to make her hear again what she had said.

She corrected herself. "I did not mean 'team.'"

And that simply, I knew that she knew that Edie was dead.

Any response I could have made would have been insufferably banal — that is how I thought in those days. So I said nothing.

She felt obliged to explain. "Michael has spoken to me. That his mother died not a year ago, I know. That she died in her automobile, I know that."

"There was a collision on a mountain road," I said. And then I surprised myself by adding, "It was an accident," as if Mrs. Healy had wondered, as if I had. In fact, I never had wondered about that. Nothing in Edie wanted to die.

This first explicit reference to her death in — what, four or six months? Is that what drew me into this other woman's aura? I had yet to begin to grasp what Michael's situation might be, yet now, on that chill bench, in damp, blustery air, I found myself examining her face.

Again I saw wreckage in her eyes, which, using her cigarette as a prop, she then lowered. Nothing, I sensed, wanting to die in her either.

"I know that Michael's mother was a good woman," she said. "He has told me how close they were, how he misses her. He has told me how she cared for him when he was ill."

"I'm surprised he told you that," I said. "My son is reticent."

"It is a good thing, Mr. Montgomery, to talk about this." She raised her face toward me again, but now with a certain defiance — as if I, an American male, *believed* in reticence. A certain defiance, but also her face seemed unprotected, which made unthinkable any expression of the resentment I felt at her intimacy with my son. Not resentment — jealousy.

"I am sure you are right, Mrs. Healy," I said carefully. "I appreciate your kindness to my son. But I need to know now where he is. What is happening?"

"You are afraid for your son," she said, "but not only because he did not come home this weekend."

"This week was the first time I let him take the car." Now I recognized something else to be afraid of — not that he was hit by a reckless driver, as Edie was, but that he was the reckless kid on the road, hitting someone else.

She went on, "Fear, Mr. Montgomery, can be an expression of grief."

I had to look away. Reticent with *me,* is what I should have said about Michael. How could he have discussed such feelings with this stranger and never with me? Yet look at how I, too, was reacting to her.

The weather had turned dark again, the wind gustier. Clusters of wing-shaped seed pods swirled at our feet. Still looking away, thinking about the war father of her child, I asked, "How do you know that about grief?"

"You ask me that?"

Again I assumed she was rebuking me, the profaning interloper once more. But when I looked at her, to my surprise a faint smile had transformed her face, a resigned expression that asked, below the surface, Where would I start to answer such a question?

Impossible. To change this impossible conversation, I stood up.

The winged seeds had been sucked into a whirling funnel between us. "So then," I said, "let's discuss the simpler things. Gross alarm. National security. The danger of my being followed. By your husband's agents? Or some enemy's? My son's disappearance. The breach between you and your husband regarding your son. What the hell is going on?"

She stood, too. She took something out of her pocket, an old-fashioned cloche hat. It had started to rain. She put the hat on without a thought for arranging her hair, then, ducking, she moved past me to dash away, as if the water would hurt her. I went after her, snagging her elbow, the gentleman showing the way. The ridiculousness of such pairing was in the quick authority with which she led me inside the Russian Chapel, pulling the door open, not tentatively, as I had, but as if she had done it dozens of times before. Once more, the relative darkness of the Byzantine interior blinded me.

A flame flared in her hand — her golden lighter. She lit the candle she had shown me and placed it in a cup on the vigil rack in front of the icon. She lit several of the candle stubs. Only now I noticed that the icon showed the face of the sorrowful mother of God — burnished skin, golden braided hair parted in the center, a red robe, eyes cast demurely down toward the lower left corner of the gilded frame. Mrs. Healy stood before the icon with her back to me for a long moment — enough to make me wonder if she was praying.

I thought of Edie. St. John the Divine. Not prayer, but mere refuge.

When Mrs. Healy turned to me, the wavering light was at play on her face, and now her skin, too, was burnished.

The mood cracked as soon as she began to speak. "They found your son's car last night," she said briskly. *You want the answer?* was her tone. *Here it is.*

"Where?" I asked. "Are they all right?"

"They found the car. Only the car."

They. Her use and my use of that one word, referring both to our kids and to the shadow figures who pursued them, confused me at first. Then, once more, the refrain: *What could Michael have to do with any of this?*

"In an ordinary car park," she was saying. "The car was normal, parked and locked. My husband's flight bag was not there, nor were the young people."

"You have to slow down. *Who* found the car?"

"Military police. American military police. Not German. German police have been told nothing. My husband's men who came to the house last night reported on this. I heard them. Your son's car — a blue convertible. An American car."

"Yes."

"They were looking for it all through the day yesterday on the routes west, toward Nürburg. But the three were not going there at all. The sports car club, yes. But not them. The MPs found the car in a city to the north, which is what . . ." Pausing, she searched for a word. The flickering light, shadows dancing, underscored the unreality of what was unfolding, made me think of the other chapel, the other nightmare from years before, polio. ". . . what heightened concern."

"What city?"

"Helmstedt."

I had never heard of it.

"Helmstedt," she explained, "on the border of East and West, at the Allied access corridor that runs through Soviet Germany."

Soviet Germany. As I repeat the phrase she used, I recall that it was a common term for East Germany — the DDR — in those days. To us, that vast continent stretching east beyond the Curtain — Prussia, Silesia, Lithuania, Poland, Ukraine, the entire way to Azerbaijan and Turkmenistan — all of it was "Russia," and all of it was Red.

"Helmstedt," she was saying, "is the last place in West Germany where the duty train stops."

"What the hell is that?"

"The American military train into Berlin. It is why my husband is telling you nothing. Telling no one. To avoid alerting authorities in the East. Apparently Rick, Michael, and Kit left the car and boarded the train. Probably in the late afternoon yesterday. A train passed through Helmstedt at four o'clock. Three hours later, having crossed through the DDR" — she pronounced the letters the German way — "they would have arrived in West Berlin."

"West Berlin, Jesus Christ. Three kids can't go to West Berlin on their own." I had traveled there myself around four times in the course of the year, always by airplane, always with a sense of high frontier. Berlin was the pin of the grenade that Khrushchev was waving in Kennedy's face. As if to emphasize that, Communist border guards only the month before had shot and killed a pair of hapless drunks who wandered into a forbidden zone between sectors. There were regular stories of West Germans disappearing during visits to the East. Americans were discouraged from traveling to Berlin without reason, and no Chase employee could go there without authorization from me. "Impossible," I said.

Mrs. Healy nodded at my statement, but it was a contradicting gesture. "If they go by the American Army train, they can. On the autobahn, they would have been stopped by U.S. military police and by Communist *Volkspolizei*. But not on the train, a *military* train. The United States government refuses to let the Communists interfere in any way with its military access to the city. You may have gathered that." The resolve concerning Berlin, the grenade in his face, was Kennedy's way of refusing to blink. "The duty train," she said, "is the main symbol of American will, and so Americans ride it freely."

"But these are kids." What didn't I know about the high noon of geopolitics? What didn't I know about the hijinks of American teenagers set loose in Cold War Europe? What didn't I know about Michael's capacity for deceit and stupidity?

"Each one has an American passport," she was explaining. "And as dependents, each has American military identification. For purposes of the duty train, they are military personnel. Even your son."

Jesus Christ. It was true. I'd had to obtain the military ID for Michael as part of getting him into the high school at Wiesbaden. Officially, he was the son of a Defense Department contractor with the senior civilian rank of GS-19, which was, in fact, *not* true. If there was deceit and stupidity here, it had begun with me.

"Such American identification and a ticket," she said, "are the total of what is required. And the ticket, naturally, like admission to the base theater for the latest films, like bread in the commissary" — she was speaking now with a bitter edge, sounding like a German of the occupation — "costs very little. My husband's colleagues concluded last night that Rick and Michael and Kit are in Berlin, where the search for them goes on."

"But why Berlin?"

"A teenage road trip? What is the new American hero's name? Jack Kerouac. Jack Kerouac in Europe." She was summarizing her own speculations. "West Berlin, the utopia of pure resistance. The city without *das Heuchler*. The destination of young freedom lovers. German youth are draft exempt if they live in West Berlin. Therefore anarchists, Socialists, cowards come — not for the cabaret, as before, but for the coffeehouses and jazz clubs, like New York. The young have a hundred such reasons to go to Berlin. But my husband has another theory."

"That your son," I ventured, "has his own history there. His own unfinished business involving a family named von Neuhaus." This goddamned family had sucked Michael into this foolishness, *their* unfinished business. I calmed myself to ask, "Wasn't it in Berlin that you were living when you and General Healy met?"

Her looking away from me was an articulate refusal to discuss that past. "One says only 'Neuhaus' if the family is being referred to as such," she instructed in monotone. "The 'von' is a connective, used only as a link with the forename. Americans are always making this mistake, and now ignorant Germans are making it also."

Was this true? How many times had I heard the dead man in Frankfurt referred to as "von Siedelheim" that week? But that had mostly been at the bank. I almost asked her, but her expression stopped me. There was such weariness in her that all at once she seemed an old-world matriarch explaining to a mulish new servant the intricacies of life in the *Schloss*. All Germany was her estate. At that moment, I disliked her intensely.

She said, "My husband's theory concerns the sort of thing that might draw the interest of any young person — a spectacle, an occasion of excitement and adventure."

"What, then?"

"Do you know what day it is?"

"What day?"

"The date today."

I had to stop. The date today? Hell, I hardly knew the month by then, the year.

"May first," she said, as if that explained something. "The first of May, Mr. Montgomery. The great festival day of world communism. This afternoon is the May Day parade in East Berlin, already announced to be a mass display of Soviet power. A display for President

Kennedy, the first time ever on television. The Red Army marching up Stalinallee to Alexanderplatz, the tanks, the missiles, the trucks pulling guns, the banners with portraits of Lenin, and the streets lined with a million *waschecht* Berliners. *Waschecht,* a word which is meaning 'washing true.' You say 'colorfast.' Red."

"Tanks, missiles, guns," I repeated, knowing now where the issue lay. Karl Marx, misunderstood! Michael got that bullshit from this other kid, and now he was in danger because of it. But I did not know the half of it.

"Yes," she was saying, "and your son will be there with the son of the man in command of American military intelligence, a boy carrying a bag with silver stars on its tag. My son, a native of Leipzig, now behind the Iron Curtain, yet now with an American name. Your son with identification that is not true. Both of them dressed — how? Blue jeans and tennis shoes. Behaving — how? In a manner to draw immediate attention to themselves, with the Soviets looking for points of complaint. What do you think now, Mr. Montgomery?"

This was thirty years ago, yet I am still capable of reliving the quite physical sensation that came over me then, the weakness in my legs, a near loss of consciousness. Michael at the mercy of the Soviets. *I can't cope with this.* Who had said that to me? Edie, of course. At last I understood what she felt.

Our separate thoughts had become a wall between me and Mrs. Healy. When I focused on her face again, it seemed once more the impassive face of the burnished icon — suspended, aloof. Surely I was dreaming, as I had so often dreamt of the *Stephen Case,* that torpedo slamming out of nowhere.

But her steady, cold voice said otherwise. "When my husband's colleagues left our house last night, assigned the mission of recovering his bag while rescuing our son, David and I were made to confront how we are different. Not in our wishes or fears, but in our situations, and therefore in our feelings."

"The boy is *your* son," I said. The eyes of the icon above us were hidden, while this real woman's eyes were light brown, flecked with green. Her eyes were clear, steady. Feelings, yes. But no question of her not coping. "And your husband," I said, "is playing golf this afternoon."

"Do not misunderstand that," she said. "David has no choice. He would go to Berlin himself, would be in Berlin already, but East German agents track him everywhere, and he knows it. Clerks at Lindsay are Stasi or KGB. Drivers. Gardeners. Cooks. David must do nothing to draw attention to the fact that his son is missing, much less that his son is almost certainly in Berlin, soon to be in *East* Berlin. David has no choice but to entrust to those others a task he would much rather keep for himself. Out of love."

As she spoke, an emotional undercurrent ran in the opposite direction from what she was saying. I sensed that I was hearing the reiteration of an argument, justifying a reasonable course of action that to her was utterly to be rejected. "If David were to go to Berlin himself, it would worsen Rick's situation — and Michael's and Kit's — making them more likely to be noticed by the Stasi, making them more vulnerable to accusations if they are noticed."

"Accusations?"

"Our children, if they are taken, can be taken for spies."

"Which is preposterous, of course. As we would quickly establish."

"Perhaps," she said, even more coldly. "Perhaps not."

She left it to me to see the problem, the one with which we'd begun. "The bag," I said. "The bag and whatever is in it."

"Which is my husband's concern. And as he points out, our children are not children. Still, they, and they alone, are my concern. My husband has two concerns. I have only one. And my husband is condemned to wait by the side, and condemned is his word. Because he is well known to the Russians, to the Stasi. I am not."

"Nor am I."

"That, Mr. Montgomery, is what we have in common. It is why I am here."

My mind went all at once to the Kurfürstendamm in West Berlin, the broad shopping street that showcased capitalism deep behind the Iron Curtain. Chase, under my predecessor, had provided financing for the Lindenhof, the newest building on the avenue, the tallest in the city, and I had been there for the gala opening in December. The happy crowd that had thronged the ceremony had struck me, in its enthusiasm for the glittering new Berlin, as a version of the crowds one imagined cheering at the openings of the ponderous edifices Albert Speer built for Hitler. The question of their former enthusiasms was one we never raised with our German colleagues, but it lodged ominously below the surface of our collaboration, and it could jump out at unexpected times.

"I am going to Berlin," I said, adding to myself, *where Michael needs me.*

"Once I met you this morning," she replied, "I saw that if you knew what was happening, you would go." Nothing demure in this woman. Nothing soft. No question now of downcast eyes. Her son, too, in need. That was all. "And I," she said, "am going with you."

Part Two

4

W

HAT MY FATHER SAW in me as need was simple readiness. Yet I am now a little past the age that he was then. I have my own grown children, and I begin to see things from his side as well as mine. Teenagers have a way of making parents both wise and crazy, and so, naturally, my own teenage years look different now. In my case, alas, the crazy reasons to worry were real. If my youthful naiveté had been only that, but the context made my actions thoughtless beyond measure, and if they had ended tragically, they would have been unforgivable. For a long time, they did seem so. It was only your father, before he died, who made a final forgiveness possible; only he, given what had happened, who could have offered it — to himself as much as to me and Kit. Someone had said to the three of us, "Don't you be the thing that brings a hair-triggered weapon out of its holster." But we were that thing.

My father and I are alike in understanding history as the frame within which our quite personal story unfolds. We are telling it all these decades later because once again Berlin has been in the news, beginning with the long-overdue breach of the Wall that brought us all together again. The Wall went up, in the first place, not long after the fateful two days in which everything happened.

Oddly, the literal breakthrough of the Wall on November 9, 1989, the end of an era if ever there was one, occurred on the fifty-first anniversary of *Kristallnacht,* the Nazi savaging of Jewish shops and synagogues. I say oddly because *Kristallnacht* was of course the beginning of the era, but also because, speaking personally, the Shoah and what led up to it has been a focus of my work. I write for the *Atlanta Constitution,* and have published three books on politics and history, the most recent an account of artworks stolen from Jews, how the great museums of the world took full advantage of the genocide.

I am conditioned, perhaps, to see the shadow of that past everywhere, and so, regarding Berlin, the coincidence of dates struck me less as odd than as inevitable. The flukes of history make us love it, but also fear it. That first diabolical Novemberfest seemed fittingly reversed when hundreds of thousands of young Germans, grandchildren of the perpetrators, took to the streets to smash not glass but drab concrete. They danced on both sides of the Brandenburg Gate, monument to Prussian glory. But Prussian glory had been swamped by the twentieth century, which only goosed the frenzied happiness of the young democrats who scaled the Wall, of the accidental graffiti artists who splashed the cement barrier with whatever paint came to hand, an anarchy of color released upon the gray monotony of a prison that had passed itself off as half a city.

The destruction of the Berlin Wall, as it happened, was also the destruction of a wall in my memory, the events that divided our lives into the before and after of who we were and who we became. And because your father was there with us at the start, helping to create the people we are, it is crucial that you know of him as he was, taking this remembrance as a measure of what he then accomplished with his life. We misunderstood his reaction all those years ago, thinking it foolish, when, as history shows, it was noble.

You were too young last year ever to have your own memory of the Wall coming down, so let me tell you. Tens of thousands of men and women rushed through the hole that opened when the *Volkspolizei* chose not to fire at the first doofus to hoist himself up to the ledge atop the Wall, jitterbugging and calling back to those who'd egged him on, "*Aufkommen! Aufkommen!*" Within days, the once omnipotent Erich Honecker resigned as East German party chief, Hungary and Czechoslovakia declared their borders open, and Mikhail Gorbachev, watching from Moscow, shrugged. And once again, after the rude interruption that lasted three decades, the massive tectonic shift from East to West resumed, the largest movement of people ever to occur in Europe.

That movement had begun in 1944, with the mad flight of pan-icked Prussians, Silesians, and Sudeten Germans ahead of the onrush-ing Red Army. "Feet," as they say in Atlanta, "do your thing." At war's end, the migration quickened as if the central plain of Europe had been tilted on its side from the Urals toward the Atlantic, spilling westward women, children, and what men survived. Between 1945 and one night in August 1961, almost five million Germans fled from the East through Berlin, the boldest of them marching under that same chariot-crowned Brandenburg Gate. The gate was the em-blematic transit point marking the continental divide, but at the time of our May Day visit to the city, a few weeks before the Wall went up, there were something like eighty places where the momentous bor-der crossing could be made. I read later that three thousand East Ger-mans, mostly young and skilled, were then making it every day.

After August 13, there were seven crossing places in Berlin, and they were ruthlessly controlled by *Vopos* whose authority was as ab-solute as the armor of Soviet tanks with engines idling not far away. *Republikflucht* was defined as a major crime against the Socialist state, and guards were authorized to prevent flight by shooting to kill, which they did more than two hundred times.

The Wall became the defining symbol of the Cold War, for us in the West as well as for your people. In the rhetoric of Western leaders from John Kennedy to Ronald Reagan, it was simply evil. Yet to citi-zens throughout Berlin, beginning early on, the hulking concrete and wire construction, running 103 miles through the city and in a full circle around its western half, was informally known as the Peace Wall. Your father told me that at the time of our reunion. In the West, there would be a journalistic obsession with the "death strip" as the very symbol of demonic totalitarianism, but in fact the barrier repre-sented a practical solution to a vastly destabilizing problem. The Wall stopped the East-West refugee flow in its tracks, effectively saving the eastern provinces of the nation for an eventually reunited Germany, while defusing the terrifying confrontation that had turned Berlin into the Cold War "flashpoint." In one day, each side implicitly rede-fined its commitment in Berlin, with the Soviets yielding their claim to the whole city and with the Allies equally abandoning the East. The Wall did this. If the Soviets had not thrown it up, there were reasons why the Americans could have. Indeed, despite all their public protests, Americans not only valued the Soviet Wall, but had, in deep secret, encouraged it. What a country.

That surface enemies were subtle partners in maintaining what was necessary for peace is one of the great untold stories of the Cold War — and it is the hidden assumption of the story my father has begun, and that I pick up. The clandestine collusion between Washington and Moscow eluded us at the time, of course, but it was very much to the point of what happened when I joined Ulrich as a counter-refugee, bucking the flow to go from West to East. What know-it-alls we were. We knew nothing.

Subtle collusion between Washington and Moscow does not mean that their confrontations were less than terrifying, and the spring and summer of 1961 were, until the Cuban missile crisis the following year, the worst of it. It is hard to remember now, with Russia in social and economic free fall, but in those days the Kremlin seemed the center of a nation of evil geniuses. At the slightest whim of their madness, so we felt, they could blow us to smithereens. Only weeks before we took off for Berlin from Wiesbaden, for example, the Soviets had demonstrated their superiority by launching the first man into space. The name Yuri Gagarin was on everyone's lips that month. And only weeks later, Nikita Khrushchev would humiliate John Kennedy at their summit in Vienna. A shaken Kennedy came home from that encounter to announce on television it was time to build bomb shelters — a month's anticipation of the drab concrete of the Wall, but this concrete was to be poured in the cellars of American schools, factories, places of business, and homes. For the first time, a U.S. president was openly warning of nuclear attack, and in response, we the people began to stock up on canned goods. "Berlin is the testicles of the West," Khrushchev declared. "When I want to make the West scream, I squeeze."

When I was a kid using the guest bathroom at my mother's parents' house, a mansion on the North Shore of Long Island, I was always drawn to the tidy stack of back issues of an American magazine that sat on the cool porcelain shelf of the toilet tank. It was called *Reader's Digest,* and its pages were laced with pithy oddities that I loved. One was a feature called "The Most Unforgettable Character I've Met." The stories of resolute amputees, say, or of prostitutes-turned-nuns made it seem a particular achievement — not to be unforgettable, but merely to have encountered someone who was. The Unforgettables: it became a category against which I measured teachers, doctors, nurses, and physical therapists. My mother, once she died, epitomized unforgettability, but she hadn't while alive. All too soon, certainly by that spring of 1961, I found myself unable to recall with precision what she looked like, which was why I took to carrying her picture in my wallet, as if she were my girlfriend.

So unforgettability was my standard of measurement when I met Rick Healy not long after starting at Wiesbaden. We became friends when we did what none of our other classmates presumed to do, which was to ask each other one awkward but simple question. What happened to your legs? Why do you speak with that accent? Beginning then, because he told me to, I stopped calling him Rick, although everyone else continued to. Even before the events of that spring, I'd already begun to understand Ulrich as *Reader's Digest* material, and I actually thought of composing an article about him — the first of my ambitions as a writer.

On the magazine's scale, Ulrich might have been unforgettable simply by being a German-born postwar adopted son of an American Air Force general, but how much more so by his being the son of a German baroness. It seemed an impossible claim, doubly so when he urgently swore me to secrecy. If his mother was a noblewoman, then what did that make him? We were sitting alone in the cafeteria, having lingered through the lunch hour. Beyond the wall of plate glass windows beside us, a soft autumnal light washed the air. Blue-smocked workers were wiping down the tables with ammonia, but he seemed not to notice them. Ulrich had lit a cigarette, which was forbidden in that room, and I could not decide whether his defiance of such rules made what he'd just told me less believable or more.

But I accepted his claim totally once I began visiting his family home in the military compound across Wiesbaden — once, that is, I began getting to know his mother. She was "Mrs. Healy" to me. I could see that she was German, but that wasn't all. From her worldly bearing and careful way of speaking English, it was clear that she was no mere housewife, not even of the hunt club set. Ulrich's mother never referred to her prewar social status, but she was as beautiful and kind as a lonely American boy had to imagine a banished princess to be. I was ready, in that year after my mother died, to fall under the spell of someone else's.

Ulrich was tall and thin, with a striking blond beard that might have made him seem a sailor except for his shaggy blond hair, which grew even longer that year, making him seem a sailor shipwrecked on an island. Ulrich was the first boy I knew who had no apparent acquaintance with a barber. In style and attitude, surrounded as we were by bobbysoxers and soda jerks, he was unique. It was unimaginable that within a couple of years Ulrich's would be the style and attitude of a generation.

Like me, he was new to the school, and to the smug culture of American Army brats. He was there after completing all but his last year in the far more rigorous course of a boarding school in Dorset, England. When I told him about St. Dunstan's in New York, where the teachers dreamed of waking up as British schoolmasters, we agreed we had survived the same shipwreck — although it was obvious that we were both better educated than the kids around us. Ulrich explained that he had demanded of his parents the right, as a German, to attend school at least for one year in his native country before going off, according to his parents' plan, to an American university. His father's idea of saying yes, he snorted, was a year at H. H. Arnold High.

Ulrich's accent floated between British and German. That, his whiskers, and the embarrassment of his father's rank combined to make him an instant misfit in the chipper high school. Like me. We instantly liked each other. I tried hard to carry myself like a survivor of combat, but most students kept their distance. That was not generally a matter of ill will, I knew. Rather, wanting not to rudely look at my deformed legs, my callow schoolmates simply avoided me, and soon enough it was as if I were not there. I suppose that behind my back the cruel ones called me gimp, or crip, or some such thing, although if they did, I never heard it.

I knew from hearing it, though, that behind Ulrich's back they called him Fritz. And I knew that when we became friends, they called us Katz and Jammer. Ulrich might have found himself on the social margin just because of his readiness to associate with me, but in fact his quasi-pariah status was set less by his accent, appearance, or family status than by his air of condescension. He held in open contempt the athletes and cheerleaders who embodied the character ideal of the school so aptly named for a guy called "Hap."

"Hip Hip High School," Ulrich dubbed it. One day early in the year, standing before the general's oil portrait in the school foyer, he told me who Arnold was — a leader of the American bomber command who saw to the obliteration of the city of Hamburg. In one night's bombing in July of 1943 — a few days after he was born, Ulrich said — the Allies killed more German civilians than English civilians were killed in all the Luftwaffe air attacks and blitz raids throughout the war. When I asked him how he knew this, he stared at me coldly, and I knew to believe him. Years later, I would learn that fifty thousand citizens of Hamburg had died that night, and that he was right.

Ulrich was, to my knowledge, the only other student in the senior class who read novels not assigned by Miss Klein, the English teacher. Once I asked him why he was reading *The Brothers Karamazov,* and he replied that Dostoyevsky was unafraid of things as they are, which stumped me. My fears had been tied to the future, not the present. Only then did I begin to recognize things as they are as *the* things to be afraid of.

When, another time, I told Ulrich that my father and I lived in Frankfurt am Main, he held up a book and said joyously, "He is from Frankfurt!" The book was in German, but even I could take in the title as *Eros and Civilization,* the author as Herbert Marcuse, whom I had never heard of. When Ulrich realized that, he set to work on me, launching an open-ended tutorial in the theories and slogans of what would later be dismissed as the faddish New Left. To me the ideas seemed elusive, and I only pretended to grasp their urgency. Eventually, though, I began, as we said, to true-believe.

My reading tastes had set me apart from other kids, too. Rainer Maria Rilke was my idea of a writer to carry around. I took his famous letters as addressed to me alone. *You must think that life holds you in its hand, will not let you fall.* I remember how Ulrich hooted when I recited that line from memory. "Rubbish! Of course it will let you fall. What the bloody hell is polio if not life letting you fall? What is the death of your mother if not that?" Before long, under Ulrich's influence, I began to criticize Rilke as apolitical, but that did not keep me from the consolations of his eloquent sadness. I continued to read Rilke, but without quoting the letters or poems to Ulrich.

Soon Marcuse formed the pulse of our conversation, and I began distinguishing between the language of dispute and of feeling, the one public, the other private. It was an inhibiting dichotomy that took me years to overcome. "Happiness is freedom," Ulrich quoted the philosopher as declaring, and I recall nodding at the grave implications of the statement. We were sitting now in a corner booth of the Zimmertal, a becurtained *Konditorei* down the hill from the American enclave where the high school was, a place our classmates spurned in favor of the snack bar at the base exchange with its molded plastic chairs, ferociously orange. Ulrich and I were smoking our French cigarettes and drinking black coffee, hunched together over the book, dotted with pastry crumbs. Sexual freedom, political freedom, personal freedom, intellectual freedom. There was nothing in the text about freedom from crutches.

I said yes to all of it, but heard myself asking, How do we actually live when we are free? I remember repeating the question, but couldn't make my meaning clear to Ulrich. It was enough to admit to myself that his talk was weightless, which didn't matter. I liked it anyway. The happiness for me wasn't freedom. It was his company.

Ulrich was the first person from whom I heard the word "bourgeois" outside a classroom, and to my horror, that day I realized he could be talking about me. His denunciation of what he called the economic hierarchy, the waste and war it leads to, the slaveries of fascism and Soviet communism alike, but also the stupefactions of materialism, what would later be called consumerism, the hypocrisies of Victorian repression — all of it to be overthrown by the coming generation, *our* generation, the hope of a utopian future. Youth! Ulrich introduced me to the solidarity of the young.

I objected that I felt no solidarity with our ball-tossing classmates up the hill, and weren't they young? He easily turned my assertion into evidence of alienation, which was the only authentic way of being young. That idea seemed tailor-made for me. *I love this guy.* Yes, I said, to all that he was teaching me, while I dared not reveal that my father worked for the Rockefeller family bank, the very counting-house of hierarchy.

Eventually, after he'd begun to confide his secrets in me, I did tell him what my father did. Ulrich lived in a general's house. I lived with a capitalist overlord, and if my mother had been a European, she'd have been a baroness, too. We laughed and laughed at the contradictions we had in common, aware that no one else would have seen what was funny. It was only then I realized that in Ulrich, my first real friend, I had my first real secret from my father. There was no question of bringing Ulrich home to Frankfurt on a weekend, no question even of discussing him there. That recognition was my door to freedom, and changed everything.

Once, the bond I'd felt with my father had been absolute. During my various recoveries, he had carried me places until I became too heavy, and even after that I continued climbing into his lap, and he let me. All the more reason for being appalled now at what, in my rebellion against that intimacy, I did to him.

After my mother's death, he had his sorrow and I had mine, and by then there was no carrying or being carried, holding or being held. Yet for a time the simple fact of my father's presence seemed the only antidote to the pain in my chest that at intervals left me choking in the air-lock vacuum of her absence. Sometimes I would awaken soaked through with sweat, and like during my time in the iron lung, I would be terrified of suffocating. For the lung-clearing vapor of my father's presence, I had come to Germany with him instead of staying in New York and boarding at my old school, where the other boys around me had developed the vague look of statues.

But our time in Germany also coincided with my reaching an age when I simply had to have my distance. He, too, could make me suffocate. I came to admit, for one thing, how little my father and I actually had in common — an experience of which he was ignorant, yet with which I became obsessed. "There is more to life than making money," I declared to him one day that spring, a first expression of disagreement.

"Yes," he shot back. "There is having your own convertible."

A neat parry, that, since I had only moments before asked for the car as my own. We were at a restaurant on the Rhine, one of our Sunday outings.

"But making money *off* money, Dad. What kind of life's work is that?"

I was both satisfied and ashamed to see his face register my question as a blow. I did not know it then, of course, but I was desperate to defy my father because he was making me crazy, using me to plug the gaping wound caused by my mother's death. He had not killed her any more than I had, but for each of us, guilt and grief were bound together. We were companions in that complexity, but we were rivals in it, too, until events of that May Day, my true rebellion, released us from the prison of one loss into another. As if I saw that coming from the vantage of the garden restaurant, a foreshadowing, I stormed away from the table, deflecting my fresh guilt into silently cursing him as a goddamn materialist. That was a word I had from Ulrich. It had begun to matter less whether my new friend held my father in contempt than that I did.

But Ulrich gave me a language with which to define the differences between the world I'd come from and the outlines of a world I'd begun to see in the haze of my future. Except in those jolting exchanges, I could not discuss any of this at the house on Mosbacher Strasse, and thankfully my father seemed hardly to recognize those exchanges as the arguments I knew they were. What he took for my moody adolescent silences during our long drives through the vine-covered hills of the Rhine, I regarded as a dutiful protection of his illusion that his little boy still needed to be kept from harm. What a resentful jerk I was.

Later in the year, again at the Zimmertal, Ulrich declared himself to be what he called a neo-Marxist, which was the first time I'd heard that soon-to-be-ubiquitous prefix. It removed little of the bite of "Marxist," and we both knew that his Air Force father would have taken mortal offense at his defining himself that way. There is no conveying now the offense implied by such a label in 1961. In the States, the Red Scare was still on, and Ulrich's declaration meant, in my leaping imagination, that I could be subpoenaed to testify against him. Also, there was a thrilling, slightly salacious naughtiness in the statement. Still, by then I had learned to argue with Ulrich, had learned it from him. "A Marxist?" I challenged. "Like Stalin?"

"No, like Groucho," he cracked. "Groucho, Chico, Harpo, and Neo." But he was dead serious, and launched into his case. With Marcuse, Ulrich measured Soviet Marxism against what he called classical Marxism, as if it were music. He measured Lenin and Stalin against a mythical Trotsky, standing sentinel on the road not taken. The problem with Marxism was that it had yet to be tried.

Later in the decade, with the aging Marcuse seduced into the role of senescent pied piper, a legion of glib young radicals would reduce such sentiments to self-serving clichés, but in 1961 a heartfelt simple call for social justice could blow the lid off unexamined assumptions of innocence, both personal and national. I knew enough to take Ulrich's declaration as one of high commitment, and it was a milestone for me as much as for him.

Surely by now the bind is clear. I was a boy born to be good. Brave diligence — first in the face of my disease, then of my disability — was the mode of my triumph, and therefore, eventually, the measure of my character. I am certain that my mother would have loved me anyway, but that I coped so well at her behest, earning an endless litany of accolades from doctors and therapists and also teachers — wasn't that what had compounded her love with pride to make it infinite? I was raised to believe that if I did everything my mother told me to do — as she rubbed my legs with aromatic lotions, manipulating my ankles and knees to quicken the dead muscles, massaging the flaccid skin to firm it up — nothing bad would ever happen to me again. Polio had been my one lightning strike, and for all there was to hate about it, wasn't it behind me?

And then she died. What did brave diligence have to do with that? It took me a long time to figure out that the truck that slammed her off the road and down a ravine was driven by a drunken redneck kid and not by my lost twin, called forth from some mystery zone of fate. My father wanted very much to be the one who enabled me to come to that healing recognition, the knowledge that we are responsible not for the shape of the universe but only for what we do — but he wasn't. Ulrich was.

"The power of negative thinking," he declared, citing Marcuse again, "is a force for human liberation." Disobedience could be a virtue. Everyone in Europe seemed to want to move from East to West, but not Ulrich, and then not me. Recklessness could be a virtue, too. And what the hell, having lost my good legs and my mother, what else was there to lose? I never imagined that there was Ulrich, who also never imagined what his loss would be. Why were both of us so blind to what could happen?

It is the advantage of mature adulthood that we can acknowledge, through memory, the complexity of what drove us into the dangerous thickets of youth, which at the time seemed like the wide-open road. If only we could have done so then, seeing, for example, the absolute relevance of the fact that Ulrich, as a small child before memory, had lost his biological father, lost him to the wrong side of an evil war. And it was absolutely relevant, if beyond us at the time, that without his father, he had had for a crucial period the tenderness and protection of his mother entirely to himself. Her attention was the warm bath he never had to leave. From her, just when he needed it most, he had the guarantee that reality is benign, that life is trustworthy, or, as Einstein put it, that the universe is a friend.

That guarantee was betrayed, as he had to have experienced it, when she turned her tender affection toward someone else. Ulrich's mother married General Healy when Ulrich was six, but his life would take its shape from once having had her complete devotion. To subsequently embrace an ideal of "socialism," as it would be called, "with a human face" was to affirm the primordial faith that lovingkindness is at the heart of this cosmos, as he had so firmly been convinced when he had his mother to himself. By the time I knew him, his hedged longing for affection, which on a larger scale we called justice, made Ulrich like every young person. But his unquenchable belief in its possibility made him different. In that, more than in the length of his blond hair or his infatuation with Marcuse, he was my first radical. In that, he was unforgettable.

But Socialist hope goes hand in hand with rage at the cruelties of the present world: starving children, moronic mass media, the sewer of politics, the greed of the elite. Yet what could have been more enraging than the injustice of Ulrich's own life? To be the heir of a Nazi nation he never chose, burdened with its guilt, deprived of a *Volk* to love, and then to be adopted out of it by a tribune, as it had come to seem, of the new empire? The global domination and rank materialism of America could seem to be embodied, to Ulrich *were* embodied, in his father's confusing alternations between the demand for obedience and the bribery of what passed in America for status and affluence. Ulrich's rage at his father, I see now, sprang from the double bind of both resenting him and needing him, of having been rescued by him and orphaned by him, too. For who was General Healy, finally, but the one who took Ulrich's mother away, making Ulrich hate her for what she then became, an American general's dutiful wife? And why should such a boy not have been hurt and angry, with the depth of hurt and anger from which comes every act of true rebellion?

Ulrich told me why he had acceded to his parents' expectation that he would attend university in America, and not in Germany as he'd long hoped. General and Mrs. Healy assumed he would be attending Georgetown or the University of Wisconsin, to which they knew he had applied. But in fact he intended to go to a school in Boston called Brandeis. I had never heard of it. Brandeis was where Marcuse was teaching, Ulrich explained, Marcuse having never returned to Frankfurt after fleeing the Nazis. Ulrich had even written to Marcuse, who had yet to answer. He had applied to Brandeis without telling his parents, an act that made no sense to me. I was slated to attend Princeton, where my father and grandfather had gone, and I took the legacy for granted. Despite myself, my frame of reference was still firmly adolescent, assuming as I did that even our acts of rebellion would somehow be parent-sponsored.

Near the end of April, Ulrich received his long-awaited letter from the admissions office at Brandeis, but it informed him only that his application was incomplete. The parents' form was not filled out, nor was the section having to do with financial aid and method of payment. "Parent signature required for validation," read the bold letters that some clerk had underscored. Parent-financed was the point.

But Ulrich could not admit that as the issue. He took the letter from Brandeis as a rejection pure and simple. In effect, it was, since there had never been a chance that his parents would approve a plan

to go there, and Ulrich was certain he knew why. "Brandeis is a Jewish university," he told me. "Marcuse is a Jew. He teaches there because he had to reject Germany. Brandeis rejects me now because I
am German."

"That's ridiculous," I said. "How would they even know you're
German? You go to an American high school." I threw my arm in a
half-circle, gesturing at the school building behind us. We were
standing on the cinder track, alone, beside the athletic field with its
fresh crop of fragrant green grass. Ulrich had waited for me outside
my last study hall and led me down here, far from the other kids, to
tell me his news. "The people at Brandeis," I said, "would no more
think you're German than they would me."

Ulrich laughed dismissively. "Date of birth, 1943. Place of birth,
Leipzig."

"But your name is Healy. Rick Healy."

"On this application, my name must be Ulrich von Neuhaus, my
name at birth. To call myself Healy is false."

"Your mother's name is Healy now. How can that be false?"

"To call myself Healy is to be a hypocrite, a German in hiding from
what we did."

"You didn't do it."

He answered only with that cold stare of his, and for once it chilled
me, as if I, too, fell within the range of his negation. *Poof! Cease to
exist!*

We were on the cusp of a question, a nest of questions that were
beyond me then. Corporate responsibility, the moral content of
memory, the difference between regret and repentance, sins of the
father, guilt of the son — all of it. Ulrich was miles beyond me in
knowing how the past, as he put it to me once, paraphrasing Marx,
"weighs like a nightmare on the minds of the living."

After a long silence, Ulrich restated his conclusion. "Brandeis is
Jewish. I am German. Of course, with this technicality they reject me.
Of course, Professor Marcuse refuses to reply to me. And I blame
them for nothing."

With that, Ulrich turned on his heel and walked rapidly toward
the school, his pace making it impossible for me to follow. As he took
the news from Brandeis as a personal wound, so I took his striding
away — the only time he had ever used his good legs against me.

It was two days later, the last day of April, that he showed up at my door in the dormitory. The time was shortly before reveille, as the Army brats called the shrill bell that sounded each morning at half past six. But on this morning, his low whistle from the threshold of my room was enough to wake me.

"And you are coming with me," he decreed with a flamboyant hush, and as if his sentence had had a beginning. He looked first one way down the corridor, then the other. Apparently satisfied that he was unobserved, he leaned against the doorjamb, grinning. He was wearing a white shirt, a necktie, and a brown corduroy sport coat, way overdressed for a normal day at school, which was my first clue.

He carried a blue canvas bag with a shoulder strap. I knew it was an Air Force bag, which was unusual for him. The kids of Hap Arnold had plenty of government-issue paraphernalia — bomber jackets, overseas caps, knapsacks — and they seemed to take special pleasure in flaunting such symbols of the occupation on German streets, but I had never known Ulrich to do that. He always acted in downtown Wiesbaden like the American half of his identity was the thing to be ashamed of. Among Americans, he acted like his father's rank was the embarrassment. That he was wearing his father's shoulder bag, therefore, I knew to take as a second clue.

His capricious grin was irresistible. His hair was so blond that, had he been a girl, it would have seemed bleached.

"Going with you where?" I asked in a hoarse whisper. I was sitting on the edge of my bed, in my underwear, half asleep. In the bunk above me, my roommate, a clunky boy named Corky Murtaugh, slept soundly. Murtaugh was unwakable, and would be until just before breakfast shut down an hour and a quarter from now.

"Road trip," Ulrich answered. "*Wandervolk. Wanderschaft.*"

"When?"

"Today. Now."

"We have school. What are you talking about?"

"They let the football team miss school." When Ulrich said "football," he meant soccer. "Why not us? I give you my dispensation, old boy."

I laughed. "And who dispenses you?"

"You do."

"Not a chance, comrade, not a chance. Besides, I have to get back to Frankfurt today. My father let me take the car. I have to drive it home after school. I told you that."

"Indeed, you did." Ulrich's grin broadened.

"You bastard. The car is why you're here. You don't want me, you want my damn car. *Wanderschaft,* my ass. You want me to drive you so you don't have to hitch. You bastard. 'Shaft' is right." I flung one of my two pillows at him.

He caught it and held it back toward me as if it were a tray holding something precious. "Monty, Monty, my good man." Ulrich could mimic his mates from that English boarding school at will. He always feigned Britishness when he called me Monty, as if I were the field marshal. He called me that when he wanted something, perversely mocking me, since he knew I hated it. "Monty," he said. "*Carpe diem.* This is the day the Romans were talking about when they said that."

"He's right, Monty," someone said from behind him. Even before she stuck her head in the doorway, I knew from her voice it was his girlfriend.

Automatically, I pulled my bed sheet forward to cover my left leg. Instead of just being scarred and too thin, like my right, my left leg was a gnarled stick, lacking even the hint of a calf muscle. It humiliated me — I felt the heat come into my face — to think she had seen it. No girl had ever seen my legs.

She was another senior, famously named Kit Carson. No one could blame even a girl for adopting the nickname Kit, with that last name. Each one of us had a pose, and hers required dressing in black — not like a cowboy but a "modern dancer." She wore black tights under her sweater and skirt, which made her look even thinner than she was. Kit was a waif with hollow eyes, evoking Edith Piaf. I had hardly ever spoken to her, though she was also a dormitory resident, living upstairs on the girls' floor. And I understood then that she was how Ulrich had gained entrance to the building, which was off limits to nonresidents. But then, the boys' floor was off limits to girls, and there she was.

"Kit is coming, too," Ulrich said. He put his arm around her shoulder, and the easy way she leaned into him made it seem they'd been intimate, perhaps that very night. Then I recalled Ulrich telling me they had cooled it with each other a few weeks before. But what did I know? The girl thing was not part of what Ulrich and I had in common. This was before the so-called sexual revolution, but that high school had sex in the air, and the openly erotic restlessness between boys and girls was something else that set me apart. Given my physical inhibition, I assumed that sex with a girl was a card I had not been dealt. Feeling bad about it was no more to the point than feeling bad about that other missing card, my calf muscle.

Corky just then rolled over with a grunt, making the bunk rock. Perhaps he somehow sensed the presence of a female. Kit disappeared behind Ulrich, who said, "Meet us at the Zim." He checked his watch. "It opens at seven. That's forty minutes. *Mach schnell!*" And with that, Ulrich hoisted his bag, pulled the door closed, and they were gone.

I had never been in the Zimmertal at that hour, had never seen it crowded with Germans on their way to work, men and women in their various uniforms: the ubiquitous blue smocks of laborers, the black housecoats of *Putzfrauen,* the brown-and-green jackets of municipal employees. They were drinking bowls of *Kaffeeweiss* and eating *Konditorwaren.* These were people whom we Americans rarely saw at ease among themselves, and as I entered the café there was a downshift in their free-spirited talk, a signal that they registered my arrival as an intrusion. But when I jerked my way among the tables to the booth where Ulrich and Kit were already seated, the room's hum adjusted, and the workers stopped looking at me.

Ulrich had a German-language newspaper open on the table in front of him. He was reading intently, ignoring me, which made it seem normal for me to slide onto the same bench with Kit. "Hi, big guy," she said, then raised her eyebrows to indicate that she, too, thought Ulrich rude. Already I sensed her brashness, her readiness to give expression to whatever she thought.

She had a journal-sized notebook open before her, a faint blue tint to the ruled pages. She had been writing in it, and I noticed that her pen was the stiletto-like instrument that draftsmen use. With a glance, I saw that she had printed minute letters, each one inside its square, forming words on the page, lines of prose. "What's that?" I asked.

"Keeping my accounts," she answered, closing the book, letting me see the green cloth cover with its printed word, "Accounts."

Ulrich read through to the end of whatever article had snagged his attention, then muttered something to himself in German as he folded up the newspaper. It was that day's *Frankfurter Neue Presse,* and on the front page was a large photograph of a man in a glass booth wearing earphones. It would become a famous image, but I had never seen it, and assumed the paper was featuring another story about the quiz show scandals in America — the isolation booth, the headset. How Europeans loved those symbols of our decadence.

Ulrich looked up at me. "So you came."

"To breakfast, yes." I grinned. "But I have algebra at nine." I looked at Kit. "You too, right?"

Instead of answering me, she ran the tip of her forefinger along the edge of the powdered sugar on her plate, rectifying it.

A waiter came, and I asked for coffee with milk.

When he was gone, Ulrich said, with a gravity that surprised me, "These days are testing us. Now it is my duty to put the test to you."

Once more I glanced at the girl, and was taken aback when she flashed me another quizzical look, as if Ulrich's cosmic consciousness had made us allies.

"You must come with me to Berlin," he said.

"Berlin!"

Now when I looked at Kit, she said, "He just told me."

I said, "Why would I go to Berlin?"

"For the reason," he answered firmly, "you would have gone to Spain in 1937. Russia in 1917. Paris in 1789. Lads into the breach, my man. The bloody breach. Berlin is where we belong. Berlin is where words mean what they claim to mean. A blow for true justice, solidarity, the cause! Willy Brandt, the SPD, the only city in West Germany where Socialists are in charge! Going to Berlin is how we declare ourselves."

"Going to Berlin is crazy," I said.

At last Ulrich broke into his familiar grin. "Which is the other reason we must go there."

Kit shook her head. "I'm not going. Not a chance. I thought we were fixing to go to a Grand Prix race somewhere. He didn't tell me it was Berlin until just before you came in. Specially not Berlin. Crawdaddy would kill me."

"Who?"

"My old man. Great white father. Sergeant Buck Carson."

Kit spoke with the accent of the Deep South. When in English class she had recited verses from Eliot's "Prufrock," it sounded like the ruminations of a Confederate widow: "Let us go then, you and *ah* . . ." The lost world was not of the Somme, but of Shiloh. That stunning performance, two or three months before, had created an impression of fatal worldliness, adding Kit's name to the list of girls I assumed would never notice me. But now, suddenly, she seemed as young as I, and a bit of a hick.

I shook my head, too, but I was determined not to sound like her. "It isn't that my father would kill me," I said. "It's simpler than that. I made a deal with him. He trusted me with the car this week. I'm not going to let him down."

Ulrich nodded sagely. "So your hesitation is not about algebra class."

"Not hesitation, comrade. Refusal."

He looked at Kit. "And you, *Fräulein?*"

"No. I could care less about algebra. I ain't going to Berlin, that's all. Berlin is way off-limits." She swung toward me. "Why are you calling him comrade?"

Her question brought me and Ulrich together in a laugh. "Just a joke between us," I explained, and, pathetically enough, I was pleased to see that in this one sphere I had more going with Ulrich than she did.

"Joke?" she said. "As in, Knock, knock."

"Who's there?"

"Comrade."

"Comrade who?"

Kit began to sway in her seat, floating her hands, singing with pizzazz, "Come raht along, come raht along, to Alexander's Ragtime Band!"

"Alexander*platz*," Ulrich corrected, a reference that escaped me. That he'd cut her off deflated her. "Berlin is not the forbidden city, you two," he said. "Haven't you seen the billboards? 'Come to Berlin!' Young people going there pay lower taxes, and get help to find a place to live. They *want* people our age in Berlin."

"German people," I said.

"*And* Yanks," he countered. "There is a high school in Berlin, an American school like ours, named for General Patton. There are sons and daughters of American military, same as here. Thousands of Americans, all under orders to live as if everything is normal. Us, too. The Wiesbaden football team goes to Berlin. The debating team. We could be the debating team. H. H. Arnold versus George S. Patton. You could be the team captain, Kit. Look bloody well on your precollege curriculum vitae."

She shook her head firmly. The girl had become increasingly uncomfortable. She had made a perfect rectangle of her powdered sugar.

"I vote for Kit Carson," Ulrich announced suddenly. "What about you, Monty? Kit for team captain!"

"This isn't funny, Ulrich."

"Of course it isn't funny!" He slammed his hand down on the newspaper that was spread before him. "*Kadavergehorsam! Kadavergehorsam!* That's how Eichmann justified himself. The obedience of a corpse! That is what he owed his superiors. 'A good soldier acts with the obedience of a corpse'!"

The others in the café fell silent at this outburst, but like the timid occupation-era Germans we Americans knew so well, they made a point not to look our way. A roomful of people tidying up their powdered sugar.

"What are you talking about?" I asked in a voice several notches quieter than the one he had used.

"Eichmann. The trial." He pushed the newspaper around so that I could see its photo right side up. The man in the booth was no quiz show contestant. He was Adolf Eichmann, whose trial had begun in Jerusalem earlier that week. A few weeks before, the actual debating club, speaking of that, had argued before the whole school the question of whether Israel had been justified in kidnapping Eichmann from Argentina. The contrary had prevailed.

Now, when I recognized Eichmann's picture, the glass booth made no sense to me. Only later would I understand it as his bulletproof cage. Once Ulrich saw that I had taken the image in, he said, "There is the meaning of obedience. Good German obedience. The obedience of corpses."

I shook my head, offended. "This has nothing to do with what Kit and I are talking about. We're just not going to Berlin with you, that's all."

"Do you know what day is tomorrow?"

"Saturday."

"It is May Day, Michael. *Ersten Mai*. The workers' festival. Workers of the world, unite! The greatest fest in Europe will be in Berlin."

"*East* Berlin," Kit put in urgently, and to me. "He said *East* Berlin."

"Not *just* the East," Ulrich said. "Willy Brandt is mayor of West Berlin, the Socialist mayor, the only Socialist mayor in all of West Germany. The SPD always celebrates May Day, claiming the holiday for trade unions, not only Communists."

"He wants to go to the Communist parade," Kit insisted. "He told me."

"Of course we will go to the Communist parade — to protest it! To stand for true socialism. Workers' Day belongs to workers, not to the state. SPD, yes. KPD, no. USSR, no."

Ulrich was grinning again. He was pronouncing the various acronyms in the German way, and I followed only with difficulty, which he must have sensed, because he slowed down to explain. "The SPD is the party that last opposed Hitler. Then, after the war, they stood up to the Communists — the KPD. But they did so precisely for Marxist principles, which the KPD betrays. May Day is the perfect day to see the *real* difference between East and West Berlin — not the difference as imagined by shallow Americans who condemn everyone on the left."

"Wait a minute, wait a minute," I said, and I put a hand on Kit's forearm to let her know I was with her. "How do you go to East Berlin?"

"By going to West Berlin, how else?"

"Not by driving."

"By driving to the *border,* Monty. From the border by taking the train, the *American* train, which requires no visa, not of two Yank princes and a princess. Traveling by this train allows no interrogation by border guards. Being on this train is like being at the American embassy, immune. And I told you. We are the debating club. We have a debate tournament at Patton High School. Hip Hip High versus Blood and Guts."

It had taken until now for me to see that he was entirely serious, and what made me really nervous was how possible he made it seem. With his broad smile and perfectly straight white teeth, he sat waiting for me to declare myself. I was to declare myself in the light of his un-stoppable manic air, his display of cleverness, how easily he would an-swer the questions of the military police as we boarded the Army train, GIs barely older than we were.

And now I saw the point of that blue shoulder bag on the bench beside him. I glimpsed its tag, and sure enough, there were the two silver stars of his father's bottomless privilege in the world of the oc-cupation. An Army train, a general's son, an easy transit. He was right: no sweat. And I saw, with Kit, what there was to fear — that we could actually do as he proposed. I said nothing.

The waitress arrived with my coffee. When she was gone, the mood had changed. "Then drive me to the train," he said quietly. "Skip your classes and drive me to the train."

"I don't think you should do this, Ulrich. East Berlin is not a place for fun and games. Especially if your father —"

He raised his hand abruptly, cutting me off. "He is not my father."

I knew what he meant, that the general, strictly speaking, was his stepfather. Still, the declaration shocked.

"You are not to refer to him as my father." He smiled oddly. "Here you see the disobedience of a living body," he said. Only the thinnest veneer of levity carried his voice now. I sensed beneath it desperation and hurt such as he had never shown me. In his bitter bravado, I heard a pronouncement that the time had come for him to act on all that he had been telling me for months. I heard, that is, the stifled cry of a friend, and I knew at once, as the friend I wanted more than ever to be, I was bound to answer.

"Disobedience," he explained, "is how I know that I am not dead."

I faced Kit. "We can take him to the border, right? To the train?" When she agreed, I think that she, too, knew that the train that mat-tered was already moving, and we were on it.

5

TWELVE HOURS LATER, just coming on dusk, we three comrades disembarked from the Army train in the cavernous new *Hauptbahnhof* in the bustling heart of West Berlin. Our arms were linked. Kit was in the middle, I was on the right so that I could use my stick, but in fact she, too, was taking my weight, enabling me to match the sprightly pace as we marched out into, unquestionably, the most exciting city in the world.

Every way but verbally, Kit and I asked each other, How could we have hesitated even for a moment? Both of us were shouldering a small bag, for without actually declaring a change of heart, she and I had returned to the dormitory from the Zimmertal for our passports and a weekend's change of clothes. "Just to the border," we had both been saying, and then, hell, we'd each grabbed bags — "just in case." I put on a necktie and blazer. Kit came down from her room wearing a belted khaki tunic, a standard item of an airman's uniform, the equivalent of a civilian's safari jacket. It was far too large for her, but she wore it with panache over her black skirt and tights. The belt was knotted at her narrow waist. And she was wearing gold hoop earrings.

Her stylishness hit me, and I saw then the trick of her pixie haircut, what was called an Italian boy — how it displayed her long thin neck, not a boy's neck at all. The earrings drew attention to the sensual line of her throat, which was set off further by the red bandana she wore loosely around her neck, knotted above her breasts. Her getup qualified as an outfit, marked by the way she turned up the collar of her jacket. On her, the airman's jacket was sexy. And I noted the ghostly outline on each sleeve marking the places where a sergeant's stripes had been removed. So as Ulrich pointed to his father — stepfather — by carrying his bag, Kit pointed to her daddy by wearing his uniform tunic. I pointed to mine, I suppose, with that blazer, purchased with Dad the summer before at Brooks Brothers on Madison Avenue.

To my surprise, I sensed that the shift in Kit's willingness to come on this adventure was tied to the shift in mine, as if my being a companion in Berlin was what would make it safe. As I had gunned the blue convertible out of the chapel parking lot, the top down, I was excruciatingly aware of the pretty girl pressing close next to me, an all-time first. Her willowy leg was against mine, and I felt no impulse to pull back. I did not kid myself about why she was so close. All three of us were squeezed into the front seat, Kit pressed as close to Ulrich on her other side as she was to me.

It was then I recognized that I had overcome my qualms as much in relation to her as to Ulrich. This was a girl I wanted to be with, that was all. So completely had I become preoccupied with these two that, hitting the road, I never gave a further thought to my father, or to my promise.

At Helmstedt, we boarded the Army train in giddy high spirits, helped by beers we had downed at lunch in a wasp-ridden garden restaurant. The MPs who checked our passports, dependents' credentials, and tickets were, as Ulrich predicted, only friendly. But that would change. A short while after the train began to move, it approached Magdeburg, the first city inside East Germany and the effective border crossing, the place where the Communists usually halted the train.

The American guards had warned all passengers to sit quietly in our compartments with the window shades drawn. Once through the checkpoint at Magdeburg, we could lift the shades and look out, they said, but doing so before or at the border was strictly forbidden.

The train slowed to a stop, the engine shut down, and an eerie silence settled on the snug, velvet-upholstered compartment. With the shades drawn, deep shadow enclosed us. We three had the space to ourselves, which had seemed a stroke of luck on boarding, but which now, for me and Kit, became the opposite of luck, because of the license Ulrich took from our isolation. Outside, the East German border guards were presumably checking the roster of passengers. We didn't know it, but they routinely demanded to board the train, and equally routinely, the GIs refused to allow them to board — a power they could exercise in the absence of any irregularity as defined by the detailed protocols of the Four-Power Agreements.

All we knew, inside our stuffy, dark compartment, was that the procedures were taking a long time. Ulrich became increasingly agitated, and, finally unable to restrain himself, he lifted the lower edge of the window shade. He raised it no more than two or three inches, just enough to bend down and peek out. A wedge of light sliced down onto the floor.

"Tanks!" he whispered. "Machine guns! Red stars! My God, the soldiers are Russians!"

"Rick!" Kit hissed. "Holy shit, Rick! Close it!" Kit had made herself even smaller, scrunching as far into the distant corner of the cushioned bench as she could. "Please!" Her insistence was absolute — a girl with a will. Ulrich honored it, dropping the shade. The light was gone.

What seemed a bare instant later, the door to our compartment slid open, banging into its slot. An extremely large black soldier stormed in on us. His olive fatigues were crisply pressed, his boots gleaming, his helmet shimmering white with the black letters *MP* in stark relief. He had his sidearm drawn, and once in with us, he pointed the gun at Ulrich, who sat alone by the window on the bench opposite me and Kit. "What are you trying to do?" the MP demanded in a shrieking voice close to panic. "You had the fucking shade up. Didn't you get the orders?"

I thought he was going to shoot Ulrich. Ulrich, splayed against the bench, thought so, too.

Before Ulrich could answer, a brown-uniformed Soviet officer with a gangster-style machine gun under his arm burst in behind the MP, who swung around. "I'm handling this! This is mine!" And then he said something I did not understand, presumably in Russian.

Behind the Soviet officer, pressing in from the train corridor to fill the threshold, were a blue-uniformed *Volkspolizei* officer, also with a pistol, and, squeezing in beside him, another overlarge black MP. Very tall black men, I would later learn, were regularly assigned to East-West checkpoints in Europe, as they were to North-South checkpoints in Korea. Intimidation was the idea, as I understood full well. It wasn't only the first MP's skin color and size that were frightening. With his gun leveled at Ulrich, he seemed on the edge of craziness, as if taking Ulrich's act as a personal affront. I sensed that the Russian and the East German were giving the MP his leeway exactly because he seemed dangerously close to losing control of himself.

I pushed back into Kit, the two of us huddled together. The second MP forced his way into the compartment, gently pulling the Russian aside and reaching toward his agitated colleague. "Okay, Sergeant," he said, taking the sleeve of the first MP, "I got it." This man seemed calmer, and it was a relief when the first one yielded to him. The second MP had captain's bars on his collar. His sidearm was still in its holster. "Wait in the hallway, Sergeant. Cover us." The sergeant backed out, taking up a place behind the Russian, beside the German. He did not put his gun away, though, which kept everyone nervous.

I clutched my cane, which the captain made a first point of sizing up, as if deciding whether it was a weapon. His glance fell to my legs, then up to my eyes, and I saw an abbreviated version of the familiar pity I knew so well from strangers. He turned away from me, to Ulrich.

"Did you take pictures?" he asked. "Do you have a camera?"

"No, sir," Ulrich answered quickly. That he was completely intimidated shocked me, underscored my fear.

The captain unsnapped the cover of his holster, as if to draw his weapon, but as he did so, he said, "Well, now we have to let these gentlemen satisfy themselves that there is no camera. Do you understand?"

"Yes, sir."

"These are the rules, bud. You do as I say or they take you off the train, and I let them."

"Yes, sir."

"Stand up. Arms out."

Ulrich did as he was told. In the cramped space, his outstretched hands brushed each side of the compartment. He turned this way and that. No camera hanging from his neck. No camera on the bench where he'd been sitting. In the adjacent space was his bag. The captain picked it up, unzipped the main pocket, and upended it so that Ulrich's toilet kit, fresh underwear, and shirt fell out. No camera.

The captain glanced back at the Soviet officer, who was watching like a supervising surgeon. He said something in Russian, his voice a bulldozer. The captain unzipped the side pocket of the bag and again upended it, shaking. But now, out fell a small aluminum canister, larger than a thimble, obviously a film container.

I shot a look at Ulrich and saw the surprise in his face — a film canister he had never seen. I knew to mark the moment. *Oh, Jesus.*

"Oh, Christ," the captain muttered as if reading my mind. He stooped and snagged the canister before the Russian reacted to it. "The fuck is this?" he loudly demanded of Ulrich, holding the bright metal cylinder between thumb and forefinger right in front of Ulrich's nose. Under his breath, he added, "Make it good."

To my astonishment, Ulrich did. "That would be the yearbook pictures," he explained with what I recognized as a forced calmness. "We deliver it from our high school in Wiesbaden to the American high school in West Berlin. All the Defense Department high schools in Europe have a combined yearbook."

It was true about the combined yearbook, but otherwise what he said was utter fabrication. Yet what really stunned me was that Ulrich was speaking in a flat, unfamiliar accent with a firm hint of Dixie, like Kit's. There was nothing German in his way of speaking, no guttural curl, no vestige of the Gothic script I often imagined in balloons above his head. His British mimicry was familiar — "Monty, my good man" — but never American. Like most Americans, my assumption was that, the Deep South apart, our unaccented speech could not be mimicked.

"That film," he was saying, "has the pictures of our debating club. We're the debating club from H. H. Arnold in Wiesbaden." He pronounced "Wiesbaden" with a *w* sound, not a *v*, like any old American ignoramus. He blithely concluded, "They need our negatives at Patton High for the yearbook layout." Then he turned his most shit-eating grin to the Russian.

The captain turned to him, too, and spoke several sharp sentences in Russian. That might have been the end of it, but just then the *Vopo,* the East German in the doorway, put in a question, still in Russian.

The question made the captain turn back to Ulrich and ask, "What's the German word for yearbook?"

Ulrich's eyes widened. He shook his head. *German word? Me?*

I did not know why it was important for Ulrich not to be taken for a German. I did not know why a roll of film should spark such invention and deceit. I assumed that if there were problems tied to Ulrich's father, they involved his rank, which was, as I would later learn, the least of it.

There was an awkward silence in the crowded compartment, and it was just beginning to feel dangerous when Kit, her voice muffled against my shoulder, said, "*Jahrbuch.*"

We looked at her. In her lap was the pale green notebook I had noticed at the Zimmertal. It was open, and something made me take it in more carefully now. Lined paper. Neatly printed paragraphs separated by space breaks. The book seemed more than half full of writing.

The *Vopo* spoke again, in what language I had no idea, but he was still asking. To my further surprise, Kit replied, "*Bericht, Denkerschrift, Memoiren.*"

I thought of her in algebra class, her sharp answers, her readiness to risk being taken by other kids as smart. Now I realized she was more than smart. Advanced German. A rebellious kid, but brilliant.

The *Vopo* reached down and snatched the notebook out of her hand.

"Hey!" she said, but then regretted it and shrank back. The East German flipped the pages as if looking for what she'd read. "*Was ist das?*" he demanded.

"*Mein Tagebuch, mein Seelebuch,*" she answered. The story of my soul.

"Like Rilke," I put in, and instantly felt stupid.

Kit put her hand out for the book. "It's right private," she said. I sensed her anxiety in the plaintive tone with which she then said, "*Bitte schön.*"

The *Vopo* handed the book back, nodding like a satisfied teacher, which the captain took as an opening to bend down and gather Ulrich's belongings, folding them carefully back into his bag, as if only now aware of the general's stars on the tag. Drawing no further attention to the film canister, the captain slipped it back into its side pocket, which he zipped shut. He turned back to the Russian and, with a broad sweep of his hand, gestured him and the others out. With a last, hostile glance at Kit, of all people, the *Vopo* departed. Then, brushing roughly by the other MP, the sergeant in the threshold, so did the Russian with his machine gun.

Beads of sweat were streaming down the sergeant's face, and his gun was still leveled at Ulrich, his hand unsteady.

"Holster that, Sergeant," the captain ordered. The MP did so, and when he exhaled, his relief was large. He looked at his superior gratefully. I realized how young the sergeant was, and how irrelevant to him was his own mammoth physique. I identified with his obvious feeling of being in way over his head. "Go tell the trainmen to get us moving," the captain ordered. Without another glance at us, the sergeant disappeared.

I sensed the release of tension in Kit's body, the way her hipbone settled into mine, and only then noticed how I had pressed myself against her. Or was it she pressing me? Who is this girl, I wondered. I moved away from her slightly, back toward the center of the velvet bench.

Now that the others were gone, the American captain stepped away from the seat by the window so that Ulrich could resume it. The MP's voice was almost kindly when he asked Ulrich, "Do you think your old man got where he is by acting like an asshole?"

"No, sir," Ulrich said.

"If I write up a dependent, the charge goes to the father's CO, not the father. Did you know that?"

"No, sir."

"And in your case, that's just a little farther up the chain of command than I care to go. At that altitude, my nose bleeds, son. And when my nose bleeds, I get mean."

"Yes, sir."

"You're not just an Army brat. You're the son of the brass. You have a reputation to uphold, young man." The MP said this sternly, but with something like affection, too. I had seen this deference a few times before — the U.S. Army as a kind of *in loco parentis* for the children of soldiers and officers alike — but it had never relieved me as it did then. The MP said, "And speaking of upholding your old man's reputation, you should get your hair cut. Shave that beard. You look like a bum."

"Yes, sir," Ulrich said. The obedience of a corpse. After a bout of real fear, Ulrich was chastened.

"Give it ten minutes after the train moves out," the MP ordered, "before you lift the shades. Okay?"

Ulrich nodded. The officer said mournfully, "It's some damn fool thing like this that's going to start World War Three. You know that, don't you?"

Ulrich straightened his shoulders. "That sergeant shouldn't have been threatening me with a gun."

"Oh, really? He's what kept the Reds off of you, son. The hair trigger is what keeps the Reds in line. Didn't you know that?"

Ulrich couldn't quite bring himself to answer, but I could see that his anger was trumping his fear. His face above his whiskers was red. I couldn't believe he was daring even to begin to challenge this man. I wanted to yell, Shut up!

The officer seemed unperturbed. He said, "Don't you be the thing that brings a hair-triggered weapon out of its holster. Who's to blame for what happens then? Why don't you kids debate that."

None of us answered. It was a debate we would not have, because our being to blame would be so crystal clear.

He gave us each a last once-over. Locking eyes with me, he said, "Debating club, huh?"

"Yes, sir," I said, aware of binding myself to the lie.

"Good for you."

Only after he'd slid the compartment door shut behind him did I realize that the MP was thinking of my legs, the gumption it would take for a crippled kid to stand on a stage and give a speech from note cards. In another circumstance I'd have felt condescended to, but right then I was grateful to be included in the sweep of his affirmation. I was sorry he was gone.

There was so much to say once the train had begun rolling again, but in the weighty aftermath of what quickly seemed an unreal incident, speech seemed wrong. Instead, the clack-clack of the iron wheels hitting the rough joints of the tracks — rougher than ever, the first sign of inferior East German maintenance — began to pulse in the air like an amplified heartbeat.

Kit buried her nose in her accounts book, her draftsman's pen rising and falling as she worked to keep her letters smooth despite the jostling railroad car.

I sensed that we would each settle now into the solitude of transient contemplation, depriving me of the chance to ask Kit my questions: What are you writing there? And hey, how did your German get so good? Or to ask of Ulrich, conversely, Why did you pretend not to know German? I wanted to ask him about the stark fright I had seen in his face when the film canister fell out of his father's bag. But that his lies had worked made the lies seem appropriate, and it felt almost true, what we had claimed — the debating club, the yearbook.

Ulrich's lies, for the moment, had made our trip seem mundane, safe, sponsored. I briefly found myself looking forward to our arrival at the high school in West Berlin, checking in at the principal's office, being shown to rooms in the American dormitory, doing a microphone check at the podium in the high school auditorium, practicing our topic: *Resolved: That World War Three will be started by some stupid kid lying to his father.*

That thought made me shut the lid on the free association of a traveler's brooding, and also on the thin consolations of the falsehoods Ulrich had constructed. Our purpose was not a return to the protection of the American cocoon, but adventures in the anti–Wonderland of the Socialist state, the first of which we'd just had. The lies, in fact, were part of our rebellion. But I knew I would be in trouble if I was left alone to follow such a train of thought in rhythm with a train crossing forbidden country. So I leaned toward Ulrich. "How did you learn to speak like that?"

He ignored me, staring at his wristwatch.

"Hey, Rick," I said, a pointed refusal to call him by his German name, "how'd you learn to talk like that? Come on, I want to know."

He lifted his gaze to meet mine, but very slowly. "Frankly, my dear," he began, and of course I knew the inflection. In three words, he'd nailed Rhett Butler. "I don't give a damn." And then he let his face fall into that same shit-eating grin. *That's how, asshole.*

I pictured him, a lost boy, hour after hour in one base theater after another, watching *Gone With the Wind,* which was in permanent release at military movie houses overseas; watching a dozen other movies like it — *Picnic, Giant, Casablanca, Red River, Rebel Without a Cause.* I saw a boy in the dark studying and memorizing; proving that he wasn't British; trying not to be German; taking the measure of the way Americans walk and hold their cigarettes and knot their neckties; listening acutely to the way Americans onscreen talk to one another, preparing to talk that way himself when the time came. The surprise, I saw, was that it had come so soon.

Ulrich resumed studying his watch, leaving me to wonder which of his accents was real. And that led me to wonder, in the swaying clack-clack of the hypnotizing train, how I had come to think of this stranger as my friend. Ulrich had put on display the mystery of accent and its relation to identity, especially for those made self-conscious by the way they talk. Then I realized that Kit, with her drawl, would have been Ulrich's tutor, a thought that made me wonder about their relationship. They weren't acting like boyfriend-girlfriend now. Why was Kit sitting next to me?

I thought of asking Ulrich about that film canister, then admitted to myself that whatever it was — whatever had made him afraid — I didn't want to know. And this was well before mysterious rolls of film had become clichés of movie thrillers.

A few moments later, Ulrich tugged the window shade down and, with a flourish, let it go. The shade snapped up to its rod, flapping around twice, letting harsh sunlight flood the compartment. The landscape outside flashed by in a blur.

"Rick!" Kit protested, uncoiling from her corner like a spring. Her accounts book fell to the floor.

"Ten minutes, the captain said. Ten minutes is up."

"You're pushing it, Rick. You shouldn't be pushing it."

"They're the ones who pushed, Kit. Not me. You saw that guy with his gun."

"You asked for it. Don't be so damn irresponsible."

Kit's direct challenge to Ulrich surprised me. She was pissed, but there was also a core of self-possession in her, unusual in one so young; unusual, I would have said then, in a girl.

"What is irresponsible?" Ulrich asked. "A hair trigger is irresponsible. Incompetent Americans playing games at the border are irresponsible. What would have happened if the Soviets back there were as wild as the *Schwarz?*"

"*Schwarz!*" Kit said. "What the fuck! Don't call him *Schwarz!*"

"Black? He *is* black."

"You know what I mean, Rick. *Schwarz* is Kraut for 'nigger.' And I won't have that."

"I won't have 'Kraut,'" he retorted angrily.

"It's 'nigger' I can't stand," Kit said. "I've a mind to get off this damn train right now."

Ulrich laughed, gestured at the flashing window. "Be my guest, my dear."

Kit glared at him.

He said, "And stop calling me Rick."

"Whatever you say," she replied with sudden resignation. She leaned down to get her accounts book and sat back against her corner, pulling her shoeless feet under, stretching her black stockings at the knees so they showed white. She glanced at me with shy embarrassment and whispered, "I can't believe this," which I took to mean, I can't believe I'm in a fight with him. But then she added, still under her breath, "Can't believe there's racist bullshit here, too." A white southerner who hated the word "nigger."

I touched her foot with my left hand. "Ulrich," I said, "what does that guy's being Negro have to do with anything?"

"Everything, Monty," he said, but calmly. "Everything. The only reason those assholes are on duty at the border is because they're Negro — especially the NCO. Obviously underqualified for the motor pool, much less the checkpoint. Negro giants, that's why they are there. We are supposed to believe all Americans are bigger than us, all are frightening Nubians. How stupid do they think we are?"

"We?"

"We Germans. We Krauts." He looked at Kit. "The bigotry here is yours, not mine." Ulrich turned away, as if this declaration ended the argument. He pressed his forehead against the glass, inviting a change of mood, inviting us all to stare out at East Germany. This was what we'd come to see.

Only then did it hit me that we were now fully behind the Iron

Curtain. The train was flying, as if to cover the enemy territory as fast as possible, the right idea. We were passing through a country town, and I glimpsed a man on a tractor, then a man in a white apron, a baker, then a man standing by a sign, which I missed, but barber popped into my head. Farmers, bakers, barbers — a town like any other in the world. A generic town in Soviet Germany, with a generic population — women and men working, laughing, loving, dying, caring for their children and their elders, looking back at us and wondering if we are different. Such were my first impressions of the enemy.

I moved closer to the window, opposite Ulrich, intending to focus on particular objects to undo that sense of the generic. I saw a rusted corrugated-iron roof, then I saw the crack splitting a cinderblock wall. I saw a church steeple that had been shorn off, blunted like a broken sword, bomb damage from the war. Then, instead of singly, I began seeing objects grouped: vacant houses, carts without wheels, herds of emaciated cows, chicken coops clustered around weed-ridden ponds.

When our train careened through crossroads villages, people were gathered behind lowered pikes: women in babushkas holding the hands of children, the children with one thumb held firmly in their mouths. They must have come to the crossings to watch us pass, but no one waved.

I saw derelict railroad cars at sidings, rusting in place but not quite abandoned. They had sackcloth curtains on their windows or, if they were boxcars, sackcloth curtains in the doorways, indications that these railroad cars had been claimed for houses.

Even at high speed, the scenes I glimpsed were striking for their drabness. The trees had the sharp green of spring, and the sky was as blue as it ever was in what we so blithely called the free world, but the human things seemed devoid of color: the gray of the buildings, the dried mud of the roads, the washed-out pallor of housecoats and shawls. Railroad workers wore black overalls. The smock coats here, unlike the bright blue of the West German workers', were the color of dishwater.

Soon it seemed I could make out the very eyes of those who watched us pass. No color there, either. What an exception we must

have been in our flashing, carefully painted cars behind the sleek locomotive. Now I understood why the Army had polished its fittings
and scrubbed its wheels as if the train were a ship, so that even in the
few seconds it took to pass through the vision of any one Communist, the American train would cut the arc of a figment shooting
through a dream.

Shooting stars, I thought, cutting through the night sky — me, as a
boy, sitting beside my father on the dock at our lake in the north
woods, my father whom I loved. And now it struck me: the harsh-
ness of our last moments together earlier that week, how I had re-
sented him, how pissed off he was, even as he had let me take the goddamn car.

I looked back at Kit, expecting her, too, to be transfixed by the
sight of what we were passing through. Not so. She had fallen asleep.
Her foot was only inches from my hip — a perfectly shaped foot,
joined to a trim ankle and leg tucked away inside the flare of her father's field jacket. I took advantage of the moment to stare at her. I
timed the rising and falling of her small but alluring breasts, measur-
ing her breathing in and breathing out against my own.

Her accounts book had fallen to her side, toward me, and it was
open. The letters were tiny but so carefully made that I had no trouble taking them in, one clean paragraph:

*You made her set with you on the veranda, and you tole her it was incur-
able, incurable! And the hot breeze on her face pushed hair acrost her eyes, so
you could not make out what she reckoned of what you said.*

I could have read more, but I stopped because it seemed wrong,
and I found myself wanting to ask about that word "set," about
"acrost," and about "incurable." Who was "you"? And who was
"her"? But already I knew what a violation it would be to ask about
what I'd just read, even that.

I looked at her sweet sleeping face. *Where are you from? Georgia?
Virginia? Is that your father's jacket? Whose bandana? And incurable what?*
Polio, I wanted to tell her, is incurable, but it doesn't need to kill you.

To get away from those thoughts, I faced Ulrich. He was so intent,
looking out the window, that I felt I shouldn't interrupt him. But
with Kit asleep, and my thickening questions about her, I knew I had
to. Her presence next to me on that velvet bench, her foot only

inches from my leg, the sweet aroma of her body, its sly movement with each breath — it all combined to spark in me physical sensations I knew very little about and a quite unphysical longing that felt intensely familiar.

"So, Ulrich, *wie geht es Ihnen?*"

"*Sehr gut,*" he answered quietly, not turning toward me. Then he added, under his breath, "*Natürlich.*" He was aware of my watching him, of my waiting. So then he did look at me. "*Und Sie?*"

"I'm okay. Although to tell you the truth, I wasn't so sure back there." I'd calibrated my voice so as not to wake Kit. I was desperate not to wake her. "At the border," I said, to distinguish from the uneasiness I'd felt during the flare-up over *Schwarz*.

"Nor was I." Ulrich matched my tone. "You did well at the border, Michael."

I deflected his compliment with a slight recoil of my head. "Me? You're the one who pulled it off. You were great."

"I was a fool. As the MP said, an asshole." He glanced at sleeping Kit, and I sensed that he felt like an asshole in relation to her, too.

"He didn't call you an asshole."

"He said my father *wasn't* one. My stepfather."

"That's not —"

"World War Three, he said. It is possible I was wrong to want to do this."

His voice had fallen back into the edgy rhythm of a German speaking English, a hint of a *v* in "want." A German speaking English well, but as a guest in the language, not an owner of it. I had to stare at him hard to be sure there was no punch line coming. How could Ulrich be having second thoughts when I myself was — I hadn't the word for it then, but now I would describe my state as one of quiet exhilaration. The border crossing had frightened me, but deliciously so. What fear I had felt before, in hospitals, had been smothered by my parents.

"Why didn't you want them to know you are German?" I asked.

"A normal American kid. I could not have them looking a second time at me." He saw the incomprehension in my expression, so he added, "Because of my stepfather."

I thought of debating the point with him: *Actually, he's your adoptive father, not your stepfather.* Instead, I indicated his bag. "But he's your ticket. The rank is what makes them jump."

"But if they knew more than what rank he is . . ."

"Like what?"

"Like what he does. What he is in command of."

"Which is?"

"Intelligence."

Nothing suggests the innocence of those times like my prior assumption that the word "intelligence" meant only the ability to think and learn. I could see it in Ulrich's eyes when he realized that he had to explain the word to me.

"Military information," he said. "*Auskunft.* Secrets. Major General Healy is in charge of learning about the plans and activities of the enemy. He is what you call a spy. He is the chief of spies."

This was a long time ago, remember. Before spies and rolls of film had become the stuff of pulp fiction and movies. So I was only mystified by what he was saying. I let my eyes go to the window, the vista flashing by, a lake, trees in the distance, the ordinary world. I held fast to the sight and said, "If it's secret, how do you know?"

"You know what your father does, do you not?"

"Yes."

"Because he tells you?"

"Not exactly."

"Because you know, that is all."

"But your father —"

"He is not my father."

I brought my gaze back from the passing scene to look at him. "Your adoptive father, your stepfather, whatever he is, the guy who raised you . . ." Suddenly it hit me, a whole new context for understanding what we were doing. "And you're going to Berlin? You're going to the May Day parade in East Berlin, and your father is a spy?"

"Not my father," he said patiently. Then he smiled, a certain satisfaction in his expression: even I could see the outrage of what he'd done. And now I understood the meaning of his second thought.

"You *are* an asshole, Ulrich." And we grinned at each other. I thought of that film canister dropping from the general's bag, but had no idea what my question about it should be.

After a moment, he shrugged. "But also, for me," he said, "this is a kind of going home. I lived in Berlin as a child. It was where my mother and I came when we were refugees." He gestured at the window. "That is my home country. Not Germany. *East* Germany. And look, look at it, Michael." He hunched closer to the window and pointed. "Have you been seeing this? How there is no glass in the windows? Look there. The roof with tiles missing. The edge of the roof with no gutter. Do you see?"

The buildings were going by too fast. I had to consciously adjust my eyes to take in first one building, then another. We were passing a farming town. A barn. A silo. A building without gutters.

"There are no gutters in East Germany. The copper has all been stolen. Pillaged by the Russians. Since the war, and still. Look, there, see. Roof tiles again. Missing roof tiles. Even glass. See the horse carts. Why are there horse carts? Because the tractors are all gone. Stolen by the Russians! In Bonn, they say it is communism that keeps the DDR in poverty, but it is not communism. It is Soviet theft. Those gutters and roof tiles are on the houses of commissars in Minsk and Leningrad. It is what Marcuse says. There it is. Communism has not been tried."

Marcuse, Christ. It was the last conversation I wanted to have. I glanced back at Kit. Her pen had fallen into her lap, her accounts book closed beside her. Her face was turned into the corner. Still asleep.

Instead of launching into one of his political tutorials, Ulrich fell back against his seat, abruptly weary and, it seemed to me, sad. No Marcuse for him, either. "Those people we are seeing there," he said. People at yet another country crossroads, people not waving, not even the children waving. "They are prisoners. As I myself would be were it not for my mother, who . . ." He let his voice trail off.

"Who what?"

"Carried me out. From Leipzig to Berlin. Do you have any idea how far a hundred and eighty kilometers is when you are walking, carrying a child, carrying a bundle that holds all that remains to you? All that remains of a once great family of Saxony? Do you?"

"No," I said, hardly breathing.

"She cleared rubble in Berlin. The *Trümmerfrauen*. You know that word?"

"No."

"The rubble women. She got us to Berlin, but with nothing. The two of us alone. She would sit me in the pram nearby, then work with the other women, picking up debris, wreckage. My earliest memory is sitting beside a mountain of paving stones, hearing the stones click against each other, the click, click, click of stone striking stone as the *Trümmerfrauen* added to the pile." Ulrich fell silent, staring out the window.

I imagined the sound of those clicking stones, could hear it, and I knew that my own equivalent memory was far less harsh: the sound of my mother's humming as she massaged my legs.

He looked over at me. "You know her hands? You have seen my mother's hands?"

"Yes." An old woman's hands.

"She ruined her hands clearing the rubble of Berlin for a few pfennigs a day. My memory of my mother is that she was always hooded, always cloaked with coarse cloth, as if she was a Turkish woman. Only later did I understand that she was too beautiful. Women with her beauty became prostitutes to survive, but my mother — no. In every way she could, she made herself like a hag so that the Russians would not rape her." He glanced toward Kit, who had not moved, then added more quietly, "But I think they did."

I could say nothing to this. The click-click of stones — yes, I could imagine that. But this other — no. Rape? My mind jumped away from the word. And how could a baroness have become a rubble woman? Looking back now, I recognize the infinite gap that stood between me and Ulrich at that moment as an instance of the gap separating innocent Americans from Europeans who had been crushed and crushed again, and then again. We Americans, astride the world, knew nothing.

Out of the silence, and looking for a way to help him past the impossible thought, I asked, "When did your stepfather —"

He cut me off. "Eventually, she was employed as a translator for the Americans. She stopped dressing like a Turk. She began to wear perfume; I remember that. She let her hair grow back. She found her American officer. She thought him kind. Compared to the Russians, he was. He divorced his wife for her. A simple letter to the States and that first marriage ended. He has a child older than me, and he never sees her. I have never met her, my *Stiefschwester.* My mother married such a man because in Berlin in 1949 there were no German men. She married him because she thought I needed a father."

"Maybe you did."

"Yes, a *father.*" There was such depth of feeling in this dismissal that I could not imagine how to respond. I thought of shifting, to ask what he knew about his biological father, but that was an impossible question, dragging in others — questions about the war, the fate of a pretty woman in a time of pillage, shame, the real father never mentioned because never known? Impossible.

When I said nothing, Ulrich, too, fell into a weighty silence. We gave ourselves over to the click-click not of paving stones but of the iron wheels hitting the joints of the tracks.

After a while I remembered what I'd started out before to ask, and I asked it now, quietly. "What about Kit, Ulrich? *Was ist los?*"

"Loose?" He grinned. He glanced toward her.

"What gives?" I asked.

"What do you mean?"

"Between you two?"

He stared at me, then smiled broadly. "Oh, Monty, Monty."

I hated myself for blushing. I sat there embarrassed and transparent. Simply to do something, I lifted my cane, twirled it once, let it fall back into its corner.

"Oh, Monty, you sweet man," he said, then glanced at her again. From the bright surprise in his expression, I knew I had to turn and look, too.

To my complete horror, Kit's eyes were open. She was looking at me.

Without moving from her corner, Kit said coldly, "Why are you asking him?"

"What do you mean?"

"Why do boys think they can bargain with each other over girls, as if we are cows?"

"That's not what we were doing," I said weakly.

"You were asking him if I was already taken."

I glanced at Ulrich, who was grinning, enjoying this, the bastard. I was on my own.

I looked back at Kit. "I guess I was asking that," I admitted.

"Then why not ask me?"

"Well, are you?"

"No," she said with an easy glance at Ulrich. "I'm not taken, am I, Rick?"

"She calls me Rick. I spurn her." He grinned. Whatever it was between them, it was different now.

"*Ulrich*, then," she said. "Ulrich von Neuhaus." She looked at me. "Y'all know what Neuhaus means, don't you?"

"New house?"

Her face lit up. "Casanova!" Her drawl thickened when she added, "He's my bratwurst Casanova." Then she laughed hard. So did we all.

When our fit passed, she touched my leg. "No, Michael. I am not taken." Then she added, "Are you?"

I laughed out loud again — and felt myself blushing once more. "No, Kit," I found it possible to say. "I am not taken."

"In that case," she said, "I reckon I'll join you in a smoke, Michael."

"What?"

"A smoke. Or do you dip snuff? *Habst du ein Rauch,* big guy?" She mimicked smoking, pressing two fingers in a V to her lips, as if we were strangers who just met. But she had called me *du,* not *Sie.*

I retrieved my pack from the inside pocket of my blazer and offered her a cigarette. I held my Zippo for her, and she leaned into the flame. "Light in May," she said, blowing smoke.

"What?"

She put her accounts book in her bag, took another book out, and held it up for me to see: *Light in August* by William Faulkner. She opened it and pretended to read aloud, but she was quoting by heart. "If they are not innocent of sin, at least they sin in innocence." She gave me a sweet smile, then curled over the book to read.

About an hour later, just as the light of day was fading, the train began gearing down. We hadn't spoken much. Kit's calm self-possession had centered us. We had passed from isolation back into the solidarity of companionship, the three of us. *Du und Sie* — in point of fact, Kit used the intimate form with both Ulrich and me.

6

SHACKS AND TUMBLEDOWN HUTS in the shadows of dusk one moment, a bejeweled early evening skyline the next: to come out of the postwar wasteland of Soviet Germany into the frantic brilliance of West Berlin was to cross a line on the earth. To see that demarcation of the world-historic argument was to glimpse the edge of a trench into which each side was poised to plunge. Of such instants is the structure of a mind made, and after that I was a sucker for dualism, if in nothing but politics.

But here is the odd thing: I arrived in West Berlin, with its propped opulence, prepared to see it as I'd been told to, as a showcase of freedom. Berlin was the urban proof-text of free enterprise. *From each according to his ability, to each according to what he can grab.* It is not as if I did not link arms with Kit and Ulrich, our triune phalanx advancing on the train platform in an exuberant spirit of American arrival, the exhibitionism of the entitled young. But the human tide against which we pushed pushed back, forcing us out of our little bubble to see — really *see.*

All around us was the bustle of far more complex comings and goings. This train station was the terminus of major supply routes for the island city. Raw materials were offloaded in the yards outside, but here along each platform, and on the broad terrace into which each platform ran, were stacked hundreds of pallets holding cartons, bundles, and mailbags. Moving among all that were throngs of travelers, not giddy like us but grim-faced, eyes fixed, coursing to and from trains with the air of those for whom transit itself was the thing to survive. Greeters and senders-off clutched handkerchiefs, some weeping openly. Vendors stood at sawhorse benches and pushcarts selling wurst, newspapers, bottles of milk. Their customers included roughly dressed women and men mystified by the currency they held — a crowd that reeked, as one creature, of body odor. Later I would understand that many of these people had come down from the elevated train platform above, the S-Bahn line that ran from East Berlin to West Berlin, stopping first here at the *Hauptbahnhof*. These were refugees who, as fugitives, had just dared to step off the city train in this forbidden sector, part of the tide of thousands that the Wall would break in August.

The S-Bahn was the easiest way to flee the East, and if there were grave expressions on the faces of certain of the men and women around us, it was not for the danger they were in, but for the sure jeopardy into which they had just plunged their relatives at home. For those left behind, there would be loss of jobs, loss of housing, possible arrest, or banishment to the distant countryside near Poland. In that time and place, the supremely selfish act was defection.

Others of those around us were arrivals from the West, disembarking trains that had come from Hamburg and Munich and Düsseldorf. These were the young men looking for draft exemptions and training slots at Telefunken and Siemens, industrial giants that had made West Berlin the electronics center of Europe. They were girls coming for the artificially high-salaried jobs in hotels and offices. They were continental beatniks coming for the jazz clubs and cafés. And that evening, they were young Social Democrats coming for the May Day celebrations that would take place the next day on both sides of the city. All had come, in one way or another and however gravely, for what in America we thought of as the thrill of the frontier. Us, too.

To get our bearings, Ulrich, Kit, and I took up a place near a welcome desk that was manned by several people in religious garb, the men in clerical collars, the women in austere black clothing with crosses hanging from cords around their necks. Standing there, we watched the bustle before us, awed by it.

At one point Ulrich elbowed me, then pointed at the granite blocks of the wall above us. The stone was pockmarked and chipped, and a massive wooden beam also had rough marks, like those from a pole climber's cleats.

"What?" Kit said, instantly attuned.

"Bullet holes," Ulrich answered.

"Jesus H. Christ," she said, and took my arm.

"I doubt it," I said, but she gave me a look.

Ulrich repeated himself: "Bullet holes."

I felt the cold blast of a large second thought, not fear, exactly, and not regret at having come here, but about the oversimplified impression with which I had anticipated this arrival. It wasn't physical dread holding me back, but an unexpected feeling of sympathy for the worn-down world of East Germany through which we had passed. It was a feeling like nostalgia, perhaps akin to what Ulrich had conveyed as he'd looked out on alien territory that nevertheless made a native claim on him.

But what claim could it have made on me? We stood there long enough in silence for me to know. I had seen the East as a truncated nation on the losing side of history. Shot by history — no, crippled by history. I myself was no gleaming city alight with beauty, no polished locomotive — no true rebel, either, on an authentic quest. What I had seen looking out the train window was a world improperly aligned with itself, where no tree stood in right relation to any other, where roads failed to meet except at jarring angles, where hills had connections neither to the valleys before them nor to the hills beyond, as if iron curtains had fallen everywhere *within* this realm.

But that wasn't all I had seen. I had caught glimpses of my own reflection, wild flashes of disconnection there as well. I saw the line of my cheek as the defining line of my mother's face, and then, with a snap change of focus, I saw her perfect mouth outlined in a wispy cloud, smiling in the sky even there. But Mom was dead. Incurably dead.

Confronted now by the wrack line of desperate characters in front of me, and by evidence of mortal violence in the stone above, I realized why Kit had mostly slept in the train. She had put the harsh truth of this world off until now, and she was pressing my arm. To calm her, I almost said, Not incurable, Kit, and no bullets lately. But I said nothing.

Behind the welcome desk, a dozen yards from where we stood, was a pair of phone booths, and I suddenly wanted to call my father. I wanted to tell him that I had seen Mom's face outlined in a cloud. I wanted to say I was all right with this sadness, that he didn't need to worry about me anymore. But at eight in the evening, it was more than two hours after he would have expected me home with the car, and by now he would be nuts with worry. Worry and anger, the double whammy.

My heart sank. How the burden of his love bent me. And anyway, I could never tell him where I was without his thinking that I needed him, which I surely did not. Or so I told myself, squelching what little remained of the impulse to call. *Sorry, Dad.*

Above the welcome desk a poster read, *"Evangelisch Gemeinschaft."* Ulrich was talking to one of the religious women. Kit and I drew near behind, and to my surprise I heard him speaking English, even though the woman was less than fluent in it. He had dipped his voice in the syrupy southern accent he had used in the train compartment with the MP. As I listened, I realized that below the shift in what we think of as accent, he had altered the very beat of his sentences, no longer speaking with a German rhythm that jumps at open sounds, stops at consonants. Yes, syrup.

In this conversation, the woman accepted the kibitzing of the timid male cleric beside her. He seemed to have a decent English vocabulary but no knowledge of sentences. The woman handed Ulrich a number of German-language brochures, explaining each one as well as she could. Ulrich was masterful as a mulish but well-meaning American hayseed, vacantly tugging at his beard. *Ah be danged.* I sensed the fun he was having with his impersonation. Indeed, the fun was in the subterfuge, which made me think of something else. Ulrich von Neuhaus — Herr Independence — was marking our arrival in the espionage swamp of Berlin by enacting a drama that had everything to do with his stepfather's function, in a phrase of a then current book by J. Edgar Hoover, as a "master of deceit." What a thrill to join him in it. Kit, too, with her talk of dipping snuff.

When the sister spread out a map of the city on the desk, Ulrich leaned over it. Kit and I stepped closer, each to one side of our friend. I could feel myself being drawn into the game, even if I hadn't a clue yet about its rules or even how victory and defeat were defined. Enough to observe the tremor in the woman's finger as she traced what I took to be the dividing border between the Allied and Soviet sectors. I saw the serpentine lines of a river and its offshoot canals, and

I picked up the words "Zoo" and "Tiergarten" and the fan shape of the railroad tracks here at the station. Otherwise, the map was as incomprehensible as the city outside.

"Where?" Ulrich asked, then placed the tip of his forefinger on the map next to where the woman was pointing. "Oh, that's great," he said in teenage American. "Really great!" Then to Kit and me, feigning less, he said, "The church runs a youth hostel not far away."

The male cleric, his mouth a slit, muttered in German, something Kit translated with an urgency that surprised me. "Male and female dorms," she said. And she met the clergyman's cold stare, his stare at her. She lowered her voice, but all could hear when she declared, "We're not splitting up, guys. I am not spending the night someplace by myself." Having said this, she stepped around Ulrich to be between us — or was it to be next to me? Did she want me to put my arm around her? I saw tiny beads of sweat on her upper lip, and nearly did.

Ulrich was still leaning over the map, letting his finger move across it. "Where are the May Day celebrations going to be?"

Again the male cleric muttered to the woman, who said, "What means you?"

"May Day," Ulrich answered. "Tomorrow. Workers' Day."

The sister shook her head slowly, but with such an air of disapproval that I just wanted to thank them and move on. Ulrich, though, raised his bright face from the map, all innocence. "There's a big parade," he told her, as if defining the circus. "And a huge street meeting. The parade in the East, the meeting in the West. You know this, right?"

"We do not know," the man said emphatically, his first full sentence in English.

"That's fine," I put in. I took Ulrich's elbow, pulling him. "Thanks a lot," I said. "Let's go, Rick."

He looked at me, then back at the pair of evangelicals, making a decision. Nodding, he collected the brochures she had given him. The woman carefully folded the map, and when Ulrich said, in a caricature of himself, "Ah surely do appreciate your many kindnesses," she handed it to him.

We backed away, each with a shoulder bag, Ulrich with his fistful of folders. The religious people watched us, but others were watching us, too, in that drab sea of immigrants and refugees. I realized how conspicuous we were in our bright American clothing, Ulrich bearded and long-haired, Kit pert and sexy, me with my gimpy lurch. To the Berliners we must have seemed like the trio on the road to Oz. Judy Garland was a star here, wasn't she?

We crossed into a second, equally crowded hall and found places at a standup *Bierstube*. Kit insisted on paying for our beers. She untied her bandana, into which she had folded several German bills. Ulrich and I fought her off for a minute, then we each threw in some money. Kit had made her point, however. She was no one's date.

We claimed one of the several raised tables for ourselves and drank our beer. Kit said, "I mean it, I'm not sleeping in some room full of strangers or off by myself."

I said, "What if we just go to the high school?"

Ulrich looked at me with surprise. "What?"

"The American high school, General Patton. They have a dorm. We could find some kids who'd let us in, let us have a couch or something."

"The American high school?" Ulrich used my inflection, mocking me.

"It's what you said before."

"That was the *story*, Michael."

"But it sounded good. What the hell, we could do worse than hooking up with kids like us."

"Monty, Monty," Ulrich said, "there *are* no kids like us. We are the *Edelweisspiraten*."

"The what?"

Kit translated, "Edelweiss pirates." To Ulrich she said, with an air of *cut the shit*, "Which is what?"

"Anti-Soviet youth groups, when I was living here before. I was a child, but you remember something called the *Edelweisspiraten*. Heroes of resistance after the war." Ulrich grinned, but oddly, given what he was saying. "All eliminated by the Stasi and the KGB."

"That's just what I mean," I said, looking at the bullet-pocked wall. "I vote we go to the high school."

"What, for the sock hop?" Ulrich looked at Kit, appealing. "This is goddamn Berlin!"

Kit refused to look at him. She raised her glass of beer to her mouth and hid behind it. I sensed how much she wanted not to choose between us, which made me want to force her to. "What do you say, Kit?"

"I only said I didn't want to sleep in some dorm for females, off by myself with a bunch of strangers. I don't rightly see why we have to fight about it." The threat of dark weather moving in on us again upset her.

I felt guilty for pressing the point, so I playfully punched Ulrich's arm. "And I didn't say anything about a fucking sock hop, Ulrich."

"I think you want to be calling me Rick."

"Oh, so now your name is Healy, not Casanova?" But it was not smart to mock him for his impulse to pass as pure American. Pure American would keep us safe. "Look, guys," I said, "we need a base. A place to leave our bags before heading out. A place that's safe."

"Youth hostels are safe," Ulrich said.

"But you heard Kit. That won't work for her."

"Hey, don't make me the issue between you two."

I glanced at her, ready to say, You *are* the issue. But just then my eye went past her to a man at an adjacent counter. He had his beer, but what he seemed interested in was us. Meeting my quizzical stare, he smiled. He raised the glass, toasting me. He sipped without lowering his gaze.

"Jesus," I muttered, looking down. "That guy's watching us."

Kit snapped off a look, but Ulrich calmly picked up his glass. "No problem," he said. "Be cool."

I looked again. The man was still smiling at me, his teeth bright in the curl of his mouth. He was short, his dark hair in a crew cut. He wore a rumpled tan suit, a white shirt open at the collar, no tie. His nose was red, his eyes were glassy, he looked drunk. Hence the smile, which suddenly seemed more goofy than sinister. He downed the last swallow of beer and smacked his lips happily, then moved toward us.

"He's coming," I whispered.

Ulrich turned toward the man as he joined us. He claimed a corner of our standup counter by putting his empty beer glass down. Kit shifted toward me.

"Good evening, friends," he said. "Perhaps it is the case that I can be help to you." His smile now seemed real, and he appeared to be not much older than we were. He was feeling no pain, but he wasn't drunk. "Here in Berlin," he went on, "we must look to help each other. It is the only way. Welcome to Berlin." And again he raised his glass.

So did we, draining them, which prompted the man to go back to the serving window for more. While he was gone, Ulrich said again, "Be cool." We had come for the adventure, right? Here it was.

The man returned with a tray, four beers and four cardboard coasters. He served them around. When he raised his glass, we clinked with him. "To a death in Berlin," he said.

"What?" Kit blurted.

"A traditional toast," the man said, grinning. "Every Berliner's fondest wish. A death in Berlin — in the distant future, not tonight."

"A body hopes not," Kit said, and we all laughed.

"I am Josef Tramm," he said. "I please to make your meeting."

Something told me, as we introduced ourselves, each shaking his hand, that his awkward syntax was deliberate, a bit of the buffoon to put us at ease. I liked that he was so short; he had to look up at me.

"American students, I think, yes?"

"That's right," Ulrich said. "From Wiesbaden." Again that *w.* "Our fathers are in the Air Force. The U.S. Air Force."

Josef raised his glass again. "Ah, the Air Force. We in Berlin love the American Air Force. In 1948 the airlift saved us."

Ulrich touched his glass to Tramm's. "To the airlift," Ulrich said with a cocky grin. "When the same planes that had destroyed Berlin came back to save it."

Jesus, I thought, Ulrich and his damn ironies. I vastly preferred the mode of innocents abroad. *Not innocent of sin, but sinning in innocence.* I watched the German to see what he would make of Ulrich's curve.

"A point well made," said Tramm. "But Berlin suffered far more from the Russian shelling than from American and British bombing. And after the shelling, the Cossack pillaging, which is not forgotten, even in the East."

Tramm pulled a half-smoked stub of a cigarette from somewhere in his clothing. Cupping his hands around a flame, he bent to light it, then waved the match out. "To people my age," he continued, "and I was twelve during the airlift, the Americans were the 'chocolate bombardiers,' that is all. That is why we greet you warmly."

"What are you, the welcome committee?" Ulrich seemed as relaxed as Tramm.

Tramm grinned. "In Berlin there are many welcome committees. You were already greeted by the church people."

That was in the other hall. Had he been watching us there?

"I greet you on behalf of workers. I am of the *Deutscher Gewerkschaftsbund* — the DGB, the trade union council. My job is to welcome workers arriving in Berlin, which naturally is to recruit them — industrial workers, electricians, carpenters, masons. We are, you say, *desperate* for labor here. My job is to —" He put the butt of his cigarette between his lips, squinting at the smoke. The stub was so short it must have been hot to his flesh. He reached into the inside pocket of his jacket and pulled out a stack of cards, dealing one to each of us. "Here is a pass for meals and, you say, accommodation at the Free Workers' Reception Hall. Clean beds. Good food. The DGB offers support in finding jobs and houses, and protects the worker in all matters having to do with conditions and wages." A mission statement.

"We're not looking for jobs," Kit said. "We're just here for the weekend."

"Of course, of course. You are Americans. There is no question of jobs. But you are welcome. You are welcome at the Workers' Hall."

"Men and women together?" Kit asked.

"Are you speaking of yourself?"

"Yes."

"To remain with your friends?"

"Yes."

"That can be arranged. We have facilities for senior workers, what you call, I believe, VIP. It pleases me to welcome the sons and daughter of the chocolate bombardiers."

Ulrich, eyeing the card, surprised me by saying, "I have memories of the airlift."

I watched him carefully. Was he going to tell the truth? His mother looking up from her pile of rubble at the gleaming American planes, his own first taste of chocolate? But by 1948, wasn't she a translator already, working for us? For Healy?

"My father," he said simply, "was one of those Air Force pilots flying into Berlin."

"*Voilà!*" Tramm said, clinking glasses again. "*Prost!*"

What Ulrich said may have been true, in a way — of his stepfather, not his father — but still, the effect of his statement was one of deceit. His ability to lie amazed me. The complexities hinted at only moments before, the airlift reversing the air assault, were gone now, and Tramm seemed thoroughly convinced. America the eternal friend of Germany; Germany a nation solely of virtue — West Germany, of course.

Tramm was about to put his cigarette out in a tin ashtray when Ulrich offered him his pack of Luckies. Tramm took one and lit it from the stub.

For my part, I was stuck on the questions of whether he'd been watching us in the other hall, of what he'd heard us say to one another in this one. "Herr Tramm," I asked casually, "you speak English very well. How is that?"

He shrugged. "West Berlin, my friend. English is a second language here. You will find this. In the East, naturally, it is Russian."

"You speak Russian?"

"No. I myself only English. Russian in the East. Not here. And you? *Sie sprechen Deutsch, ja?*"

"Hardly any," I said. Kit and Ulrich were studying their beers.

"But I heard you speak quite well," Tramm said, "of the *Edelweisspiraten.*"

"That was me," Ulrich said. He met Tramm's eyes and held them.

After a moment, Tramm asked, "*Wie heissen Sie?*"

"Rick Healy," Ulrich answered, and he offered his hand, which Tramm shook, saying, "*Sehr angenehm.*"

I introduced myself, then Kit did, calling herself Katharine. Tramm bowed and gave each of us a quick handshake, although Kit's hand he held a moment longer. "There is much to see in Berlin, *Fräulein.* I would be honored to show — the Kurfürstendamm, Charlottenburg, McNair Barracks where the Americans live, the American high school. You say 'high school,' no? You would like to see this?"

I exchanged a worried glance with Ulrich: Did this guy know we talked about the high school?

But Tramm was smiling easily at Kit, still holding her hand. "Your bag," he said, indicating the overnight bag on her shoulder. *WHS* was emblazoned above the silhouette of an Indian and the word "Warriors." "You three are at an American high school, no?"

I could feel myself blushing. Kit withdrew her hand from Tramm's, saying, "Yes," then giving me an impatient look: Relax, bud.

Ulrich said, "We do not need to see the high school. We have seen a high school." When he laughed, Tramm and Kit joined him, leaving me to feel foolish.

"Well, well," Tramm said then, an undeterred salesman, still pitching to the girl. "You said weekend, *Fräulein*. A visit for the weekend. Very good. Very good. This is a special weekend in Berlin. Do you know this?"

"May Day," she said.

"*Jawohl!* Have you come for this? Then I am doubly happy to greet you. The great, how do you say, mass meeting?"

"Rally," Kit said.

Tramm bowed appreciatively. "The rally is tomorrow. My trade union council, naturally, is a main sponsor. I can arrange for you very special permits for places near the platform. You can hear Willy Brandt. You can see him."

"And in East Berlin?" Ulrich asked. "We were hoping to see the military parade."

"Yes, yes," Tramm said without hesitating. "It is possible. The rally at Schöneberg is in the late morning, the parade passing through Alex — Alexanderplatz — will come after noon. It is possible. All is possible. And crossing the sector border will be easy tomorrow, because Honecker wants all Berliners to see the might of the Soviet forces. I will take you myself."

"That is kind of you," I said uneasily. "But —"

He cut me off. "It is decided. Tomorrow is my holiday. It would please me. Very much."

"But —"

"For your father. I do this for what your father did."

"Not my father," I said with a firmness I regretted at once.

He turned to Ulrich. "Then for yours, Rick."

Tramm's eyes were moist with feeling — also beer. He seemed entirely sincere, a man determined to repay an old debt. "It would please me very much to do this thing for you. *Ich bin sehr dankbar.*"

"*Nichts zu danken,*" Ulrich replied, making me think, with alarm, that he had abandoned the strategy of presenting himself as a non–German speaker. But of course ignorance of the language would make no sense if his Air Force father had been serving in Germany since the airlift — which, more or less, General Healy had.

In fact, Ulrich was almost certainly up to something else, as Kit explained to me later. His use of the everyday phrase for "Don't mention it" was effectively meaningless in the context set by Tramm, whose gratitude, obviously, wasn't directed to us but to our parents, our country. Ulrich's — Rick's — was the kind of dumb mistake that an entitled American kid would make, and he had spoken that and every other phrase, Kit said, with a distinctly American inflection, not a German one. When she told me this, I was amazed at her knowing such a thing simply by listening, but her cleverness only made me appreciate Ulrich's. I was the dunce of this trio.

The German snuffed out his cigarette gingerly, sliding the two-inch butt into the flapped pocket of his shabby suit coat. Later I would learn that cigarettes had for years functioned as the only stable currency in Berlin, which explained why Berliners, even into the 1960s, still treated them like coin. Tramm polished off his beer, prompting us to do likewise, which, in turn, he took as a signal. He stepped back with a hand sweeping toward the exit. "*Diese Richtung,*" he declared. "This way."

He tried to help me with my bag, an offer I refused by brusquely hoisting it away. When he then reached for Ulrich's bag, I saw that the tag with two stars, the general's tag, was gone. I thought I must be mistaken and looked closer. But no, gone.

A watery sensation settled in my gut. *Achtung!* was the feeling, and, however vague, it came clearly tied to Ulrich's bag. When had Ulrich removed the tag?

To my relief, Ulrich shook off Tramm's effort, and by the time the ever helpful German turned to Kit, she had her strap slung across her chest like a bandolier, both flattening her breasts, which were already lost inside her father's field jacket, and making me imagine them. *Achtung!* again. From a certain angle, with her short hair and with jeans on instead of her black skirt and dancer's tights, Kit could have passed as a boy. If I said so, I wondered, would she be insulted? An Italian boy, I would say, but a boy. Yet she was pure girl to me.

We filed toward the massive arched doorway of the train station, ahead of Tramm. Already I didn't like it that he could see me without my seeing him. But then I had special cause to be self-conscious. I sensed the Germanic precision with which he was no doubt taking the measure of my limp. Cripples like me had been gassed.

My goddamn limp. Sometimes when I walked I tried to regularize my gait by pretending to be a ship sailing up the Hudson. If there was a dip-and-toss to my shoulders, couldn't it at least be rhythmic like a tidal current? But no. Not then. Not there. Rhythm was impossible. The click of my leg braces was anarchic. Not for nothing do they use the word "jerk" for my movements. I consoled myself that it was only Tramm behind me watching, not Kit.

It wasn't easy to move out of the station through the surge of cowed refugees: émigrés carrying roped bundles rather than suitcases; thick-ankled women in shapeless gray suits and stout heels; younger women with hair on their legs, matted in splotches by nylon stockings; men in caps and threadbare coats, some carrying tin milk pails, relics of the farms they'd left behind. They were a throng, literally, of *arrivistes,* all looking to change their lives. They smelled of it, the stink of worry and longing. And who was I to think, despite my trim blazer and tie, that I was not one of them?

At the threshold of the unornamented entrance, just as the cool air was hitting us, a man in a black leather jacket jumped from nowhere into Ulrich's path, stopping Kit and me as well. To the three of us he said, "Deutsche marks for dollars. Good rate. No fee. Nothing paid."

Before any of us could respond, Tramm stepped in — "*Nicht! Nicht! Nicht!*" — and pushed the man away with a force surprising in one so short. The man cursed Tramm, but he backed off, then scooted into the crowd, disappearing at once.

"Black market," Tramm explained. "Beware these people. Nothing on the street! They are thieves. It is the great problem of free Berlin. Make no business on the street."

The encounter had taken place so quickly that I felt bewildered by it, and the aftermath was no less intimidating. We were surrounded by a crushing pedestrian tumult against a backdrop of blaring horns, the random noise of traffic. The sidewalk seemed a stream of potential black marketeers. D-marks for sale! Vodka! Records by Elvis Presley!

I imagined a slew of pitches and saw in the face of every passerby a readiness to make them.

Suddenly a pair of exceptionally tall women, with their arms linked, stopped right in front of me. They wore slinky elbow-length gloves; their eyes were outlined in what looked like charcoal. One was red-headed, one was blond. Their impossibly long, curvaceous legs stretched from short skirts to stiletto heels. Tramm shooed them away. I had seen prostitutes on street corners at night in Wiesbaden, but never like this. Involuntarily, I stepped back, which was hardly cool.

"Hookers," Ulrich said with a knowing glint, but his worldly air leaked away when Tramm snickered, "*Jawohl!* But they are male! 'Surprise whores' is what they are called. But the bigger surprise is when their pimps rob you. Make no business on the streets, my friends!"

Tramm slipped between me and Kit, taking each of us by an elbow as he ushered us along. I exchanged a look with Kit, who was as wide-eyed as I.

"We're not in Kansas anymore, Michael," Kit said.

"Berlin!" Tramm said. "You are in Berlin, the greatest city in the world! The most wicked! The most *wunderbar!*"

When Tramm then adjusted his gait for me, I sensed it and felt grateful. I relaxed some, and admitted to myself that without him, whatever was coming, we'd be lost already.

Outside, the darkness of night landed hard. Now we were on a broad, bustling boulevard defined by glaring lights, a thousand, a million of them. The avenue was a double river, with headlights rushing in one direction, white water, and taillights in the other, a flow of blood. Across the avenue, up and down its length, were giant neon signs, a dance of blue, yellow, and red. Punctuating the near distance were tall streetlamps wearing halos of gold, and beyond was a canyon wall of illuminated windows in a rank of modern buildings. Light had never seemed more garish, more exotic, yet its effect was to draw the eyes ever upward, to the contrasting backdrop of the black vault of sky, against which one thing stood out above all. A spotlighted tower soared in the far distance, with a gleaming stainless steel sphere atop it, like a huge ball bearing pierced through by a silver needle.

"Whoa!" I said. "What's that?"

"The *Fernsehturm*," Tramm answered with the self-satisfaction of a tour guide. "The television tower. It is taller than the Eiffel Tower in Paris."

"Just to make people in East Berlin jealous?" I asked.

Tramm laughed. "The *Fernsehturm* is *in* the East. The Russians built it for propaganda, just to be seen, just as you have seen it. The joke is, in East Berlin they have a television tower but no television."

We three laughed — a forced laugh really, a release of pent-up tension. But it was also an expression of relief, no doubt, that we had actually done what we had so crazily set out to do. Berlin. We had come to Berlin.

A joke about the material superiority of the West? We didn't care, or if we did, Ulrich included, we weren't making an issue of it. We just laughed, and that was that. How simply we had handed ourselves over to the care of our new friend.

7

THE FREE WORKERS' RECEPTION HALL was a relatively new building in an otherwise older, mixed-use section of the city not far from the train station. Kreuzberg, Tramm said, a neighborhood that had survived the bombing and shelling, was now home to diligent Berliners and guest workers. There were tall prewar apartment buildings, apparently renovated, modest restaurants and shops, a nightclub or two, a church. The hall had been shoehorned into all of this, not quite fitting in scale or feel. It was a three-story box of poured concrete and broad plate glass windows, from perhaps half of which streamed a cold, flat wash of light from fluorescent tubes.

We arrived at around nine o'clock by taxi, having covered a distance short enough to have walked, which made me think Tramm had decided I was not up to it. He paid the driver and led us into the building as if we were dignitaries. In an expansive front room, a woman sat at a desk while about a dozen other people sat on vinyl couches and plastic chairs that ranged across a polished terrazzo floor. Potted plants stood here and there to break up the space. At a table, four men in overalls and workers' smocks were playing cards. Behind them was a floor-model radio from which came a plaintive female voice singing something sad. Except for the desk woman, everyone in the room was male, and they all seemed to have looked up as we came in.

Behind the desk hung a large banner featuring the letters *DBG* and a slogan that translated, by my guess, as "Building Free Berlin."

Below the banner was a closed door marked "*Herren Direktoren.*" When we stopped a few yards from the desk, Kit took my hand. I looked at her, read her mind: all male. She held my hand as if she were my girlfriend.

Tramm spoke briefly to the desk woman. He dealt her three of the cards he'd given us, then gestured us forward. "You are welcome." He held up a pen, which we each took in turn to sign a guest book. I signed last, noting that Ulrich had written "Rick Healy, student." Kit had written "Katharine Carson, student." I wrote "Michael Elgin Montgomery, student." My mother's face flashed before me again. If she were alive, knowing what I was doing, she'd flip out. She'd blame my father, flipping out at him, which she always did as a way not to yell at me.

Foolish thought. If my mother were alive, I would not have dared to come here; she'd never have allowed me to take the car.

When I resumed my place at Kit's side, I took her hand again, and she let me. In the merciless light from flat ceiling fixtures, the paleness of her face made her look ill. Yet that vulnerability seemed more linked than ever to her unbreakable spirit, which I had learned already to trust. Kit was at the dependable center of our adventure.

"Frau Hess will show you where to stay," Tramm said. "I will wait for you here."

"Wait for us?" I asked.

"To show you the canteen." He pointed toward a door on the far side of the broad room. "The cooking is finished now, but there is always soup and bread, good black bread. You like to eat the German bread, no?"

"Yes," Kit said. "Love it. I'm starved."

I was too, suddenly. But I said nothing.

"And then perhaps to see Berlin?" Tramm said. "Berlin at night, yes?"

Kit squeezed my hand to signal no. Before I could protest, Tramm added, "To go, you say, on the city."

"On the town," Ulrich corrected, and then, "Sure. *Wunderbar!*" The *w* wrong.

Frau Hess wordlessly led us to a staircase and up a flight. She was a plump woman on the wrong side of middle age. I noticed her hands, one at the railing, the other at her side, palm facing me. Her hands had rough, reddened skin, like Mrs. Healy's.

As she took the stairs ahead of me, it was impossible not to notice the ribs of her girdle pressing against the stressed material of her brown dress. The back straps of her brassiere did, too. I looked away to notice other things: a grilled light fixture, a black vinyl-clad banister, a pay phone hanging on the wall at the landing by the stairwell door. I looked for bullet holes, but this building was too new for that.

We followed the woman into a vacant corridor. It had the feel of a high school hallway, lined with gray steel lockers. We passed an open doorway from which piano music was coming, and I glimpsed a large room that held numerous bunk beds, some disheveled, at least one with a man asleep.

At the end of the hallway, Frau Hess withdrew a key from somewhere in the ample folds of her shapeless dress, and she opened a last door. She reached into the room for a wall switch. As tube lighting flickered on, she stood aside. We saw a small room with six aligned cots protruding from one wall, leaving a narrow aisle between the wall and the ends of the cots. Each cot held a thin mattress. Each was neatly covered with a dark brown wool blanket tucked in crisply at the corners. The room, apparently, was unoccupied.

I recognized the blankets as the same Army issue we had at the dorm at Wiesbaden, war surplus blankets stamped *U.S.* It was a good omen, and I led the way in. A large mahogany wardrobe beside a window on the far wall was the only other piece of furniture.

Frau Hess and Kit exchanged a few sentences in German, and once more I marveled at Kit's fluency. The older woman pointed back through the doorway, down the corridor — instructions, I took it, about the WC and washroom. Kit thanked her and offered her hand to shake. Only then did the woman soften. She took Kit's hand warmly and smiled. "*Machen Sie es sich bequem!*" Make yourself at home. She handed Kit the room key and left.

Kit closed the door and turned to me and Ulrich. She said with relief, "It's just us, at least for tonight."

Ulrich walked the length of the room and flopped down on the bed nearest the window. "Great! Great!" He grinned at us triumphantly. "Is this not great?"

"This is a female workers' bunkroom," Kit explained to me, "but they don't get that many women — 'bachelor women,' as she said. This could be just ours for both nights." Kit dropped her bag on the cot farthest from the window, leaving four cots between her and Ulrich. She took her jacket off and dropped it on the bed, too, an act so natural that it pulled me instantly into the fantasy of her removing that sweater as well.

I had a mad impulse to take the cot next to her, but squelched it. I crossed to drop my bag, my stake, on the one beside Ulrich's, leaving Kit an end of the room to herself, the closest thing she would have to a girl's privacy. I was, of course, thrilled just to be sleeping in the same room with her — until it hit me that I hadn't brought a bathrobe or even pajamas. Unless I slept with my trousers on, she would see my legs.

"So, did I not tell you?" Ulrich crowed. But his satisfaction, I saw, was made up mainly of relief. He had his hands clasped behind his head, his feet propped on his overnight bag at the end of his cot. The skin on his cheeks, just above the edge of his beard, was flushed with pleasure, his eyes wide with anticipation of my response. His pleasure would be incomplete if mine failed to match it. In his longing for my affirmation, I glimpsed the deeper meaning of our friendship, and it was in that, more than in our arrival, that I could join him in feeling relieved. I leaned over to punch his arm, the friendly blow, then sat on my cot. Kit took a toothbrush and tube of toothpaste from her bag and disappeared from the room.

About two feet separated the cots, and my knobby knees pressed close to Ulrich's leg. "Only one problem," I said.

He gave me a weird look. "No pillows. I cannot sleep without a pillow."

"Not the problem I'm thinking of."

"What?"

"Josef."

"What about him?" Exasperation and warning laced Ulrich's voice: *Do not fuck this up with worry, you asshole.*

"He's downstairs," I said as casually as I could. Was it because I was the only one not fluent in German that I, alone apparently, sensed something moving below the surface appearances? "He's waiting for us."

"And how, old chap, is that a problem? Josef is our ADC."

"Our what?"

"Aide-de-camp. Every general officer has one." Ulrich grinned. "Josef will open doors for us, already has."

"You don't think he's a little . . . ?"

"What?"

"I don't know."

"Monty." Ulrich threw an arm toward the ceiling, the room. "Look what he's done for us already, beginning with that black market character at the station."

"Maybe *he's* black market." But I said it without conviction, lacking language with which to express my suspicion.

"Selling what? Josef does not want anything from us. The new socialism, Monty. The family of man. This is what I have been telling you. This is what *ersten Mai* celebrates, the way *Rosenmontag* celebrates the coming of spring."

"*Rosenmontag* celebrates the coming of Lent. Big difference."

"And Josef honors the airlift. I was here, remember? Berliners love Americans. It is that simple, my friend."

"I just have a funny feeling. You don't?"

"Not on your life."

"Why did you take your father's tag off your bag, then?" I gestured toward his feet where the bag was.

Ulrich looked at me sharply, but did not answer.

I pressed. "Why? Why the phony Dixie accent? Why aren't you telling Josef the truth? Telling him who you are — that *you* are from Berlin? You signed in at the desk as Rick Healy. What the hell happened to Ulrich von Neuhaus, if you think everything is so cool?"

Instead of answering, Ulrich let his eyes drift toward the ceiling, then across it. Was he looking for hidden microphones?

When at last he spoke, it was softly, calmly. "Did it ever come to your mind that a guest whose name carried that 'von' would be less than welcome at the Free Workers' Hall?"

"So what about your father's tag?"

"My stepfather's."

"So don't give me shit about my having a funny feeling, okay?"

"Josef is good, Monty. Relax. He will make everything possible for us tomorrow."

I flopped onto my back, suddenly exhausted. "I know. I know." Exhausted and hungry. "I need some soup. I need some bread."

"Now you are saying something." Ulrich stood up with an athletic swing of his feet. "Where is the wonderful Kit?"

"The john, probably. The WC. You go ahead. I'll wait for her. We'll be down in a minute."

"Okay." Ulrich hoisted his bag, the strap on his shoulder, and he turned for the door.

"Why are you taking that?" I asked. I sat up.

He looked baffled for a moment, then his eyes looked uneasily from the bag to me and back. "I would just rather bring it, that is all." He tugged at his beard, that phony gesture he had used with Tramm, now using it with me. *Jesus.*

"The door locks, Ulrich. The lady gave a key to Kit. We should leave our bags here."

"Not mine."

"Why?"

"Because." A distressed look came into his eyes. A moment of proletarian insecurity after all. "Because I should not have brought it." Not proletarian — adolescent. "My stepfather would —" And then he just stopped talking, stopped cold.

"The chocolate bombardier," I said.

"Yes."

"And we are the *Edelweisspiraten.*"

"Yes."

"And you don't have a funny feeling. Not on my life."

He shook his head. "See you downstairs, Monty." All we're after, his manner said, is a weekend's diversion, the adventure story we'll get out of it. So far so good. "Let's have some soup."

"And then go 'on the city.'"

He laughed. "Oh, and Monty, my good man — you should be calling me Rick."

After soup and bread in a big room furnished in greasy plastic with a counter holding a large jar of pickled pigs' feet, which looked like fetuses in formaldehyde and from which only Josef ate, we did indeed go out. Not quite on the town but on the neighborhood — to a small basement jazz club about two blocks away. The air outside had turned damp with a threat of rain, and in the crowded lounge the air was thick with smoke. There were small round tables, low backless stools for jazz buffs to sit on with knees hunched, and a bossa nova trio consisting of guitar, bass, and drums. Of the forty or fifty people squeezed into the place, perhaps a dozen were American servicemen, including several blacks, which made it seem safe.

German girls wearing garish makeup draped themselves on the GIs. *Goldliebchen,* Josef called them in whispered good humor, as if the girls were nothing more than another manifestation of the gratitude of Berlin. Tramm, like the other Berliners in the room, seemed to accept the fact that white girls clung to the necks of blacks. I didn't know what to make of it, except as part of a scene that drew me in at once. I sought out Kit's eyes, thinking of her rejection of "nigger," but what would a girl from the Deep South make of this? She refused to look at me.

In fact, whites-with-blacks added to the bohemian air, embodied what Europeans cherished as the pure and primitive energy of the American jazz scene. In the States, 1961 was the year of Chubby Checker, who, in a famous remark of Eldridge Cleaver's, taught white men how to dance. But it was jazz that Berliners would always prefer to American rock, and so would I.

Music defined my generation, but in that regard, as in others, I was already on the margin, where I would remain even when the Beatles made their splash later that year. My taste in music was rooted in my permanent problem. Jazz was meant to be listened to, not danced to. Subtle movements of the head, a little toe-tapping — no twist and shout for me. Or anyone else that night, thank God.

Josef and Ulrich quickly downed several beers, as if to catch up to the other patrons. Kit ordered a Coke, then another, while I nursed a single beer. I found it impossible to talk over the music, and knew better than to do so in any case. But the bossa nova could not keep Tramm from a steady loud patter addressed, embarrassingly, to the three of us. The genius of Brazilian and American music, the technical perfection of Telefunken amplifiers, the hot-club scene in West Berlin — on and on Tramm pontificated. To my surprise, neither the musicians nor our fellow patrons seemed to care. As usual, the disturbance was imagined, imagined by *me,* a function of my masterly uptightness. Soon Tramm was expounding on the Marshall Plan, funding for 180 new bridges within the city limits of Berlin alone. He had gone from being our tour guide to our professor. As the evening wore on, I half listened to him and half let my mind drift.

Ulrich would not have liked where my mind drifted. I watched with disguised interest as a leggy German girl at the next table fondled her GI. Her amazing legs were shaven, but the hair in her armpits wasn't, a sight that made me embarrassed for her. The girl clutched a shot glass in one hand and let the other rest in the soldier's lap, occasionally applying gentle pressure, making him groan. The unsought image in my mind, meanwhile, was of Ulrich's mother behaving in such a way, in just such a place, with her Yank, David Healy. When he groaned, did he think it was love?

I hated the idea of Ulrich's mother as a *Goldliebchen,* ordered it out of my mind, but no use. Every German girl in the room, seemingly at foreplay, made me think of her. The association was an offense, but I couldn't shake it. Finally I decided to go. I raised an eyebrow at Kit. She nodded.

Ulrich and Josef were speaking loudly to each other in English. Ulrich — Rick — had succeeded in seeming only American, although several other young men in the room were long-haired and bearded, and they were German. Was it a German style, I wondered, and not particular to Ulrich? The waiter brought a fresh pair of ceramic beer steins to the table just then, and so neither Josef nor Ulrich hesitated to let me and Kit go. *Auf wiedersehen.*

Outside, it had begun to rain, a soft midnight drizzle, which felt clean. We linked arms to walk, taking the rain as only the young know to do. We turned our faces to it, licking the air, laughing.

"Do you know what a raincoat is?" Kit asked suddenly.

Because half my mind was still back with the leggy German girls, I thought at first she meant some euphemism for condom, but no, not Kit. "What?" I said.

"It's what your mama makes you wear when she's afraid *she'll* get wet."

I laughed with her and said, "Come to think of it, they never explain what's so great about staying dry."

Getting wet in the middle of the night seemed just then to be precisely the point of coming to Berlin, and the best part was having no need to say so. As we walked along, I was aware of her hip by mine, mine bumping at each step. For once I stopped hearing the click of my braces, almost forgot what they were for. The feeling was, if I could have, I'd have skipped, skipped gleefully through the gathering puddles, Gene Kelly singin' in the rain.

But who was the dead opposite of Gene Kelly if not me? In those days, too, the opposite of Paris was Berlin. Instead of skipping, I channeled my exuberance into a cocky twirl of my cane. I wished we could just slow down so that these moments together would last longer.

We paused under the overhang outside the Workers' Hall. We were alone. "What did you make of it back there?"

"Nice guitar," she said.

"I mean the couples."

"The girls with the GIs? Good thing my pa wasn't there. Great white father. Emphasis on white."

"He would have — ?"

"My daddy started out as a mill worker in Montgomery. Best thing the war ever did, it did for him, even if he's too thick to know. The Army got him before the Klan could. But some things he won't abide. He'd kill me if he knew I was even in there."

"So you're from Alabama?"

"Yep."

Despite our damp clothes, the chill, I wanted to stay out here with her, pretend this was a date. But I could not think of the next thing to ask.

Kit said, "What else do you want to know?"

"Your folks are in Turkey?"

"Ankara. Pa's a flight-line mechanic at the air base. Ma hates it there. Base housing is Quonset huts."

"You going back there after graduation?"

Kit shook her head. "They think I'm going home to Montgomery, to live with my granny, work as a carhop at the A&W."

"But you're not?"

She shook her head again and turned away from me. She stared out into the rainy dark, leaving it to me to ask more. "What then?"

"Rick didn't tell you?"

"No."

"It's what we did together. Him at Brandeis, me at Ole Miss. Rick helped me work up the nerve."

"To do what?"

"Apply to college without permission. We both did that, but not starting from the same place. College is a fur piece for someone like me." She grinned. "'A fur piece.' Get it?"

I wasn't sure I did, but I nodded.

"Might as well be a fur coat."

"But you got in?"

"Yep. Ole Miss. Oxford, Mississippi. Full scholarship, work-study, the whole shebang. Next September, whether the great white father likes it or not. And it *will* be not."

"You haven't told them?"

"I'm working on it."

"But they'll be proud."

Kit snorted. "Ole Miss," she said. "My pa thinks it's a football team. Period."

"And you?"

"To me it's Faulkner country, that's all. Faulkner lives in Oxford. I wrote to him. Rick made me do it, just like he wrote to that guy of his."

"Marcuse."

"Right. I wrote Faulkner. I told him I was coming, get ready."

"*Light in August.*" I was about to lie, say "I love that novel" like a callow date.

"What?" She looked at me with such interest that I could not lie to her.

"I know you're reading it," I said.

"'My, my. A body does get around. Here we aint been coming from Alabama but two months, and now it's already Tennessee.'"

"What?"

"The last line of *Light.*"

"Oh. I thought maybe it was yours, what you're writing."

She gave me another look.

"I saw you. I saw what you're writing, a glimpse of it."

"A body does git around, big guy."

""The story of your soul.'"

"Did I say that?"

"Yes."

"And you said Rilke. Thanks for saying that. It made the *Vopo* leave me alone."

"I *do* read Rilke," I said. "*Letters to a Young Poet.* Though I'm no poet."

"Don't be so sure. Who else but a poet would stand out here like this, freezing his durn butt off?"

I laughed, aware of how chilled I felt, but when she turned and opened the door, I was disappointed.

She gestured at the sign: "*Frei Arbeiterschaft Halle.*"

"At least it's free," she said.

Once in the room, our ease with each other evaporated. I went at once to what I thought of as the boys' end, and misunderstood when, turning around abruptly, I found that Kit had followed me there. But she was only going to the wardrobe, which she opened. Inside, she found a stack of folded towels. She took two, tossed one to me, and returned to her end of the room, leaving me to wonder if she had any idea how uncomfortable I'd become. As if I *had* lied to her.

Separately, without comment, we each toweled our wet hair. Then, while Kit went down the hall, I opened the wardrobe and found hangers. I slid one into my damp blazer and hung it up. I went over to the window and watched the rain fall through the cone of light cast by a nearby streetlamp. The window was open a few inches, and I could smell ash in the air — what Berliners had smelled for years, I would be told, every time it rained.

Kit came back, and I took my bag with me to the WC down the hall.

When I returned to the room, the overhead light was off. Now the light from the street was the only illumination, a faint glow. Kit's corner was entirely dark, and it took me a moment to realize that she was already under her blanket. I was crushed that this time alone with her was now going to end in sleep, but relieved that she would not see me without my clothes. I went to my cot, undressed facing away from her, removed my leg braces, careful to put them down without a sound, and slid under my blanket. My good GI blanket. I was equally aware of the scratchy wool on my legs and of the three vacant cots between me and the girl.

I was wearing briefs and an undershirt, which made me wonder what she was wearing. I knew nothing firsthand of the female body apart from the sweet implications of clothing; nothing of breasts, nipples, the curve of the hip. I had pictured it, of course — the camera-book nudes and statues, the furtive sessions with girlie magazines. But what was a vagina to me beyond a fancied wound between legs? Or the clitoris, of which I'd never heard. When I pictured a woman's naked body — as I did then Kit's — it had no hair anywhere except for the head.

"A penny for your thoughts," she said, her disembodied voice floating in the darkness. I almost choked at what I'd have had to answer if the truth was even remotely on my list of things to say.

"Mothers," I said — I don't know why. And at once I rebuked myself. Playing on her pity for a boy who'd lost his mother — is that what I was doing?

"What about her?"

"Not my mother," I said, a lie told to deflect an emotion I wanted no part of. "I meant Ulrich's mother."

"Ulrich's mother? What about her?"

"Her being German. I was thinking of her back there in the club."

"With those German girls?"

"I guess so, yes. I mean — well, not literally. Those girls were hookers, right?"

"Just desperate kids, Michael. I mean, what would we be doing if we lived here? Imagine."

"That's what I was thinking about Ulrich and his mother when they lived here after the war. What they survived, what they went through."

"Mrs. Healy is good to me."

"Me, too."

"You've been through a thing or two."

"Not like that, though. You could see it in Ulrich's eyes today, the way he looked out that train window."

"And the way he's getting blasted tonight."

"I guess I don't blame him," I said. But what I felt was gratitude that he was still out there, gratitude to Tramm for keeping him out. "I just mean, I can't really picture Ulrich's mother acting like those girls."

Kit laughed. "But it sounds like you *did* picture it, big guy. And what the heck, why not? Mrs. Healy *was* a *Fräulein,* and if you know her now, you know she *was* a pretty one. And General Healy, or Major or Captain or whatever rank he was then, was a handsome Yank flyboy. And sure they went to clubs. Why the heck not?"

"Not flyboy, Kit. Spy. Do you know that? Ulrich told me that today in the train while you were asleep. Ulrich's stepfather is a spy in charge of spies."

"I wasn't asleep."

"Jesus, you too?" One unexpected turn after another — why was I loving it so? "You're a spy, too?"

"What, because I pretended to sleep? I just needed a little time to myself, was all."

"But Kit, have you noticed something about this trip? Nothing is what it seems to be."

"Substance versus surface, big guy. Not 'this trip' — life. Nothing's what it seems to be in *life.* The hateful duplicity of all that we experience, which happens to be Faulkner's subject."

"And yours."

"The moral disease of the human condition."

"Incurable."

"What?"

"You said 'incurable' in your book."

"What book?"

"The one you're writing."

"Now who's duplicitous!"

"I told you I glimpsed it. Only glimpsed. You mind?"

"What I write in my accounts is private, bub."

I did not answer. After a long silence, I said, "I'm not talking about your book, or Faulkner. I'm talking about us. Ulrich pretending to be Rick. You and me — a debating club, for God's sake. Josef Tramm — a union rep? Yeah, right."

"Don't get paranoid on me, Michael."

"It's Berlin, Kit. Paranoia everywhere."

"Okay, so maybe we're all spies. Maybe those girls in the club were spies. Maybe when she was young, Ulrich's mother was. Maybe she still is. Let's pretend it's a movie. Ingrid Bergman."

"Marlene Dietrich."

"Romy Schneider."

"But it's not a movie, Kit. Ulrich's whole thing in coming here, what we saw in him on the train — it's more than what you and I are up to."

"Maybe. Maybe not."

"No, for sure it is. I mean, the guy has all these ghosts in his brain. The Edelweiss Pirates, what the hell is that? Adolf Eichmann. Herbert Marcuse. The chocolate bombardier. Rubble women. Talk about incurable."

"No one was talking about incurable, Michael."

"You were."

"Because I said 'disease'? Is that what you're asking?"

"You mean like my polio?"

"I didn't mean that."

"It's okay, Kit. I know I had polio. You don't have to worry if you refer to it. That's obviously no secret, though everybody treats it like it is."

She didn't say anything. It seemed like her turn, and so, for a few moments, neither did I. I could hear her breathing.

Was it over? The day? The time with her? Had I blown it by actually saying the goddamn word out loud? To keep our talk going, I said quietly, "Earlier today, I thought of *The Wizard of Oz,* and then you quoted from it. You were Judy Garland."

"You're Ray Bolger?"

"The scarecrow?"

"We were talking about Rick."

"'The power of negative thinking is a force for human liberation.'"

"If you say so."

"That's Ulrich's motto, Kit. Marcuse. That's what we're doing here. Negative thinking in relation to the German past. Negative thinking in relation to American materialism. Negative thinking in relation to his old man. All that negative shit — 'the disobedience of a living body.' You heard him. It's why you and I weren't going to come at first, why we started out this morning by saying no."

"But we do negative thinking of our own, I guess. Huh?"

"Like about *your* father?"

She didn't answer. I pressed. "What was that about the Klan?"

"The Klan is just one tree among many in the woods I come from."

"But you hate it. So you're here."

"Something like that. I was cussing this whole thing on the train, but now I'm glad we came."

"Even if you're headed for a Communist parade?"

"Yes. And you're glad, too, Michael. I can tell. You can't fool Dorothy."

"I am glad. I love it, actually, being here." I paused, admittedly for effect, before adding, "Especially now."

Those two simple words marked a move away from the others and toward us — which is why, no doubt, we each fell silent again, each staring up at the shadowy ceiling, each breathing so the other could hear. You, I thought. Not Ulrich. You. You, Kit. Not me, either. Tell me about you.

At last I said, "Your mother. What's she like?"

"Oh, she's real southern, a country gal. Daisy Mae and all that. Dogpatch. My folks are what you guys would call hillbillies."

"No, I wouldn't."

"No shame in being hill people, Michael. It all depends on where you're starting from. You start in a place very different from me."

"How do you know that?"

She laughed. "Written all over you, big guy. There are mill workers and there are owners. Some differences not even being an Army brat smoothes out."

"I'm not an Army brat."

"Which makes the point."

"No shame in that either?"

"Right."

"But we were talking about your parents. Your mother."

"Daddy whistles Dixie when he wants something from her. And she delivers." Kit's laugh now carried a hint of the lewd, a hint of her parents' raucous pairing. "Sometimes he calls her Dixie Cup." But her jovial esprit had come out of nowhere, and even in the dark it seemed counterfeit.

"What do you call her?"

"Mama. Most of you guys say 'Mom.' But I call mine 'Mama.' I love that word 'Mama.' Mammary. Marvelous. Magnificent. Amazing."

"What do you mean, 'you guys'?"

She laughed again. Kit was enjoying this — what, this dissection of differences? I had been feeling so *like* her, but now she was emphasizing how we were unalike. A way of pushing me away? "You Yankees," she said. "You Yankees. You say 'Mom, Momm . . . Dad, Daad.' We say Mama. We say Daddy." I sensed her in the dark, her head propped on an elbow, facing toward me. "Knock, knock," she said abruptly.

"Who's there?"

"Marmalade."

"Marmalade who?"

"Marmalade everyone but Daddy."

I got the joke, but I did not laugh.

She snorted and fell back on her cot. "Although not in my house. A Dixie Cup can't fight back."

I heard in her inflection an echo of her father's demand, a hint of her mother's surrender. And that said what about Kit? Another way we were alike? The weight a kid feels from the tension between her parents, or his. A mill hand. A racist. The great white father. Her disdain for her father was very clear. And mine?

"I'm surprised at you, Michael," Kit teased. "Laughing at a joke like that."

"I didn't laugh."

"I noticed. Why, because it's raunchy?"

"Was that raunchy?" I asked, trying for fun and affection. If I'd had a pillow, I'd have thrown it across the room at her. "Why does this feel like a game of keep-away?"

"Because there are certain things we are not talking about?"

"Exactly."

"That's the Army brat's way, Michael. You live a lot of different places. You see a lot of different people. You keep having to fit in over and over. You're very careful what you show to folks. Wiesbaden is my tenth school."

"It's my third."

"There you go. An Army brat gets to choose which of her sides to show. When I'm with Ma and Pa, I'm Katey-Ann, Miss Keep-the-peace-at-any-price. With Granny, I'm Katharine, the girl who fetches. My folks think I'm going to take care of her in Montgomery, for my room and board."

"But?"

"I love Granny," Kit said, "but come September, I'm a freshman at Ole Miss, and that's that. And the first thing I'm doing is, Knock, knock —"

"Who's there?"

"— on William Faulkner's front door in Oxford, so I can ask him if he needs help with the chores."

"What do you mean?"

"He's an old man. He's going to need help with his chores, and I'm going to do them for him. And before I'm through, I'm going to get him to read my novel."

"*That's* the thing we aren't talking about, your novel."

"Which you were reading without permission."

"I didn't know it was a novel."

"Bits and pieces of one. Still private."

"I'm sorry."

She fell silent again. After some moments, I said, "Knock, knock."

"Who's there?" Not mere pleasure in her voice now, but true delight.

"The little old lady."

"The little old lady who?"

"You don't know it?"

"The little old lady *who*, big guy!"

"And when Mr. Faulkner answers the door, you tell him you are good mountain folk, which is why you can yodel. *Liddle-oldle-ladee-whoo!*"

"Jesus, Michael, you are *good*. I'm great, but you are good."

"And you can tell Mr. Faulkner that you've been to damn Berlin!"

"Even *East* Berlin, if we get away with it tomorrow. Can you believe we were behind the Iron Curtain today? The damn Iron Curtain, Michael!"

"We're still behind it, Kit."

"Could you believe Rick at the border? That asshole."

"Talk about obedience of a corpse. I'll tell you something — I was scared there for a minute."

"For a minute? Jeez, big guy, I'm still scared."

And we laughed again, hard. A couple of kids at camp after lights out, scaring each other, creating the potent intimacy of night secrets, our confessions to each other. Two kids admitting to being scared. And then, in the good silence that follows laughter, waiting to see what else we would admit to.

But the silence thickened, and I thought, with sudden if regretted weariness, that we might be going to sleep now.

But there came her voice again, floating in the darkness. "What about your mother?"

"What?"

"You said your mother before, I heard you." She paused before adding, "I know she's dead, Michael."

I had to stop. Hadn't she been the one to bring mothers up? With her crack about raincoats? If she knew my mother was dead, then was her reference a deliberate opening, the sly offhand remark, say, a shrink might make to help? Wizard of Oz, wizard of pity — was she someone, really, to trust?

"How do you know that?" I asked.

"Ulrich told me. He told me not to tell any of the other kids. He told me you don't like people to know about it. I haven't told anybody."

"I don't want people feeling sorry for me. I hate that."

"Nobody does."

"Yes, they do."

"Because of your legs, you mean? Okay, I take it back. You're right on that one. How can people not feel sorry for you because of that. Of course we feel sorry for you, Michael. You're crippled."

I was hardly breathing as she said this. It was the first time anyone, even including blunt Ulrich, had used that awful word with me. Awful word, yet the truth. The sound of it in that dark room brought an unbounded feeling of relief. "I do okay," I said.

"You sure do," she said.

After a long moment, in a different voice, she said, "Knock, knock."

"Jesus, Kit. What's with you?"

"Knock, knock."

"Who's there?"

"Mahatma."

"Mahatma who?"

"Mah hat 'n' mah cane! I'm goin' for a walk."

I didn't know how to react.

"Get it?"

"Cane."

"I forgot today, Michael. Completely forgot. That you have it. Your cane. Like it's disappeared. Because of the way you are. You are amazing."

"Polio has its advantages, believe it or not."

"Like what?"

"Like . . . like it made me really close to her."

"Your mother?"

"She took care of me. She . . . took . . . really . . . good care of me."

"You must miss her."

It wasn't at all horrible to me that my eyes spilled over then. Tears coursed down my temples into the wells behind my ears. Unbounded relief, yes — even if made possible by this girl's not being able to see me. I hadn't cried in months, and never, since Mom, in another's presence. Not even my father's.

Now, as I write this, looking back through the years at the figure of that boy, bereft in a strange bed, I wish I could do for him, across time, what the girl across the room had no way of doing — reach through the dark and only touch him, to let him know that the pointed chaos of such feelings is what we were put here not to withstand, but to express. What I did know was that the shedding of tears in response to her, even if she did not understand, was what I had come to Berlin to do.

Lying there completely motionless, my legs as if paralyzed, my arms at my sides, my head flat, without a pillow — I flashed back to those first months in the pulmonary unit of St. Luke's Hospital; my life in an iron lung, a time when I was certain I would spend *all* of my life in an iron lung. I had been able to imagine that prospect only by imagining also that my mother would be always there beside me, to wipe the streaks from my temples, to smooth back my damp hair, to sponge my forehead with her hand. The wetness on my face now brought back the consolation of her presence, as if she were the one in the room with me here.

"I miss her a lot," I said, yet felt consoled for the first time since hearing from my father of my mother's death, a consolation mediated by the gorgeous girl across from me. "Why does it help to say so?"

"I don't know, Michael. I've never lost anybody. But I know in other things, it helps to say so. That's why I write my little novel."

"Don't call it little."

"Well, it's not big." She laughed self-deprecatingly. And then, with her sense of what was needed to break me from grief, Kit told me how she had started writing because of Faulkner, who taught her, she said, that the most interesting people are the ones who are broken inside. The brave ones are at war not with the world but with themselves. She was speaking with a forced literary self-consciousness, a girl wiser from books than from life. But I could have listened to her forever.

Finally I said, "Will you tell me?"

"What?"

"About your novel. What's it about?"

"I don't know you well enough."

"Writers read their work to strangers all the time."

"I know, but you're not a stranger, either. You're sort of in between. I would need you to like it, but I don't know if you would."

"I would."

"Don't say that. If you automatically liked it, what good would that be?"

"So who is incurable? Tell me that, at least."

"That would be telling you all of it."

"Is it about you?"

"It's about my mother. That's all I'm gonna tell you. Don't ask me anything else. And no, you can't read it."

"Okay, okay."

"It's why I felt so . . . when you brought up mothers."

But I had not been the one to do that, I was sure.

"Michael?"

"Yes?"

"*This* is sort of like what writing does. This talking. It's new to me, to talk like this."

"Not even with Ulrich?"

"Especially not. I like Rick, but he makes me nervous when he gets mad."

"I get mad, Kit. At my dad."

"That doesn't count."

We laughed.

Then I said, "Being here in this room in the middle of the night with you. Talking like this. I've never done this before either. It feels right, Kit. But it feels illegal."

After a further silence, she said quietly, "I know."

It helps to say so — wasn't that what she had just told me? What I wanted to say then seemed absolutely and utterly unspeakable, illegal, *verboten*. How to say "I like you, Kit"?

Except, of course, by saying it. I said nothing.

I let my face fall to the right, away from her. *Human culture, Monty, assumes man's alienation from his sexuality.* I let my eyes drift in the un-differentiated light outside the window, light defined only by the floating mist, tiny drops of water carried by specks of cinder and ash that remained in the air of Berlin.

Unconsciously, I had lifted my left hand up and out of the blanket — perhaps a way of not touching my erection. I became aware of my forefinger softly rubbing the left side of my face until it was dry. I imagined my finger as if it were Kit's, as if she were the one — not an angel, not my mother — to come to me. And with that, or something soon after — more fleeting thoughts of Ulrich quoting Marcuse, of my father, of Tramm, of Kennedy and Khrushchev, of Elvis, even, singing "GI Blues" — I went to sleep.

When I woke to a noise and a jolt of my cot, my first thought was, Kit, you have come to me.

But it was Ulrich. He bumped past me and fell heavily onto his cot, fully clothed and still clutching his bag. The stench of vomit poured off him. Almost immediately he began to snore.

I lay rigidly on my side, my face in the foul wash of his exhalations. I did not move. I sensed someone standing motionless at the foot of my cot — Tramm. I did not turn to look at him. He made no sound, and I knew somehow that he was watching me. In the diffused light from the street, I was as visible to him as Ulrich was to me. An old hand at paralysis, I knew I could make him think I was dead asleep.

Tramm then came into my field of vision, a stone-sober man moving quietly with intent. Ignoring me, he stopped over Ulrich. He lifted Ulrich's hand and started, I thought, to remove his watch. Jesus. A simple thief.

But that was not it. Tramm was removing the strap of the bag Ulrich had clutched to himself. The strap was entwined in Ulrich's arm, like a child's sleeping-toy. Tramm could move it only so far, but soon he had it free enough to open the bag's zippered side pocket.

That was the pocket with the roll of film that the MP had made such a fuss over in front of the Russian at Magdeburg. Tramm had to have been directed to that pocket, as he had to have been told of our supposed interest in the high school. There was no way his knowing that was a coincidence. So Tramm now knew from us tonight that the melodrama in the train compartment at the border, with Ulrich announcing us as the debating club, the roll of film as the yearbook photos — knew that we had lied. He knew we didn't give a shit about the high school.

From the way he was now sliding his hand inside the unzipped pocket, back and forth, back and forth, I realized that the film canister was not there.

Tramm urgently opened the bag's main compartment and felt inside it, pushing his blind hand into the clothing. No roll of film. It was as if I were watching a movie, the villain outsmarted by the good guy. Ulrich had been ahead of me all day. Was he even now only seeming to be conked out?

But no. His breath was so foul, his snoring so grotesque, way too much, he couldn't be faking.

Tramm sank to one knee at Ulrich's cot, remained motionless for a long moment, staring at Ulrich. What boss would Tramm report this failure to? He craned his neck forward slightly, and I sensed that he was about to frisk Ulrich, his clothing. The prospect alarmed me, as if I, too, had a part to play in the hide-and-seek of the film canister, whatever it was. Instinctively, I groaned and tugged at my blanket, a warning, as if my waking up would threaten Tramm — which apparently it would have. He froze again. He was looking at me.

I smacked my lips, twice, then settled again. When, seconds later, I peered through the slits of my eyes, Tramm was closing the zippers of the bag. He tucked it back into Ulrich's side. I half expected him to sleep on one of the vacant cots between me and Kit, but I heard a click, the door opening, and click, softly closing. Tramm was gone, although it took me a full five minutes to dare to roll over and look. Yes, gone.

I brought my left wrist up to my face, to see my watch. Fifteen minutes before three. I made myself wait a full thirty minutes more. Then I threw my blanket back and found my trousers at the foot of my cot, folded but damp from the rain. I clutched the trousers in one arm. In my bare feet, without my braces or cane, I moved haltingly to the door. Yet I made my way soundlessly through it. Along a bright hallway, I steadied myself on the wall as I went. In the stairwell, I found the pay phone. I let my trousers fall out of their fold, fished in the pockets for the coins I knew were there, and dropped them into the telephone slot. I inserted four, a guess at the cost of a long-distance call. I dialed the number of our house on Mosbacher Strasse, knowing already, with no conscious planning, exactly what to say.

I was going to tell him that I was sorry about calling so late, sorry about our argument, sorry about the breach of trust with the car. I was going to explain that I would have called sooner, but I had not been ready to apologize, had not been strong enough — and now I was.

I was going to tell him that I was in Berlin, afraid of what I was doing here, but also that I was more alive with this adventure than I had ever been before. I was going to tell him that with Ulrich von Neuhaus I was safe, that we had a game going, and that we were winning.

I was going to tell him that, yes, tomorrow I would cross the forbidden border — and everything from then on, I was certain, would be different. And above all, I was going to tell him about Kit Carson, that for the first time in my life, in wishing for a woman, it was not Mom.

The phone rang and rang, in that strange German way, and my father never answered. I did not imagine what he was doing, already, to come after me.

Part Three

8

WE WERE IN a refitted DC-3, the airplane that had become iconic in the haze behind Bogart and Bergman, how it had seemed to be nosing upward even while still on the ground. C-47 was the military designation — C for cargo — but the plane I had booked through colleagues in Frankfurt was owned by the Bank of America, the San Francisco bank whose European holdings made Chase Manhattan's seem like chump change. Bank of America openly controlled several dozen companies in West Germany, not counting its even more extensive silent partnerships with German banks. They had a small fleet of DC-3s and -4s based at Rhine-Main, halfway between Wiesbaden and Frankfurt, and it had been a simple matter to tag one on short notice that morning.

The plane's appointments were meant to impress, and normally the plush swivel seats, arranged in cocktail-lounge style around small Formica tables, would have held investors, union officials, or government ministers. Today General Healy's wife and I were the only passengers.

The jovial pilot, a retired Army Air Corps veteran, had told us he averaged four flights a week to Berlin, but during the airlift he had flown four roundtrips a day, and could still hit Tempelhof blind. Mrs. Healy and I boarded the plane barely more than two hours ago — less than three hours after we left the Russian Chapel — and as we did, the pilot saluted as if we were the commander and his lady. *Bank brass, Army brass — what's the diff?* The youthful copilot had doubled as our steward, and reappeared in the cabin only moments ago to lock down our swivel chairs, help us with the seat belts, and collect our coffee cups.

"I wish you would call me Paul," I said now.

Mrs. Healy was looking out the window as our plane banked down over Berlin. I glimpsed the towering half-arches of the airlift memorial at Tempelhof, where we would land soon. But Mrs. Healy was seeing other things, things I knew better than to try to imagine.

"You should call me Paul," I pressed. "We will shortly be in company where I won't want to be using your last name. Am I correct about that or not?"

She brought her face toward me, but her eyes still carried the weight of what she'd been seeing. "Who?" she asked. "What company?"

"A colleague of mine. A Berliner. A banker. Hans Krone. Very well connected across the city, famously so."

"How well do you know him?"

"My bank, Chase, owns a controlling interest in the Commercial Bank of Berlin, of which he is head. I meet with him several times a month, always in Frankfurt. In effect, I am his boss."

"And you trust him?"

I had to laugh. "I trust him totally for what I need him for. I've never needed him for espionage."

"Nor will you today."

"Which returns me to my point. We don't want him or others to even imagine espionage, right? This is just three kids on a lark and a couple of pissed-off parents reeling them in. No question at all of 'national security,' as your husband calls it. Right? So we're leaving the general out. In which case, who are you?"

"Ulrich's mother. Rick's mother. Can it not be left at that?"

"All right," I said. "We'll see." I did not keep the skepticism from my voice. On the other hand, I saw the problem. If she hoped to fudge things about her husband, perhaps it was because she was savvy enough to know that in Berlin, it was better to avoid explicit deception. Enact the truth, would be the strategy, but limit it.

She said, "I have never beheld Berlin from the air before." She let her gaze drift back to the window, the scene below.

"I find that surprising, given your husband's work."

"We left here shortly after we married. I never wanted to come back, and have not. As for David, given his work, as you put it, he could not return here. He became too senior."

"He knows too much? He can't risk — what, their truth serum?"

She aimed the razor of her look at me, a look that said, Don't you dare mock my husband or his work.

I felt chastened. "I just cannot believe I am doing this. I'm one of those hapless Americans who find it impossible to imagine the world of spies as actual, existing outside of bad fiction."

"It exists in Berlin, Mr. Montgomery."

For a few minutes, we let Berlin be what there was between us, as the plane banked over the desolate, compulsively squared-off urban landscape of the Eastern sector. One broad boulevard, lined with twin ranks of new, blockish buildings, stood in contrast to the mostly barren streets that intersected it, vast acreage that had been cleared of rubble but never built upon. Indeed, pyramids of that rubble marked every few blocks, like the tombs of dead rulers. That one boulevard in the Communist showplace was Stalinallee. From the air it resembled the false-front street of a Hollywood backlot set.

Mrs. Healy said, "My first arrival here was on foot."

"Carrying your son?"

"Yes. Slung across my body in a shawl. Not a proper shawl. The remnant of a blanket, as if I were a Turk. As if he were an infant. He was three years old."

"1946."

"Yes."

"Why Berlin? Wasn't Berlin pretty much leveled at that point?"

"Leipzig," she said wearily, "was 'pretty much leveled.'"

In my own life, that year was the joyous beginning, Edie and I on Saturdays in Central Park, each with a hand holding Michael's hand, Michael swinging his feet off the ground between us, his healthy perfect feet. Through that year, well into the next and the one after, the word always in my mind, as in the minds of most of us who'd returned from the war, was "home."

"But Leipzig was your home."

Without looking my way, she smiled wanly. I realized that in addition to the squared-off stretches of wasteland that still defined one half of the city below, she was seeing a reflection in the window, the wasteland of memory. I could not know it then, but she was surely seeing flashes of the particular horror that had driven her, like a frightened animal, into the herd of refugees fleeing west. The leveling of Leipzig, in her case, in her family's case, had not ended with the war. It was a nightmare story, a ghost story, a horror story I would not hear until years later, although I think she was inclined for her own reasons to tell it to me then — a stranger sitting near her in an airplane. If so, it was an impulse she resisted, except obliquely. I did not know at the time what to listen for, although now, in recording what she did tell me, I see what cast the shadow in her expression, all of it having been made explicit by someone else.

"The word 'home' had no meaning in this country then. We Germans had forfeited any right to such a word, any relationship to what the word once implied."

She turned to me. The distance between us, as between our two worlds, was enough to hold an ocean. "Berlin seemed safer. A starving city, a smoldering city — yet for me, for my child, it *was* safer. And Berlin was where I could learn . . . what I had to learn."

"Which was?"

"Ulrich's father, his natural father I mean, had disappeared. Like all of the German men. I had not seen him since . . ." She paused just enough for me to note the care with which she sorted through the ways to express — what, the mystery of their bond? "Since Ulrich was conceived. I had to learn what had happened to him. I did not know if he was alive or dead. I did not know . . ." Her voice drifted off.

Again she was referring to the man as Ulrich's father, his natural father, not as her husband, not as anything in relation to her. The significance of this distinction, observed both then and earlier in the day at the Russian Chapel, was lost on me. But it was a distinction I noted each time. "And did you learn?" I asked.

"Yes. Eventually. Not at first. At first I only survived. *We* only survived. Faceless among the mass of Berlin's women and children. Women and children without men. Women and children without names. I felt safe among them. But we were not safe. Not yet. Not until we found a place among those who could protect us."

"Americans."

"Yes. It was that simple. Americans made us safe. A common feeling in Berlin."

"You went to work for the Americans."

"I became a translator."

"Because you knew English?"

"I had been at university."

"And you met General Healy."

"Colonel Healy then." She smiled. "I could not bring myself to call him David. *Colonel* Healy. Not *David* for a long time. He was extremely kind to us. His kindness awakened me from what was known in Berlin as the 'sleep of the women,' the living death of our kind. At first it was a simple matter of fresh milk for my little one. David brought fresh milk for Ulrich, a miracle. I never knew where he got it. For me, he brought a feeling of being protected. And he was able to find out what had happened to Ulrich's father when the Russians came. There were Soviet files that —" She stopped, clearly checking herself.

But now that she was telling me her story, actually telling me, telling someone, a stranger on a plane, she wanted to go on. "I was devastated. I had loved Ulrich's father very much. A youthful love. All through the war, I had been terrified for him. Then I learned I was right to be terrified for him. One spends years fearing the worst, and then, when the worst reveals itself, it is far, far worse than one dared imagine. He was not meant for the army, certainly not meant for the Nazis."

"What was his name?"

She looked at me, deciding whether to say. Then she answered. "Wolf. His name was Wolf. In those years when we were young, it was a name that made us laugh. So untrue of him, that name. He was the opposite of wolf. He was, you say, a thinker. A philosopher. A protégé of Edmund Husserl. He was brilliant, the youngest Herr Doktor Professor at the University of Leipzig, and I was his promising student. It would be too much to say I worshiped him, but not too much to say that I defined myself by him. I was so young. Like me, he was from a landholding family, a proud family. But our families, it would be seen, were not hard enough. *We* were not hard enough.

Our families had been made soft by privilege. And also he was a man of the mind — another kind of softness. He was not equipped for the realities that unfolded in this nation, that fell upon this nation. That is what, having come to Berlin, I would learn. But I am speaking too much."

"No. You are not." I waited.

Finally she resumed. "He had become like the nation. He *was* the nation, the Reich. That is a word one never hears anymore, have you noticed? Reich. What was done routinely by Germans for the Reich in 1945, no German would have done — almost no German — in 1940. Certainly not Wolf. When I knew him, unthinkable! The war was a complete disaster for him, even more than for others. The war destroyed him — this is what I learned."

"From Soviet files?"

"Destroyed him, my husband, even before it killed him."

"He was your husband?"

She started when I said that, as if I had caught her in an indiscretion. A crimson flood rose in the skin of her throat, overtaking her face, her face seized for a moment with true fear. Which she then swallowed, a draft of poison.

Why? How had wedlock, instead of its shameful opposite, become a source of mortification? How had her marriage to this man become a secret to protect? Why, even now, was she terrified? Soviet files?

In my experience that year, no German of my acquaintance lived with any discernible attachment to the past. As I recall, that very week the trial of Adolf Eichmann had convened in Jerusalem, Israel's forcing of a long-deferred moral reckoning. We did not know it then, but that trial marked the beginning of Germany's turning back to face its history. This woman, for reasons I did not see yet, had never been able to turn away.

"Your husband died at the end. In Berlin?"

She nodded.

Why, I wondered, had she used that euphemism with me — *he never returned from the front*. The German habit of lying. I knew not to press that. "Berlin at the end," I said too easily, "was a nightmare."

She shrugged, conveying the impossibility of continuing this conversation. "It was *all* a nightmare," she said bitterly. "Berlin is nothing more than where people like you were finally able to see it as such."

"And being here brings it all back to you?"

"How could it be otherwise?" She was at the end of her patience with me. The willing stranger in the airplane, tossed up by fate, was a dunce. "Ulrich is his father's son. There is the curse. To have Ulrich at risk in Berlin . . ." She could not finish her sentence, or would not.

The plane dropped suddenly, approaching the airport. Her hand went to the armrest of her chair, clutching it. She was finished talking. What she had told me mainly was that my son was in even more jeopardy than I had feared, that I grasped nothing of what it might involve.

On landing, the plane bounced once before settling into its long rollout, and I noticed Mrs. Healy's clutching fingers go white for some seconds. Fear, yes. But also absolute control. The plane engines reversed loudly, cutting our momentum, then eased, making it possible for me to hear her when she shifted toward me to say, "It is Charlotte, Paul."

Von Neuhaus? I nearly asked. But that name, taken by her son in rejecting the name Healy, was her family's name, she had said, not her first husband's. "Please call me Charlotte," she said simply.

And that is how I introduced her, as one of the other parents, to Hans Krone, who stood waiting at the foot of the flimsy short stairs that had been rolled up to the plane. The sun was bright, but Krone was wearing a tan cotton overcoat that emphasized his bulk. He was a shrewd man, large enough to be physically intimidating, and he was known for his readiness to pull the trigger on a deal. He took his power for granted, and, as a member of a close-knit West Berlin elite, well he might. A new oligarchy had established itself in West Germany during the economic boom of the fifties — the steel barons of the Ruhr, the sanitized industrialists at Krupp and Bayer, and the key commercial bankers who, controlling liquidity, were the true princes of the new Reich. In ways that we *Ausländers* were aware of, but for all our stakeholdings never part of, these Germans worked closely together, even took care of each other. They shared an implicit bond defined, exactly, by what separated them from us. At a certain point, the clients of the occupation had become its proprietors, albeit proprietors who as yet were content to indulge us *Ausländers* in our illusion of conquest. As long as it helped with cash flow, they would.

Krone, presiding over the financing of the construction frenzy in West Berlin, was one of these princes. He and his kind controlled more of what made for life in the new Germany than the government did, not least because, in addition to handling the throttle of the economic locomotive, they were the engineers of the economic turbines running underground, commonly known as the black market. Involving millions of dollars, the black market by 1961 flourished especially in the East, since the official economy there was moribund. The failure of the Communists to supply basic needs and wants to their population made the black market inevitable, which is why moral scruples about illegality on the part of outsiders like me were irrelevant. Surreptitious exploitation, of currency fluctuations particularly, fueled a discreet auxiliary engine of the Berlin banking boom, and I knew that Krone was a prince of that realm, too. I had nothing to do with his illegal activities across the sector boundaries of the two Berlins, accounts that showed up nowhere on his books, much less on mine, but I assumed his reach into his peer elites in the Communist world. Indeed, in asking for his help today, I was counting on it.

None of this needed to be referred to. With me, Krone had always been direct. His friendliness had implied neither deceit nor ingratiation. I liked him, and in fact it was a relief to feel the warmth of his uncomplicated, affirming handshake.

When it came to women, German businessmen were afflicted, in a famous phrase from another context, with the disease that presumes itself the cure. Their sly, winking discretion intended to honor the appearance of a rigid post-Nazi morality, but like inquisitive confessors they managed to be both puritanical and lewd at once, if only by implication. There was no chance that Krone would bat an eye at my abbreviated introduction of my companion as the mother of Michael's chum. I had briefed Krone by phone, telling him the simple truth that my seventeen-year-old son had gone to Berlin without permission, probably for the May Day celebrations in the Soviet sector, and I wanted to find him. I'd told him that Michael was with two other American kids, but apart from descriptions, I had not identified them. I could sense in Krone now, even in his brisk greeting of the woman beside me, the assumption that there was more to her presence here than that. And who was I to tell him he was wrong?

A car was waiting for us on the tarmac, a gleaming black Mercedes.

Unlike mine, this one was a recent model that had at last forsworn the traditional bulbous hood and fenders for a boxy sleekness with the barest hint of fins. This style shift to American aerodynamics, the illusion of speed even while standing still, could not occur in Germany without a simultaneous shift away from the deadweighted past symbolized by the classic Mercedes design. And we Yank bankers had conveyed to the denizens of Stuttgart the virtue of built-in obsolescence, which is the economic point of style. All of this, to your father, would have been an instance of capitalist waste, except for what was being rendered obsolete. Those old Mercedes fenders, after all, had never seemed more themselves than when flying flags that bore the swastika.

The driver, in black suit and cap, stood by the right rear passenger door, holding it for Mrs. Healy, while I crossed to the other side. When I slid in next to her, ahead of Krone, she was waiting to make eye contact with me, to flick an eyebrow, alerting me. To what I hadn't a clue, then realized she wanted no discussion in front of the driver. To keep up with her, I was going to have to sharpen the edge of my paranoia. In General Healy's household, apparently, the assumption had to be that servants were enemies.

In response to her muted anxiety, I covered her hand with mine, a less intimate act than it might have been because she was wearing her tan gloves again. It was an automatic gesture, even with her. Often I had reassured Edie with such a touch, but in this context I intended it in an impersonal way, only to convey that we had no choice but to trust Krone's methods, whatever they were. But Mrs. Healy lost no time in withdrawing her hand from under mine. There would be no calling this woman Charlotte unless we were not alone.

Krone joined us in the back, settling his ample frame on a swing-down jumpseat opposite me. The driver had taken his topcoat. His suit was a well-cut, double-breasted navy pinstripe carrying a hint of Savile Row. The midday heat had not registered on me until now, when Krone snapped his handkerchief out of his breast pocket to wipe his large forehead. In America, but for those pinstripes, he would have been taken for a football fan, a man living for the glory days of his own gridiron career in school. The warm smile with which he had greeted us at the foot of the rolling staircase was gone.

"This is a very tense time in Berlin," he said. After wiping his face, he carefully wiped his hands. He returned the handkerchief first to its creases, then to its pocket in three perfect steeples. His fastidiousness made me think briefly of Edie.

"First of all," he went on, "you are correct, absolutely correct, to be concerned about your children. I have a son and a daughter, and I have sent them only this week to spend the summer, at least the summer, with my wife's brother in Geneva. Things cannot go on as they are."

The driver was at the wheel now. Krone touched a button in the door panel, and a glass partition slid soundlessly up from its slot in the driver's backrest, sealing him off. Mrs. Healy glanced at me, her point made.

The car began to move, smoothly, fast.

"What do you mean, Hans? The reports I have from you could not be more upbeat."

Krone now held my eyes with a certain coldness. He was a man of some Jewishness — not much, but enough to have prompted his spending the Nazi years in London. He spoke English with the same curt formality with which he dressed. "We live in two realms here, Paul." I could, in another circumstance, have taken his show of patience as condescension, but I didn't care about that. "There is the realm of commerce, and there is the realm of daily experience. You and I, in our normal transactions, have reason to be concerned only with the former. But that is not the case today, from what you have asked of me. Normally, we at the Commercial Bank succeed by emphasizing our success. But in this divided city, success has become our greatest danger. Commerce in West Berlin is the miracle that never ends. *Of course* in our reports that is all we say, and it is true. The last thing we want is to undermine confidence in investment. So yes, by all means, upbeat. That is what you expect, no? What New York expects?"

His eyes remained fiercely locked on mine, to make clear that until now he had given me exactly what I had wanted from him. If now I wanted something else, he would not be held responsible for any contradiction.

"And daily experience?"

"Berlin is the best investment in the world. But we are talking now about something else." He glanced at Mrs. Healy, this Charlotte, and turned back to me. "The unraveling rope."

"What?"

"Berlin hangs over the abyss by a rope. A rope which unravels. It is a rope no more. Berlin hangs by a thread. Do you know how many crossed this week?"

"Crossed?"

"Into our sector, from East to West. More than five thousand. Last week, almost as many. Since winter, every week, thousands of the very people Ulbricht needs most — the young, the skilled, the motivated, the intelligent, the courageous. They are flocking west. The DDR cannot allow this to go on. And not only the DDR. Hungary. Poland. Czechoslovakia. All losing their best people through Berlin. It is *Moscow* that cannot allow this to go on. The border will be closed. It must be closed. And then, of course, the devils come loose. All hell cuts loose."

Krone looked fully now at Mrs. Healy, a deliberate display of hesitation.

I said, "As I explained to you, Charlotte is the mother of Michael's companion, one of his companions. Her concerns and mine are identical. You can speak freely."

But something was bothering him. What? That I had not used her last name?

The car had turned onto one of the broad, well-ordered boulevards of West Berlin. It was empty of traffic. A Saturday afternoon with no people out?

"Explain about the crossing to me," I said. "I know the Communists control their zone. How do so many get out so easily? I don't get it."

Krone shrugged. "Outside of Berlin, no one understands this. In *Bonn* they do not understand. It is because Berliners, going back to the war, live in one sector and work in another. Families live partly in the Soviet zone and partly in the American, or British, or French. The subway and elevated trains cross East and West every minute. At Potsdamer Platz, workers and students cross from one side to the other every day. This is the way the city lives. And the benefit to the Eastern sector is the tax that is levied, theoretically, on every person crossing in — the forced currency exchange that amounts to tax. East German marks are worthless relative to West German marks. To go into East Berlin, one must purchase East German marks with all the Western currency one is carrying, but a minimum of twenty Western marks. This is the main source of liquid currency for Honecker and Ulbricht. Therefore, the *Vopos* are concentrated on points crossing *into* East Berlin, in the city center — Potsdamer Platz, Friedrichstrasse. The dozens of points for crossing *out* elsewhere in the city, other S-Bahn and U-Bahn stops, for example, are relatively unguarded. The law still requires currency submission, but mostly and practically that involves entrance, not exit. East Berliners know how to play this game, and East Germans coming from outside the city, and Poles and Czechs, they learn it fast. The crackdown Honecker must be preparing will involve only people from the East. The border will be sealed against them. Not against us, you see? From us he will still need dollars and marks. And if he allows Americans and Britishers continued citywide access, then NATO will have no complaint. Only Bonn will have the complaint, because the border closing against the DDR means the end of the dream of Germany as one nation — Adenauer's dream, but Khrushchev's nightmare. The only question is whether Kennedy will listen to *der Alte,* to Adenauer, when the time comes. If he does, *then* the devils are set loose."

"Kennedy is committed to Berlin, Hans. I promise you that decision has been made."

"But committed to *West* Berlin or to *all* of Berlin? That is not decided, Paul."

"What are you saying? You want in Berlin what there is at the Iron Curtain? Klieg lights? Unmuzzled dogs? Razor wire? Machine guns? Watchtowers? You want all of that *here?*"

"We Berliners, Paul, have simple hopes. Stability. Predictability. And a possibility for something better in the future. If not one Germany now, as *der Alte* wants, at least let there be two. We want East Germany to remain *German.* If all Germans who want what we here in West Berlin want — freedom, democratic structures, the decent life — if all such people leave the East, then the Soviets will simply populate it with Slavs. East Germany will be Slavic Germany, which is not Germany."

There was a familiar curl in the way Krone said the word "Slav," inevitably evoking how once the word "Jew" had been spoken. That Krone was to a degree Jewish himself only reinforced the point; the Nazis had murdered six million Slavs, too. In Krone's mouth, one heard an implication of what, in the word, had brought it into English as "slave."

He must have sensed my uneasiness, because he veered from the thought. "But the main concern that we have in the Western half of Berlin is simply to live. The war that Adenauer would welcome will last five minutes here. The fifteen thousand American soldiers are in Berlin only to trigger the American response, which of course, once that garrison is crushed by Red Army tanks, is a nuclear attack on Moscow — and all that follows. Compared to that, what are klieg lights? What is razor wire? A sealed border without a war. It is what you should want as well."

"I don't want a sealed border until my son is home with me in Frankfurt."

"Well, your timing is good. You have arrived just ahead of the moment of truth. Why do they call it that?" He grinned. "Odd phrase, but compelling. Moment of truth. No equivalent in German." He looked over at Mrs. Healy, as if for concurrence. She knew better than to blink. Krone went on, "Everyone knows that Ulbricht had to allow access back and forth between the sectors until today, May Day, his big propaganda fest. All the Stalinist apparatchiks from Moscow to stand with him on his platform at Alex — Marshal Zhukov, Marshal Bulganin, their great parade, Soviet tanks, a flat truck to carry a large toy *Sputnik,* big trailers hauling green missiles. They say Yuri Gagarin himself is in Berlin today."

Gagarin had become the first man in space less than a month before.

"A great show of Soviet power for the whole city to see, the whole world — that is May Day. And of course to Berliners, *ersten Mai* also celebrates the day our city was liberated by the glorious Soviet heroes in 1945. So today, yes!" Krone leaned toward me. Beads of perspiration had once more appeared on his forehead. "But tonight? Tomorrow? The question about klieg lights and razor wire is not *if,* but *when.* The saying for weeks has been, 'After May Day.' That is why more refugees crossed last week than ever. Because it will be impossible *nach ersten Mai*. Well, *ersten Mai* is now."

"Great," I said with an exasperation unique to the parents of ingeniously mischievous teenagers. "How did they plan this so well?"

I looked at Mrs. Healy, who ignored me to ask Krone, "Are there signals of this tension? Anything unusual?"

"*Everything* unusual. First, if the border is to be sealed, entities on both sides of it are working to secure their methods of operation, if you receive my meaning."

"I don't," I said.

"To secure their, as they say, assets on the other side. Espionage, Paul. An industry in Berlin, one of our major enterprises. And second, each side is working to learn what it can about the other's assets-in-place before the curtain falls. Frenzy. And rumors. Wild rumors."

"Of what, for example?" Mrs. Healy asked.

Krone studied her for a moment before answering. "Of, for example, a shocking penetration in East Berlin of the offices of the Ministry of State Security."

"Stasi," she said.

"Yes. The rumor is that there was a fire at the ministry, a death, a death of a senior official prompting major security measures."

"When?" Mrs. Healy asked calmly.

"Earlier this week. Monday or Tuesday. So the rumor has it."

"A fire?" I asked. "An accident?"

Krone laughed with an air of *You Americans!* "There are no accidental fires at ministry offices in Berlin. Not in East Berlin, not in West Berlin."

"Was this at Karlshorst?" Mrs. Healy asked, a question that meant nothing to me except that she knew to ask it.

"I would not think so," Krone answered. "As I say, we are only talking about rumors, which lead to guesses. The ministry has offices in a dozen places in East Berlin." Krone interrupted the flow of his speculation to face only me, to explain what he apparently assumed my companion would know. "The Gestapo had forty thousand agents to keep under surveillance a population of eighty million. Stasi has nearly three times that many agents to watch a mere seventeen million. Stasi is everywhere in the East. They make the Gestapo seem amateur. By comparison, the Gestapo was kind."

He turned back to Mrs. Healy, already aware of her as versed in this language. "Karlshorst, in the Soviet compound, Mielke's offices, yes. But unlikely to be penetrated. And the rumormongers would surely have passed along that detail. Therefore, less notorious offices . . . more likely someplace like . . ." His hesitation was for effect. I did not know what game he was playing, but his partner in it was certainly not me. He and Mrs. Healy were circling one another. "Like, perhaps, Schloss Pankow, the former palace, in the heart of a residential area, where the *Arbeitsgruppe Ausländer* has its headquarters."

"What is that?" I asked.

"An office in charge of all matters relating to foreigners inside the DDR, including East Berlin. Which is why I am, shall we say, acquainted with it." He bowed. "At times it falls to me to be one of those foreigners. A man in my position, we have dealings with the *Arbeitsgruppe Ausländer*. We have subtle ventures in East Berlin, Dresden, Leipzig, four or five other cities in the DDR. We must travel. We must interact with certain officials."

"Subtle ventures?"

Krone's gaze became steely. "Extralegal, Paul. Commerce in the zone between zones, if you receive my meaning."

Black market. Bribery. Zone between zones. A classic instance of criminal rationalization. I said nothing.

"This is work of my own," he said coldly. "Not related to my work for Chase. Not related to the Commercial Bank. Not related to you, Paul. I only refer to it now to indicate the range of my connections, which is relevant to my ability to provide you with the help for which you have turned to me."

"I see that."

"So time is short," Mrs. Healy said. "Our sons need us. How do we find them?"

Krone responded as if he'd been waiting for her sharp inquiry. "*Sind Sie deutsch?*"

"Born in Germany, yes," she answered. "But I am an American citizen. I am the mother of an American citizen, the dependent child of an American officer, a child at risk in this city. You have made me understand the risk very well. Now I want to know how you can help me find my son."

Krone nodded, apparently reassured by her crisp authority. "If the youngsters have come for the May Day fest" — he shot his cuff, revealing a gold cufflink, a stainless steel Omega watch — "then we have just time enough to go there, which is how I have instructed the driver. Chairman Ulbricht and his Central Committee and august guests from the Kremlin are just finishing their borscht and goulash under the chandeliers of the *Rathaus*. They are moving outside to the reviewing stand which looks out over the great market square, which for hours has been crowded with what they will say was two hundred thousand people but is closer to fifty thousand, no doubt including your three children. Are you feeling lucky?"

"Not particularly," I said.

To my surprise, since we were still in prosperous West Berlin, the car pulled over to the curb and stopped. The driver jumped out and, as he moved around to Mrs. Healy's door, Krone looked out the window, saying, "Ah, we are here."

To one side was a tidy park with pebbled paths, benches, and flower beds choking with tulips, daffodils, and lilies. To the other was a broad set of once elegant but now badly rusting cast-iron stairs heading up to an overhead platform. Paint was flaking off a sign that read, "Tiergarten."

The driver opened Mrs. Healy's door, but she did not move.

Krone explained, "We cannot drive into East Berlin without drawing attention to our party. Am I correct in understanding that as undesirable?"

"Yes, you are," I said.

He indicated the stairs. "We are one stop away from the Soviet sector. To cross by S-Bahn, we are like everyone else. It is how we go if we are merely tourists."

"That's what we are."

Mrs. Healy started to get out, but Krone said, "One moment."

From the floor beside his foot, he picked up a small briefcase and opened it. It was empty. Balancing the case on his knee, he reached into his suit coat for his billfold. He took out one note, and then two others like it, and he held them for us to see. Three bills, each twenty deutsche marks. "This is the admission. We must exchange this for East German marks, twenty D-marks each. Otherwise, we should leave all money here." Krone took a wad of bills out of his wallet and dropped them into one slot of the briefcase. I did the same with my money, into another slot, and then Mrs. Healy, removing the cash from her purse, did likewise. "German money," Krone said, "American money, everything." Then he handed a twenty-mark note to each of us. "And you have your passports, yes?" We both nodded, and then so did he, snapping the briefcase shut and twirling a small built-in combination lock. He reached across to touch my arm. "We are what we are, Paul. You are my banking colleague, here from Frankfurt for meetings." Still touching me, he looked at Mrs. Healy. "You are my colleague's friend. Let the officials draw their own conclusions. The less said the better. They are imbeciles at these crossing desks. They know nothing. They will ask a question. They always ask a question. Keep it simple. If possible, keep it true. But do not mention your children."

"Of course not," Mrs. Healy said, that authority again.

Krone nodded at her. "*Sehr gute. Jawohl?*"

Pointedly, she made no reply, and that apparently pleased him.

Mrs. Healy got out of the car. Krone caught my eye to wink, obviously, about her shapeliness. I turned away from him, quite aware of it myself.

9

W E FOLLOWED Krone up the ratty iron staircase. It shook frighteningly on its bolts, but at that moment the danger from an ill-maintained item of public accommodation seemed the least of our problems. Indeed, the wobbly stairs seemed to amuse Krone, and with his large frame he shook them deliberately as he ascended, pounding his feet like a kid. "Become accustomed to such wreckage," he said over his shoulder. "The S-Bahn is administered by authorities in the East, according to the terms of the 1948 treaty. East Berlin municipality — corrupt, inefficient, bankrupt — maintains stations and tracks even in West Berlin, which is to say does *not* maintain them. That is why these stairs shake, why the train rattles, why the tracks do not meet each other smoothly. You will see." He laughed. At the top of the stairs, before a rusted turnstile, he waited.

A dozen yards away was a small booth with a uniformed figure behind a grille — a woman in a tattered blue hat. She was staring in our direction, but was so impassive it seemed possible she did not see us. Krone laughed again, clapping my shoulder. "The S-Bahn is *already* East Berlin, you see, even here above our beloved Tiergarten, the most exquisite city garden in Europe." He handed us each a token and led us through the creaking turnstile. All the while, he kept speaking loudly, as if he were a tour guide. And then I realized that that was the effect he was going for. Apart from the dull woman in the booth, however, there was no one on the platform. So if he was acting a part, it was for my sake and Mrs. Healy's. He was preparing us.

"With the S-Bahn administered and manned from East Berlin, you see why conditions are so poor. Very dramatic, really, the S-Bahn all the way past Wannsee and out into the DDR, yet also bumbling along above the cafés and boutiques of the Kurfürstendamm. People from the East coming this way in the morning for work, returning at night. At this time of day, even not a holiday . . ." He gestured broadly at the empty platform, moving lightly on his feet, a kind of dance step. Krone was good.

His routine was cut short by the sound and vibrations of a train crashing into the station. The lead car had the word "Friedrichstrasse" crudely printed on a board affixed above a single headlamp, the glass of which was broken. The entire platform structure had begun to move, and the sensation of steel plate trembling under my feet brought the *Stephen Case* to mind, the train platform having taken a torpedo.

"Shake, rattle, and roll," Krone called over the noise, and, as if he'd read my mind, he made a show of taking a legs-akimbo stance appropriate to the swaying deck of a ship.

The train slowed to a stop with an ungodly screech. There was not a lubricated gear, a balanced wheel, or an unworn brake pad anywhere aboard. The cars were brown, round-topped relics of the Weimar era, made of slatted wood, not steel, wood that had not seen a paintbrush since Hindenburg.

The doors opened unevenly, some only halfway, all with the groan of swollen wood against warped iron grooves. We stepped through the door nearest us, to be greeted by a lone figure, an East German policeman in knee boots and peaked hat. He held a machine gun in the crook of his arm. A fat cigarette clung to his lower lip, with a thin stream of smoke causing him to squint, yet his eyes were steadily upon us, as if he had been lying in wait.

Despite the James Dean pose of that cigarette, I sensed the policeman's nervousness, and recalled what Krone had said about the general tension here, the universal expectation of something deadly. Torpedo indeed.

Squelching my fear, I took Mrs. Healy's elbow for the moment required to move into the car. We imitated Krone in turning our backs to the policeman, each reaching to grasp a cracked leather strap and taking up a position to look out the window. Not out. In the station, the window was a slate mirror in which to see the *Vopo* eyeing us. The door closed, the train jerked into motion, and very quickly we were out in the brightness of the midday sun, a relief.

The windows had become windows again, not mirrors. They were cloudy with dirt, but the sight that opened before us was breathtaking nonetheless. We had a clear view down the length of the opulent shopping street, the Kurfürstendamm. In the distance, I glimpsed the looming Lindenhof, a skyscraper of olive glass, the building Chase had underwritten and that I had helped dedicate in December.

The Ku'damm was marked by four lanes of gleaming automobiles divided by a center rank of youthful linden trees, which were show-ing off a fresh crop of pale green leaves. The sidewalks below were a riot of colorful café umbrellas and awnings. At eye level, I saw the bright signs and flags attached to the multistory buildings. The neon displays, illuminated even at midday, were not nearly the kaleidoscope they would be at night, but for that they were a more outrageous as-sertion of Western extravagance.

This glimpse of color gave way in a blink to the gray open stretch of a weed-ridden field beyond which sat the hulking ruin of the Reichstag, a sight that no one of my generation could fail to recog-nize. Hitler had set it afire in 1933, blaming its destruction on the Communists, successfully sparking an electoral victory from which the rest of the awful century had unscrolled. And forever after, the Communists, thus branded the mortal enemy of the monster himself, would claim the loftiest perch of the moral high ground — not just as victims of Hitler, like Jews, but as active, deadly opponents. The Reichstag had become, in effect, a permanent memorial to the heroic Communist resisters.

Just as quickly as it had come into view, the building was gone. Now the train careened onto a timber-and-rod trestle bridge, cross-ing the muddy Spree, which marked the border there between East and West Berlin. It seemed less a geographic boundary than a tempo-ral one, for all of a sudden the view was of the yawning jaggedness of bombed-out buildings, ruins, and rubble of the sort cleared in the West fully a decade before. I saw an entire city block of roofless build-ings, of walls stripped away to show the interior spaces, once vivid wallpaper made gray by weather. A second similar city block quickly followed, and then a warehouse district, the drabness of which was relieved only by a huge bright poster showing the unsmiling face of Walter Ulbricht above a red star and a red hammer and sickle.

I looked at Mrs. Healy. She, too, was staring out at the passing scene. "Colorfast?" I said. Really, the only color out there was the red on Ulbricht's poster. She looked at me vaguely, missing my reference to her phrase that morning.

And then snap! The scene outside went completely black, the window once more a reflecting glass. The policeman behind us was exactly as he had been, with his fat cigarette, his machine gun, his cold eyes on our backs. The rattling noise of the train had doubled, which was how I knew we had entered a terminal. Friedrichstrasse station, I guessed.

As the train abruptly slowed, the single weak light bulb behind us flickered, then went out, plunging our car into total darkness. My free hand went automatically to my breast pocket, to cover my billfold. The jolt of darkness disoriented me. How would I ever find Michael here?

The car stopped. My eyes adjusted. Not darkness now, but the shadows, as it were, of night. Krone led us out onto a narrow platform that reeked of ash. Cinders in the air made me squint, and when I looked back, to my surprise, our squinting policeman had never moved.

With a few other people who had been on the train, we walked to a set of stairs that took us down to a starkly lit chamber that seemed a basement room but could not have been, since we'd started well above street level. We lined up at a set of grilled turnstiles, patiently passing through into another, far larger, brighter chamber, also windowless. This room was encircled by an iron-grid catwalk near the ceiling. A pair of blue-uniformed policemen stood opposite each other, looking down at us. They, too, cradled machine guns, but unlike the guard on the car, these two were openly nervous, their eyes darting down to us, then to each other. They were young and scared and therefore truly intimidating.

Krone nudged us away from the passengers toward a doorway to the right, leaving the others in a line before a doorway on the left.

"West Germans and foreigners this way," Krone explained. He tossed his head toward the others. "They are East Germans, poor devils." A dozen or so men and women, drably clothed, preoccupied at that moment with retrieving passbooks and identification from purses and pockets; they were decidedly uninterested in us.

The doorway led to an iron staircase that took us down into yet another large room, about street level. In its center was a towering desk behind which a female guard sat — another threadbare blue uniform, not cut for any woman. She was sour looking, of indeterminate age. Beside her, standing on the raised platform, was a green-uniformed, helmeted soldier. He held the end of a chain that was attached at its other end to the throat of a Doberman pinscher. The soldier and his dog watched us approach as the woman studied papers on her desk.

Krone reached back to me and Mrs. Healy. "Passports, please," he said loudly, an obvious display of English. We handed them over, and Krone in turn passed them up, with his own, to the woman at the desk. They exchanged a few words in German, then Krone motioned us along without waiting for the woman to return our passports. In such a sea of hostility, a passport can seem like the log that keeps one afloat — and I almost protested. Instead, I followed Krone's lead through yet another door. As we went, he said, "This would be far more complex on a normal day. Today they want us in the East to see their great parade."

In the next room was a bank of cashiers' windows along the far wall, like at a racetrack. Several dozen people stood in four lines, and we joined one. Within minutes, we had each filled out a form declaring what currency we carried, and we had each purchased the minimum quota of East German marks.

In a way, it was the defining ritual of our passage, since the Cold War itself had begun as a currency dispute at the outset of the occupation of Germany in 1945. The Allies had agreed to institute a new reichsmark for all transactions, including the pay of their respective armies. American soldiers could redeem these marks for dollars, although Soviet soldiers could not redeem them for rubles. This led to a brisk black market between Ivans and GIs, with the American treasury providing Soviet soldiers with dollars, which meant that the

United States was indirectly paying the costs of the Soviet occupation. To avoid that, Washington simply announced, one day in the late summer of 1945, that it would no longer redeem Soviet-issued reichsmarks, a move that instantly impoverished several million Russians — and started the currency dispute that had continued up to the moment of our arrival at the cashiers' windows in East Berlin.

From that room, we moved to a dark, narrow corridor that reeked of disinfectant. Male and female *Vopos,* their attack dogs standing by, cursorily searched us. I was behind Krone, and was startled to see him throw up his hands, allowing one policeman to pat him down while another eyed the form he had filled out. They took Krone's wallet. The interest was not in weapons but in currency. Anything they found in excess of what his form declared they would confiscate, adding to the admission charge. But it was also clear that undeclared currency would put you at their mercy — the main reason, I saw, for the whole cumbersome procedure. As the policeman took my billfold, I felt a twinge of worry that somehow the bills I had left behind in Krone's car had suddenly materialized again. When the *Vopo* returned the billfold to me and I slipped it back inside my jacket, I noticed that perspiration had soaked my shirt.

At the far end of that corridor was a final desk, where our passports, having been mysteriously brought forward, were returned to us without comment by another dour, age-uncertain woman. With the passports, we were each given a receipt stamped with the sum of money we had exchanged and a notation marking the amount of foreign currency we were legally carrying — zero. These receipts we would be required to show upon exiting East Berlin, when, equally clear, we would be subject to search again.

Moving through a last set of creaking turnstiles, we found ourselves out in the cavernous main hall of the train station, a warehouse-like area, depressingly drab but for a cone of mote-filled sunshine slicing down from a central skylight. Altogether, the open space was an antidote to the choking claustrophobia I had felt in the transit areas. Dust, ash, and an even sharper blast of disinfectant soured the air — disinfectant already my association with the public interiors of East Berlin. Yet breathing had never seemed so sweet.

I looked around at the people. No one seemed to be watching us.

The hall was a massive postwar construction of concrete and girders, undistinguished in every way, as if thrown up by the engineer corps without an architect. There were wurst wagons, a standup coffee bar, and several beer windows. Ticket windows blanketed one wall. There were soldiers, some in the green of East Germany, some in the brown of the Soviet Union, red stars on their hats. There were *Vopos.* The few civilians in evidence were crossing toward the large doorway through which drifted the strains of band music from outside.

Krone was anxious to get out there, but halfway across the hall, I stopped him. I pointed back to the transit area through which we'd come. "The kids had to go through that?"

The image of Michael limping from the towering desk to the cash windows, past the guard dogs, under the hateful eyes of machine gun–toting *Vopos* — all waiting for what mistake? The image of my son, my boy, my child, here without me. "To get into East Berlin they had to run that gauntlet?"

The normally ingratiating Krone met my eyes coldly, as if impatient that I should have been surprised to be intimidated, even afraid. What the hell did I think the world-historic conflict was about if not something frightening?

Krone said calmly, "The young people went through that or its equivalent at half a dozen other transit points, although I suggest the likelihood of their having done so here" — he gestured toward the square where the music was coming from — "if their object is the parade, which one assumes it is, since they are boys drawn, no doubt, to marching bands and tanks. So yes, just like that, presuming they did cross into East Berlin this morning, or at least" — he grinned, daring to tease me — "presuming they crossed legally."

This entire account has as its implicit subject my unreadiness to be the parent of a mature person capable of coping with the vicissitudes of life, even as tied to the uneven contest of world politics. But, as Edie might have said: Politics, shmolitics. Michael's distance from me had nothing to do with Stalinist police, and his jeopardy, as I felt it, was that of an unstable walker taking his uneven steps too close to an edge. Never mind that the edge was the armed border between two Germanys, and the danger the machine guns cocked to enforce it. *Oh Michael,* I might have cried in a dozen other circumstances, all relatively mundane, yet crying still, *where in God's name are you?*

In other circumstances I would have been angry. Here I was only afraid.

Krone led the way out into the dazzling light of the early afternoon. I followed Mrs. Healy, whose stride was so purposeful that it was impossible to imagine that she harbored anything like the fleet of fears that had rafted themselves to me — which is how little I knew at that point. Her dread had the advantage of being tied to what was real. And truly lethal.

Outside, the sight of a throng of people — a sea of color — transformed my perception. I listened for a buzz of anticipation, but did not hear it. Instead of the communal lightheartedness of a typical crowd, this one gave off an air of anxious gravity, which I registered like weather. We had come upon them from the rear, thousands and thousands, and could see how they were pressing forward, away from us, as one creature. The crowd stretched across a vast open square — Alexanderplatz, what Krone had referred to as Alex. On the far side, like a matching bracket to the *Hauptbahnhof*, stood a large, red-brick building, the traditional *Rathaus* of Berlin. Its pair of towers reached into the blue sky. It appeared that the building had been reconstructed since the war, a centerpiece of this Socialist showplace that was marked on another side by a soaring television tower, the *Fernsehturm*, a needle spire topped with a great steel globe. I had seen the tower before, but only at a distance. From immediately below it seemed unreal, and the clouds moving behind made the thing seem ready to fall on us.

But the focal point of the square was the *Rathaus* façade, which was draped half by a huge flag — the black, red, and gold of the DDR, its hammer-and-sickle seal encircled by golden sheaves of wheat — and half by a fluttering banner showing the iconic face of Walter Ulbricht, East Germany's own Lenin. His eyes stared blankly out over the crowd and seemed, like the eyes of some Byzantine Christ, to have been waiting to lock upon us. *You!* those eyes seemed to say, and I looked away.

In front of the *Rathaus,* facing us and visible above the hats, scarves, and bare heads, was the elevated reviewing stand, draped in red bunting. A line of — to us — small old men in gray topcoats and uniforms, homburgs and peaked hats, stood looking out in our direction. Across the distance, they resembled a row of stern-faced stacking dolls. In fact, they were looking at the parade going by just below them, the parade that was as yet nearly invisible to us. All we could see were flags and streamers carried by invisible marchers. We watched the colors dip as they passed the center of the reviewing stand.

To the right, just coming into view, was the pointed tip of a massive green missile, angled upward, a giant's cartridge aimed at heaven. This was the first of a succession of such weapons in the parade, and soon we could see them coming in a rolling line, a full battery of missiles. Their profile was easily recognized by a newspaper reader of the time, for these were Soviet surface-to-air missiles, proud cousins to the high flier that had brought Gary Powers down the year before. I nearly nudged Mrs. Healy to tell her this, but I recalled that the U-2 incident had brought her husband out of cover as an intelligence officer. I realized again how much more heavily all of this fell on her than me. Everywhere she looked was an implication of threat, whether past or to come.

Krone took us each by an elbow and proceeded to push through the crowd. "The point is to search for them, no? They are the self-centered young, so it is unlikely that they would remain back here, unable to see. Wouldn't your sons and their friend push forward to draw close to things?"

"My son is lame," I said. "He walks with difficulty, carries a cane."

"All the more reason to look for them closer on. A boy with a stick — Germans would be kind to him. Even East Germans."

They were not kind to us, but Krone's display of authority was like a wedge as we moved through the crowd. Strangers deferred to him simply because he let them see he expected them to do so. Moving constantly, we were able to efficiently pass through. At one point a universal gasp of amazement, followed by robust applause, drew our attention back to the parade. We saw a line of four huge, trailer-borne intermediate-range ballistic missiles. We did not know it then, but these weapons were of the type that were soon to salt the cane fields of Cuba. After the initial applause, the crowd fell ominously silent for the moments it took the missiles to pass by.

Then there were formations of dark green Soviet tanks, their steel treads clanking, turrets emblazoned with gleaming red stars, phallic muzzles proudly angled up. Next came phalanxes of soldiers of the

National People's Army. Their goose-stepping sent a surprised chill through me, which Krone registered. He explained that in Berlin the goose step evoked not Nazis but Prussians, with whom East Germans were still allowed to identify.

For most of an hour we elbowed our way through the crowd, Mrs. Healy looking for her Ulrich, her Rick; me looking for my Michael. After scanning the front edge of the crowd, where the kids would most likely have been, I began to feel discouraged. Exhausted, too — I hadn't slept the night before. *Michael, where are you?*

Drawing close to the reviewing stand at one point, we could see the facial features of the Central Committee and Politburo members. If Yuri Gagarin was there, I did not see him. I wondered about the senior Stasi official Krone had referred to, dead in a fire. Was he supposed to be up there? And then I thought of Krone's saying there were no coincidences in Berlin, no accidents in Stasi offices. What about Frankfurt, I wondered. Mrs. Healy had asked what day that fire happened. What about the shooting in Rhine-Main Hall? What day was that?

We could see that the civilian apparatchiks on the reviewing stand wore beribboned medals on the breasts of their topcoats, just like in Herblock cartoons. We also saw that some of the dignitaries were Chinese, perhaps North Korean, and I wondered if the Asian Reds planned, as soon as the festivities were concluded, to get the hell out of flashpoint Berlin?

Judging from their impassive but alert expressions, the ruling elite of the Communist world seemed no more authentically enthused on their great day than the twenty-five or thirty thousand subdued people below. The leaders gazed out like spooked sentries. The throng wore the taut face of an entire society, dead afraid.

Many of the young people we saw wore the blue shirts and red neckerchiefs of the so-called Free German Youth, but they lacked the crazed enthusiasm of the Hitler Youth they had succeeded. It was impossible to imagine the timid kids who gave way at Krone's gesture barreling down the street smashing the glass of Jewish-owned storefronts. The point was that none of the German young wore penny loafers or blue jeans, chino trousers with little belts in back, crewneck sweaters, or button-down shirts. None of them, I was at pains to notice, wore leg braces or stout brown orthopedic shoes. None of them carried canes.

"Hello, Charlotte," a bearded, bespectacled man said, stepping out of the crowd to block Mrs. Healy's way. His blond hair struck me, and I had the feeling I knew him, but I did not recognize him. With the collar of his worn tweed jacket turned up around a black turtleneck sweater, he looked like a professor — a German professor. But his accent and his ease in approaching Mrs. Healy were pure American. Sunlight glinted off the lenses of his glasses, making it hard to focus on his face.

Mrs. Healy seemed unsurprised. "Hello, Hal," she said.

"We'd better talk," he said, "but we shouldn't do it here."

An encircling wall of Germans pressed us, their blocky unfashionable clothes, their stink of sausage and beer, their blank eyes. East Germans clearly aware of us as Westerners.

Hal made a show of studying me, then Krone. I sensed it when he decided to ignore us for the moment.

He pointed to a small grove of birch trees on the edge of the plaza, toward the base of the television tower, away from the parade. "Perhaps there." He turned and led the way. Mrs. Healy followed, then I did, and behind me, Krone. I realized that two other men, at least two, were moving in sync with us toward the trees, at a remove. One of them wore a tan windbreaker that looked American, the other wore aviator sunglasses.

The grove of trees had been planted around a granite tablet mounted on a rough concrete base, a memorial of some sort. The trees were young, the branches low. Because the foliage blocked the view of the parade, people had avoided the compact space, which lent a kind of privacy to it. Hal faced Mrs. Healy, me, and Krone. His two companions took up positions on the edge of the grove, and then I saw a third.

"You can't be doing this," Hal said abruptly. "The general —"

Mrs. Healy cut him off. "The general is my concern, not yours."

"I beg your pardon, but he told me this morning that you understood the importance of maintaining the routine." All at once I recognized him as the officer I had glimpsed in General Healy's car, leaving the house at Lindsay. The beard was false, but convincing. "The general has no idea you're in Berlin. He'd be furious. The risk —"

"The risk, Hal, is our son's." Mrs. Healy's calm only made the man's agitation more pronounced. She touched his sleeve. "This is the father of Rick's friend," she said, indicating me.

"I know who he is."

"This is Colonel Cummings," she said to me. "My husband's executive officer."

Evidently their relationship had more texture than the usual one between a general's factotum and a general's wife. Cummings, I guessed, had been with Healy for a long time.

She went on, "You are here looking for Rick, Hal. So am I. What do you know? What have you learned?"

Cummings glanced at me, then at Krone. As if Hans were not able to hear, Cummings asked, "Who is this German?"

I answered, "An associate of mine, our escort."

Without hesitating, Cummings addressed Krone. "Would you excuse us, sir?" Cummings lifted a finger toward the man in sunglasses, who stepped toward Krone with an extended arm, indicating *over here*. Krone looked at me, and I nodded. He allowed himself to be shown to the edge of the grove, apparently out of earshot. I would be aware of him throughout the conversation that followed, watching us.

"First of all," Cummings said to me and Mrs. Healy both, "you should assume that every German you meet here is Stasi. Trust no one."

"Mrs. Healy is German," I said with an edge that surprised me.

Cummings did not miss a beat. "Look, Mr. Montgomery, you are in way over your head. I don't know what you think is going on, but I promise you, you haven't got a clue. This is dangerous, and not only for the youngsters."

Mrs. Healy stood with her hands in the pockets of her trench coat. She was as immobile as stone, staring down. Of course it was true that I knew nothing. But what did she know? The piece of the story that would explain everything to me?

When I spoke then, it was to Cummings, but she was the one I meant to address. "Why don't you tell me what's going on, then? We *have* crossed a border here, and my ignorance at this point serves no purpose."

"Impossible," Cummings said.

Mrs. Healy stepped closer to him, closer to me. She put her hand on Cummings's arm again. "It is all right, Hal. I am sure of it." Then she looked at me. Now when she spoke, it was with the air of a briefing officer, a hint of another life she had led. "Ulrich inadvertently took a bag that contains a roll of undeveloped film, tourist pictures. But along the edge of the film is a reduction of microfilm that contains sensitive material, which is all you need to know. It is all that I know about it."

Microfilm, I thought. Cary Grant. Am I at the movies?

Cummings picked up the explanation, which made me realize none of this was true, or, if true, it was so incomplete as to be false. Not *at* the movies. *In* one. "If Stasi or the KGB were to find that film on Rick, the intelligence loss would be extreme, to say the least. But of more pressing concern" — Cummings shifted to meet Mrs. Healy's gaze — "of *far* more pressing concern to General Healy is Rick's welfare. You know that, Charlotte."

Mrs. Healy, instead of replying, looked down.

Cummings turned to me again. "The certain fact is that Rick would be taken by the Communists to be a professional. They would, I promise you, *not* assume his presence here was some high school joyride. They could only assume that he was in Berlin either to pick up that film or pass it on to someone. He would certainly be arrested, charged with 'illegal relaying of information.' He would be brought to trial for 'illegal agent activity.' Given who his father is, and given the present state of East–West tensions, such a proceeding would be conducted as a show trial, a shameless propaganda exercise. The only hope would be that they might not want to draw attention to what is on the film."

"Which is?"

Cummings laughed.

I said, "And General Healy kept this roll of film at home?" That seemed an obvious lapse, but then I thought of that darkroom. He had it at home to develop it himself? But I left the sarcasm in my voice as I pushed further. "He left such a sensitive roll of film where his son could, as you put it, inadvertently take it? How is that, Colonel? Maybe the general has something of his own to protect here. 'National security' was his mantra with me. Has the general himself breached it?"

Mrs. Healy touched my arm, not in a particularly friendly way. "My son is what is important," she said. "As is your son. As is Katharine." To Cummings, then, she issued an order. "Tell us what you have learned."

Cummings recited his brief. "They arrived on the duty train at 1915 hours last night. They were picked up in the station by a labor council functionary, an SPD recruiter named Tramm. We know he is a Berliner with his whole family living in the West, but we still have to assume he's Stasi. He took them to the labor council hostel last night, where they stayed. They left the hostel in Tramm's company this morning at about 0900, aiming to go first to the SPD rally at Schöneberg, then over here for the parade. We learned all this only about noon. Since then, we haven't had any more luck in finding them than you have. Odds are they're in this crowd. Or were. Or were stopped trying to get here. The *Vopos* have arrested a couple of hundred people in the last three hours, drunken pugs from the FRG, black market buckos, assorted goofballs. Our kids could be in the net, hardly noticed."

"Americans? Hardly noticed?" I said, but both Cummings and Mrs. Healy ignored me.

"If Tramm is Stasi," she said coolly, "would it not be certain that they are being held by now?"

"The question is the film. Does Tramm know of it? For that matter, does Rick know of it? Again, assuming they make the connection to the general, they wouldn't dare hold Rick without a violation — a carton of Marlboros, a copy of *Playboy* . . ." Cummings indicated the potential length of the list with a shrug.

"Especially considering," I said slowly, playing the only card I held, "the state of Stasi paranoia since the fatal fire. Isn't that the background noise against which this concert is being played?"

Cummings did not flinch. "What fire?"

I refused to look away from him, and I did not answer. Finally — what I was waiting for — he shot an accusing look at the woman beside me. The charge was clear enough: Why are you telling this dumb bastard?

Before Mrs. Healy could react, giving me the next clue of what in hell was going on, a screeching noise broke over the square, an ungodly roaring from above. Like all the thousands around us, we looked up, but in order to see we had to shift quickly to the edge of the memorial grove, to be clear of the foliage canopy. In the blue sky, swarming from the east beyond the *Fernsehturm,* was a cloud of war planes, dozens of olive-green aircraft flying in close formation. All at once, half a dozen of the planes peeled off and down, swooping toward Alexanderplatz as if to strafe us. I recognized these planes as MiG 21s.

They descended like kamikazes, which I had seen once from the bridge of the *Stephen Case* as they dived into a sister ship. The MiGs came down so ferociously that I took Mrs. Healy's hand, and instinctively she pulled close to me. Like the throng around us, we had begun to duck, but just then the planes pulled up. For the barest moment they were close enough for us to see the fire of their engines, feel the heat of their afterburn on our faces, and smell the sweet odor of their fuel. Then the jets curled back up to the sky where they belonged.

They rolled together, swooping up, up, up. In perfect synchrony, they slipped back into the last rank of the mass formation as it made its way across West Berlin. As the engines' roar faded, the crowd saluted back by breaking into its first authentic cheer, a throaty roar of its own that said, Thank the gods of revolution, for you have spared us!

In the aftermath of the roars, I became aware of Mrs. Healy again, how I was holding her, my arm around her shoulder. Cummings was watching us with cold disapproval. Mrs. Healy stepped away from me.

"Where are you staying?" Cummings asked.

Staying? We hadn't yet considered it, and when neither of us answered, Cummings misunderstood, and felt obliged to explain, "So I'll know where to contact you when we find them."

Hans Krone had watched all of this from the edge of the grove, between Cummings's men. We had moved closer to him to see the fly-by, but he was still apparently out of earshot. Yet now he piped in with the answer: "The Kempinski."

Cummings looked at him with a questioning expression: How had the German heard?

But Krone was smiling broadly, an ingratiating assistant waiting to be thanked. He walked toward us. "The Kempinski, on the Ku'damm. Our best hotel."

"And if we need you?" Mrs. Healy said to Cummings.

"Call your husband," he answered.

He turned his back on her and strode out once more into the thick bustle of Alexanderplatz. His men dallied a bit, one feigning interest in the grove's memorial plaque, the other shielding his eyes from the glare outside the shade of the trees. In this way, the agents allowed Cummings to go ahead a few paces, and when they followed, each headed into the crowd at a different angle. Soon they were swallowed up by the milling throng, which was dispersing.

I faced Krone. "He thinks you are Stasi."

Krone snorted dismissively, snapping his handkerchief out of his breast pocket and applying it to his perspiring brow. When he met my eyes, I said, "And I am prepared for the possibility that he's right. But I'll tell you something, Hans. I am depending on you. I have no choice. If you let me down, I will destroy you."

The sunlight glinted down through the trees. In another place, the play of light and shadow might have seemed lovely, but the air between me and this German banker, whom I hardly knew at all, seemed threatening. I had spoken without an instant's forethought, yet I knew that what I'd said was true, and so, I sensed, did Krone.

"My dear friend," he said, "it is a grief what these times require of us. Still." He smiled at me, but not without a twitching at the side of his mouth. "I understand."

The last of the airplanes was gone, and a band struck up its march not far away. I turned to Mrs. Healy. "Cummings obviously has a squad of men here, to have learned what he knows. In Schöneberg. At the SPD hostel. You and I are superfluous on the street, hoping to bump into the kids."

"But what else?"

Instead of answering, I faced Krone again. "I have the impression, Hans, that you know what Cummings was just telling us. You shouldn't have been able to hear from where they had you standing, but —"

"Have you worked in the bourse, Paul? The stock exchange? I was a young man, a caller, on the floor of the exchange on Threadneedle Street during the Nazi years. Have you ever tried to hear anything on the trading floor?"

"You read lips."

"Traders bought and sold on the nod, but chits required numbers to the fraction, and it was my job to get them. In that noise, of course one read lips — but without even knowing one was doing so." He had folded his handkerchief again, and now put it back into his pocket.

I said, "It would confirm Cummings in his assumption about you. You gave it away when you answered his question about the hotel."

"But he missed it, did he not?" Krone glanced at Mrs. Healy. "American agents are not infallible. I spoke up then because I wanted you to know that I — how shall I put it? — anticipate."

"So you took it in — Tramm and so on."

"More or less. Tramm, yes." He faced Mrs. Healy. "And your husband, of course. The well-known Colonel Healy. Or, as I gather, General Healy now. You should have told me. It makes the thing clearer. The problem, I mean."

"Let's assume Tramm *is* Stasi. Assume the kids have been detained. Marlboros or something."

"Or the film," Mrs. Healy put in.

"Do you know what's on it?" I asked.

She looked away.

Krone said, "It is obvious — not the particular, but the universal, for sure. Given who General Healy is. I told you, both sides are scrambling. You say 'scrambling'? Ahead of the border closing that any moment comes. Prized information about assets-in-place. Informers. Each side taking one last survey of the other before it is too late. One last penetration. I promise you this, Mrs. Healy. Your husband is remembered here."

She refused to look at him.

"If your sons are carrying film, be certain the film will be found. If the film is, as we say, *Käse,* then" — he stopped, made a point of waiting until Mrs. Healy looked at him — "you have more to worry about than embarrassment to your husband."

It was a nasty moment, and Krone's readiness to skewer her made me angry. But it mystified me, too, that even my bank colleague was privy to things that were kept secret from me. Mrs. Healy, in not replying, made her disdain plain. I had to remind myself that she was German and Krone was a Jew. Did that account for the hostility heating the air between them?

"If the kids have been detained," I said to Krone, "do you have a way of finding out? A way that wouldn't tip off the East Germans if they haven't noticed them?"

Now it was Krone who glanced quickly about to be sure no one was listening, no one reading his lips. Although the crowd in Alexanderplatz was breaking up, even as a band played on, we were still relatively isolated in the grove.

"From Schöneberg, the colonel said. If they were coming here from Schöneberg, they would have come, not as we did by S-Bahn, but by U-Bahn, crossing at Hackescher Markt. The procedures would have been the same — currency tables, passports, *Volkspolizei,* et cetera. If Stasi wanted to hold them with flexibility, the possibility of a minor detention, but perhaps leading to something more, Hackescher Markt is where it would have happened. A routine interrogation, a routine detention — those Marlboros. A middle initial missing from a signature. A penknife construed as a concealed weapon. Of course, if they were not Americans, they would simply disappear."

"And as Americans?"

Krone looked at his watch. "Eventually, the U.S. consulate in Dahlem would be notified, but if that had happened, one presumes Cummings would know it."

"And if a roll of film is an issue?" I asked. Mrs. Healy and I exchanged a look. Her expression was keenly reined. Still, I sensed her anguish, as if we were friends with access to each other's secrets.

"Hackescher Markt," Krone repeated. "Perhaps an inquiry is in order into transactions occurring there this morning."

"Of whom?"

"Why do you dear people not have a coffee while I make a telephone call, or perhaps two telephone calls. I shan't be long."

He looked through the filigree of leaves to the top of the television tower. "There is a tourist café up on the *Fernsehturm*. It goes around like a carousel. It is where you are expected to go now if you are what you pretend to be, a place to spend your East marks."

We began walking toward the tower, leaving the trees behind. Krone had fallen easily into his tour-guide mode. "East Berliners do not go up there. The view of two cities, for them, is too depressing. You from the West are expected to marvel that the elevator works. So be off. A cup of rotten Russian coffee, half Turkish. A bowl of watery borscht. A piece of strudel, cooked yesterday. A cigarette or two. Before you have finished, I will have joined you."

10

S O HERR KRONE is our Virgil?" She said this with her lips above the rim of a cup of tea, a good china cup that she held at her chin, as if for its moist warmth.

We were seated at a table by the floor-to-ceiling window of the rotating tower restaurant. The waiters wore tuxedos, and mostly stood idling in corners or at the service counter. It was late afternoon, too early for diners. What crowds had been drawn by the May Day celebration had dispersed from here, too.

The restaurant was a carpeted ring around the tower's core, from which came the soft purring of the engine that powered the movement of the room. We turned so slowly it was as though the flat world outside were doing the revolving. The tables, including ours, were covered with white linen, slightly threadbare, a bit gray from rough laundering. Most were empty, although a trio of burly, prosperous-looking men sat drinking schnapps at a table across from us, the end of a leisurely meal. Visiting West Germans, probably, versions of the men I rode an elevator with every day in Frankfurt. At another table, a pair of matronly women sat with their tea and tortes. They were easy to take as wives of Politburo members, in from one of the upper-echelon suburbs, extending their outing.

I had been in restaurants at the tops of buildings in New York, and they, too, made me dizzy. This one seemed less a skyscraper restaurant than the luxury dining room of one of those monstrous dirigibles that the Germans had so loved before the war. Outside our window, Stalinallee ran east to the far edge of the city. I recalled reading that it was wider than the Champs-Élysées, but its housing blocks and government buildings lacked not only the mansard splendor of the Champs but also its cushioning twin hedge of trees. On both sides of Stalinallee were the stretches of ruins and vacant lots and pyramids of rubble I had seen from the plane. There were warehouse clusters and a pair of massive cemeteries — grim enough to make one wonder why the authorities would allow tourists up to this perch to view them.

"I'm sorry, what? Virgil?"

Her eyes remained on the city below. She'd made her remark, clearly expecting no response. Just as well, since once more I was struck by the thing that was not to be discussed, her rare beauty. Was it possible that I had first set eyes on this woman only this morning?

The silence between us built until it, too, became an expression, as I felt it, of the inadvertent intimacy that now defined our partnership. "Tell me what you see when you look down there," I said, picking up where we'd left off in the plane. I touched the ash of my cigarette to hers where it sat streaming smoke in the faux-crystal ashtray.

"The Soviet sector," she said, "was the most heavily bombed because the old Reich chancellery, the new Reich chancellery, the Führer's bunker, the *Rathaus*, Albert Speer's constructions at Wilhelmsplatz — it was all concentrated in the eastern half of the city. *Stossers* — you say 'boosters' — of the West Berlin miracle tell you this not at all. The Soviets were designated custodians of the abyss. When I first came here, the rubble was obscene. What you see there now is cosmic order by comparison." She sounded like an objective reporter, an academic historian, that evenly paced, that unemotional. "The city was full of ghouls," she added. "One of them was me."

She sipped her tea. She had, of course, taken off her gloves, and again I noticed her hands, fingers splotchy and thick, nails blunted, knuckles too knobby for rings. Now I noticed that she wore no wedding ring.

"Why did you come here?"

She looked away from me. Why did everything I asked fall on her like interrogation? Was I really that oafish? Or were the boundaries of what she had to protect really that expansive? I had begun my probing hours before by asking her that very question.

This time she said, "To swim in the Spree." She put her cup on its saucer and sat back against the chair. "That is what we called it — arriving in Berlin from the East, crossing to the American sector. Radio Free Europe called it the 'dash for freedom.' The Voice of America called it 'voting with our feet.'" She took up her cigarette, inhaled, then, with the acrid French smoke a veil, she repeated, "We called it 'swimming in the Spree.' The river was the dividing line."

"It still is."

"Yes, but now there are bridges."

"Krone makes it sound like the bridges will close. Do you buy that?"

She shrugged.

"You and your husband haven't discussed what may happen here? Or, now that the May fest is past, could already be happening?"

"I told you. My husband and I do not discuss these things."

"I don't believe that. You know about the film."

"Only because it involves my son. That is the only reason." She was angry. The way she put her cigarette in her mouth made it clear: *No more of this.*

We watched as the river came fully into view, our perch rotating to the west. In the far sky, the red disk of the sun had begun the slide toward its slot on the amazingly flat horizon. The sun's glare obscured the distant landscape, but nearby, below, the beautifully laid-out Tiergarten was turning toward us, just beyond the Spree. West Berlin.

"There was not one tree standing in 1946," she said, referring to the park. The past, apparently, she would speak of. "The trees in the Tiergarten were a gift from the queen of England in 1948. We gathered in groups to watch the British soldiers, gardeners in helmets and combat boots."

"We?"

"We women of the work crew. All work crews in Berlin were women then. The British soldiers loved us for their audience." She laughed, a surprising sound. "The soldiers were kind. They allowed Rick to help them. He took great pleasure in planting these small shoots, smoothing the dirt around each one. He formed the mistaken impression that rifles were garden tools, that soldiers planted things. I did not find it necessary to correct him. But he did not believe me when I told him the shoots would grow to be trees. That is because he had yet to see a tree."

"I remember when Michael was that age. I didn't believe he would ever grow to be a man."

"Because of the polio?"

"No, before that. He just seemed complete to me already as a little boy."

"But he was not complete, was he? Michael is complete now." She said this with an assurance I can only describe as motherly, hinting at the bond of intimacy this stranger had established with my son. And how, then, could she be a stranger? Was her clear feeling for Michael the current on which my feeling was being drawn to her?

"It is a problem for you, I think. Your son is a man now. A young man, but a man. But you do not know this."

Her speaking to me so matter-of-factly seemed somehow normal, and suddenly I saw why. "That is exactly the kind of thing that Edie, my wife, would have said to me. She was always explaining me to myself."

"Which I think you did not like."

"At the time, true. I used to tell her that I thought she was hyper-critical. To which she would say it wasn't criticism, just the truth." Unexpectedly, I laughed. "And the funny thing is, that's what I miss most about her. The way she spoke directly to me, uncensored. If I showed up at the breakfast table with the handkerchief misfolded in my pocket, she would reach over, take the thing, and make it neat, which irritated me no end. Now I am surrounded by people who, if they see the flaw in how my handkerchief is folded, are paid handsomely not to mention it."

Mrs. Healy leaned toward me. "You have folded your handkerchief well this morning."

I found myself smiling. "When Edie told me that, it made me very happy."

"You were the one with whom she felt free to be herself. From what Michael has told me, she never made him feel he had any flaws whatever. In his mother's mind, he told me once, he was perfect. Which was a very large gift to him, as he knew very well how far from perfection he was. His mother's love was what was perfect, as he felt it. That is why he is so mature. Accepting of himself. Of others."

"Michael misses his mother, that's for sure."

"Michael became a man when she died. Her death made him a man. Perhaps that is why you have not seen him that way as yet. While he is a child, she is still somehow with you. When he is no longer a child, she becomes a mere memory. A beloved memory, but only a memory."

"Strange, Edie feels present with me — with you. I mean, talking about her with you makes her seem . . ." I had to stop, to allow the rush of my emotion to flow on ahead without me.

After a moment, more calmly, I said, "I haven't talked about Edie like this. I haven't spoken of our arguments, of how difficult —" To my horror, I felt a burning behind my eyes, and pinched it off. I looked away, out the window. The view was of the Kurfürstendamm, and I saw my own building, the Chase building, the Lindenhof.

"'Real love, compared to fantasy,'" Mrs. Healy said, "'is a harsh and dreadful thing.' It is normal to feel her presence when you speak of her truthfully. The difficulties were no denial of love, were they?"

I shook my head.

"They are the condition of love. You and your wife — the difficulties, the flaw, it was Michael's polio, I think. No?"

"That is true. We dealt with it very differently. No matter what she made Michael feel, it was a massive imperfection in her mind. Edie felt terribly guilty, as if the disease were her fault."

"When you knew the fault was yours."

"Yes."

"So, since you were both at fault, you punished each other."

I brought my eyes back to hers, amazed. No one had ever said such a thing to me, nor had such a thought ever crossed my mind. Yet I saw her simple statement as the exact truth — truth of our marriage, truth of what we were doing to each other, up to our last moment together. The slamming of those doors.

But Mrs. Healy wasn't finished. "Do you not see?" She leaned toward me again, as if examining my face. "You were hard on each other to avoid being hard on Michael. You worked very well together — to protect him. It was how you had to do it. Your love for each other would have meant nothing if it was at his expense. So I repeat, 'Real love, compared to fantasy, is a harsh and dreadful thing.' Dostoyevsky."

I sat back, still with that feeling of amazement. But I also felt embarrassed, caught again. Caught at being human. I forced a laugh. "What are you, a shrink?"

"Shrink?"

"Psychiatrist."

"How American of you, Paul. To think that grief is a medical condition, a mental illness. To discuss these things — you do this only with a doctor?"

How was it that now she had called me Paul?

"And you?" I said. "With whom did you discuss the things you had no words for? In my experience, grief, since you bring it up, has been a long silence. I do not believe you are so different from me in that."

"I know that silence."

"And then, here in Berlin, you found a man who lives by silence. Who is professionally bound to speak to you of nothing."

"That is not so. Of the things that matter to both of us, we speak freely. Because of David, I have not depended on my son for the things a person must have — feelings of dependency, mutuality, partnership."

"And you think I have?" I felt a rush of the old resentment, imperfection being flagged. "You think I depend on Michael?"

"It would be natural in this period. And, as I say, Michael is not a child. His strength would be a comfort. His simple presence, I imagine, a consolation. I am not judging you, Paul."

"I do enjoy his presence. I've been living for the weekends this year. I need his presence, Charlotte. Why does it feel like a confession when I tell you that?"

"The grief you feel for the loss of your wife is also grief that Michael is trying to get free of you."

What a fool I was. Overly aware of having just used her first name, as if now we were friends, I took her statement as a grave accusation. "Does Michael tell you that? That he's trying to get free of me?"

"He does not have to tell me. The thing is clear. It is normal. The same is true of my Rick."

"But your husband is not Rick's father."

"Rick is getting free of me. It is what they do. It is what we did."

"By getting ourselves in serious trouble? I don't think so. I am not in Berlin enacting an Oedipal drama. I am in Berlin because my son needs, at the very least, my support, and perhaps rescue. Michael is in a danger zone, whether he put himself there or was sucked into it."

"Sucked into it?"

"By your son, the gravitational pull of a boy Michael emulates, a boy whose world — well, look." I gestured at the window, at the scene outside, the abyss of the Eastern sector coming once more into view. "I am thinking of what you said before: 'Ulrich is his father's son. There is the curse.' I don't like thinking of my son in the pull of someone else's curse."

"Nor do I. I am sorry Michael is involved with this."

"Which father?" I asked then, sharply.

"What?"

"The curse of being the son of an American spymaster, or were you thinking of Wolf?"

Her silence was her answer.

"Why is it a curse to be the son of a philosophy professor who died for his country?"

"I did not mean 'curse' literally."

"But something is going on here that involves your first husband, your time here after the war. The gravitational pull of a celestial body that ceased to exist?"

"You are American. Things are simpler for you. Feelings of grief? Get a shrink. Feelings of anguish, guilt, dread — don't think about it. America is all future, no past. Is that not the point of your country? It is difficult for you to understand that here in Germany, certainly here in Berlin, everything involves the war. The war is the past that will never go away."

"But which past? First you told me that your husband died at the front. Then you told me he died here in Berlin."

She lit a fresh cigarette, shrugging with an exquisite indifference. "At the end, this was the front."

"That's not what you meant. You intended to deceive me. At first, in Wiesbaden, you recited from a script of your late husband's life, what you tell everyone. 'He died at the front.' It was the accident of your being ambushed by the sight of Berlin from the airplane that prompted you to say the other thing."

"I trusted you with 'the other thing.'"

"And I am worthy of your trust, Charlotte. Tell me why it is a secret that Wolf died here."

She shook her head once, decisively.

"You said Wolf had become like the nation. What he would not do in 1940, he did in 1945. What did he do?"

"Where were you in the war?"

Hadn't she asked me that before? No. Healy, in the vestibule of their home. She had not heard. She was not testing me.

"The Pacific," I answered. "The Navy."

"And you, Paul? Would you have approved the attack on Hiroshima in 1940, as surely you approved it when it occurred in 1945? That is all I meant. The war had its diabolical momentum. Even with the Jews. In 1938, at *Kristallnacht,* all Hitler wanted was to expel them. Eichmann, what they are saying now in Jerusalem — elimination, that grotesque word 'extermination,' *Ausrottung* — all of that came later. All of that came *after* the war had already destroyed us, destroyed us as human beings, destroyed our morality."

"So it was the war's fault?"

"How dare you say that to me!" The flash of her anger purified the air between us. She smashed out her cigarette. "I am not deflecting the fault! I am telling you how it was."

"So is that what Wolf did? The Jews?"

To my complete surprise, she laughed. Her anger dissipated. She said with strange mirth, "No, Paul. Not the Jews. Nothing to do with the Jews."

"Krone is Jewish."

She shrugged. *Who cares?*

"He spent the Nazi years in England."

"He knows the new Berlin, I can see that."

"Why have you not been back here?"

Again a shrug. Exquisite indifference.

"Your husband?"

"I suppose so, yes."

"Which one?"

"Are you trying to trap me?"

"I'm trying to measure the hole my son fell into, that's all. You know the measurements, but you won't tell me."

"It is a rule of life, Paul. You get not what you look for. You get what you find."

"Dostoyevsky?"

"Healy." She smiled. "And do not ask which one." She reached past the ashtray to touch my hand, a gesture that reminded me of Edie. She, too, after the rough weather of our effort to talk to each other, could come out like sunshine. I kept my hand where it was, palm down on the cloth beside a water glass. She let her hand remain blanketed over mine.

"Hello."

It was Krone, who was standing several paces away, like an anticipating waiter. How long had he been watching us, reading our lips?

Mrs. Healy pulled her hand back, although only I seemed to feel we had been caught at something.

Krone joined us, pulling a chair from an adjacent table. He snapped a finger, and a waiter came over at once. "Scotch whiskey," Krone said.

The waiter shook his head. "Vodka."

"Bourbon," Krone countered, and I realized he was playing a Berliner's game, the cross-border one-upmanship, the parrying for control.

"Vodka," the waiter repeated.

"*Wacholderbranntwein.*" Krone winked at me, and mouthed, "Gin."

The waiter shook his head impassively. "Vodka."

"*Ach so. Ich möchte ein Bier, bitte.*" He winked again, and for my benefit said, "In that case, a beer."

The waiter went off. Krone bowed toward Mrs. Healy, then turned to me, speaking fast and low. "They were detained at the *Eintritt* desk. At least one of the three is at risk for being charged with failure to declare currency, which can easily be compounded with smuggling charges and black marketeering."

"How do you know it was them?" I asked.

"A boy with a beard? A girl? A boy with a cane? Leg braces?"

"Goddammit," I said. The explosive word seemed to split me in two, as if half my body now floated out the window, a mystical soul above Berlin, looking down not on a city but on a large steel hulk slicing into the sea, a smoking ship sinking while its klaxons screeched and flaming bodies leapt over the rail into an ocean of burning fuel oil.

That was what had terrified me when the *Stephen Case* went down — the sight, from my place on the upended bridge, of the sea afire, the impossibility of water in flames, an absurdity I would comprehend only later. "The Pacific," I had told her of my war only moments before. "The Navy." Answers that said nothing.

The other half of me, which had stayed in the restaurant with Krone and Charlotte, said, "They are being held?" An idea as impossible as water on fire.

Krone had raised his hands toward me, palms outward. Now he slowly lowered them, shushing me. "That is what I am telling you," he said softly. "I spoke to a friend who witnessed it in the station. My friend saw the three young Americans being challenged, then taken away by *Vopos*. A German man in a worker's cap was with them, not detained. That would be Tramm. His being able to walk away means Stasi for sure."

"*Wo sind sie?*" Charlotte demanded, and then another imperative question, also in German.

"Can we do this in English, please?" I asked.

Krone, again with the quieting hand gesture, said, "Extreme alarm would be premature. This may be minor harassment, designed to embarrass the Building."

"The Building?"

"American headquarters at Dahlem. GIs are often held for a few hours if they are flip, if they do not declare their unopened pack of cigarettes."

"You're the one who spoke of tensions approaching a climax. After May Day, you said, the border will close. Both sides maneuvering for position."

"It is still May Day," Krone said. "There are thousands of Westerners in East Berlin right now, like us. Tourists. Nothing will happen at the border today, not tomorrow morning. But tomorrow night, Sunday night, when all good Socialist workers are at home . . ."

Charlotte seemed indifferent to the question of border tensions, as if her worry transcended the armed push–pull of East–West politics. Eventually I would learn in what way that was so. But just then, watching her hand go to her cigarette, her fingers shaking as they had not before, I understood that it was up to me to respond to what Krone said.

"When was this?" I asked. Do this calmly, I told myself. Show nothing. Be a banker closing a deal. A Spartan with a wolf in his shirt.

Ah, wolf! There was an association to note, but not to express.

"They were detained after noon," Krone answered. "Before the festival began at Alexanderplatz, well before we arrived."

"That was hours ago."

"What witness?" Charlotte asked.

Krone's stern expression said he did not like being probed, but after a second look at her, he answered, "A cleaner in the station. A *Putzfrau* who sees everything."

"East Berliner?"

"Naturally. Although her son has crossed to West Berlin. He works in a factory I control. So his mother is grateful to me. She kisses my hand."

"A peasant woman."

"If you like."

"So she comes from the country, with other family members still in Soviet Germany." Charlotte's expression was one of dull simplicity, worn down by having to pluck out threads of the obvious. Krone returned her look with one of irritation. "We must assume," Charlotte continued, "that Stasi knows of your inquiry. If the *Putzfrau* kisses your hand, she kisses theirs as well."

Charlotte said all this with willed detachment, but I could sense her anxiety. All aristocratic hauteur was gone. Hers were the eyes of a woman ready to recognize a peasant as a sister — the eyes, say, of a starving child's mother scouring the ground beside a shuttered market stall for an overlooked potato.

What was the equivalent of water aflame for her? The discovery in the rubble of a shoe that still had a maggot-ridden foot inside? A decision calmly made to toss the shoe on the pile of harvested stones?

Looking at Charlotte, seeing her as I had seen her in the Russian Chapel, a haloed face at home with suffering, I felt ashamed to realize that, had she ever found such a shoe, she would have gathered the other rubble women to bury it with a prayer.

I touched her sleeve. "If the Stasi knows we are here poking around, that's good. We want them to know. We want them to know *right now* that these kids have parents who are here, parents the Stasi has to deal with." I leaned toward her, sensing weakness for the first time, weakness I could only misunderstand. "We are here to bring our kids out, Charlotte, and we will."

"I don't —"

She was about to disagree with me, so I cut her off. "It's too late to think they don't know who General Healy is. They've seen your son's ID. We have to *land* on them with who your husband is. We have to land on them with Chase Manhattan Bank. This is no trio of drunken GIs looking to score on the black market." I turned to Krone. "They don't do this with my son. Do you hear me?"

"Yes, Paul. So do the waiters."

"Good. Not with my son they don't." Feeling, yes. Expression, yes. Feeling and expression, however, for the sake of power, a dazzling rush of power. I gripped Krone's forearm and saw him wince. "You have to make them deal with me. Get me to them."

"To whom?"

"That is what I am paying you to tell me, Hans. They have our kids. They know we're looking for them. They are waiting for us."

"I doubt the latter point, Paul. Despite Mrs. Healy's intuition, the people on whom I depend are not Stasi."

"Not intuition," Charlotte said. "Assumption."

She raised her eyes to Krone's, allowing us to see what was written in them — the stories of children dying by the roadside, of pits full of unclothed bodies, of young men shot dead at border crossings. Her assumption, clearly, was that Krone was Stasi, which would account for her sudden deflation. She had entrusted herself to me, and I had delivered her over to the enemy. And why should she not have been drained of fierce authority? Her nightmare was coming to pass.

But not mine, not yet. Why the kids' detention seemed the end of the story to her I could not know, but to me it was the beginning. "It doesn't matter," I said. "We want them to know. Even if there are 'illegal agent' charges because of something Ulrich was carrying, we have to react like what we are — parents concerned about our children."

I had said this too loudly, and she whispered, "*Sie sind keine Kinder.*" She had picked up a toothpick from a cup in the center of the table and was staring at it. Her face was crimson. I was the father of a bystander. Compared to Rick's mother, I had nothing to worry about.

The waiter arrived with Krone's beer, a foaming clay stein the color of pewter. Krone took a long swallow that signaled a need beyond thirst. When he lowered the stein, a line of foam marked his upper lip. He took his handkerchief and dabbed at it. All the while his eyes were on me.

I said, "You were telling us before about — what did you call it, *Arbeit* something?"

"*Arbeitsgruppe Ausländer.*"

"The office for foreigners, you said."

"Yes."

"So, for example, three Americans detained for currency irregularities."

"Not necessarily that. No, no, not that at all. That would be border police."

"But the *Arbeitsgruppe Ausländer* would have preempting authority, surely."

"Yes, but —"

"And your contact there was — ?"

"Colonel Erhardt. Colonel Rainer Erhardt, the deputy chief. But Paul, our relationship is of necessity entirely discreet."

"Then you shouldn't have boasted of it to impress me. I am impressed. I want you to take me to him. Where is his office?"

"Schloss Pankow," he answered quietly. He glanced out the window as if to point the place out, but we were facing west again.

"That is where the fire was," Charlotte whispered. "You said before, the fire was there."

"Indeed so. And Erhardt's chief, Colonel General Sohlmann, is the officer who was killed."

Charlotte snapped the toothpick in two, an involuntary reaction.

I checked my watch. It was not yet five. "Take us there, Hans."

Krone shook his head. "No. I have never met Erhardt there. He would be under immediate suspicion."

"Not if I'm with you. The office in charge of everything concerned with foreigners — where else should an American father go if his son has disappeared in East Berlin?"

"But if I —"

"You are my local factotum, Hans. Is that not so?"

It was a humiliating designation, but just then it was accurate. Hans, nodding, even welcomed it. He raised his beer to his mouth and chugged. How far he'd come from the cozy urbanity with which he'd greeted us at Tempelhof.

"Let's go," I said when Krone's stein hit the table. This time he wiped his upper lip with his sleeve.

He and I started to get up, but Charlotte stopped us. "I can't," she said.

She held the two halves of the toothpick, each one between a forefinger and thumb, pressing against the splinters.

"I cannot go with you there. It is impossible."

I settled back into my chair. "You are Rick's mother. They know who he is. It tells them nothing new if you come." If you don't come, I added to myself, that tells them something, too. But what?

She shook her head. That was it.

"Then go to the hotel," I said.

"Yes." She was no more surprised by my authority than I was.

I asked Krone, "What hotel did you say?"

"The Kempinski. On the Ku'damm. The car will be waiting at Friedrichstrasse. The driver will take you."

She nodded, put the toothpick halves neatly in the ashtray, then picked up her gold cigarette lighter and dropped it in her purse.

I said, "Why don't you wait here for a few minutes after we leave. If only one person is following, he will have come after us."

"It does not matter," she said, slipping a tan glove onto her left hand. "I am accustomed to the shadows of watchers." She tugged on the second glove, then glanced at Krone. "Perhaps they will take me for a *mozhnos.*"

If this was a test, Krone no longer cared. He looked at me. "A swallow," he said. "A Soviet term for what your CIA calls a 'sister.' A female who lures an agent." Krone turned back to Charlotte. "Unless, of course, the agent being lured is female."

"A 'crow,' in that case," she said with a bitterness I had not seen. "I will go and sit in the Tiergarten. I will look at the trees that were gifts from the queen of England, and that my little boy helped to plant. Then . . ." She looked directly at me, her expression transformed by dependency. She brushed a strand of hair away from her face, an elegantly unselfconscious move with which she brushed away her need, becoming once more a self-possessed patrician lady. ". . . I will wait for you at the hotel."

"And Cummings?" I asked.

"The initiative is his. Presumably he will have learned what we have learned. Meanwhile, he assumes I am being followed." She said this with a hard glance at Krone. "I will protect the truth of what I am — not an agent, a mother."

"Consistent with that," I said, "you could come with me."

"To Schloss Pankow? Impossible."

Why? But I knew not to ask in front of Krone. Whatever he was to me — and I wasn't sure — he was something else entirely to her.

Krone started, a sudden recognition. "Ah. I booked only one room. Under the name Montgomery."

She looked quickly at me. Was she thinking of the scene later when her husband would call and find her in another man's hotel room?

It was just that prospect that had prompted Krone's abrupt disclosure. Even now, to him, anything was possible between me and this world-weary, mysterious woman. Was that a measure of a Berliner's implicit moral anarchy, which came with life lived on the edge of an abyss? Or was it tied to a Berliner's knack for reading what was written on the air? A hotel room, a rendezvous between two anguished people, the movement of fear into the realm of desire. Whatever such things were to Krone, what were they to me?

Charlotte nodded, snapping shut her purse and saying under her breath, "*Sehr gute.*" Then she turned to me and said, "It is better if I do not use the name Healy. Better if I leave all my names behind."

"Right. You can take the room. I will call you later. If your husband calls —"

She stopped me. "I will be calling him."

"Of course," I said, sounding like a perfect fool. But it was not my puerile imagination when her suddenly wet eyes stayed with mine for an instant longer than necessary.

11

S CHLOSS PANKOW, Krone explained as we approached it, was the former palace of Prince Elector Joachim II. He pronounced the name as if I would know it. The building, he said, was an exceptional example of early-nineteenth-century architecture. Krone had sublimated his anxiety again in the pose of a tour guide. Or was it his anxiety that was itself the pose?

The palace, he said, was built to resemble a stone castle of a much earlier time, with towers, turrets, and crenelated roof lines. One wing was deliberately left unfinished, to evoke the ruins of the Middle Ages — a hallmark of the Romantic period. "The odd thing," he said, "is that when the Soviets reconstructed the *Schloss,* they restored the ruins, too, which is quite a joke in West Berlin. Stasi and its brandnew ruins."

It had taken us perhaps ten minutes to go by S-Bahn east from Friedrichstrasse to a stop marked Heinerdorf, in the heart of the Soviet zone. From there it was another ten by foot to Schloss Pankow. En route we passed a new cemetery on one side of the rough avenue, and on the other the stucco buildings of a hospital complex. Both the cemetery and the hospital had been built on the formerly sprawling parkland of the palace estate.

A spiked iron fence set off what remained of the palace grounds from the avenue. A guard booth marked the entrance, and as we approached, a soldier stepped out. He wore a crisply pressed gray uniform, a steel helmet, and the golden epaulettes of some elite unit. He held a machine gun in his left arm.

Krone, with the panache of one empowered by another's authority, went right up to the guard, handing over his own visa and my passport. I missed most of what Krone said, but I heard his reference to Colonel Erhardt, which was enough to prompt the guard to hand back our documents and wave us through. I glanced back to see him return to his booth and pick up his phone.

We crossed into what would once have been an elaborate terraced garden but now was a large, crudely paved parking lot running up to the huge building. The lot was full. Some cars were the olive green of state officialdom, some had police lights on their roofs, all were unimpressive minis. Yet these cars were the height of luxury in East Berlin.

The building was four stories high and, despite its provenance, was far more hulking than palatial. The monotony of its dark granite façade was broken by large windows. Archers' slits between each pair of windows had been filled in with daubed cement. From a central tower flew the red flag of the DDR, and from several smaller towers other flags fluttered in the early evening breeze. As we drew into the building's shadow, I felt the temperature drop, the chill onset of night. Out of the fading sunlight, the *Schloss* seemed especially sinister. I thought of Kafka, and the weak grasp I had on the false confidence of my stride.

Far to the right, jutting out from the main part of the building, were the "ruins," a faux-Gothic remnant of wall with an archway that led, from what I could see, nowhere. The wall was anchored by a half-built Norman keep, a folly whose whimsy seemed out of place in East Berlin. From the tower a huge banner hung, showing the goateed, unsmiling face of Walter Ulbricht.

Soon we were at a second guard station, where two more members of the military elite stood with their machine guns. Before Krone spoke, one of them waved us through.

We crossed a planked drawbridge traversing the vestige of a moat. Like the paved-over garden behind us, the ditch had been flattened and shoddily lined with asphalt. On second glance, I saw that the drawbridge was no Romantic relic. Its hinges were wet with oil, so the bridge could be pulled up to seal the entrance against the onrush not of an invading army but of an unleashed mob. The thing to fear most was a population deprived of automobiles, even small ones.

We went through the open archway into a tunnel that led into a spacious inner courtyard the size, say, of a country club's set of tennis courts. The image was prompted, no doubt, by the startling sight of close-cropped grass carpeting the area. The grass was split by the neat, pebbled driveway on which we entered. The surrounding walls seemed made of windows. A border of flowering shrubs lined the courtyard. Benches sat every few dozen yards all around, but they were unoccupied. Indeed, not a soul was anywhere to be seen. Kafka indeed. All the drivers of the cars outside, all the bureaucrats at desks and file cabinets behind the windows, all the apparatchiks and commissars, where were they?

In the far right corner of the rectangular courtyard were gently flapping tarps attached to lumber scaffolding; apparently the restoration was still under way in that section of the building. The canvas tarps covered the façade there, its four full stories. The horizontal roofline at that point was interrupted by the lone upright figure of a sentry standing with his weapon, looking toward us. Even across the distance, his cool observing eye intimidated, and I focused on what was before us.

The driveway led to a surprisingly modest doorway in the center of the *Schloss*. As we approached, our feet crunched the gravel, an overly loud sound to my ear. Sure enough, there was movement behind a row of ground-level windows to the right. When Krone saw me turn toward the windows, he said quietly, "The barracks of the Dzerzhinski Guard, the Stasi SS. They are not here to guard against you Americans or us West Germans, but against citizens of the glorious Socialist republic. They want you to see them watching you."

"And you, Hans," I muttered.

"It is the *feeling* of being watched that keeps the East the East. A feeling that belongs to dreams, but not here."

"You know about the barracks because you've been here before? Or was that a dream?"

He did not answer.

"Hans, you said you never meet Erhardt here."

"Erhardt is not my only client, Paul. Now, do you actually desire to discuss this right into the building? Or can you trust me?"

"I don't have a choice, do I?"

He stopped. "Look. Chase Manhattan engaged my services. You

depend on me for ties to Berlin finance. Berlin is not Vatican City. Berlin finance is not the Holy Office, and I am not the Virgin Mary. Which is precisely why Chase Manhattan depends on me. You either cease pretending otherwise, or we halt this enterprise right here."

"I take your point. But I am depending on you to level with me."

"Nothing I have told you is false."

"But you don't tell me everything."

He laughed. "Until now, that is why you paid me so well."

"Right. Until now. And one other thing, Hans. The Holy Office — isn't that the Inquisition? Where they burned heretics?"

"Yes. And Jews." He stared at me hard, almost scornfully, as if I were Roman Catholic. Then he grinned, slapped my arm, and set us walking again.

We were soon in a spacious entrance hall, at a desk, with Krone once more presenting our documents to a guard, who pointedly compared the photographs with our faces.

There was razor wire in the way the man looked at us. He never uttered a word. Then he stood and disappeared with our papers through an adjacent door. Some moments passed. I became aware of a faint, acrid aroma in the air. I worked to identify it — the smell of stale ash, the blowback of an aged coal burner, cinders falling from the sky, the aftermath of some inflamed astonishment — or not. Something mundane, more likely.

Out of restlessness, I surveyed the once grand foyer. Plaster moldings on the walls and ceiling, reliefs, and fluted faux columns topped by Corinthian capitals — all the elaborate work had been lost in a careless overcoat of dull beige paint. I noticed a large bronze plaque on the wall opposite the doorway. It had clearly been mounted after the walls had been painted over. With a small stand holding a vase of fresh flowers before it, the ornamented metal plate — about four feet wide, six feet high — seemed like a shrine or the back of an altar. Names in two columns were engraved below the familiar seal of the DDR. "*Moabiter Märtyrer*," read the heading above the columns of names. Below were a few lines of text, impossible for me to decipher, but presumably an epigraph extolling heroism. At the very bottom of the plaque, in letters to match the heading, was the date: "*1 Mai, 1945*."

Krone was beside me. "What's this?" I asked.

"Moabit was a notorious Nazi prison in Lehrter Strasse, long gone, never replaced. It was where they kept the so-called political criminals — KPD, Communists. That is whom this commemorates. The DDR glorifies the Communist anti-Nazis as the founders of the Socialist state. The only Germans who fought Hitler." There was sarcasm in his voice.

"And why not glorify them?"

Krone shrugged. "Moabit was a spa compared to Buchenwald." He tossed his head toward the columns of names and at the same time touched the back of my neck with his forefinger. "Who would not prefer a bullet in the back of the neck to choking asphyxiation, naked, befouled, in the crush of a gas chamber?"

At that, he turned and strode back to the desk. Such an emotional expression was rare for him, I sensed, but I found it perplexing. To me, Nazi victims were alike in being Nazi victims. But was it so simple for Jews? For Communists? Could the victims be in competition? Degrees of victimhood? Certainly no American had the right to ask such questions.

But what about that date, May Day 1945? Wasn't May 1 the date of Hitler's suicide? The day before the Soviets overran Berlin? A riddle in time: What happened on that single day of Berlin's interregnum?

I glanced toward Krone, wanting to ask what was being commemorated here, but his back was to me, and I hesitated. I looked again at the plaque, the text, but my mulish mind could not translate most of the German. Several words registered — no more.

A noise told me the guard had reappeared. I turned. Instead of the soldier, I saw a gaunt young man in a dark suit, white shirt, and tie. Horn-rimmed glasses gave him the look of a graduate student, his gray pallor that of a patient in a sanatorium. On second look, he was not so young, and there was nothing weak about him. He was interrogating Krone. My passport and Krone's visa were in his hand. As I stepped toward them, I realized the man was speaking Russian.

A surprise. Moscow overlords usually stayed behind the scenes in East Berlin, their armored divisions in the suburbs, their troops in the Soviet compound in Karlshorst. Was Stasi different? A KGB subsidiary for sure, but was Stasi under overt Soviet supervision? Or was it surveillance? Was the Russian's presence related only to the pressures of May Day, or was this a hint of the coming border crisis?

And what was I to make of it that Krone was answering fluently? He pointed toward me, and it was clear that I was the subject of the exchange. Krone had given himself over to the role of an American VIP's toady, and I sensed it as he exaggerated my importance. The complete sycophant, he had drawn his hands together, even bobbing forward as he spoke. The only words I recognized in what he said were "Chase Manhattan," "Rockefeller," and, after a quick insistent exchange, the German phrase *"Arbeitsgruppe Ausländer."*

After the Russian looked me over — his eyes were frog-like behind his lenses — he led us through a doorway and up a broad, brightly lit stairwell. The soldier followed behind. Our steps echoed up the shaft.

At the third landing, the top floor save one, we went through a door into a wide corridor filled with bustling men and women. The Stasi bureaucracy was one of the largest in Soviet Germany, and at last was showing itself. Dozens of people — some in uniform, some not; some carrying accordion files, some wire baskets; some pushing wheeled trays laden with boxes — were toing-and-froing from room to room, up and down the length of an apparently endless hallway. The civilian men wore baggy serge suits and scuffed shoes. The women wore heavy pleated skirts, sweaters over blouses, hair on the upper lip. I heard snatches of German, yet intuitively I knew, here again, that some of these functionaries were Russian. Although if Russian, they would not be mere functionaries.

Once I adjusted to the sight of the Stasi workers, such a contrast to our isolated approach till then, I relaxed some. This must be like a corridor in the Pentagon, or in Whitehall in London. It was what I expected. Never mind what nightmare each brown case file represented, each folder in its tray, each dossier. Abstracting from its actual outcome, what was more mundane than a bureaucracy at work? Now, to find Michael in its maze. Michael, whom I pictured grinning at the wheel of the car. *Where are you?*

Our Russian escort led us down the center of the corridor, his authority implicit both in the way the sea of workers parted for us and in the way they avoided looking at him. He acknowledged no one.

Every door we passed was closed except for the occasional one that happened to open as someone went in or out. Even then, we could glimpse only interior vestibules off which, presumably, other doors opened into the offices proper. All the doors were marked just with numbers. There was nothing to be learned from looking.

What they weren't able to keep from us, however, were the motes of dust in the air. As we made our way along, I noticed — overriding the general aromas of mildew, body odor, cheap cologne, and rose water — an intensifying smell of ash.

Finally the Russian stopped, opened a door, and held it for us. We went through and found ourselves in a narrow inner hallway, perhaps thirty yards long. At its far end, toward what I realized would be the corner of the building, was an ancient tapestry that had been hung to serve as a blocking wall. We approached it. The tapestry was threadbare in places, and if the colors were ever bright, they had long since bled together into a faded gray-green. It showed a hunting scene, a cornered stag, hounds, horses, a man with a horn. The tapestry was hung to come within three or four feet of the floor, and in that space I saw a stretch of the same canvas tarp I had seen outside. The stench of ash was coming from here, from whatever rooms the tapestry sealed off. Now I recognized it: the smell of a doused fire.

The Russian stopped again, knocked once on a door, and, without waiting for acknowledgment, opened it. He stepped aside for us. We entered a cluttered work area with half a dozen men at desks and typing tables. They ignored us.

The room seemed to press in from the sides: the walls were lined with metal file cabinets, which were themselves stacked with cardboard file boxes. In front of the window, facing away from it, was a tattered leather couch. The man gestured toward it. We went there and sat. The armed guard remained by the door through which we had come, and the man disappeared through another door.

Krone, beside me, adjusted himself restlessly on the couch, a large man at the mercy, as it were, of pinched underwear. Then I realized he was maneuvering to come closer to me. He coughed and kept his hand at his mouth, and I leaned toward him.

"With the Russian here, Erhardt and I can never have met. It is up to you." He coughed again and edged away from me, but I snagged his arm.

"That fire," I said, nodding in the direction of the sealed-off corridor.

"Yes. The fire is why the Russian is here. The KGB is watching Erhardt." He coughed again and moved away.

Two feet separated us on the couch, and we did not speak again. The light washing in through the high window behind us faded quickly. Soon twilight gave way to evening, and evening to night. One by one, the typists and clerks in front of us yawned, closed their drawers, covered their typewriters with towels, and pulled the strings on their little lamps. They retrieved their thermoses and lunch cans and snapped shut their satchels. Without a glance at us or our guard, they left the room, having bid no one good night. Heading home to their dismal flats after another day of serving the cause of world revolution.

Without the desk lamps, a dusty low-wattage bulb in a ceiling fixture did little to fend off the gathering darkness. I wouldn't have been able to read by this light.

An hour passed. When I thought another had, I checked my watch, but could not see it. By then, Krone and I and the soldier, still at the door, were the only ones there, each in his silence, each in his personal shadow.

When Erhardt's office door finally opened, the man who showed himself was in uniform, the uniform of a senior officer — braid at his shoulder, beribboned medals at his breast, gleaming brass buttons. The officer was short and bald. His face was thin, cut at an angle set by an ax-like nose. He actually clicked his heels and bowed slightly in our direction, a movement that drew attention to the right sleeve of his tunic by setting it swinging. The sleeve was folded in half and pinned up. He'd lost an arm.

Krone and I stood. When the officer looked at Krone and said "Herr Montgomery," I saw at once that he was Colonel Erhardt, pretending not to know who Krone was — a message for Krone. It was all I needed to know that what Krone had claimed about their surreptitious relationship was true.

I said, "I am Montgomery." I stepped forward, indicating Krone. "This is Herr Krone, my associate."

Erhardt remained at his door but stepped aside for us. As we crossed the threshold, he offered his left hand, like a bishop offering a ring to kiss. However much business he and Krone had done together, it was as if they had never laid eyes on each other. Yet we were here, weren't we? Erhardt had found a way, even with a Kremlin falcon on his shoulder, to meet Krone's demand. Krone was good. As I went past Erhardt, I realized that he was good, too.

The dark-paneled office was large and better lit. A conference table with eight chairs dominated one end of the room, and in one of those chairs sat the Russian. He was holding a pencil poised above a notepad on the table in front of him. How it must infuriate these Stasi big shots, I thought, when Moscow swoops in to jerk the leash. The Russian's relative youth, and even his gauntness, I saw, were to the point of the insult being delivered, and the function of that insult was control. It wasn't only that the Russian was here to watch. He was here to make a show of watching. In how many ways, and how mortally, I wondered, was Erhardt being squeezed? And what a nightmare for him now to have Krone show up out of nowhere.

At the other end of the room, by the window, was Erhardt's desk, one end of which was taken up with half a dozen telephones. How could these people threaten us, I thought, when they haven't figured out the multiline phone?

Erhardt went behind his desk and sat.

There were no chairs for me and Krone. As we stood before his desk, I realized how this arrangement would make a petitioner of everyone who came before Erhardt in such a way. He had been a man with real power, but now? The deputy director of the office in charge of all matters concerning foreigners: What would a sealed border mean to him? What did the fire in the adjoining office mean? What did it destroy? And if that fire killed Erhardt's chief, Sohlmann . . . My mind leapt sideways and back. Why had Charlotte flinched at Sohlmann's name? Why had she refused to come here? My questions tumbled over one another.

Erhardt glanced at a one-page brief that was centered on the desk before him. Then he looked at me.

"Your son, he is absent?" he said.

"My son, Michael Montgomery," I replied with what calm I could muster. For some seconds it was as if the interview were occurring underwater. Words bubbled out of me, and I could barely breathe. "Age seventeen, a student in the American school in Wiesbaden. He came to Berlin for the weekend, a school excursion. I am told he was detained with two other American students at the station."

Erhardt eyed me with studied indifference. "That is under the authority of the *Volkspolizei,* the East German People's Police — the *Hauptverwaltung Aufklärung,* the main administration for border security. If your son violated border procedures, it has nothing to do with this office."

To my surprise, Krone spoke up. "That is my mistake, then, Colonel. I was under the impression that the *Arbeitsgruppe Ausländer* is concerned with all matters involving noncitizens of the DDR."

Erhardt shook his head. "Not border violations. Certainly not. NVA also has authority. *Nationale Volksarmee.* Stasi is not concerned with borders."

"But what possible violations are we talking about?" I asked. "Three American teenagers are here for a parade. And now they are arrested. In custody. Where? Charged with what? I demand to know what's going on."

"Herr Montgomery —"

"No, wait a minute, Colonel. I have come to you to keep this thing simple. I have not as yet contacted the American authorities. I have not involved the consulate, nor have I been in contact with my associates in Washington. That is because I assume there is a mistake here, the bad decision of a minor functionary at a crossing point under high pressure because of May Day. *Vopos,* NVA, Stasi — I don't care who. A small mistake that can be quickly corrected by *you.* Corrected without becoming an incident. It serves my purposes no more than yours for this to become an incident."

"I have told you my situation, Herr Montgomery. My office has nothing to do with your son's circumstance, whatever it is."

"It does now, Colonel. My next stop from here is the American headquarters in Dahlem, and you are the person I will name as responsible for the kidnapping of three American children."

"Children?" Erhardt's one hand went to the empty sleeve, where he hooked his forefinger into the fold.

"Yes, children. Minors. Ineligible to vote. Unable to buy a drink."

"Old enough to serve in the Army, I believe." His glance went to the corner of the room where the Russian was sitting, then back to me. "Although I understand your son would not be a conscript, for other reasons."

"That's right, Colonel. My son's being a cripple will be a big part of the story when this becomes public." Cripple. A word I never used about Michael. Why had I used it now? Because of the German's missing arm? I veered from the thought. "Now perhaps you can explain to me how you know that about my son, if this matter is of no concern to you."

Erhardt smiled and looked at Krone. "Your associate, Herr — ?" He was making a point not to know the name.

Krone touched my arm. "I told them that, Paul. Downstairs."

"And you, Herr Montgomery," Erhardt said. "You departed for Berlin when?"

"Today. This morning."

"But *before* your son had been, as you say, kidnapped. No? Why is that, sir?"

He had me, and I knew it. I found a way to say, with dead calm, "I have business with Herr Krone. You can understand that."

I let my eyes shift to the right, toward the Russian. Would the KGB distinguish between run-of-the-mill black marketeering and treason? Not after a fire in the Stasi inner sanctum, which had the Russian sitting on Erhardt's one good shoulder. You, too, Colonel, have business with Krone, I said in every way but words.

Erhardt said, "I am a father myself. I know what it is, the worry you have." He leaned forward, openly consulting the page on his desk. "That is why I troubled to learn what the situation is. As a father." He reached his one hand to the corner of his desk, to punch the button on the base of a gooseneck lamp. It threw a wedge of golden light onto the paper, and he began to read aloud the German text while Krone leaned toward my ear, translating. *Two Americans, Hackescher Markt, currency violation, detention pending appearance before the people's magistrate, which will not take place until Monday.*

When he looked up at me, he smiled again, but still without warmth. He resumed his English. "It is inconvenient, Herr Montgomery. But also insignificant. Dozens of these each month. There will be a — what do you say? — financial penalty."

"Fine," Krone said.

"Yes, fine. A small amount. Your son will be released on Monday."

"Three Americans," I said.

Erhardt looked again at the page. "No, two. A man and a woman."

"There are two boys and a girl."

"No. My information is otherwise. Perhaps it is that the second boy was not arrested."

Krone touched me. "If they counted the one as a native of Leipzig, he would not be in an *Ausländer* report."

I looked sharply at Krone. Why was he bringing up Leipzig? "He's an American citizen."

"I am only speaking to the possibility —"

I turned back to Erhardt. "*Three* American children."

Erhardt shrugged. "I have no record of three. You will have to take it up with the *Hauptverwaltung Aufklärung*. I have done what I can do. I have done too much."

"I am not waiting until Monday."

"Herr Montgomery, your son stands accused of violating the laws of the *Deutsche Demokratische Republik*. I said a moment ago that this is a minor violation. But perhaps I spoke inaccurately. It is better to say that there are no minor violations of the law in this nation. We take the law as serious —"

I slammed my fist on his desk. "Don't give me this garbage, Colonel! You have kidnapped these Americans. I want them released."

"Nothing occurs until Monday."

"I want to see them. I demand to see them. I demand that you arrange for me to see them."

"You perhaps must then take this up with the American consulate, as you said." Erhardt's finger went back into the fold of his empty sleeve.

It was as if Krone took that slight gesture as a signal. He touched my arm, then leaned over the edge of Erhardt's desk. "As one Berliner to another, Colonel; as a man appealing to your sympathetic heart — let me ask you to use your influence on behalf of these young people, on behalf of this father. I know you can help. I am asking you to help as a fellow Berliner."

Erhardt said nothing for a long time. I could hear the Russian breathing from his place across the room, and I was sure Erhardt could hear it, too. Finally, he stood. His desk chair clattered back. He looked at me and said, "We do not want an 'incident,' as you term it. I will learn more. I will inquire about a visit to your son —"

"All three," I said. "I want to see all three."

"Out of respect for your position, Herr Montgomery, I will do this."

Krone handed Erhardt a business card. "I will await your call."

Without looking at it, Erhardt put the card on the sheet of paper on his desk.

That was it.

I wasn't sure it was enough, but it was all we were going to get. Krone and I turned and crossed toward the door. By the time we reached it, the Russian was there ahead of us, pulling it open. We walked through without breaking stride. The Russian slipped ahead of us and led us back the way we'd come, with the soldier following.

Downstairs in the foyer, I stopped Krone. The Russian, having held a door, was several paces behind. "Hans, before we leave, I want you to ask this man where Michael is."

"He will not tell us."

"Ask him."

Krone, dutiful assistant, did as he was told. That gave me the moment I wanted to step across to the bronze plaque I had noticed before. I focused on the explanatory paragraph, looking for the words that had faintly registered in my brain. I saw them now.

Von Siedelheim.

The name was buried in the account of the *Moabiter Märtyrer*, in the next-to-last sentence of the paragraph, near the bottom of the plaque.

Von Siedelheim — a martyr in 1945, in Berlin.

Von Siedelheim — the name of the man I had seen murdered only last Monday in that Frankfurt lecture hall. I had replayed the instant of savage violence again and again, the torpedo striking below the waterline of my already listing mind. But now, what had reasonably been taken to be a neo-Nazi assassination in Frankfurt was stripped of political meaning, coming into view as telltale white bubbles streaking toward my son.

Krone joined me. "He has nothing to say."

But he did. The Russian snapped a word in our direction. "*Bitte!*" A command. He was pointing at the door.

Krone pulled me.

We went out into the night. Light from windows on all four sides of us — the Stasi graveyard shift — established the margins of our passage, made it possible to see.

The soldier behind us remained at the doorway as we moved into the unlit courtyard across which, in a rectangle of light by his sentry box, another soldier waited, watching.

With the slow, steady gaze of an officer scanning the ocean's horizon from the bridge, I took the measure of the eerie world of Schloss Pankow at night. But inside I was trying to grasp the implications of what I had just seen.

Von Siedelheim. My mind flashed again with the image of that tall, handsomely balding aristocrat taking a bullet in the back of the neck, the crack of the single pistol shot, the shocked intake of breath of a thousand witnesses, the spurt of blood from the man's exploded face as he fell forward on the lectern.

I stopped walking.

We were in the center of the courtyard. Krone continued on for a couple of paces, his shoes crunching the gravel. Then he stopped and came back to me. The pair of sentries watched from opposite ends of the driveway. The dark silhouette of the crenelated building, with flags still flying from its towers, loomed over us. But we were alone.

"Paul," he said urgently, "we must get out of here."

"What was it you said about a bullet in the back of the neck?"

Krone looked impatient, resentful. My question made no sense to him, but he stifled his reaction.

"At Moabit. Bullet to the back of the neck, you said."

"Yes. The favored way Nazis executed political criminals. Traitors were hanged. Jews were gassed. A method for every category of enemy of the Reich. The KPD took it as a point of pride to be shot in the neck."

"Shot from behind?"

"Yes."

"And what day was the fire?"

"What?"

"The fire here, when Sohlmann died. When was it?"

"Tuesday night, Wednesday morning."

A day after the shooting of von Siedelheim, events connected by a name on the wall, a name on a bankers' program in Frankfurt. Markus von Siedelheim — a developer of trade with impoverished Africa — martyred, it was coming clear, by racist neo-Nazis.

And this other von Siedelheim, this earlier one, martyred, too. A Communist murdered by the racist Nazis who started it all.

To leave all my names behind — Charlotte Healy's words came back to me. I felt a surge of hatred for General Healy for leaving her unprotected, but his reaction — "national security" — at last made a kind of sense. The murder in Frankfurt had set an emergency in motion, I saw that much now.

And whatever Healy was protecting — a roll of film? — it was not his wife and not her son.

Overhead, the dark sky was full of stars, a measure of how little light the city of Berlin threw even now. I was suddenly aware of the vast infinite wonder of the night canopy. I could have been on the bridge of my ship on that blowing ocean. On the dock by the lake. I was in the presence of some unseen reality, conscious as I was both of the negative strike of my anger at Healy and of a fresh desire to consecrate my life, as if for the first time. To what? The rescue of Michael, that was all.

"All right," I said to Krone, "let's go."

But he had just put his hand firmly against my chest. "Whatever you are thinking, Paul, be careful. If Erhardt is helping us, it is not because of me or what I can bring against him. It is because he needs something, needs it desperately, with the KGB pressing him — and he thinks you can bring it to him."

"What?"

"You tell me."

And there was the reason for my anger at General Healy. Erhardt wanted what Healy had, and Healy's wife, her son, a girl named Kit, and my son were caught in its snare, whatever it was. National security? A roll of film? The coming crisis of border closure? A May 1 anniversary of 1945? The cause of a mortal fire in the devil's own sanctum sanctorum? Charlotte's fear of the name Sohlmann? What?

214

Each question was its separate prick of light in the radical dark, like the stars above. Yet I could not imagine the design, the architecture, what gave those lights the order of constellation. In my ignorance, would I lead Colonel Erhardt to the cosmic secret, with Hans Krone as the guide? Was he my Virgil or theirs?

All I knew for sure was that in America's valiant war against brutal, godless communism, Charlotte and Rick were on their own, and with them so was Michael. The snare was tied to some long-dead martyr, a man still bound to America's enemy, and therefore mine. He was a man whose family was somehow still at risk.

Markus von Siedelheim, murdered on Monday, assassinated, executed.

Von Siedelheim. Completing the name I had just read on the bronze plaque, not Markus, was *Wolf.*

Part Four

12

THAT FIRST NIGHT they kept us in a small room in a big house someplace near a railroad crossing, which we knew because there were regular blasts of a locomotive whistle right through until midnight, plaintive wailing sounds that could have been coming from our own throats, we were so afraid.

Kit and I were together, but not with Ulrich. We had been interrogated again, one at a time, in the early evening, in a musty basement room of the same house, and Ulrich, after they took him away for his turn, had never come back. The woman who brought us a tray of food — again soup and bread — told us he was being held in another part of the house, but that was all she would say. We worried that Ulrich was the one in real trouble because, as Kit put it at one point, the trigger was his bag and the gun was his father. Stepfather, I corrected her.

Being with Kit kept me from going insane, although before the night was over, I was sure I had slipped into a dream state in which everything that happened, bad and the unexpected good, was imagined. Even now, in relating the events of that frightful yet exotic night from the vantage of a mundane middle age, I find it hard to believe I am referring to what happened to me.

They arrested us at the transit point in a subway station. Before crossing from West to East Berlin, Josef Tramm had instructed us in how to fill out the temporary visa applications. He was standing beside us when the East German policemen began their search, and at first he acted like our protector, with a few gruff exchanges in German, as if announcing us as VIPs. The police ignored him. They made Kit take off her father's khaki field jacket, which Tramm protested, but when they then searched its flap pockets and handed it back to her, I realized that they had not wanted to risk touching her breasts. The *Vopos* were not much older than we were.

They searched Ulrich's bag with no special show of interest. I watched as they turned to the zippered side pocket, which I had seen Tramm search the night before. Even in my paranoia, I had not imagined that they would find a white envelope that held a wad of dollars — twenties and tens. The shocked look on Ulrich's face, his immediate denying exclamation in German, told me what I already knew. When I turned to look at Tramm, he was gone.

Of course, it was cash Ulrich had not declared on his visa application. He continued his protesting denials as Kit and I exchanged a stupefied look. Stupefied and stupid. Her dark, wide eyes were always ready to be surprised, yet this time they showed her absolute bafflement. This was so, as she told me later, because in her anxiety she had pictured just such a thing. And now it had actually happened! She stepped toward me, took my arm in her firm grip, and whispered, "Damn, Monty, damn!"

One of the *Vopos* took Ulrich's arm, but Ulrich shook him off, looking wildly around — looking for Tramm, I knew. A second policeman moved in on him. Kit and I backed away. The *Vopos* took Ulrich's arms again, and now when he struggled one produced a nightstick out of nowhere and brought it down on Ulrich's head.

Ulrich staggered but didn't go down. Both policemen began to beat him, a succession of quick blows to his face and head, one using the stick, the other his fist. I had never seen such mayhem, and my reaction was only visceral. "Hey," I said, and unconsciously raised my cane, pointing at the nearer policeman as if it were a weapon. He slammed the nightstick against my cane, knocking it out of my hand. It clattered loudly on the floor, bouncing away.

He turned back to Ulrich and clubbed him once more. Ulrich slumped, out cold, as the other *Vopo* held him. Blood streamed down his face. My arms were jerked together behind my back by someone I did not see. I saw an expression of pure terror on Kit's face. I wanted her to look at me, but the blood on Ulrich had seized her, and I knew that, as horrible as this was for me, it was even worse for her. Why did I sense that? She had seen blood like this before.

Suddenly Kit was pulled away, out of my field of vision, all of this accompanied by German imperatives — the language, to my ear, never more itself. My arms were yoked behind me by a set of manacles closed around the bones above my elbows, causing an excruciating pain in the nerves and muscles there. As I was being hauled away, my eyes went to the crowd of people who had witnessed our arrest, Germans from West Berlin as well as from East Berlin, faces that would come to mind years later when I read of that famous bystander detachment.

Behind the people was the tunnel entrance through which, only moments before, we had come from the subway into the cavernous transit hall. Now I saw a man making his way against the flow of May Day traffic pouring out of that tunnel, and I knew that it was Tramm, heading back to West Berlin, his job done. We never saw him again.

In short order, Kit, Ulrich, and I were thrown into the back of a windowless van, all three manacled in the same way, but with Ulrich still unconscious, bleeding.

When the *Vopos* slammed the doors shut on us, we were plunged into darkness. The stench of fresh vomit filled my nostrils, and for a moment I feared that I, like some recent occupant of the van, was about to puke. When I successfully stifled the nausea, I felt the power of my own will, what we called in those days mind over matter. To my surprise I thought, I can do this.

"Kit, where are you?"

"Behind you. Over here."

"Are you all right?"

"Rick is hurt, Monty. Rick! Rick!"

I shifted in place, finding them. As my eyes adjusted, I made out Kit. She was leaning over the slumped form of Ulrich. A loud rumble shook the steel plating under us, the engine starting. When the van lurched into motion, Kit fell back, audibly banging her head against the metal wall.

"Are you all right?"

"Shit, Monty," she said. "What the hell."

On my knees, I was able to get over to Ulrich. With my hands useless behind me, I nudged him with the knob of my left knee. "Ulrich! Ulrich! Can you hear us?"

He groaned.

"Good man, Ulrich! Way to go, comrade! Do you hear me? It's Michael. Monty."

"Oh, God," he said.

I put my face down to his, unsteadily and off balance with the bumping of the van as it careened along over rough and broken pavement. "You're okay," I said. I placed my cheek against his head, my nose into his hair, which was wet with blood. "The bleeding stopped, comrade," I said, only hoping it was so. "You're going to be okay." But I was panicked, thinking, Shit, what if he's really hurt?

"Quit calling him comrade, Monty," Kit said.

"Let me wipe your face, Rick," I said. I put my shoulder against his head, pressing.

He groaned and pulled away.

"I'm sorry," I said.

Ulrich pulled himself up. "No, *I* am sorry. Oh, God." He rolled onto his side and came to his knees. "I am so sorry."

"Don't be crazy," Kit said from her place by the wall.

"Are you still bleeding?" I asked.

"I don't think so. I am just sorry. Sorry."

"Why should you be sorry?" I asked.

"It is because of my stepfather," Ulrich said. "The bastard. The bastard!"

"It was Tramm," I said, "not your stepfather." Ulrich's anger at his stepfather made no sense to me. On the contrary, didn't we need the general more than ever? As an American big shot, wasn't he our best chance of getting out of this? "You've got to tell them who your stepfather is. They won't mess with an American general."

"Oh, Monty, you really amaze me."

The old snap in his voice relieved me. I was glad to have something to disagree about. He was okay. "Tramm is the one who screwed us," I said. "He's the one who planted that money." If you made a mistake, it was with fucking Tramm, not your stepfather.

"Yes, Tramm put the money in there. But this is all a work of theater. Tramm played his role. Now they play theirs, and we ours. But

222

for what audience? For General David X. Healy. This is why I do not need to tell them who my stepfather is. They already know. And not just because of my ID, either."

"What do they want?" I asked.

"I do not know," Ulrich said, but with a new note of defeat.

"That film?" Kit said.

"Shh!" Ulrich said. Until then, it hadn't occurred to me that we could be overheard. All at once the question hit me, the one that should have the night before: Where *was* the film? Why had Tramm not found it in Ulrich's bag?

Ulrich had slumped back against the wall of the van. Unlike me, he was able to steady himself against the jostling, bumpy ride. My left thigh was pressing painfully down onto the metal of my right leg brace, and when I tried to adjust, I fell over, knocking against Kit. "I'm sorry," I said. I looked for her face. Her eyes were closed. Back into that nightmare of hers, whatever it was. *Incurable.*

When I regained my balance, I turned back to Ulrich. Something in his slumped posture made me ask, "What's wrong?"

His voice, when he answered, was strangely disembodied. "I came here to get away from him, from what he does, from what he represents, from what he made my mother become."

"You shouldn't have come to Berlin."

"Berlin is the one city where he cannot follow. And Berlin is *my* city."

"Well, you can have it," I said, trying to lighten the mood.

Some moments passed. To my surprise, Ulrich had begun quietly sobbing.

"Rick," I said. What pain he must have been in.

But it was not the beating that made him cry. "I cannot get away," he said. "I cannot get away from him. Not even here. I cannot. I cannot."

The van swerved, taking a turn fast. Kit fell against me this time, and as she did, a strange, guttural groan escaped her lips.

"Kit, are you all right?"

When she didn't answer right away, the question resonated in the close air. *Are you all right?* I remembered the words, a woman's voice coming to me from a threshold, a light behind her figure, a kind of halo around her head, making individual strands of hair stand out like silver threads. Those words had always soothed me, no matter what. *Are you all right?* They soothed me now, just to have spoken them.

"No," she said finally. "My arms. My arms have gone numb. My hands. I can't move my damn fingers. Something's wrong."

"It's the clamps. They've cut your circulation. You have clamps on your arms. You know that, right?"

"Monty, my arms are paralyzed."

I heard the panic in her voice. Oddly, her agitation had a calming effect on me. "The manacles on your arms, Kit. Here, turn toward me." I swung around so that my back was to hers, to take her arms in my hands, one at a time. "Can you feel that?" I massaged her upper arms, first one, then the other, my hands moving up and down over her elbows, kneading the flesh around the metal cuffs. How thin she was, how easily I could make out the contours of her bones. "Is that better? Your arms are just asleep, that's all."

"Why does it smell like vomit in here?"

"Somebody before us. Drunk. May Day. The parade. Do you feel that? Can you feel me touching your arms?"

"Yes."

"Then you're okay. You'll be okay." My fingers found hers, intertwined with them, kneading and pressing. "You're okay, Kit."

All this while Ulrich, apart from us, was softly crying against the wall.

"How come my arms are tied, Monty, and yours aren't?"

"Mine are, Kit. Same as you. That's why I have my back to you."

"You do?" She looked around at me. "Holy shit." Then she laughed, and I realized with a rush of absurd self-satisfaction that she was grinning at me with some kind of admiration. That I was coping. At that moment, I believed in myself because she did.

It had yet to occur to me that if I uncovered unexpected resources of strength or resolve in myself, they had not been put there by someone else. Yes, I was afraid. Yes, I was sure that, not for the first time, my body was about to fail me. But Kit seemed more real to me than my premonitions. Her simple presence was the vertical axis by which I measured balance, her presence and the stunning fact that she had turned to me in need. And I was meeting it.

Here is proof that beauty is a trick of the mind: in the dark, in that terrible moment, Kit seemed beautiful to me, beauty itself. I rejoiced in the sweet sight of her near invisibility.

The van rolled down into what seemed an underground garage. The garage also was dark, so that when they opened the van doors, it felt like night. I had to remind myself it was the middle of the day. I could see Ulrich's face more clearly now, and was relieved that the blood had dried. He seemed to have regained some physical resolve. Indeed, I was the only one to stumble and bump the cinderblock walls as they herded us along. Ulrich tried to help me, but without the use of his arms there was little he could do. The clicking of my leg braces had never seemed so loud. Without my cane I had to lope along with an exaggerated stride. I knew what rhythm to strike, but I knew also that the gait made me look spastic, and I hated to have Kit see me that way.

They pushed us into a dimly lit elevator. Fliers were crudely taped to the walls of the elevator car, showing faces of mean-looking men, head-on and in profile. Mug shots. Wanted posters. There were about ten of them.

I leaned toward Ulrich and whispered, "Police station." One of the *Vopos* poked me in the ribs. "*Sei still!*" And I shut up.

On an upper floor of the building, they led us into a kind of hearing room, with a long table at one wall, three vacant chairs behind it. Opposite the table were three or four rows of straight-backed chairs. One of the policemen pulled three of these forward, closer to the table, while two others, from behind us, unlocked the manacles on our arms. Oddly, it was when I brought my arms forward that I felt the sharpest crack of pain in my shoulders, but that quickly gave way to the undiluted physical relief it was to be free. That feeling passed, too. We sat, with Kit between me and Ulrich.

I turned toward him, trying to appear casual. He sat slumped, inert, his eyes on the floor. This deflation, on the heels of his frenzied happiness before our arrest, should have warned me of what was coming, but I knew too little still of the ways we come unglued.

Just then, a mustachioed man in civilian clothes entered. That he had a white handkerchief steepled in his suit pocket reminded me of my father. The man's eyes met mine and he nodded. He walked to the table, taking one of the three chairs behind it. He carried a thick manila envelope, which he placed square on the table in front of him.

"Good afternoon," he said, and though he smiled at me there was something sinister in his expression. "You are Herr Montgomery?"

"Yes."

He unclasped the envelope and upended it. Our passports, ID cards, visa forms, and wallets tumbled out. Last came the white business envelope I had seen before, with the money. He lifted it and said, "This envelope is for your club?"

"What?"

"Your school group. What is it called? The Pirates?"

My heart sank. I could not think of what to say.

"The Edelweiss Pirates?"

Kit put her hand on my arm. Ulrich did not react. He was still staring at the floor.

"That isn't our group," I said. "We are the school debating club." How easily the lie came to me, a kind of truth by now. "We came to Berlin to debate the team from the American high school here. In West Berlin."

He smiled and nodded. I felt a wash of cold fear on my neck. I was saying what he expected me to say.

Ulrich raised his head. "The bag is mine," he said. "The money was in my bag. These two have nothing to do with it. You know this. You are interested only in me."

The man's smile thickened as he turned his gaze to Ulrich. He spoke to him in German, something I missed.

Ulrich's reply, also in German, given calmly, was a denial, I knew that much.

The man lifted the white envelope and slapped one end of it on the table. "Two hundred dollars in ten-dollar notes, twenty-dollar notes. Officially, ten DDR marks to the dollar. Unofficially, one hundred marks to the dollar. Your two hundred dollars, with the well-planned rendezvous, would fetch twenty thousand marks, which you then, in the West, trade for two thousand dollars."

"We don't know what you're talking about," I said.

"Quiet, Monty," Ulrich said.

"And you, *Fräulein*? Do you know the penalty for illegal currency activity?"

"Don't answer, Kit," I said. To the man I said as firmly as I could, "Josef Tramm put the money in the bag. And then he made sure it was not noted on our visa forms. He was with us at the border, and you let him go."

"Montgomery!" Ulrich barked. He brought himself up, squaring off before the interrogator. "If I tell you the money was mine, will you let these others go?"

The man smiled benignly. He answered in German.

Ulrich replied in German.

"Speak English, please," I said.

Finally Kit spoke. "We want to see the American ambassador."

The man laughed. "The American ambassador is in Bonn, *Fräulein*."

"The American consul, then. The military attaché. Somebody."

He said, "The American authorities will be notified. Regarding you" — he rifled through the papers in front of him, picked up one of the passports, opened it, and made a show of matching it with Ulrich's face — "you are German born. *East* German born."

Ulrich said nothing.

I said, "He's American. An American citizen. Tell him you're American, Rick."

"Monty, he sees my passport. He knows what I am. He knows everything."

"Not everything," the man said, and his eyes went gray, locking on Ulrich. I sensed he wanted something from Ulrich, but he wasn't going to say what. I thought of Tramm the night before, looking for the film. Fucking roll of film. The film was what they wanted. And Ulrich was mute.

Later, after they brought us to the house — again a garage, and we did not see surrounding buildings or streets, but it felt like a house you'd find in a pretty nice neighborhood — they resumed interrogating us. This time they took us one by one into the room in the basement. Without my cane, I had to move from place to place while holding on to the wall. It was all right with me that they never offered to help.

The interrogator was a different man, but again a civilian, a chain smoker. He spoke excellent English, I remember. For part of the time during my session, a woman was also in the room. She would be the one who later brought me and Kit soup, after Ulrich had failed to return.

In this second interview it seemed that the guy was just going through the motions, at least with me. He asked where we stayed in West Berlin, what we did before crossing the sector border, what I thought of Willy Brandt's speech at the Schöneberg rally. I asked him for a cigarette, which he gave me. It was German and tasted rotten, but the hit of nicotine felt great.

He asked me about Ulrich, and when I shrugged and said I didn't know him that well, he did not press me. He seemed not to care about me — and he never mentioned Chase Manhattan Bank. They took Kit after me, and when she came back, she said it was the same with her.

"Except they asked if Ulrich was my boyfriend."

"What did you say?"

"What do you think I said?"

"'Mind your own beeswax,' probably."

"Nope."

"What?"

"I said you are."

"Boy, you sure know how to throw the enemy off. Talk about a 'fur piece.'" She didn't laugh. Had she just made some kind of declaration? Then I had a new thought, and I announced firmly, "Everything I told them was true." As I said this, I cast my eyes first to one corner of the ceiling, then another. I mimed the act of holding a microphone. Kit nodded. With her, this could be a game.

She said, "*Ich auch.* True, all true. I don't think it's smart to lie to them. I really don't." She made a stretching motion with her hands, the fish that got away. Now, in telling this, I wonder why it did not occur to us — if they could be listening, couldn't they be watching?

She drew close to me, to cup my ear with her hands. I felt the warmth of her breath on the side of my face. What I thought of already as her particular aroma — part soap, part tobacco, a hint of musky perfume — floated by my nostrils. When she whispered, the words went into my ear in a succession of puffs. "I didn't want them putting me in a room by myself. I wanted them to know it was okay with me to be in the same room with you. They think I'm a beatnik anyway."

She pulled back. We turned away from each other to look the room over. It was sparsely furnished, with a deal table, four straight-backed chairs, a narrow day bed against a wall. The bed was covered with a gray blanket. A tattered brown bolster made it seem a couch. This was more a servant's quarters than a prisoner's cell.

Kit put her mouth back to my ear. "That woman seemed nice. I told her I can't be alone. She said it didn't matter. She said they might leave us together."

"Good," I whispered. I still assumed Ulrich would show up, after they were finished interrogating him. It would be the three of us. Kit could have the couch, no problem.

She moved to the table and pulled out a chair. She unbelted her khaki tunic and shrugged it off. Her black turtleneck sweater displayed her small breasts. In a normal voice, she said, "The lady told me we'll be here until Monday, when they take us to a judge. The judge is in charge of informing the U.S. government. She said it's our own fault for screwing up on a holiday."

"She said that?" I took a chair, the table between us.

"Not 'screwing up,' but that's the gist. Did they ask you about the yearbook?"

"No. They asked you about that?"

"The club. The yearbook. The whole shebang."

The roll of film? The story Ulrich had made up about club pictures? These were questions I wanted to ask, but knew not to. And then it hit me, the role to play. "God, that's right. What's going to happen when we don't show up at the high school in West Berlin?"

Kit winked. "Nobody actually expects us in Dahlem until tomorrow. And the debate isn't until Monday. Maybe we'll still make it."

"Oh, sure. Just like that. They let us out."

"Resolved: Walter Ulbricht is not such a bad apple after all."

"Jesus, Kit. Why aren't you scared or something?"

"Monty."

"Okay, okay. Resolved: Why do people write novels about incurable diseases?"

She stared at me hard, then, with a shrug, put her reaction aside, whatever it was.

"That's no debating proposition," she said with fake nonchalance. "Not in the form of a question, *Dummkopf.*"

"Why do they?" I pressed. What disease? Who has it? Will he need an iron lung? I wanted to know everything. Her "little novel," my glimpse of it, seemed the key to the mystery of what was pulling us together. Not disease, I hoped. "I want to know."

She rolled her eyes: *With an audience?*

"Really," I said.

She shrugged. *Okay, big guy.* "Because writing is the opposite of banking. That's why you love Rilke, because his letters weren't to a young banker."

"Writing is the opposite of war," I said, warming to it. "Which makes you the rebel, since you're the Army brat."

"Air Force brat. Big difference."

"You *are* a beatnik."

"Thank God my daddy doesn't know where I am. What's your daddy doing about now?"

"My *daddy?*" I laughed.

"Really. I mean, he knows, right? What's he doing about this mess you're in?"

"No idea. Out of his mind, probably."

"Pissed?"

"Trying not to be. He feels guilty when he gets pissed."

"Why the hell would that be? Jesus, Monty, God put daddies on the earth to be pissed off. Being horny and rip-roaring mad — that about covers it with those guys. And beer."

Was she doing this on purpose again, emphasizing what made us different? "My father feels sorry for me. He doesn't think I can handle it when he gets pissed. He doesn't think I can handle a lot of things."

"You do all right."

I grinned at her. A grin entirely forced. "You think so?"

Blood rushed to her face and she looked away from me. She reached for her jacket, fumbled in the pocket for cigarettes, pulled out two, and handed me mine.

"What?" I asked.

She shook her head.

I leaned across the table, close to her, a cloud of smoke between us. I whispered now, but with insistence, "What?"

She looked right at me. "I told the lady you needed me," she said very quietly. "I said you'd lost your cane. I said you needed help. It's not that I meant it. I just didn't want to be alone. That's what popped into my numb skull."

"*Needed* you? Because I can't handle things?"

"That isn't what I meant. You're handling this shit better than I am. That's why I had to lie."

I made an urgent gesture at the ceiling: *Don't say you lied!* And then, whispering, I said to her, "But what a funny lie. I'm not sure what my legs have to do with the mess we're in. Is it that you think at some point we'll have to run?"

"Monty."

I had to look away from her. It was the burning behind my eyes that had me scared.

We sat there smoking, not talking for what seemed a long time. The truth is, I went under, sinking into my impassive shell, into a quite familiar feeling. Often that year, when driving with my father through the tailored, vine-covered hill country of the Rhine, he would say something that would have that effect on me, something completely lacking in malice, like, "You should consider fine arts in college. You have the sensitivity for it."

And I would choke on words I was unable to utter: *Sensitivity? Since when is that something to put on your résumé? Since when is that a virtue?* Virtue, I would think then, from the Latin, meaning manly.

Art begins in a wound, the novelist John Gardner would tell us years later. And wound was what I would hear in my father's use of the word "art," which would sink me every bit as much as the damn torpedo had sunk him. Not business. Not science. Not premed. Nothing requiring toughness. Fine arts — what, like watercolors? Me in a smock and beret. All I wanted, when my father looked at me, was that he not see woundedness.

And now, Kit too?

Out of the silence, she said, "He's probably like that because of your mama."

Mama. How my mother would have laughed to have that word applied to her. But what Kit said wasn't true. My father had been like that with me ever since I could remember. Kit was just trying to change the subject. So I let her. "I have a picture of my mom," I said, reaching for my wallet. But the police had my wallet. Police, *Vopos,* whatever they were.

In addition to everything else — my passport, my military ID, my fifty bucks, my driver's license — the police had my mother's picture. It showed her at the helm of our Lightning, the *Desperate Lark,* the wind feathering her dark hair. I'd taken the photo myself one summer day just as we were approaching the starting line of a race at the lake. I was her crew, and I'd been counting down the seconds to the gun even as I clicked the camera. I caught in her face that determination to prevail at all costs. Only now do I realize why that expression should have been so precious to me: it was to her determination to prevail on my behalf that I owed everything.

"Well, I *used* to have a picture of my mom. Speaking of pictures."

But of course we had just been careful *not* to speak of pictures. *Jesus.*

"Where's Rick?" Kit asked suddenly. "He should be here by now. They didn't take this long with you or me."

I did not know what to say. My intuition told me Ulrich was in real trouble. Between his stepfather and his being German born and his unpredictable attitude, anything could have happened. Especially since I wasn't with him. I sensed even then how Ulrich had come to depend on my inbuilt prudence as a check on his craziest impulses. It was, from his side, why we were friends. I was drawn to him because he had everything I lacked, those crazy impulses certainly, but also his exotic masculinity and overt rebelliousness. Not to mention a beautiful mother who was alive.

My worry matched Kit's. Without me, would Ulrich be at the mercy of the thing that made him strange? But what good had I been to him the night before, when he had so stupidly let his guard down with Tramm?

The night before I had not worried about Ulrich because, let's face it, I had been preoccupied with Kit. I was alone with her again, but it was different now because the dangerous game was under way, and Ulrich, far more than the two of us, seemed ready to get hurt. The point being — this was no game.

The room's one window — it showed nothing but a cement wall, and sky above — had gone completely black in the time we had been together there. We were sitting in shadows.

I stood and crossed to the door for the wall switch, snapped it. Harsh light from a cheap plastic ceiling fixture washed the room, turning the windowpanes into a set of ebony mirrors. I glanced at Kit, who grimaced. It was far too stark, like both the interrogation rooms we had seen that day, and so I flicked the switch off and returned to the table.

In the darkness we sat in silence, watching the glowing tips of our successive cigarettes. Now and then we heard a mournful train whistle. I had forgotten that the hands of my wristwatch glowed in the dark. We had been in custody for nearly eight hours, in that house near the railroad tracks for three. Ulrich had been gone for almost two.

It was more than an hour later when we heard a key turn in the door lock. The *Hausfrau* turned on the light and entered with a tray of bread and soup. It was then, in response to Kit's question in German, that the woman said that Ulrich would be spending the night in another room of the house, that he was fine, that we should not worry.

Though I could not quite follow what she was saying, I sensed that it mattered to her that we not be upset, and when Kit had translated the woman's words, I really wanted to believe her. She was heavyset and not that old, and her most prominent feature was a dark mustache, which made me feel sorry for her. Which made us even, I guess.

An hour after that, a key turned in the lock again. Kit and I were still seated opposite each other at the table, a saucer full of cigarette butts between us. When the woman opened the door, I stood, bracing myself on the chair. This time she did not turn on the light. She was dragging something into the room. By its shape I recognized a rolled-up mattress with a bundled blanket and pillow.

I drew myself up and said, just as I had rehearsed it in my mind for an hour, "We demand to have our friend with us."

The woman looked at me uncomprehendingly. Despite myself, I softened at once. "*Bitte schön*," I said. "*Freund, bitte.*"

Sadness suddenly came into her expression. She let the bedding fall like a corpse at my feet. "*Für Sie*," she said to me, and then she nodded at Kit. There.

Kit said, "*Dankeschön.*"

The woman returned to the threshold. Light poured in from the hallway. She turned to look at us with what I took to be a grandmotherly concern. Years later, I would recall the potent, needy connection I felt with her at that moment — my version of Stockholm syndrome.

She seemed about to say something personal. Instead, she nodded brusquely and, with curt gestures, indicated the WC down the hall. It was her job now to supervise our last trip to the bathroom before locking the door again.

Kit got up and left the room. The woman, following her, disappeared.

All at once, it felt like a replay of the night before, as if Kit and I were an old married couple with our routine. I spread the mattress on the floor against the wall across the room from the day bed. The table would be between us. With more difficulty than I would have wanted witnessed, I arranged the blanket and pillow on the mattress. Then I straightened myself again and took hold of the back of my chair. Now what?

The room seemed desolate without Kit, and for a moment I feared that she, too, would simply not return. Betrayed first by Tramm, then by the *Hausfrau*.

I tried to squelch that worry with an assertion of calm, like stifling nausea, mind over matter again. And perhaps I had some perverse need to establish, if only for myself, that despite Kit's claim to the *Hausfrau,* I did not need her. But I did — and knew it. She wasn't coming back. She wasn't.

I channeled my growing panic into agitated busyness. I squared up my mattress and arranged the blanket again. I hung my blazer on the back of a chair. I unbuttoned my sleeves and rolled them up. As I went through these motions of delay, I was acutely aware of the difference between this night and the night before. There was no question now, for example, of undressing. No lowering of my trousers, unstrapping my leg braces — none of that, thank God. When Kit and I had taken our swim in the unearned intimacy of the "female bachelors" room of the union hostel, we had done so in a spirit of adventure. Now there was no pretending, after boozy jazz and a soft rain in moonlight, that we were a young couple embarked on the old journey. No softness here, no jazz. We were in goddamn awful trouble.

Kit returned.

She went directly to the day bed and sat down, looking at me. I stared at her stupidly before I realized she was waiting for me to leave. I went out, and with the *Hausfrau* behind me, found the WC down the hall. By the time I returned, Kit was under the blanket on the bed.

I looked back at the German matron, but, as if she had spent her day's quotient of empathy, she refused to meet my eyes. Slowly she closed the door, restoring the room's darkness and sealing it with the click of the lock. I made my way to my end of the room, found a chair, and sat.

From the day bed, Kit said, "Jesus H. Christ, Monty." Her voice was thick with anxiety.

"I know," I said. "Me too. And the H means hell. Where the hell is Rick?" I called him Rick, thinking of the snoops who would be listening in on us. We had to emphasize his being American.

"I'm scared," she said. "I'm really scared."

"They wouldn't hurt him, Kit. They wouldn't dare. An American? A general's son?" I could say that, couldn't I?

"People just disappear, Monty. This is the Iron Curtain we're across."

My thought was, Maybe *we've* disappeared. But saying that would have made it seem true. I said, "I feel like we've let him down."

"What can we do? We're just hanging on ourselves here."

"They want us to feel like he's on his own, you know? As if we're not in this with him."

"But we are."

"Right. Rick's being okay is why I came to Berlin."

"Me too."

"That and the debating club." I laughed quietly, and was relieved to hear her laughing, too. But then I thought, Fuck it, they never believed that debating shit.

And speaking of lies, she had told them I was her boyfriend, which brought me back to my very first question. "About Rick," I said.

"What?"

"You didn't tell me what happened between you two."

A long silence. Then she said, "How can we talk about stuff with Big Brother listening?"

"Just talk, Kit. They only care about things we have nothing to do with. Talking about *our* stuff makes the point."

"So what about him?"

"You tell me."

"Have you seen that hole in his wall?" Kit asked.

"What, in his bedroom at Lindsay?" So she'd been in his bedroom. "Yes, I've seen it."

"I was in there when he did it, Monty. He punched that hole in the wall with his fist. It scared me."

"He has a temper. So do I."

She laughed. "Not like Rick you don't. You're a gentle guy, Monty. You give off gentle vibrations, it's the thing about you. Don't you know that?"

I sensed her flowing my way, but could not imagine how to meet her. "Rick," I said. "Rick is dealing with a lot of shit, Kit. You know that. His stepfather —" I stopped myself, another deflection. *Not his stepfather. Do not talk about his stepfather.*

"And his *real* father," Kit said.

"What do you know about that?"

"Nothing. But he had a German father first, right? And when you think about what sets Rick off — the Eichmann trial, a Jewish university, that Jewish radical . . ."

"Marcuse."

"He's a Jew, right? So maybe, who the hell knows, Rick's real father, you know . . ."

"Killed Jews?"

"Have you ever noticed that about the Germans we meet? How none of them ever knew about the concentration camps. Do you believe that?"

"So you think Rick's problem . . . ?"

"Is with his real father. Why the big secret about the guy? Rick's mother won't even talk about him. It makes Rick crazy. *Vergangenheitsbewältigung* — have you heard that word?"

"That's not a word. It's a paragraph."

"'Coming to grips with the past.' It's what they say about the Eichmann trial. Rick said it about himself that day when he hit the wall with his fist."

"And it scared you."

She did not answer me.

"The sins of the father," I said.

"And the stepfather," Kit said, her voice barely above a whisper. "Rick feels guilty because of both of them. Death camps *and* Dresden."

"But that's crazy. Am I guilty if my father forecloses on widows?"

"Yeah, right. In Frankfurt, capital of the *Wirtschaftswunder*, mortgages for widows, sure."

"And you're guilty if your daddy . . . Kit, what wicked things does Sergeant Carson do in a Mohammedan country? Make moonshine?"

Even in the dark, I sensed how my question opened into a room she didn't want to enter. Again she said nothing. Her great white father.

I veered. This was like sailing. "It's the point of being young, isn't it? That we get to start over?"

"The past is never dead, big guy," she said, recovering. "It isn't even past."

"Who says?"

"Billy Bob Faulkner. William to you. My daddy would kill me if he knew what Faulkner's books say."

"About colored people?"

"For one. And about how Eupheus Hines beats his old lady purple. 'Universal bones,' Monty. 'Universal bones.' That's what Faulkner calls it. The cruelty in folks. Incurable cruelty. Specially men."

The word hung in the shadowy space between us: incurable.

"I thought it was your mother who was incurable," I said. "I thought it was her disease you were writing about."

"You *did* read my damn book, didn't you?"

"One paragraph."

"Some paragraph. I'll tell you what my mother's disease is — it's my father, *his* incurable cruelty."

"That's why the blood in the van got to you. You've seen blood like that before."

"In the kitchen. In the bathroom. On the porch. Always on my mama."

"I thought you said she was his Dixie Cup."

"And what do you do with a Dixie Cup when the ice cream is gone? You crush it with one hand. Haven't you seen that?"

"Yes."

"Haven't you done it?"

I had. The sweet sensation of the wax container crumpled around its wooden spoon. I could not say so, gentle me.

"And with the other hand," she went on, "you punch a hole in the wall. We've had fist holes in the wall in every house I've ever lived in."

"Did you explain that to Rick?"

"No."

"But it's why?" Why she wasn't his girlfriend anymore.

"Yes."

"Because of your old man."

"I get scared. I can't help it. Not of Rick. Just of, like, what I'm feeling, which isn't Rick's fault. He would never take his problem out on me, I know that. I love the guy. But he's too intense."

"Like at the border, when he tried to fight them. Jesus. When he trusted Tramm."

"You blame Rick for that?"

"Not *blame*. How could I blame him? Whatever happens next, Kit, and however much the past — I don't know — all of that is off the table as far as I'm concerned, because this is already the best damn thing I've ever done."

She took that in. Then she said, quietly again, "I could never talk to him like this."

"About your secrets?"

"Which ones?"

"That your father hits you?"

Silence.

"Right?" I pressed.

She said, "I've never told that to anyone. How did you know?"

"It's what your book is about. The feeling you're scared of."

"Whoa, what is this, ESP?"

"Writing about it as a way of saying it will never happen again."

Kit laughed. "If my daddy was here tonight, he'd have his strap out."

"Because you're behind the Iron Curtain?"

"Because it's like midnight or two A.M. or something and I'm in bed in a room with a boy."

I laughed. "A boy *across* the room, a boy in a chair. And anyway, your daddy wouldn't mind it being me." Not intense enough. Intense emotion — what was that line?

Kit said, "I don't know about that, him being able to read my mind and all."

"Meaning?"

"He'd know I'd be wanting y'all to come on over here."

"Us all?"

"Or do I have to come on over there?"

"No," I said. "No, you don't." But I did not move. She remained where she was, waiting. And I — I waited, too.

We remained there in the silent dark, apart from each other for a long time. At last, I knew I had to move or speak. Still, I could do neither. What was given me then were a few lines I had sometimes recited to myself while drifting into sleep but had never said aloud. I said them now.

> "I am not yet wise in grief —
> so this great darkness makes me small.
> But if it's you . . ."

I stopped. Always before, "you" had been my mother. But no more.

> ". . . make yourself fierce, break in."

"Like this?" she said, startling me with a touch on my shoulder. She had crossed to me without a sound. I could hardly make out her form. She took my hand and gestured me to my feet. Not speaking, she began to unbutton my shirt.

When I was bare-chested, I opened my arms. Like that, she was inside my embrace. To my amazement, her own skin was naked against mine, the pressure of her breasts against my chest, the fleshy firmness of her nipples.

"Jesus, Kit," I said. I started to pull away, but she held me.

239

"Make yourself fierce, you said."

"That was Rilke."

"It was nice."

When I lowered my face to hers, her mouth was ready. She wasn't the first girl I had kissed, or the second, but she might have been the third. I knew nothing.

We kissed again, then simply held each other. The skin on my chest had never seemed more sensitive.

I whispered, "I've never been naked with anyone."

"We aren't actually naked yet."

She was wearing underpants. When she pulled back now, it was to get at my belt buckle. My belt, in her father's hands, would be a strap.

I let her unfasten my trousers, aware of it as she brushed against my erection. She pushed my trousers down, and I sat in the chair as she began to pull them off. I stopped her. "My shoes," I said. "My braces."

She knelt and began to untie my ugly orthopedic shoes. I let her do this because I knew that when my legs were exposed, she would not be able to see them in the dark. I leaned forward to release the leather fasteners of my braces. Very quickly then, my shoes, braces, and trousers were off, and Kit once more drew me up to stand with her, both of us naked except for underpants.

Taking my weight, she led me to her bed. We lay together on top of the blanket, on our sides, facing each other. I kept my legs back, away from her. We mirrored each other, her face an inch or two from mine. I could not read what was in her eyes. We kissed. I touched one breast, brushing it lightly with the back of my hand, so tentatively.

"Bee stings," she said.

"What?"

"They're so small."

"They're beautiful."

"Compared to what?"

I laughed. "To what I've only imagined."

"And this isn't even daylight."

"Which is just as well," I said.

She moved closer to me, pressing the length of her body against mine, taking my erection against herself. I moved back against the wall.

240

"What?" she asked.

"This is good, Kit. Just being with you like this."

"Is enough?"

"Yes."

She pushed close to me again. She put her mouth on mine, her tongue alive in a new way. I found her breast with my hand. My other hand went around her, to her ass, pulling her to me. But matching my arousal was a mounting inhibition, which came to me as a question: Why is she doing this?

I pulled back. "Why?" I asked. "Why are you?"

"Because I just love contact sports. And this is one *you* can play."

"Oh," I said with a bitterness that surprised even me.

"Legs are not what counts in bed, big guy."

"Who's talking about legs?"

"All right. Let's talk about something else. What about grief? 'Wise in grief,' you said."

"Rilke said. And what he said was 'not yet.' "

"But it's true. It's true of you. You *are* wise in grief already. It makes you kind and caring, and you know things nobody ever told you because it's true, you *are* wise, that's exactly what you are. I've never met a boy like you."

"You feel sorry for me."

She went rigid. "Oh, Christ."

"I mean you —"

She pulled away. "Jesus H. Christ, Monty. I'm not the visiting nurse, you know."

"Nurse? Why do you say nurse?"

"Oh, come off it, big guy. You told me to get fierce. It so happens that turns out to be easy for me — with you. I like you!"

"I forgot. I'm your boyfriend."

She sat up. "What is your problem?"

"I just don't want you —" I was flat against the wall, pressing into it.

"I don't, Monty. Okay? Feel sorry. That's what you're worried about, right? If I feel sorry for anybody, it's myself. Stuck in Berlin with a *pair* of sawdust Casanovas."

"Casanova. New house. Ulrich."

"Rick isn't here, though. Not now. Can't we leave him out of this — you and me?"

"You brought him up."

"You, Monty. It's *you* I'm with. It's you I want to be with."

"Because of my grief."

"Which *you* brought up." I sensed her deciding to say what she was thinking. Then she did. "You know, Michael, you really ought to get over it."

"What do you mean?"

"About your legs."

"Get over it?"

"Your legs are only a problem if you let them be. We *all* have things we would change, Monty. About where we come from. About who we are. About our bodies. Look at me and my small boobs."

"Your breasts are great. I love your breasts."

"You can call them boobs, Monty, now that you've met."

"They rise up out of your ribs like mounds of life itself."

"Tits, Monty. And too small. Cut the crap."

"They're perfect."

"Unlike your legs, you mean?"

"I never discussed my legs. Not with anyone."

"That's not true. You discussed them with your mama."

"Not discussed, exactly."

"But she knew. You let her see what you felt. It wasn't that she was magic, Monty. No miracle worker. If she knew about your legs, it was because you let her know. What you had going with your mama was something you did for yourself, as much as her doing it."

"Why are you saying this?"

"Because you can do it again. You can do it with me."

"I'm working on it," I said.

"Me too, Monty. I wasn't kidding about my boobs. It ain't polio, but it still bugs me. If your mama was here, wouldn't she tell us both to get over it?"

"Yes."

"Well, then." Kit leaned forward and pulled the blanket away from my legs. Her nakedness hit me again, and I had an erection again.

"Let me look," she said. Then added, "Mother, may I?"

242

"It's dark."

With that she got up and went over to my pants. She came back with my Zippo and flicked it. She sat next to me and held the flame before our faces, so that I would look at her. She was entirely in earnest, knowing this could not be a game with me. In the light, I saw how small her breasts really were, but I was right. They were beautiful.

"So, may I?" she asked.

"Yes."

I watched her, a silhouette moving down the length of my body, the lighter flame making a halo at her burnished face. She ignored the bulge in my underpants and moved the flame to my legs — my real private parts. First she examined the smooth skin of my left thigh, the bony protrusion of my knee, and then, moving slowly, the gnarled flesh below my knee, the web of purple veins, white scars, red welts, the uneven ridge of my shin bone — the most familiar terrain I knew. It silenced me to watch someone else explore it.

Unfamiliar, impossible to keep on the margin of my concentration, were her breasts, each flowing forward around its nipple as she bent over me. Each was shaped to fill a champagne glass. Breasts, I thought. I could never call them boobs, tits, knockers — crudities that had never seemed, despite Kit's ease with them, more profane to me.

I reached to touch her, setting my fingers at play, lightly, in her hair.

I studied the shape of her long, thin neck — Nefertiti, Audrey Hepburn, a swan. I watched the flickering glow of the Zippo flame as it washed back onto her face. A diamond of light danced in the green cone of the one eye I could see. Her expression, a tender curiosity, reminded me of a certain nurse who had, one summer, regularly changed the dressings on that leg, but she had always exclaimed, as the pasty skin appeared from under the peeled-back bandage, "Oh, good! It looks good!" She had said that even when I knew that that part of me looked dead, ready to be burned. *Oh, dead! It looks dead!*

Would Kit say "good" when it wasn't good? No. Kit was looking at my leg not with medical detachment but with the interest of a patient examining her own leg, trying to find the spot that had been hurting her.

But then, for an instant, I was afraid she would do something equally sentimental as saying "good," something condescending — like kiss me there on my bitter flesh, touch me on the sharp edge of my bone.

She did no such thing. Yet in examining me, her face was close enough to my leg that I could sense her warm breath on my ever sensitive scars.

Looking back, I know what I could not have known then, that it was indeed the moment, as she'd said, of my getting over it. My legs would still be ugly, a permanent curse, a disability. But never again, not for one second, would I ever wonder if they defined me.

She closed the cover of the Zippo with that hollow snap, and for an instant, without the light, she disappeared. But she came back, bringing her face to mine, drawing the blanket forward as she did, covering us, clothing our nakedness. She put her mouth by my ear and whispered, "Knock, knock."

"Who's there?"

"I love you, Michael."

The surprise was that I was not surprised.

I touched her cheekbone without seeing it because her face remained close to my ear. "I love you, Katharine."

And then silence for a long time, a deep, consoling silence in which I listened to her breathing.

After a while, I freed my right arm from the blanket and reached to her. My hand found her cheek, and with the back of my fingers, I rubbed it softly. To my amazement, her cheek was wet. "You're crying?"

"Not with sadness. With feelings. Lots of feelings."

"Intense emotion."

"You betcha. All of them."

"You're okay now, Kit. We're taking care of each other."

"You sure are taking care of me, Monty. I'd be cooked by now without you."

"'Then your great transforming will happen to me,'" I recited, completing Rilke's stanza, "'and my great grief cry will happen to you.'"

"It just did," she said softly.

244

I let my hand caress the back of her neck, and without consciously deciding to, I gently drew her head to mine. We lay together like that in silence, her face nestled between my cheek and shoulder. Later, I would wonder what this embrace, this whole encounter, had to do with sex, but not then. Knowledge, carnal knowledge — not the same thing. The naked intimacy was all we wanted, all we needed. And it turned out to be as true of her, despite her sexy moves, as of me.

I felt the moisture of Kit's tears puddling at my clavicle. Despite her "big guy" breeziness, she was weeping again. *Incurable.* She continued to do so, almost soundlessly, until she drifted into sleep.

13

B Y THE TIME the *Hausfrau's* key turned in the lock the next
morning, Kit and I were dressed and sitting on our separate
sides of the room. Kit wore her black turtleneck under her
father's jacket. I was safely buttoned into my blazer and tie. The
Hausfrau wore the same brown sweater over a shapeless dress and
the same sturdy shoes. Now she smelled of cooked cabbage, which
seemed odd so early in the morning.

But what time was it? Daylight was filtering in through the cloudy
high window, and my watch said eight o'clock, but the dependable flow of minutes and hours had been interrupted. I could not
trust the clear signs that it was morning. If the woman had said
"*Guten Abend*," I would not have been surprised. In fact, she said
nothing.

And if she had conveyed a hint of sympathy the day before, today
she seemed only irritated. She stood in the threshold staring at us, a
thick pillar of disapproval. Did she assume we had betrayed her laxity
by huddling together under the one blanket? Would she believe that
our intimacy had been, if not chaste, not sexual? But why would she
care? The woman was no nun. And what were Communist morals in
any case? Had she been privy to our time together, she would have
laughed at us pregenital puppies, wildly short of understanding who,
overnight, we had become.

Without having planned to, I blurted, "Where is our friend?
Wo ist — ?"

Kit finished my question, "*Unser Freund?*"

The woman looked blankly at me, then at Kit, who spoke several sentences in German. Except for the word "American," I missed it. When the woman still did not reply, Kit said to me, "I told her we demand to see the American ambassador."

"Consul general," I said. "In Berlin, it's the consul general."

Kit mouthed the word "asshole" at me, and I felt stupid and crushed. She grabbed her bag and went to the door, having understood ahead of me that our mute matron was waiting for us to go down the hall to the WC.

While Kit was gone, I made one more stab at learning something. *"Unser Freund, sie gemütlich, ja?"*

Her dismissive look made it clear that I had used a word wrong, but she knew what I was asking, and she still did not answer. I tacked, spoke in English, unable to believe that she really could not speak it. "Ulrich's father is an important American. You should tell your bosses that. You shouldn't be messing around with that kid. You'll be sorry." Even I nearly laughed at my thin threat, a boy reduced to the intimidation of the playground.

By the time, after Kit, I returned from the bathroom, she was wearing her bandana neckerchief, a small stylish touch. I wanted to wink at her, a bit of style myself, but she would not look at me.

A simple breakfast of warm milk and toast had been set on the table, and we ate it greedily. Then the woman took the dishes away, and once more locked the door behind her when she left.

The absence of visible guards made me wonder if we had made a mistake in not trying to escape. Then the image of a broad, roughly plowed field crossed my mind, as if the house beyond the cement wall were surrounded by farmland — the picture of a hobbling boy in a blazer, the girl having to waiting for him, dogs giving chase, gunfire, helicopters, tanks. Then what? Kit finds a branch for me to use as a cane? Kit risks her own survival to hang back, lending me her shoulder?

I looked at her. Though we were alone now, she still refused to meet my eyes. No one had ever warned me about the morning-after *tristesse* of lovers, even lovers who stopped short. But here it was. She sat facing away from me, immobile, as if there were something in the wallpaper to decipher. *Knock, knock — no one home.*

All at once I began to feel afraid again, really afraid. Afraid of what had happened to Ulrich; of what would happen to us; of my father, how pissed off he'd be; of Kit's father, how he would hit her. Then I realized that her version of fear like this was what had taken Kit away from me. There was no speaking of it. There was only sitting there, an ocean of anxiety in us and between us.

An hour, perhaps two, elapsed after the key had turned in the lock, but when the lock clicked again and the door opened, it was not the *Hausfrau* but two green-uniformed *Vopos*. At their brusque order, we gathered up our things. They ushered us out of the room and down the dim corridor. As I steadied myself against the wall, one of the *Vopos* poked me to hurry me along, prompting Kit to snap at him in German. "It's okay," I said, loping. I smiled at her, hoping for a smile in return, but not getting it.

With one *Vopo* leading and one trailing, we went through a door and down the creaking wooden stairs we had ascended the day before. We found ourselves in the same basement garage, the chilly stench of it. A windowless van like the one that had brought us there sat waiting.

When I followed Kit into the van, I heard her yelp of pleasure before seeing what prompted it. Ulrich was there, huddling in the far corner, his knees drawn up into his arms. Kit went right to him, stooping to put her arms around him. I wasn't jealous at all — I loved Ulrich, too.

He sat with what for him was an extraordinary impassivity, accepting Kit's embrace but not returning it. Otherwise, he seemed all right, no signs that he had been beaten again. When the guards slammed the van door shut behind us, we were plunged into darkness. Like before.

I pulled my lighter out, made its flame our center.

"Where the hell have you been?" Ulrich said, and I was relieved to see him grinning.

"Were you in this house here?" I asked.

He shook his head. "Someplace else, I think. I've been in here for an hour at least, and they've been driving. But they could be fooling us."

"Are you okay?"

He nodded.

The van lurched as the engine started, and we bounced against one another when it began to move. Kit was still holding on to Ulrich. The noise of the motor vibrating through the sheet metal made it seem safe to talk. I snapped my lighter shut, as if darkness would guarantee our privacy. I leaned closer to Ulrich. "Did they interrogate you?" I whispered.

"For a long time. Through most of the night."

"About what? We've got to get our stories straight. They didn't ask us about hardly anything."

"The yearbook. Did they ask you about the yearbook?"

"Yes," Kit said. "But we stayed with the story."

"The film, Ulrich," I whispered. "What the hell happened to the film? That's what they want."

"And what is it, anyway?" Kit asked.

"Do not do this to me," Ulrich pleaded. The anguish in his voice was more pointed for coming in the darkness. "You are asking me like they asked me."

"But we only have a few minutes here," I pressed. The fear was swooping in again. "You fucking *have* to tell us what is going on."

"I do not know!"

"Monty," Kit said, and I felt her hand on my shoulder. I sensed that she had a hand on each of us.

I said, "In a few minutes we're going to be separated again, probably in front of that magistrate, and each of us won't know what the others are saying. Come on, guys."

"Not the magistrate," Ulrich said. "It is Sunday."

"Jesus Christ, Ulrich," I said, "they're Communists. They don't care about the Lord's day."

Ulrich pushed back against my agitation by replying with dead calm, "The magistrate is tomorrow. They are taking us somewhere else today. They have until tomorrow to do what they want with us."

"Do they know who your father is?"

"My stepfather, Monty. My fucking stepfather."

"Oh, fuck you, Ulrich, with that crap. Father, stepfather, you know what I mean."

"Nevertheless, the distinction is not unimportant."

And then, like that, a new question came to me: What about his actual father — was he in this too, somehow? But I didn't know how to ask.

Kit squeezed my arm, which I took as a signal that she and I were together. Yes, in a way we *were* interrogating him.

"Well, either way," I said, "do they know? That's what I'm asking you. Do they know?"

"Of course! *Natürlich!*"

"Then that's why the yearbook doesn't fool them. I saw Tramm going through your bag for the roll of film. The film is why Tramm set this whole thing up."

"Did you give it to them?" Kit asked.

"I do not have it," Ulrich answered. "I do not know what you are talking about."

"Hey, Rick," I said. "It's us. Kit and Monty. Jesus, man."

"I have no film. I do not know about film."

Despite its dullness, there was a desperate edge in Ulrich's voice that doubled my alarm, a hint of how little I knew of what he'd gone through — not just last night, but over the years.

Kit was still pressing my arm. She said quietly, soothingly, "Okay, Rick. Good enough. But we have to keep our story straight. If there's no film, why is there a yearbook? Why are we the debating club? Maybe we should just go back to the truth. May Day. The Red Army parade. Marcuse."

"It is making me crazy not to be able to see you. Who else is in here?"

"No one. Just us," I said. I lit my lighter again.

Now, when the golden circle of light brought us alive to one another again, I was shocked to see Ulrich's face wet with tears. There had been no such emotion in his voice — which seemed impossible. I clasped him by the back of the neck. "Hey, comrade, you're okay. In fact, you're better than okay. You are great. You are doing great!"

"This is all my foolishness. This is completely my unforgivable foolishness. And I do not know what they are doing" — Ulrich looked up and locked his eyes on mine — "with you. I told them to let you go. This has nothing to do with you." He faced Kit. "Or you."

"Or you, either," Kit said. "You haven't done anything, Rick. Don't let them make you think you've done something."

250

As if that was what had happened to him, Ulrich lowered his face into his hands, muffling words that I heard as "I am afraid." His head and shoulders began to shake with sobbing. How far he was from my cocky tutor, berating me, his mulish pupil, with the slogans of a pop radical. Where was the power of negative thinking now?

As I watched him, I felt a deep pity, and also an embarrassment that was new to me. The word that sprang to mind — a word very much of the era — was "brainwashed." They had done something awful to our friend.

As if to protect Ulrich's dignity, Kit touched my arm, indicating I should put out the Zippo, which I did. Whatever else, immediate and remote, prompted Ulrich's distress, the truth is that he was giving vent to what all three of us were feeling. But Ulrich had not been consoled as I had been last night by Kit. I'm not sure where I stood with her just now, but I had experienced the consummation that matters most. I could not remember what Marcuse had said about sex and revolution, but I knew he was right, whatever it was.

In the unsteady darkness, Kit and I balanced against the jolting of the van by leaning together, but our leaning was over Ulrich, to hold him. I was aware of the physical feel of each of them, but differently. My left hand reached around Kit's ribs, the tips of my fingers extending just to the wire of her bra at the rise of her left breast. Her right hand was on my left thigh, above the wasteland of my lower leg, no secret from her.

"It's okay, comrade," I said again.

"Don't call me comrade," he hissed.

"All I mean is, we're with you all the way. Honest to God."

This was as solemn a promise as I had ever made. Indeed, that I pronounced it as "we," certain that I was speaking also for Kit, moved the statement, more than its rote evoking of the deity, from mere promise to vow. We three slumped together then in silence, a desperate trio in the corner of the lurching vehicle.

Minutes later — or was it an hour? — the van seemed to jump a curb. Then it went steeply downhill, tossing us, brakes pumping, snapping us alert. We must have been going down a ramp.

The van halted abruptly. Seconds later the door was pulled open.

The dim light of a large garage filled the metal cubicle. I glanced at my comrades. Ulrich was wiping his nose with his sleeve, stifling his emotion. Kit was rubbing her eyes against the light.

Guards in uniforms unlike any we had seen before stood at the ready by the open door. They carried machine guns, and one of them, as he ordered us out, used his as a pointer. Kit was the first to climb down. I was amazed by her apparent self-possession, as if she knew what was coming and knew we were up to it. The girl who was afraid to be alone was, in her chosen company, indomitable.

With a dancer's grace, she reached back to me — less an offer of help than an act of choreography. It was the most natural thing in the world to take her hand, then to lean on her. As I clumsily hoisted my-self out of the van, of course, the illusion of fluid movement broke. Then we both turned to watch Ulrich climb down behind us — he sullenly refused help — and Kit held my hand until one of the guards struck my arm with the stock of his gun.

Instead of the baggy green serge of the *Vopos,* whose uniforms came from the quartermaster's pile, these guards wore tailored and crisply pressed gray tunics and fitted trousers falling neatly over pol-ished black boots. Their black helmets shone. On their shoulders rode golden epaulettes. At their belts were chromed bayonet sheaths. They ordered us to move. We followed one into an ill-lit corridor while the other came behind.

The soldiers wore steel taps on the heels of their boots, causing the click of each footfall to echo with a sinister lack of synchrony. At a succession of heavy doors, we banged through. At each threshold, the decor of the linked hallways improved, from unpainted cement block to block painted gray; from painted block to walls surfaced with a mustardy stucco; from naked bulbs hanging by cords to ceiling fixtures fashioned, saucer-like, of pressed tin. Finally we halted in an almost handsome, wood-paneled vestibule before an elevator cage featuring cast-iron florets and brass fittings. The gate slid open, and we went in.

The elevator operator wore a dark blue smock and a felt cap with a bill — decidedly civilian, proudly proletarian. He closed the gate, leaving the two guards outside. He tended to his throttle with his back to us. As the elevator ascended through the grilled shaft in the gyre of a winding staircase that showed vestiges of opulence — a brass banister, crystal wall sconces, however dull — I caught Kit's eye and whispered, "Not a jail. Not a police station. Too fancy."

"*Sei still!*" the elevator operator said, half delighting in his interlude of authority, although not daring to look back at us. He reminded me of Charlie Chaplin or Stan Laurel.

I nudged Ulrich. He would be the one savvy enough to guess where they had brought us. When he looked at me, I mouthed, "On Sunday? Court? Questioning? What?"

He let his eyes drift to the slowly moving needle indicator above the gate, a gauge showing that the building had five floors including the basement, where we started. When the needle approached 2, the operator dropped his throttle and the car slowed with a hiss, softly bounced a couple of times, then stopped. The machinery sighed. With a pronounced dip of his right shoulder, the operator pulled the gate open. A man in a black suit, white shirt, and black tie stood there waiting for us. He looked like a mortician.

He wore heavy black-framed glasses that drew attention to the unhealthy pallor of his bony face. Not only the frames were thick; so were the lenses, which magnified his eyes out of proportion with the rest of his face — a man of several disjunctions. He said nothing, just gestured with one hand, a simple movement that revealed him as someone accustomed to being obeyed.

We went across a small lobby, through a door, and out into a broad, vacant corridor. It was illuminated by one dim ceiling fixture, but the hallway proper was a shadowy tunnel that went on and on into darkness. To the left, only a few dozen feet away, the corridor ended not in a wall but in a hung tapestry toward which our escort directed us.

The tapestry showed a medieval hunting scene — a wounded deer, a huntsman in breeches, dogs with blood dripping from their muzzles. As we approached, I smelled something acrid, as if the tapestry had recently been rescued from a burning building. Before we drew nearer to it, the man in black led us through a door into a narrower hallway.

As in the basement corridor, I moved with one hand skimming along the wall, my leg braces clicking, and the other hand gripping Ulrich's arm. Despite the clamp he'd fixed on his emotions, he still seemed disoriented. He was nevertheless all the support I needed just then — Ulrich and Kit, all the support I would ever need.

Ironically, it was because he had proved to be less than stalwart, once we were arrested, that I began thinking of him as a true friend, a guy like me. His presence at my side, his firm arm under my grip, was helping me — and I knew I was helping him. His need was calling from me a strength I did not know I had.

When the next door opened ahead of us, showing a small room crowded with furniture, Ulrich brought his free hand to my forearm and pressed it. *Friends, friends forever!*

When I looked at him, he nodded. I mouthed "comrade" at him, the word he'd swatted away, but now he grinned.

A conference room. Its wood-paneled walls, long table, and leather-backed chairs gave it the air of a place where important meetings were held — unlike the crude interrogation cells we'd seen earlier. The room had a large Palladian window looking out onto a grassy courtyard awash in the light of midday. Across the grass was another wing of the same building, huge. We were in some kind of old palace.

The man in the black suit had said nothing up to this point, and now he only gestured toward the table, indicating chairs for us on the near side. Four other chairs stood opposite. Once we were seated, the man exited the way we had entered, closing the door behind him. A second closed door broke the wall on the other side of the table.

I leaned toward Ulrich, but his hand shot up, stopping me from speaking. He cast his eyes to the ceiling: *How can you keep forgetting?* They were always listening. I looked at Kit, thinking that they had even listened to us the night before. She had her left fist inside the cup of her right hand on the table in front of her. She was staring at her hands, a way of not looking at me.

I turned back to Ulrich. "*Edelweiss,*" I said, touching him. Who cared if they heard us?

"*Piraten,*" he answered. We were like chums in a clubhouse, checking the secret password — an association all three of us must have had, because we burst into laughter.

I took out my cigarettes and offered them around. My friends each took one, then I did. We smoked in silence, letting the nicotine work its magic on us, the potent rush followed by the chemical ebbing, which we mistook for calm. When Kit blew a smoke ring, it hung in the air before us. I tried to match it, imagining that my ring could go through hers. But I choked on the smoke, which made us laugh again. Some pirate.

Then we were quiet, still, each of us holed up inside. Okay, I thought, imagine something good.

The U.S. consul general. Ulrich's stepfather. The Marines. An intervention, after all. The cavalry. Rescue. Free.

What else would explain their bringing us here on Sunday? I warmed to the argument, a debate-team captain after all: What else would explain the disappearance of our guards? The reunion with Ulrich? The posh surroundings? The resentful withdrawal of the mean-spirited man in black? The only answer to every question: the Americans have come for us.

*

14

WHEN THE DOOR opposite, across the table, opened at last, it never occurred to me that the first person to enter, after the now familiar bespectacled man in black, would be not some Eisenhower or Wild Bill Donovan or Hap Arnold or either Dulles brother, but my own father.

And, goddammit, what did I see as the table between us stopped cold his rush toward me but the old anguish in his eyes, the most familiar sight of all — the worry, the expectation of disaster, the sure conviction that, in my case, all was lost, lost forever. And how could my heart not have sunk at the sight of him?

"Michael!" He moved a chair aside to lean closer. If he could have moved the table, he would have. I recognized the coiled energy, the power that would collect in his fist, say, as he squeezed the tiller of the Lightning to make it go faster in a light wind. Some races we won simply because he willed us to, which was why, approaching the finish line, in addition to being thrilled, I could be intimidated.

My father was dressed in a gray suit, and his rep tie was like mine, but as always he exuded that peculiar American masculinity, embodied in the understatement of style, while I still only aspired to it. The foundation of a man's style lies in his shoes, and I yearned for penny loafers. My blazer and tie made the blocky orthopedic shoes protruding from my chinos that much more ridiculous. My father's shoes, as I knew without looking, would be English cordovans, slim, perfect.

Is it necessary for me to state here that I dearly loved my father? That I lived for his approval? That I understood myself in terms that I had from him? But in these hours, all thoughts of my father had dropped away, and now, instead of feeling rescued, I felt ambushed. His goddamn worry, what a burden it was. *He worries, therefore I am.* His worry — therefore his presence — was the last thing I needed.

"Hi, Dad," I said. But I did not move.

Right behind him was Mrs. Healy, who brushed past my father as she entered the room. She wore a fitted tweed jacket over a long brown skirt, and with her tan kid gloves she seemed ready for the paddock. She had often struck me as really good looking, especially for somebody's mother, but there was an unworldly implication of anguish in her face — an emotion transcending my father's mere worry — and it made her all the more beautiful. She said nothing as she moved quickly to the end of the table and around it. Ulrich was on his feet and moving, too. They met at the table's head, opposite where the man in black stood watching. The desperation with which Ulrich and his mother embraced set them apart from the rest of us, as if Kit and I were mere teenagers charged with curfew violations, while Ulrich was a man charged with murder.

"Please to separate," the dark-suited man said, his gruff accent, even in three clipped words, sounding not at all German.

Mrs. Healy and her son ignored him. A helmeted soldier in the crisp gray uniform appeared in the doorway. He entered efficiently, but before he could move to Mrs. Healy, my father stepped ahead of him. It was my father who took Ulrich's mother by the shoulders and pulled her back. "Charlotte," he said. "Not now."

I had experienced my father's tenderness many times, and I had also witnessed it occasionally in his responses to my mother, even when she came at him in anger. But the intimate way he approached Ulrich's mother seemed entirely new to me.

"Let your mom go, son."

What? My father's authority with them surprised me.

The soldier behind my father had frozen in place, deferring to him.

Ulrich was crying again. As his mother released him, my father said, "We're going to get you out, Rick. You're going to be okay."

"Please," the dark-suited man said, but with sharp impatience, a clear imperative.

Ulrich came back to his chair between me and Kit, wiping his face with his sleeve, ashamed.

Mrs. Healy and my father went to the chairs opposite us. My father pulled one out for her, an unconscious gallantry that seemed out of place. I had to stifle a visceral resentment, my father with his banker's manners, everyone a potential client. What a phony he was.

"Okay," he said, leaning my way. "Here's the situation. You guys are all three going to be all right."

Again his authority surprised me. "Dad, how did you get here? Where's Ulrich's dad?"

Because of the tense reaction in my father, and in Mrs. Healy, too, I realized at once how stupid it was to mention Ulrich's father. Ulrich's father the master spy. Obviously, my father was here because Ulrich's could not be. I sat back holding the red flower of my face — *fucking asshole* — and resolved to just shut up. *Just shut the fuck up.*

"There's been a mixup," my father said. "We've spoken to the authorities, and it will be rectified quickly."

Rectified, I thought. What a pompous word.

My father's gaze was on Ulrich. "Rick, you are being charged with failure to declare currency at the border — not border, but sector demarcation. Because it's a question of sector, border regulations do not apply. The lines between Berlin sectors are not international borders, or at least the U.S. refuses to recognize them as such. That's the heart of the mixup. You guys have stepped into a political minefield."

"Minefield?" Ulrich asked with alarm.

"Metaphorically," my father answered. He was the soul of calm. "And the trick is to go out the way you came in, a step at a time, by the book. The book, in this case, is the Four-Power Agreements, which say the Allied Control Council must be represented at your hearing, but they also say internal sector regulations apply, so your hearing cannot be held until the standard magistrate session. It's a formality. As an American citizen, you are not subject to DDR authority, exercised solely."

"But if the sector line is an international border?" It took me a moment to catch the drift of Ulrich's question, of why it was frightening.

My father answered, "That is the point of dispute. But it's a larger issue than you, and it's something the Allies aren't prepared to yield on. The point is, Rick, we'll have you out of here by this time tomorrow."

"What do you mean *Rick?*" I asked. There went my resolution to keep quiet. And then, with the mystified expression they all turned on me, I realized they thought I was raising the banality of Ulrich's name. I added quickly, "What do you mean *Rick* is charged with the violation?"

The distinction had been clear in my father's words and in his addressing them to Ulrich alone, speaking of "exercised solely."

"Yeah," Kit joined in on my side. "All three of us are charged."

Mrs. Healy was sitting stock still beside my father, staring at her hands clasped on the table in front of her. She had not removed her gloves, and for the first time I sensed that she was ashamed of the rough ugliness of her hands. We all have things, Kit had said, that we hate about ourselves.

Then I looked at my father's hands. I thought of his fierce grip on the tiller — *Hard alee!* His voice had that kind of determination in it when he finally answered Kit. "No," he said, "only Rick is charged. That's also part of the mixup. You and Michael have been held by mistake. They claim they didn't know whom to release you to, but now they know."

"What does that mean?" I asked.

My father did not look at me at first, a hesitation that told me he had heard quite well what was in my voice. I thought of the moment he had come into my room at the house on the lake, to ask me to come downstairs where he told me about the phone call from the state police; told me that it had come nearly two hours before; told me that he had already been to the scene of the accident without me. "Why didn't you take me with you?" I had demanded. He was unable to put his answer into words, which I knew anyway: Because you are not strong enough to withstand the blow of your mother's death. You are my weak and wounded son, and now you will be weaker and more wounded than ever.

"What does that *mean?*" I repeated when he did not answer.

"It means you are coming with me. Now." He faced Kit. "And so are you, Katharine. Only Rick is being charged. The currency at issue was in his bag. Only Rick remains in custody."

Mrs. Healy brought her face up. She found her son's eyes. "Tomorrow for sure," she said. "You will be out."

"But that's crazy," I said.

"No, it's not, Michael. It is the way it is." My father said this with his simple authority, as if he were telling me all over again that Mom is dead.

Okay. Right. Mom's death — a fact of life. Get over it. Something to accept. No choice. But not this. I do not accept this. "But the currency violation," I said calmly. "That was my money, not Ulrich's." The lie came as easily as the feeling. What was Berlin but one lie after another, harmless lies adding up to their fucking opposite. Berlin, for all these lies, felt like my first real experience of the truth. My truth.

"Mine, too," Kit said. "The money is mine, too."

"We put it in Ulrich's bag," I said, "without his knowing about it. His was the only bag we had."

Ulrich put his hand on my arm, the bone of it. Then he pulled back, a clear signal of indecision.

But on his other side, Kit, who had the nerve to light one cigarette from another as she spoke, picked up the beat as surely as I had laid it down. She said, "We heard you could make a killing on the black market."

I looked across at her, loving the way her father's jacket decked her thin shoulders, the overlong sleeve cuffed back like an artist's smock, the sexy bandana. The girl's self-possession was a marvel to me.

Not to my father. "Don't be ridiculous," he snapped. He may have seen right through us, but his irritation showed that we had him.

He glanced at the man in the dark suit, who was still standing at the foot of the table, listening to every word — but doing so, it seemed, through the slit of his mouth.

Pathetic Dad, I thought. Didn't he realize they would be listening to us even if the zombie apparatchik wasn't hanging over the table like a Commie gargoyle?

"So Kit and I have to be at the hearing, too," I said. "We remain in custody."

"Michael —" Mrs. Healy began.

But I interrupted her. "Even if we are guilty, Allied Control takes over our case, right?" Looking at Ulrich's mother, my eye went to a line of perspiration that had formed on her upper lip. I had to look away, even if it meant looking at my father. "Because we are U.S. citizens, all three of us. Right?"

As I said this, I may well have grinned — the point I'd scored. In recalling this scene now, I wonder if my extraordinary sense of invulnerability was a matter of entitled American exceptionalism or the mark of a virgin boy still flush with the exuberance of having been naked with a girl and survived.

My father's hand was suspended, palm outward, a foot or so above the table, and as he spoke it remained poised like that, as if he were swearing an oath. He and I occupied different realms altogether. He spoke slowly and calmly, the way he always did when he was pissed, really pissed.

"The undeclared currency was not yours, Michael. Nor yours, Katharine. Nor was it Rick's. We know that it was planted in that bag by the unidentified man known as Tramm, who brought you to the sector boundary. We know this. And so do the East German authorities."

He glanced again at the man, which is when I understood that he was not of "the East German authorities." He was Russian. At the time, I could not fully grasp the significance of such a distinction within what to us was the monolithic Communist enemy. Later I would get it — that to the East Germans, Communist or not, the so-called Soviet Military Mission remained in 1961 an unwelcome occupation force. I would get it also that by then we Americans amounted to something similar, if subliminally, to West Germans — although West Germans who defied Americans were not kidnapped, made to disappear, written out of history. The night before, that had been my terror — that we had "disappeared," and here I was daring them to make it happen.

My father, afraid at that moment of what *I* was doing, not Russia, was speaking with measured gravity. "That the dollars were planted has been acknowledged in discussions we have had. The authorities are prepared to stipulate the likelihood that the man known as Tramm was a West German provocateur, an agent of the intelligence service of the Federal Republic. But that assumes your continuing to deny any knowledge of the dollar currency in excess of what you declared, as you have done until now — all three of you." My father lowered his voice and stared at us. "Changing your story at this point, out of loyalty to Rick, is a mistake for him as well as for you."

Somehow I found it possible to keep looking him full in the face, his smooth-shaven, handsome face. He was self-assured but also guarded, as if an inch below his composure was an expression of rank mystification. Was that hint of bewilderment a sign of what had gone wrong between us?

At the lake. That night he had asked me to join him downstairs on the porch, where we could talk, as if we could not talk in the knotty-pine box of my room. Each of us sitting in a rattan chair, the sky black through the screen, no star cutting an arc, no star falling. When he told me that Mom was dead, I found it impossible to look him in the eye, impossible even to find his eye. I realize now that the porch's many other places for our eyes to settle was why he'd brought me down there. In my room, we would have had to look at each other.

Blind. Mute. I had been equally unable to give voice to what flooded into me, a terrifying feeling of rage, rage at him. *Mom is dead! Here was what I could not say. Because of you! You made her mad again! And this is what happened!*

My father was staring back at me across the table. Familiar as that face would become years later, when it was mine, it seemed then like the face of someone I hardly knew. It was, of course, how I must have seemed to him. Absolute and mutual incomprehension. I said, "I'm not leaving Ulrich, Dad. That's all."

"Me neither," Kit said, God bless her.

"You do Rick no good by staying here."

"His name is Ulrich," I said, stupidly, passionately.

My father ignored this. "We are getting him out tomorrow. I promise you."

"Do you keep your promises, Dad?"

"You know I do, Michael."

"So do I, Dad." I put my hand on Ulrich's arm and kept it there. Ulrich brought his face up, and the three of us sat there looking at my father and Ulrich's mother as if we were immovable. I guess we were.

Mrs. Healy said very quietly, "Thank you, Michael. Thank you, Kit."

After a long silence, my father said, "All right. But it is important not to change your stories. About the money. Forget this crap that it was yours. Tramm put it there. Tell them the truth, Michael."

I nodded, but I knew that he was still in charge, or thought he was. Still fucking in charge. What I said then surprised me, a pristine expression of my anger after all. "The truth? Tramm? The BND? That the money was planted by a provocateur of the *West?* That's the *truth?*"

From the way he flinched, I could see that my father was afraid of what I was doing. Tramm was a Stasi plant and everybody knew it. Would I use that to upend the deal they had made? My father was afraid of *me*.

A first-time feeling for both of us. A shattering of some pact of falsehood that we had made. What an odd satisfaction it was to finally be coming back at him. Especially odd then, since I knew very well that all he wanted was to take care of me. But that was exactly what had made me angry. I wasn't stuck in an iron lung anymore, waiting for Daddy to come and unlock it.

At the time, I had no clue about any of this. At the time, all I had were wave-like feelings breaking over me, a torrent of emotions that closed off from my conscious mind the countercurrents swirling just below the surface — but below.

So, yes, my father was afraid that I was going to bollix the tidy deal he'd struck at his own private Potsdam Conference, but he was afraid beyond that, I sensed even then, of something else I could do — do to him. What?

Force out the truth, I might have guessed at the time, of what he had done to Mom? *You made her mad and she died!* I was too young to imagine for a moment that his fear was tied, not to her, but only to me. I am a father now myself, and understand what it is: the mortal dread that a once needy child can live without you. Not only can, but must.

My father was nothing if not self-disciplined, and he found it possible to bracket the chaos of his emotion, stilling it with a patently false calm. "Just tell them the money was not yours. That it was *none* of yours. *That* truth, Michael. Don't play games with these people. Do you hear me?"

"Yes, Dad. I hear you."

"Good. You will have no lawyer. The hearing is not public. Allied Control will have a representative standing by, an American officer from the Army provost marshal's office, but you will have to handle the back-and-forth of the hearing yourselves. Rick declares his innocence. You two back him up. Tell them about the guy who brought you to the checkpoint, Josef Tramm. It's not for you to know or say who he was. That will confirm what they already have. Then they will release you." The three of us sat quietly, taking this in. My father glanced again at the apparatchik. That he was privy to this briefing did not matter, since tomorrow's hearing would be *Berlinsky* charades in any case.

Kit broke the silence. "Why isn't the American embassy handling this? No offense, Mr. Montgomery. No offense to you, Mrs. Healy. But at the dorm they tell us if we get in trouble, we should always call the embassy."

I was grateful for the kindly air with which my father nodded at her. "We've talked to some people, Katharine."

"Her name is Kit, Dad."

"Kit. What they tell us is that for now this is better handled according to the set procedures. Mrs. Healy and I are here as a matter of parental concern. If your father and mother were in Germany, they could be here, too. We're just parents, Kit — which is best at this point. The U.S. government is aware of what's happening, but if this became a formal matter outside procedures already set by the Four-Power Agreements, it would become political. We want to keep it in the confines of Berlin, Kit. Not Washington. Not Moscow. Berlin. East Berlin, West Berlin, a mother, a father, some kids in a jam. That's all."

"Not innocent of sin, but sinning in innocence," Kit said. She said it with a totally straight face.

"Whatever you say, Kit," my father answered, but warily. And then he added, "So far it's a small matter. We have to keep it that way. Do you understand?"

"Small potatoes," Kit said.

"Don't misunderstand. I mean, just for —"

"No, I get it. Small matter. Mox nix."

"For the sake of the dismissal we expect tomorrow."

"She understands, Dad."

"And if you have a phone number for him, I'll call your father. I'll call him right away, this afternoon."

"No," she said emphatically.

"No need for that, Dad," I put in.

But he was studying Kit.

I craned my neck to catch a glimpse of her. She was staring back at my father with clear, firm eyes. Her courage was what I saw, and her resolve. I imagined her facing down her own father like that. Great white father. Fathers were put here to be pissed, she had said. She was put here to stand up to them.

Looking at my father then, I saw that bewilderment. Her old man whips her, Dad, I thought of saying, let's leave him the hell out of this. But what did my worried father know? I was sure he had never hit anyone. Suddenly I felt sorry for him. A dead wife. A kid who tells him nothing. Worse — a kid who lies.

To get him off Kit's case, but also in a rush of my own guilt, I said, "I'm sorry." He looked at me with surprise, and I went on quickly so he would not think I was sorry for staying with Ulrich. "About the car, I mean. Sorry for taking off in it."

And then, seeing the rank irrelevance of my confession, I laughed. To my relief, so did he. "Not to worry, Michael. You'll be happy to know the car is safe where you left it in Helmstedt. Although you left the rear window down." He grinned the old shit-eating grin, the parent who knows everything.

"All is finished here," the man in the dark suit said, and he clapped his hands once. My father jumped, a reflex that shocked me and made me admit the awful knowledge that my father was afraid of that man. Really afraid.

Ulrich leaned forward, not reaching to his mother but to my father. "Please," Ulrich said, "make them put me back with Monty and Kit. They are keeping me alone. I cannot be alone again. Please."

Kit and I found each other's eyes behind Ulrich. I saw a shining depth of feeling in her, the same gratitude I felt for what had passed between us. The simple intimacy of the night before was not to be repeated, and that was all right. Smoke rings. Perfect for a moment. Gone.

My father said, "I will make a point of it, Ulrich."

And apparently he did, because when they returned us to the same house that afternoon, the house within earshot of a railroad crossing, Ulrich would be in the room with me and Kit.

Late at night, with Kit asleep on the day bed by the wall, Ulrich would begin by thanking me for what my father had done, but he would also express resentment toward his stepfather, who had done nothing for us, and toward his real father for being absent forever. In my whispered response, I would ask him to tell me both their stories, and he would answer it was impossible, impossible. "Later," he would say. "Later. I will tell you everything." Given what happened the next day, it was a promise he would not keep.

We stood up, the three of us, on our side of the table, and Mrs. Healy and my father on theirs. Only then, as I gripped the back of one of the chairs for balance, did he notice that my cane was nowhere in sight. "Where's your stick?" he asked.

I looked at him helplessly. Please, Dad, I wanted to say, but did not.

My father turned to the Russian. "My son carries a cane. Where is his cane?"

While the man looked from me to my father uncomprehendingly, the door behind my father opened. Someone listening from another room knew that we were finished. The door swung wide and I saw another man in uniform, this one with ribbons and braid and red boards on his shoulders, some officer. He was a short, thin man whose bald head and sharp nose made him look like Adolf Eichmann.

Then I noticed his empty sleeve, an amputated arm. An arm ripped from its socket by Nazis? Or by Stalin? An arm lost, in any case, to evil, to war, to the violence of men. Not to a virus just ahead of the vaccine, the lucky bastard.

My father had turned back to me, seriously agitated now. "What happened to your stick, Michael? What are they doing —"

"It's all right, Dad. Never mind. Jesus."

During this brief commotion, with the room's attention on the officer's arrival and on my goddamn missing cane, Ulrich and his mother had circled to the foot of the table and were embracing. Suddenly all eyes went to them. The one-armed officer and the Russian exchanged sharp words I did not understand. Ulrich had his mouth to his mother's ear and was whispering. It was so obvious that I expected the apparatchik to bark an order at them, or the officer to step between them, but each one remained where he was, watching, as the mother listened to her son.

Kit banged her chair against the table, and I knew she was trying to draw attention to herself. "Mr. Montgomery," she said loudly. "Something else. Would you help me with something else?"

We all looked at her, all but Ulrich and his mother.

"They have my accounts book. Would you make them give me my accounts book back? I need it."

"Your accounts book?"

"I really need it." Kit had her left thumb inside her right fist and was gesturing like an agitated child. I thought she was going to say it had her novel, the story of her soul, an incurable woman whose disease is a man. But she surprised me. "It has my letter to Faulkner in it," she said. "I'm writing to William Faulkner because I am going to be his page next year." Kit turned toward the man in the dark suit and spoke to him in German, a sentence constructed around the words "William Faulkner." The man only stared at her, but the point was, he was no longer staring at Ulrich and Mrs. Healy, to whom, in fact, he had never barked "No whispering!"

My father said, "I'll ask about it, Kit. I'm sure you'll get it back."

"I need it now. I have to set down some things."

"Kit's a novelist, Dad," I said, as if that explained her urgency. To my knowledge, my father had never met a novelist. My father hadn't a clue, even, that I myself had begun to imagine a life as a writer. Kit would get her accounts book back, but not until the next day. Still, it would be time enough for her to do something precious with it.

Ulrich pulled away from his mother's embrace. She took him back for the instant required to kiss him firmly on the cheek, a cheek that had the moisture of his tears.

I looked out the window at the afternoon light. I wanted to memorize the light, not imagining that it would fade, but understanding that the sky would never look this clear again. Even then I knew it was *right here* that I had learned who I was, had become who I am, and that whatever happened now, I would never be the same again.

"What about your stick?" my father asked. They had him halfway out the door.

I felt pity for him then. What a burden it was to be such a worried father. "It's not important, Dad." Not my stick, of course. I was speaking of my very legs.

Part Five

15

THIS WAY, Charlotte." I took her elbow. We had just crossed from the stairwell to the round entrance foyer, its walls — now I saw it — the color of smoke. Hans Krone and our escort, the gaunt, bespectacled Russian, were close behind.

Krone, seeing my detour, stopped the Russian with an innocuous question, giving us a moment's opening. Charlotte had no idea where I was leading her until we stopped in front of the bronze tablet, "*Moabiter Märtyrer.*"

"I wanted you to see this," I said. "I saw it yesterday."

She looked at the lines of text, afloat like tea stains on a plaque the color of a caramel apple. Out of the margins and the spaces between the letters, as out of silence, rose the list of names, the explanatory paragraph, the date — May 1, 1945.

She slowly backed away, gloved hand to her mouth, forefinger knuckle between her clamping teeth. This, or something like it, was what had kept her from Schloss Pankow yesterday. She would not be here today except to see Ulrich.

She turned from that one particular name to cast an accusing look at me, a look full of hate and defiance. Then she moved rapidly across the foyer, through the door, and out into the bright afternoon. Her skirt flared at her calves with every clipped step she took.

I caught up with her in the broad, grassy courtyard. A squad of gray-uniformed soldiers was moving through its drill a few dozen yards away. Aware of the difficulty in closing those last few inches between my grasping hand and her sleeve, like that old Greek paradox of the arrow never reaching its target, I lunged, took her arm, and forced her to slow down. "Show nothing," I said. "You are showing too much."

She fell into step with me, but only because I was right.

Leaving the squad to its maneuvers, we crossed the courtyard, ahead of Krone and the Russian. We passed the sentry and entered the shadow of the archway that led through the front wing of the palace. In that disappointed tunnel, the air became wind, a last pressure against us, and together we bowed slightly into it — to get out, out into the crescent-shaped parking lot with its thin herd of dwarf autos.

Krone's Mercedes was there waiting for us, an incarnation of escape. The uniformed driver, in the universal chauffeur's cap, was at the wheel. When he saw us approach, he hopped out and came around, but Charlotte was at our door ahead of him. She opened the door, flung it wide, got in. I followed.

Even as she made room for me on the seat, sliding away, her right hand shot back toward me, poking the air near my face. "Silence!" she commanded. "Do not speak!"

Krone, following behind, was stooping to join us, aiming for the jump seat on which he had ridden before, but I stopped him. "Hans, ride in front, will you?"

He stared at me. "There are things to discuss." He then let his eyes flit briefly toward the Russian, who was watching us from a dozen yards away. Krone said, "That one is KGB, from the *Kommandatura*. Erhardt is terrified."

"Later."

"But I —"

"And turn on the radio, Hans. Turn it on loud."

He looked at me with the disappointment of an unneeded hunting dog, then nodded brusquely. He closed our door, then hoisted himself into the front seat with an awkwardness that made it clear he had never ridden there before. The driver got behind the wheel and, without so much as a glance at Krone, started the engine. As we began to move, I leaned forward. "The radio, Hans."

He pressed the dashboard button and an operatic chorus poured into the air, something of Bach's. I pressed the button on my armrest that raised the partition between front and back seats.

When we were sealed off, I turned to Charlotte, but her shoulder was angled away from me. She was staring out the window, as if the landscape of the wrong side of Berlin might hold some interest. Rubble nostalgia? I could see the whorl of her ear, its pearly shimmer. I could see the line of her cheekbone, the luster of skin without makeup. But I could not see even one eye.

"Charlotte."

She ignored me. What had Krone said? *Kommandatura?*

The car had come quickly to speed, and the stucco wall of the nearby hospital flashed by like unspooling ribbon. I glanced out the rear window. No one. From what I saw, ours was the only moving car in East Berlin.

Turning back to Charlotte, I asked, "Who is von Siedelheim?"

She whipped around toward me. "Silence!" The order came in a hiss now, and her eyes darted forward to Krone, to the driver.

All that had gone before, every revelation — her life as a rubble woman, Healy's rescue, even Healy's film in the bag that Ulrich took — was nothing compared to this. Von Siedelheim. *Moabiter Märtyrer.* Wolf. Bullets to the back of the neck. Tied in this knot were threads of the secret of secrets, twisted into the rope of the noose around the neck of her only son, and therefore around the neck of mine.

"No," I said quietly but firmly. "The time for silence is past. No more silence between us."

She stared at me helplessly, then once again her eyes went to Krone.

"He can't hear us," I said. The choral passage on the radio filled both cavities of the limousine. "Listen," I said. "It's Latin. *Deposuit potentes.* 'He hath put down the mighty.' It's the *Magnificat,* your Virgin icon. We are as safe here as we were in her presence in the Russian Chapel." Only the day before, yet the chapel now seemed to give us a shared history, that first instinctive coming together that drew its energy from what we could not put into words. When language fails, longing takes over, a thing I knew from Edie. Indeed, it was Edie who had made me listen to this exuberant canticle until it was mine, too. Not religion, but music. "'He hath exalted the humble and the meek,'" I translated.

Charlotte nodded. "Bach wrote this for Leipzig. I heard it sung in Leipzig every Christmas."

"You hear it now." Flutes, drums, strings. Voices. "So do they." I indicated Krone and the driver. "Which means we can talk."

For the first time, she brought her eyes directly to mine. Her eyes were fluid, enormous, searching mine.

"You can trust me, Charlotte. I promise."

She smiled. "And you keep your promises. So does your son. Your son is magnificent."

I didn't think so at the time. It wasn't that simple to me, not yet. But I left my complications with Michael aside. "And yours," I said, "yours is in trouble. What trouble, Charlotte?"

I think she was going to tell me, but just then the pavement turned rough, and with wheels rumbling, the driver slowed. I saw that we had come into Potsdamer Platz with its cobblestones. That quickly, having crossed through the trafficless streets of a Sunday afternoon in what the Soviets called democratic Berlin, we were approaching the checkpoint of the American sector.

Automatically, we turned from each other, reaching for our passports, the entry receipts. I pushed the button to lower the partition and handed the documents to Krone, who took them without comment. I raised the partition, waiting for the kiss of its seal.

Charlotte had moved away, and again sat facing the window. She watched as our car pulled into the slotted line. The border police wore long green trench coats and peaked hats. Rifles were slung at their shoulders. The cars ahead moved forward slowly but steadily, a candy-striped gate rising and falling at each one. When our car pulled to the barrier, the soldier bent to the driver's window, glanced at the proffered set of documents, at the pair of us in back. He then straightened to wave us through.

As if it were the soundtrack only of time in the East, Bach's canticle was just then winding through its . . . *in saecula saeculorum*. Before we had pulled fully away from the checkpoint, the chorus finished its *Amen* with a decisive snap, and all at once the air was blank. Behind the Iron Curtain, silence on the radio could seem not a void, as in the West, but a positive statement, a broadcast version of a soundless scream. The silence went on and on.

Charlotte looked at me with an expression that said, There, now we will be overheard. But what the silence sparked in me was a fresh urgency, the warning I had yet to give her.

I slid next to her and put my arm around her shoulders, like a boorish date. I brought my mouth to her ear. She seemed to understand what I was doing and did not resist. "Whatever Rick told you back there as we were leaving," I whispered, "they *let* him tell you. They *wanted* him to tell you whatever he told you."

She started to pull away from me, but I held her. I was aware of Krone turning to look back at us, and perhaps so was she, because suddenly she relaxed against me. She put her hand on my leg. I continued to whisper, "What they wanted Rick to tell you is probably why they let us in to see the kids in the first place. So now you know the secret, whatever he told you. And they will expect you to act on it now. And they will be watching, following."

Her finger shot toward Krone: Him.

"It's the film, isn't it? Rick told you where the film is."

She made no reply, but I was aware of her body stiffening against me. The honeyed perfume of her hair filled my nostrils.

She brought her hand up to my face, her fingers at my cheek, what could have been a tender caress. But I knew the gesture for what it was, an obscuring of Krone's view of my lips.

"So you must not do it, Charlotte," I said. "Let the film go until tomorrow, until after the kids are out."

"What film, darling?" she whispered.

Darling? "What?"

She adjusted her face so that now it was her mouth at my ear. "Tell them," she whispered, "to take us to the hotel."

I began to pull away from her.

But with both her hands at my neck, she held me. And then a sudden change of mind. "No, wait! Don't tell them yet."

And to my amazement, she brought her mouth around to mine. With her lips parted, she kissed me, and I tasted the sweetness of her saliva.

Her leg pressed against my leg, from ankle to thigh, a first promise of her long, muscled body. As she adjusted, forward and over on the seat, to more fully embrace me, her mouth all the while on mine, I felt the fullness of her breasts on my chest. My hands closed, one on her back, one on the curve of her hip.

I responded with lavish willingness, pulling her to me, so that she would know, despite my surprise, how I had wanted this. This obliteration of the confusion I had felt, or rather, the suspension of it. Confusion would return in short order — it always does. For the moment, no one was asking how this carefully unacknowledged hunger had come here, like an animal, to be fed. Her hunger, apparently, as much as mine.

My one hand went under her tweed jacket, into the silk, I thought, of her blouse. But it was not silk, not her shirt, but her satin camisole, which rode up from her waist. Then that hand was on her flesh, incandescent to the touch of my fingers, which then measured the hollow perfection of the small of her back.

Krone was watching us, I knew it.

And then I realized that Charlotte knew it, too, because she pulled her face back. Sowing mine with kisses, her mouth moved across my cheek to my ear — the ear away from Krone. Instead of devouring it, as I wished, expected, she whispered with cold urgency, "Now! Now tell them to take us to the hotel!"

To fool Krone about the hours ahead of us, the woman had — was this possible? — just fooled me.

At the Kempinski, I followed her across the lobby, her heels clicking on the bright marble, that brown skirt swirling at her legs, her leather shoulder bag swinging with each step like a slanted pendulum. She walked with the assurance of a well-to-do shopper returning from a spree. At the desk, she asked for her key and, right beside her, I asked for mine, as if we were not shoppers now but fellow conventioneers returning from sales conference.

By the time I had arrived at the hotel the evening before, she had the privacy sign on her door. At the desk, she had left a note for me, together with a bag containing a new shirt, underwear, and socks, as well as a razor and toothbrush — purchases she had made for me at a department store. Her note had proposed breakfast in the hotel dining room the next morning. I had been afraid that I would be unable to book another room, but people who came to Berlin for May Day were not the type to stay at the Kempinski. Charlotte's room was on the seventh floor, facing the Kurfürstendamm. Mine was down the hall, a room with a window on an air shaft. I had slipped a note under her door, thanking her for the clothes and saying "Yes. See you at breakfast."

276

Now, when the tuxedoed clerk handed her the stout brass room key, he also gave her a folded piece of pale blue paper, which she took without any show of interest. She put the note in her bag without reading it.

As the clerk passed me my room key, Charlotte covered my hand with hers. "My room, darling," she said, then laughed brightly, a woman without a care in the world. "It's in your name anyway."

"Whatever you say, *Liebchen.*" I winked at the clerk, which was surely overdoing it, but what the hell. Charlotte and I linked arms.

In the elevator going up, in addition to the operator, were a pair of dour old ladies, one of whom reeked of talcum powder. The other leaned on a thick rubber-footed cane, which made me think of Michael.

The ladies got off at five, making it seem we were alone. The elevator operator, a short man in the round, stiff-sided cap of his kind, looked like an organ grinder's monkey and appeared to be just as oblivious. When the doors closed after the ladies, I said, "I don't like it that they took his cane away."

"I think he is coping well with that," she said, "as with everything." Her confidence in Michael seemed total, and that alone was enough to set her apart from Edie, not to mention from me.

I was more than irritated at my son for his spirit of cavalier recklessness. I knew that my irritation was beside the point, but still, my simple view was that he should have been out of East Berlin by now, with me. I had taken a room with twin beds, expecting him to sleep here tonight. Charlotte had her reasons for feeling differently — Rick not alone — and I understood that. But there was also something spacious in her response to my son, whom I suddenly envied for that.

At the seventh floor, the operator pulled the doors open for us. Charlotte said, "*Dankeschön,*" and led the way out. When the elevator doors had closed again, she dropped my arm.

She went immediately to her room, content to show me her back. She unlocked the door, and then left it open for me to follow her in. The room was large, far more elegant than mine, decorated in a sort of muted art deco style, with sleek surfaces, mirrors, variations of black and beige. A canopied double bed anchored one end of the room, a settee arrangement the other. A highly enameled black-and-white chandelier marked the room's center. On the far side of the entrance was a set of French doors, slightly ajar, open to a balcony. A filmy curtain billowed in the soft afternoon breeze.

Charlotte walked to the French doors, opened one side, and turned, waiting for me. "Step out here, darling," she said. "I want that you should see this, *eine schöne Aussicht.*" A beautiful what? Her demeanor, blowing hot and cold, for show and not for show, had me off balance by now. I went past her, out onto the balcony, as she wanted. We went to the stone balustrade and looked out over the tidy rooftops of Berlin's most prosperous district.

Across the avenue was a new tall building made of glass the color of the Caribbean, and a block to the west was an even taller one, newer, also glass, the color of olives, like the new skyscrapers nestled behind Rockefeller Center. I realized it was the Lindenhof, my building, the one I had helped dedicate in December. I had never seen it from an angle like this.

From directly below, the bustle of the Ku'damm carried up to us, a glad cacophony of horns, streetcar bells, the general buzz of traffic, and the voices of strollers and café patrons up and down the boulevard.

Side by side, leaning on elbows, facing the view, we were also fully in view ourselves. That, too, I realized, was her point. She put her hand on my arm, an easy, familiar gesture that had nothing to do with what either of us was feeling then. But whether we were being observed or not, she felt free to talk here, and said so. "Here we are alone," she said.

"Charlotte, they are not omnipresent."

"You are the one who warned me," she said brusquely. "But foolishly, you warned me in front of Krone."

Krone. I leaned to look down at the curbside where I had said goodbye to him only moments before. He had not bothered to conceal his resentment, convinced as he was that I still needed him, the insult he took from my instructing him not to return for me until morning. His quick glance at Charlotte had conveyed his disapproval, but despite his peevishness, I was sure he'd bought it — the blood urgency of our afternoon rendezvous.

"Let go of it, Charlotte. Krone is trustworthy. I am certain of it."

As she replied, her face remained in profile to me. "Krone is Stasi. That was the point."

The point, of course, of her kissing me, the point of "darling."

I watched her as she calmly took in the stunning vista. My every intuition told me that Krone was what he claimed to be. If I was wrong about Krone —

"Ridiculous," I said, not bothering to keep the anger from my voice. Ridiculous was, in fact, how I was feeling. First my son toying with me, now her.

Instead of answering, Charlotte pushed away from the balustrade, turned, and walked back into the room. Once more she waited at the door for me. I followed. She closed the doors, then pulled the curtains closed, first the sheer layer and then the heavy brocade drapes, which plunged the room into shadow. She went to the wall switch, snapped on the black-and-white art deco chandelier, then pulled an ottoman over from one of the chairs, positioning it just below the hanging light fixture. She gestured at the ottoman with a swirl of her wrist.

I stepped onto it, a surprisingly firm pedestal that brought me up so that my head was level with the chandelier. In its workings, I saw at once what she wanted me to see — a small black knob attached to a thin cord winding into the hole from which the electrical wire ran. A microphone, of course. I stared at the thing as if it were aware of me doing so.

I was back for a second on the *Stephen Case,* on the bridge, stretching like this to see. To see. Where was the telltale white streamer in the blue water? Futility itself — because by the time you do see, it is too late.

I looked down at Charlotte, dumbly.

She put her finger to her lips and made a pointing gesture at the microphone. *Leave it in place.* A contradiction of my impulse, which was to rip the thing out. She shook her head. *If you rip it out, they know.*

I nodded. She took several steps back and turned. She walked past the bed and through a door into what had to be the bathroom.

I did not move. Ridiculous, I thought. Standing on my cushioned stool, wishing it were the bridge of a ship, a rampart, but seeing it, *seeing* it for the ridiculous thing it was: an ottoman from India, land of elephants. And just like that, I realized what I was, and what she was. I was a circus animal doing tricks, waiting now for the sound of my trainer's whip.

The sound coming from the bathroom was that of a sudden gush of water slapping a plastic shower curtain. I hopped down and went to her. If she did not want me to join her, would she have left the door ajar?

The bathroom was the size of an office, a display of ostentation that at a later time would seem thoroughly American, but which then smacked of the decadence of old Berlin. At one wall a pair of gleaming alabaster sinks were set into a sheen of black countertop. Opposite were a toilet and a bidet of Carrara pink, and the third wall was taken up with the tiled counter of a dressing table. Its cushioned wire chair stood before a large gilt-framed mirror. Attached to the wall beside the mirror was a slung telephone, pink in color — in those days, any color but black was unusual. A second large mirror dominated the wall above the sinks, so that when I focused at last on Charlotte, languid against the dressing table, I also saw reflections of her to my right and left. Beside her was the bathtub and its drawn shower curtain on which water was beating, a sound that filled the space.

She had removed one glove, presumably to turn the shower knob, and was now removing the other, a deliberation that seemed to have overtaken her concentration. The effect of seeing her head-on and in both profiles simultaneously was dazzling. The mirrors were an absolute showcase of her beauty.

But against the gravity of her fierce expression, the very idea of beauty, hers or anyone's, seemed banal. As if to underscore the frivolity of mere appearance, the fresh sight of her blunted but heroic fingers drew my gaze away from her face.

I pushed the door closed behind me.

"There are no wires in here," she said. "I have examined closely." She dropped her gloves on the table beside her.

"But you run the noisy shower anyway. You can't be too careful, is that it? What makes you think it is Krone?"

"You saw him with Erhardt."

"Yes, and I saw Erhardt sweating blood in front of the Russian. What Krone said is true. He owns Erhardt. He can destroy Erhardt. It's why they dealt with us."

"No. You were right before. They dealt with us because they expect me to lead them to what they want. I know that. Of course I know that. But neither Erhardt nor the commissar booked this room. Krone booked this room, Paul. Krone. I found the microphone five minutes after checking in. There was no time for anyone else to put the microphone there. Krone is Stasi."

I stared at her. She had to be wrong, but I could think of no way to rebut her. And I am ashamed to admit that my thought went at once to: If Krone is Stasi, what does that mean for Chase?

To hell with Chase, I told myself. "That makes no sense, Charlotte. Krone booked this room for me. He did that before knowing anything, before knowing who you are."

"But he knew by the time he left us at the *Fernsehturm*. He was away from us for most of an hour. He came back agitated. Do you remember that beer, how desperately he lifted that stein?"

"Exactly. If Krone were Stasi, would his hands shake?"

"My hands do not shake. That does not mean I *am* Stasi."

"Your hands shook at Schloss Pankow, Charlotte — although not in front of the Russian. Your hands shook in front of the tablet at the entrance. The Moabit martyrs. Why is that?"

She reached into her bag, which stood open on the vanity behind her. She took out her cigarettes and, with an easy flick of the wheel of her gold lighter, lit one, a show of transcendent calm. I sensed it as a ritual act, designed to cover up — no, to manage — a deep insecurity. When she exhaled, the smoke rose to the ceiling, where it was lost in the cloud of steam that had begun to pour out of the shower.

"That has no relevance to what you and I are doing."

"Oh? Isn't that what kept you from Schloss Pankow yesterday? You were afraid of what the tablet reveals."

"Which is what?" she asked with slit eyes.

"This parody of lovers that you had us enacting began when I asked you in the car about von Siedelheim. You kissed me to shut me up about von Siedelheim. Why?" I stopped, but only for a breath. "At a convention hall in Frankfurt a week ago, I saw a man named von Siedelheim take a bullet in the neck. And then I learn that a man named von Siedelheim was one of a group taking a bullet in the neck in Moabit prison just before you came here in search of your son's father. And this von Siedelheim was named Wolf."

Her expression could not have been colder. "What makes you think this Wolf, as you say, took a bullet in the neck?"

"That's how the Nazis executed Communists. That's what Moabit was, a prison for Communists. Every prisoner was executed just as the city fell to the Soviets, which the bronze tablet commemorates."

A startled buoyancy came into her eyes for a moment — a woman of feeling after all. But before I understood it properly, that clue to her swirling inner state was covered up again.

I thought I was on a starboard tack, so I pressed on. "Does General Healy know your first husband was a Communist?"

I waited, but she said nothing, which seemed answer enough to me. The expression on her face, all three of her faces, had gone to stone, simply stone. I thought of the carved face of that czarina, looking out from the lintel of the Russian Chapel above Wiesbaden, where I had asked how she knew of grief and she slapped my question away. As I recalled that moment now, I would recall this one in the future — no slapping away, just her immutable inscrutability.

All right. If she was not going to start answering, I was not going to stop asking. "Does General Healy know that Wolf's . . . brother? cousin? was just executed in the same way? By whom, Charlotte? Secret Nazis? The cabal that protected Eichmann? And why doesn't Rick know that his father's name was von Siedelheim?"

This question landed a blow. "How do you know what Rick knows?"

"You told me as much when you said Rick signed his runaway letter 'von Neuhaus,' your name. Why haven't you told your son who his father was? What is the shame in Wolf's having been a Communist against Hitler? And wouldn't it be to Rick's advantage now if Erhardt knew? Jesus Christ, Charlotte, Rick's father is on the Stasi honor roll."

She shook her head firmly. "No. It would not be to his advantage."

"Because whoever his father was, his stepfather trumps it. But they know who his stepfather is. They know about his stepfather's flight bag, the thing that started this. They know about the stepfather's roll of film. What? The list of agents-in-place in anticipation of the sealing of the border? Whose agents, Charlotte? Ours or theirs? Or does it matter? Is that the secret you are protecting? Or are you protecting the secret of your husband's incompetence for having lost it?"

"I am protecting no one. But I am *trying* to protect my son. Trying to."

"I was right about Rick, wasn't I? He just told you where the film is."

She did not answer — which, again, was the answer.

"And I was right that Erhardt and the KGB watcher let him tell you, because now they expect you to lead them to it."

"You were right to warn me." She turned and mashed her cigarette in a porcelain ashtray on the dressing table, then turned back to me. "But I have no need of you telling me to be careful."

"I can see that. I admit, you've taken me by surprise. Clearly, you've learned a thing or two from your husband over the years." When she said nothing, I added, "Or is it he who has learned from you?"

"Do you dare ask me such a question?"

"You said that to me before, Charlotte. When I asked you about grief."

"I am asking you to leave me alone."

"What do you expect of me? That I should walk out of here and hope for the best? That I should slink down to my room and hide so that your subterfuge will work? I disappear and then you go into the other room and make noises for the microphone so that whoever is listening will believe what Krone told them — that the two boys' parents are celebrating the prospects of their release with an afternoon tryst?"

"No, Paul." She looked away, but an ardent roseate tide flooded her neck, rising into her jaw and cheeks. In the mirror to my left, her eyes came right to mine, the liquefaction of her former cold resolve. "How could I do that?" she asked, stunned, I knew, by my blunt crassness.

But her retreat now to girlish innocence angered me more. "How could you fake the love fest alone, you mean? Easy, Charlotte. The agents in their earphones are men, no doubt. And men only want to hear the sounds of the woman in throes."

"Please."

"You're offended? So am I. You set us up here this afternoon so that you could slip away a little later, to get the film for your husband, or perhaps for the free world. What did you imagine I would be doing? Am I supposed to stay here and, at the proper physiological intervals, resurrect the sounds of eros? Tell me what you expect of me, Charlotte."

"Let go, Paul."

"But I am not holding you."

"Of your son. Let go of your son."

"What has that to do —"

"Everything! You hold on to your son to hold on to your wife. But she is dead. You should let her go, too."

"Charlotte, I can't —"

"Michael has moved on from you, Paul. And he has moved on from his mother. He wants only to let go of his grief and to live. But you will not allow it."

"He needs me."

"Your son has made his own choices. And he is more than capable of living with them. And you cannot stand the feeling. It is what makes you ferocious with me."

In recalling this, I see now how I proved her point then by slapping my hand against the cold stone surface of the sink counter, jarring the bones in my wrist and forearm. "My son is in jeopardy! He put himself there because of your son. What is the jeopardy? You have to tell me!"

"I cannot."

"Why?"

Our eyes were still locked together, but through the mirror, which now wore the haze of steam from the shower.

She did not answer. I held my stinging wrist in my other hand, and I told myself — an old trick I had often used with Edie — Down, boy, down. "We are speaking different languages," I said. "What translation do we need here? German-English? Woman-man? Mother-father? Or is it spy and ordinary Joe?"

She laughed. "Ordinary Joe."

"I'm out of my element here. You see that. And if it makes me 'ferocious,' I apologize. But I'm lost. I don't know where I am."

"You are in Berlin, Paul. This is what it means — to be in Berlin."

"Which is why you left."

To my surprise, she took my simple statement as a blow, registering it physically. That slouched, elegantly world-weary woman was transformed in an instant. She had the bereft expression of a rubble woman, hankering for nothing more than not to be hit again.

Her voice had become almost inaudible when she said, "I never left. You see, I tell you to let go, recognizing how we are alike, because I myself never let go."

"Of Berlin?"

"Of all that Berlin did to me. I tried to leave, but I could not. David knows this. All these years with him I have been pretending. I never let go of Berlin. This is what I must confess now. I confess this to you."

I could not know then what she had just told me, and so I only looked at her.

Our silence became a kind of impasse, more painful in its way than the harsh exchange — to recall the cruelty of my words to her shames me — that preceded it. Moments passed. And more moments.

Finally, she drew herself up from the edge of the dressing table, coming to her full, impressive height. She folded her arms primly in front of herself. "You are right about the microphone. I must give them something to record. Otherwise they will know. They will —"

She brushed past me to pull the door open and go into the bedroom. She left the door open behind her, and a current of cool air rushed into the steamy bathroom, dispelling the shower cloud of which I had been barely aware.

16

FROM WHERE I stood in the bathroom, I watched as she crossed to the bedside table and turned on the light. She picked up the phone and dialed zero, waited, then spoke several sentences in German, the last of which she punctuated with the word *Dankeschön*. She hung up.

As she walked out of my line of view, she shrugged off her tweed jacket.

"I made a booking for dinner, Paul," she called. Her voice was loud, appropriately so, entirely offhand. "Half seven," she continued. "Is dinner in the hotel all right? They say the dining room is superb."

"All right," I said, marveling at her transformation, but failing utterly to match it. I said the curt words loudly enough to be heard above the shower, in the other room, but I knew that my voice, compared to hers, was false, stilted.

The shower, as far as the microphone was concerned, was now for me. Realizing that made me feel, once again, ridiculous. Ridiculous! I might as well have been poised on that circus stool, standing as I was in a steaming bathroom with my suit coat still on, my tie, my perfect creases gradually losing their edge.

I closed the bathroom door, as if for privacy. But from whom? Her? The listening strangers, whoever they were? The ghosts of her Berlin?

Only then did I notice her satin nightgown hanging by a pair of shoulder straps from the door's back hook. A forbidden garment, the sight stopped me. She had bought it for herself the day before, when she bought my shirt. The gown was the full length of her body, the color of burnished gold, a lace filigree at the neckline, a fold of material for her breasts to fill.

Involuntarily, I touched the garment, touched it where her hip would take its warmth, pinched it between my forefinger and thumb. The smooth fabric brought rushing back the sensation of balm on my fingers, what I had experienced in finding my hand at play upon her camisole in the car.

The last of whatever resentment I had felt at being made to seem her trick pony drained away, because the simple intimacy of this woman's need was real, even if her desire was not. It mattered not at all that the mystery of her need did not include me. I was here to help her — that was all — help her not to be dragged under by the ghosts of this city. Whatever the shadows of the local past, she and I did have a bond that protected us from them — the absolute future that was our children.

But her satin nightgown. I leaned toward it and brought the fabric to my nostrils. I recognized the perfume of her skin. Desire of this kind, I thought, like the gloss of silk to lovers who have left their clothes behind, is beside the point. I did not know it yet, but I was wrong. Desire is what separates human beings from the ghosts they fear. I let her satin gown fall from my fingers, and it twirled slightly, the hint of a dance.

When I turned, the varied images of myself in the mirrors were a puzzle. I would remember the odd sensation later in that decade when the maze of mirrors emerged as a cliché of the literature of espionage. I saw myself, in one surface reflecting off another, as a man seen from behind, his dark, close-cropped hair well up from his collar, the silver at his temples, the square shoulders of his sorrowful gray coat — none of it familiar. To this stranger, I would gladly have put my question, which at that moment would have run something like, If she is right about Krone, is she right about you?

Let go? Let go of Michael? At the fresh thought of my newly unyielding son, I had to sit. I lowered my haunches onto the cool marble ledge of the counter. *Michael, where are you?* I addressed this second question to the man with his back to me, aware of it as my first question. Two nights ago, at the beginning of this story, it was a question of physical whereabouts, but it had become a question of the interior geography across which we are chased by ghosts. *Michael, where are you?*

Here in this city, came the answer, this city of ghosts.

And are you here in flight from me?

That was a question — *how you flee from me!* — that I never knew to put to his mother, but I should have.

Edie, what about me made you run?

And there it was, a connection too blatant even for me to miss: Edie's flight from me had literally killed her, and wasn't a replay of that, *with you, Michael,* what terrified me now? Michael running from my anger, like Edie. *You killed her, Dad.* That was what he had been saying to me in every way but words.

This stranger just sat on the edge of his counter, looking away from me.

And how, I wondered, had the unknown woman in the other room come so surely to the knowledge of what I was doing, of who I was, of the fear that made me dangerous, but only to those I loved?

An impossible train of thought. To stop it, I stood and took my suit coat off, rolled my left shirtsleeve, reached inside the shower curtain, and shut the water off.

I found a towel, and as I dried my forearm and hand, I was determined to keep my gaze away from the man in the mirrors. Instead it fell, quite by accident, on Charlotte's leather bag, which still sat beside the ashtray on the dressing table. On the lurch of a wrong impulse, I dropped the towel and went for the bag. I opened its mouth fully, and there, atop a billfold, compact case, change purse, and a welter of other womanly things, was the slip of paper she had been handed at the desk, still folded, still unread.

Her request of me, that I "let go" — what is the opposite of my letting go?

This is. I reached into the bag and took the paper and unfolded it and read what was written there. The block letters with a slight backward slant read, "Do not forget that I am your V & V now." And it was signed "D." At the top of the paper was an abbreviated version of the hotel letterhead. At the bottom, near the right-hand corner, was the notation "1145" and a pair of initials, an operator. A phone message, therefore.

I folded the note and started to put it back into her bag, but that would seal this as a despicable act of snooping, and then I would find it impossible to remain in her presence, having done such a thing. Unless, of course, I could blame it on the stranger in the mirror.

And so, as though I were her page — odd word, that girl Kit had used it; "Faulkner's page" — I carried the folded slip of paper into the bedroom.

At first I was startled because the room seemed vacant to me, Charlotte gone, not on the bed, not on the settee, not in either of its companion chairs. Startled, on the way to panicked, that she had gone out into the wilds of the city without me.

Then I saw her, a dark form sitting upright on the floor in the far corner, a dozen paces beyond the furniture, beyond the French doors, which were still closed over with the drapery. She was as far from the unilluminated but in all ways electric chandelier as it was possible to get in that room. The light from the small bedside lamp, with its cloaking amber hat, did nothing to dispel the shadows across the room, and I could not see, until moving closer, that she had her long legs drawn up under her skirt, her elbows on her knees, her fingers spread to form a cradle for her forehead. She had unfastened her hair, and its free downpour screened the sides of her face. As I approached, she unfolded herself to lean back into the angle where the walls met. Her auburn hair now brushed her shoulders, and I remembered that this was how I had first seen her yesterday morning, her hair still damp from the shower.

Despite her air of gravity, or because of it, there was something regal about her; the corner into which she leaned could have been a throne. With her gaze on the middle distance and whatever figments floated in it, she wore her patrician hauteur like purple.

I walked to the French doors and stood over her in silence. When my eyes had adjusted to the shadows, I could see how her cream-colored blouse subtly outlined the contours of her breasts, and my mind went to the burnished folds of her nightgown, the aroma of the fabric, which was her aroma.

She looked up at me, her face expressionless.

I held the paper down to her without comment — I, the page, the squire.

And she took it. In that corner there was not enough light to read, and so, crooking a finger in the drapery, I pulled it back slightly to allow a wedge of sunlight to slice down upon her, a stage effect. She brought her hand to her brow. A million motes of dust floated in the sail-shaped brightness, like the figments she had been staring at before, her vision missing nothing.

As she unfolded the note, I felt appalled that I had read it first, even though its message meant nothing to me. I had to look away now, as if belatedly, to honor her privacy. If she noticed, she'd have seen it as a hollow gesture, shamelessly after the fact. Reading her mail. Sniffing her garments. What was I becoming here?

I looked through the drapery opening to the view outside, restricted as it was. As it happened, the small segment of cityscape that presented itself was centered on the Lindenhof, across and up the Ku'damm. The impression the Lindenhof and other buildings had made before, when we stood on the balcony, was of offices closed for Sunday. But now my eyes, as if newly trained, went right to a window where, behind the olive sheen, there were lights. I saw a flash of movement, and then I saw what might have been a man standing and looking out, a pair of men, one of them stocky, looking this way. And was that flash a reflection from binoculars?

Hans Krone.

The Commercial Bank had taken four floors of the Lindenhof, well up in the building, perhaps there. Krone's office — there! Krone's office overlooking the hotel room he had arranged for me.

Krone, my Virgil. What a fool I was, a self-important ass to have thought myself Dante. Did Dante condemn his Beatrice by asking her to trust his vain foolishness? Krone, no Virgil, was Judas! Binoculars! A bolt of self-loathing rose in my throat like bile. If Krone is Judas, I asked myself, then who are you? Jesus Christ, indeed.

Having registered all of this without moving, I let the drapery fall. I welcomed the return of shadows.

Looking down at Charlotte, I almost said, You are right, right about everything.

But she had lowered her face onto her knees. The slip of paper was on the floor beside her, open.

Her shoulders were moving in the gentle tide of her inaudible sobbing. I went down on one knee and put my hand on the back of her neck, on the angle of skin that lay uncovered where her hair had fallen away to either side. Through that pink membrane, I felt the current of her blood flowing, warm. And I felt the slow ebbing of her grief, whatever it was.

After some moments, I swung around to sit beside her on the floor, easing my weight against the wall, inviting hers to shift against me, which, with a movement as natural as gravity, it did. With one arm, I held her in silence for a long time.

Her head at rest on my shoulder, her tears dry on my shirt.

It was a simple matter to bring my face down, sheltering her face from the room, my mouth beside her ear, her mouth beside mine.

"V and V?" I asked, a whisper. There seemed to be no question of our being overheard; no question, either, of her not answering.

"*Verhältnis und Verwandten,*" she whispered in reply.

I had no idea how the words were spelled — for this writing, I look it up — yet they struck a familiar chord, as if I'd studied them in my Berlitz. "What is that?" I asked.

"An expression. In English you say 'kith and kin.'"

"David is telling you that —"

"He is my family now."

"Emphasis on *he.*"

"Yes."

"That doesn't go without saying?"

"I told you. I never left Berlin, never really left. I thought I did. David thought I did. But I never left Berlin. That is the revelation of *ersten Mai,* 1961."

"And 1945? The curse of Rick's father — Ulrich's father. You said that before, 'curse.' What curse? That he was a Communist? And then the Communists became the enemy? What?"

"Paul —"

"Were you a Communist, Charlotte?"

She laughed nearly out loud, a burst of air in my ear. "Of course not."

"'Soviet files,' you said. You came here to learn what had happened to Wolf, and your American found Soviet files for you, which answered your questions. And Sohlmann, the Stasi official killed at Schloss Pankow this week, how does he —?"

"Paul!"

"You've shown me the pieces, Charlotte. Now show me how they fit."

"Let go, Paul. Let go of everything. If you let go, we can just be here together. *Be* here together. Can that not be enough?"

"No past? No future?"

"Not until . . ." She hesitated, then said, "Tomorrow."

"And David?"

"David is my rescuer. He gave me milk for my child, and I will always owe him that. He finished my story for me, too. But there is the problem. I never finished the story myself. He took me from Berlin, but that was not enough. David and I are like you and Michael, which is why I know what Michael feels. What David wants is impossible, and that truth comes clear only here. If there is a curse, that is what it is."

"Berlin."

"I am in Berlin and David is not. It was always thus. I confessed this to you. I wanted to love him, my rescuer. I tried to love him all these years, but . . ."

She fell silent. I supplied the line she had offered me: "'Real love, compared to fantasy, is a harsh and dreadful thing.'"

"And now David is hurt, very hurt."

"You 'confessed' to him?"

"Yes."

"When?"

"Last night. By telephone. That is why he sent the message. Why I did not read it."

"A worried father, like me. A worried husband."

"But with nothing he can do. Everything is out of David's hands. And like you, David finds this very difficult."

"And all of this, between you, is because of Wolf? Wolf is what keeps you 'in Berlin'?" I felt her stiffen next to me. "Because you still love him, your Leipzig professor, your honored war hero, your son's father, even if he is dead. Or perhaps *because* he is dead."

Abruptly, Charlotte pulled back. I felt a rebuke coming, for pressing her again.

But I was wrong. She brought her face to mine, our noses nearly touching. She put her hands on each of my cheeks, clutching my bones. She looked into me, a gaze, not a stare. "Paul," she said in the whisper that had become our vernacular. "Wolf died a terrible death in a terrible time. He was at Moabit prison, yes. That is his name on the bronze tablet at Schloss Pankow, yes. But Wolf has nothing to do with love — mine or anyone's. I will say nothing more about Wolf except this. He is not what makes me like Michael or like you — I am like you both; I see how *both* of you feel — because your wife was very different. Your Edie. I know that."

"What do you know?"

"That you and she punished each other as a way to avoid punishing your crippled son. What you did, you did for love."

"And you and Wolf?"

"Leave it at this: my dead husband was nothing like your dead wife."

"But you and I . . . ?"

She shrugged against me. "Similar, perhaps."

"You are like me because the past has its grip on you."

"We do the gripping, Paul."

"I see that, because of you. And believe it or not, I am letting go because of you."

"As am I. Because of *you*. When I turned to you in the car, it was not only for Krone. Here is my real confession. It was for you."

Our kiss then belonged to both of us.

As did the quick passion with which we tried to swallow each other. Soon we were pulling at clothes, tumbling across the stretch of bare hardwood that was the margin between the wall and the thick, soft carpet against which we brushed. I was a man out of practice, and I recall that it came as a surprise to me that Charlotte's bra fastened at the front. We both laughed when we had to stop so that she could unclasp it.

The sight of her free white breasts brought a gasp from the well of my throat. I lost that sight as she pressed against me, pulling off the last of my shirt — the shirt that she had bought for me. Then she was unhooking my belt. Then we were naked, and I was between her legs, over her, in her, aware of every bodily sensation, including the breath-stopping pressure of her thighs at my waist as her long, smooth legs locked around me, her legs which so kept the pace of our rocking that it was impossible to say who set it.

I forgot that there were reasons to stifle our noises, and reasons not to. The sounds Charlotte made as she approached her succession of hills — not only the guttural rapidity of breathing, but the timed slaps of her open hand onto the floor beside us, a rider's whip hand — were a next level of pleasure to me. That pleasure was like a beloved summer house I was returning to after winter, and in one of its rooms I met an old envy, familiar from a thousand times with Edie, how a man can only marvel at the supreme self-possession of a woman's ecstasy, her lover a partner, yes, but an awed bystander, too.

To Charlotte and me, if I may presume to report for both of us, our raucous coming together provided the perfect release; was an exquisite expression of need and longing; a transitory but consoling fulfillment of both; an act of love, even, though the word was nowhere in the air between us. An act, while it lasted, of simple purity, pure simplicity. But oh, the sounds! The sounds surely suggested something else. Not once did I wonder, as she grew louder and louder, if, after all, she was thinking of Krone and his knot of Stasi listeners, to whom our sweet, redemptive passion could have been only fucking.

"I used to think that hair didn't grow on women's legs," I said, "like their faces." I was rubbing my foot along the smooth skin of her calf, the bent knuckle of my forefinger along the high ridge of her cheekbone. This was later. We had moved to the bed, had drawn back its blankets, and the cool, crisp sheets had received us as if we alone were meant for them.

I had suggested with a whisper killing the microphone in the chandelier, but she said no — what is left to hide? And besides, it is better for the children if the Stasi think us naïve.

I could tell from the way she answered that she had already thought about it, and I might have wondered why, but didn't. Anyway, she said, who cares what the Stasi hear, what they think?

We made love again then, with more deliberation, more delight, more tenderness, and more attention. Aware of the microphone above us, I made my moves this time in near silence, and was struck that, despite her disclaimer, so did she.

Now, enacting the cliché of our kind, we were smoking, our bodies half up, leaning against the cushioned headboard. "Really," I said, "I used to think that."

She laughed. "And then you came to *Deutschland* and met the *Fräulein*."

"My secretary has more hair on her legs than I do."

She brought her foot to my leg while drawing on her cigarette, then let her foot fall away, the utter complacency of sexual satiation. As she exhaled, I watched the smoke stream out of her elegant lips.

Beside her, away from me, was the bedside table and the glowing small lamp, which alone kept the room from darkness. With the drapes still drawn, it could have been the middle of the night. In silence I watched her smoking, aware of the way the table lamp backlit her profile, from her face down to the quite pointed form of her uncovered breasts.

"You know why that is," Charlotte said, and it took me a moment to realize she was still thinking of my offhand remark about unshaven legs.

"Why?"

"Razors have been rationed in this country during forty of the last fifty years, because German steel went to guns. When razors are rationed, how readily do women procure them, do you think?"

She paused, and I was unsure if she expected me actually to answer what was, after all, no question. But before I did, in any case, she added, "There was hair on my legs and under my arms until I met my American."

Her simple statement threw me. I looked away and stared at the glowing tip of my own cigarette. She spoke so matter-of-factly that I could not discern what, if any, feeling she was expressing. To my regret, her words sparked feeling enough in me, a feeling I did not want. Her American. Healy. Her rescuer. Her "V & V," kith and kin. Ulrich's well-meaning stepfather. Her husband.

A good guy, obviously. And here I was in bed with his wife. But what kind of man lets his wife take on the Stasi by herself? Healy, I had concluded, was a military man of supreme duty. I knew the type. However unwillingly, hadn't he put "national security" ahead of his family? And hadn't he pressed Charlotte to do his Berlin dirty work for him, reversing some breach that he had caused? And anyway, hadn't he abandoned a first wife and child of his own? So who was innocent? What had that girl said? They sin in innocence.

And now wasn't Charlotte indicating that if there was infidelity here for her, it was in relation to unfinished passions tied to her dead husband, not Healy?

Such was the cluster of rationalizations with which I could have brushed my qualms away. But in fact I needed no such rationalizations. My qualms did not survive a next glance at her naked form. The unabashed ease with which she lay next to me, uncovered if not precisely exposed, was enough to obliterate forever any idea that language, accent, nationality, even history are the particularities that matter. Instead, the slight mound of her abdomen, the crater at her navel, the twin ledges of her rib cage, her languid breasts, and the erect buds of their nipples — all of this defined her. At that moment my capacity to take it in defined me.

The unselfconscious show of her repose seemed as erotic, in its way, as had her earlier frenzy. I found myself becoming hard again, as if my foot gently running up the hill of her lower leg was the very height of foreplay.

I reached across her to put my cigarette in the ashtray between the lamp and the telephone, a movement that made her adjust, but that also brought a smile to her face. She handed me her cigarette to do likewise. With me leaning across her, it was a simple matter for her hidden hand to steal down my body to my stiffened penis.

"What?" she teased. "My grim talk of fifty years of German steel, is that what brings you up again? The grimness, darling, or the steel?"

"Neither. It's the thought of you — needing an American." I kissed her. "I wish I could have been your American."

"But you are, *Liebchen,*" she said, laughing and pulling me onto her again.

296

And with a laugh of my own, I sang, "To look sharp every time you shave, to feel sharp and be on the ball . . . ," the Gillette jingle that would have meant nothing to the uncomplicated German girl she seemed to be just then. I began by kissing each of her shaven armpits, which tickled her and made her even wilder. The laughter this time, even more than the sex, was what made us friends.

Later still, forgetting to whisper, she said, "If I call the front desk and tell them to ring us in an hour, we can sleep now and still keep our dinner reservation."

It seemed a thought out of the blue, but in fact I had begun to doze. I didn't care about dinner, but I said, "Sure. Good idea." I found my wristwatch on the floor on my side of the bed. The time was a quarter past six. She made the call, then snapped the light out.

She kissed my forehead. "Sleep well," she said, then turned away from me, bunching her pillow under her head, a woman who, in sleeping, needs a little space.

I was not sure how much time passed — not much — before I vaguely registered that she had slipped out of bed and crossed to the bathroom. The hazy thought pleased me because I assumed somehow that she would return wearing the burnished satin nightgown, a sexy domesticity as a complement to her nudity. Through the closed door I heard the faint sound of the toilet flushing and the whine of a faucet that I took at first to be the sink. But, coming more fully awake, I realized it was the bidet.

When the bathroom door opened again, she had turned out the light, and so her form was a shadow as she walked purposefully to the far side of the room where our clothing lay folded on the chairs. What is this?

I sat up, threw the blanket back, and would have spoken, but she came right to the foot of the bed, to stand close enough for me to see her forefinger pressed against her mouth. She was already wearing her bra and underpants.

I got out of bed and went past her to the bathroom, turning on the light, closing the door against her. I was not prepared to see myself in triple images again. I went to the toilet, urinated, went to one of the sinks and splashed my face with water. As I was toweling myself dry, still trying to stretch my brain to the new thing, the door opened and she came in, almost fully dressed. Only the last buttons of her blouse needed fastening. She closed the door behind her, careful not to let it click.

"What?" I asked.

"I have to leave."

"You deceived me."

"No." She closed her blouse as we spoke.

"You wanted me asleep so that you could go. Go where?"

"I wanted you asleep so that you would not ask me."

I wrapped the towel around my waist. "Well, I am asking."

"And I am not answering. You must not think there is anything you can do to stop me."

"What changed you?"

"Nothing changed me."

"This was your plan all afternoon?"

"Yes."

"So it was a lie, all of it."

"No, Paul. Almost none of it. Dinner was a lie. And sleeping. Nothing else."

"And you wanted them to hear so they would believe, as I did, that you weren't going for your husband's film, that you are capable of putting your son first."

"My son *is* first."

"What is on the film, Charlotte?"

"Do not ask me!" she hissed.

"Agents. The battle order of spies. Soviet plans. KGB, Stasi — who cares? Why does this matter so much to you? Let them play their game. 'Let go,' you said. Why can't you let this go, at least until tomorrow afternoon?"

"You fool!" she whispered bitterly.

The word seared me. Yet it also cauterized the wound of my ignorance, my pathetic readiness to be hurt by what I did not know.

"They will not release Rick tomorrow or *ever*," she said, "until the film is dealt with one way or another. I *must* deal with it." She turned to go, but I stopped her.

"Charlotte."

"No. And do not ask. Ask nothing."

"Let me come with you."

"This is for me to do."

"I respect that. Just let me be with you."

"I will explain nothing."

"I won't ask. I promise."

"And you keep your promises."

"As you know, because you have seen that in my son. He learned it from me." I found it possible to smile at her. Each of us was aware of the new place to which she had brought me — she and also Michael. The change in me had come from both of them.

She studied me with her careful eyes, no stare but a long, unmoving examination. Then, quite simply, she nodded. She turned, opened the door, and let me go through. She moved back to the dressing table and its mirror while I found my clothes and put them on in silence.

When we left the room, Charlotte wore her tweed jacket and brown skirt, the leather bag on her shoulder. Her hair was up from her neck, as before, but she had covered it with her cloche hat. I was in my suit and tie, as before. We might have been the demure couple in the hotel brochure except for the hint of stealth with which we moved into the hallway, closing our door without a sound.

Assuming that we would do better slipping down the stairs, I was surprised when Charlotte punched the elevator button. While we waited, I said quietly, "You left a wake-up call. The phone will ring."

"Does not matter. By then" — by 7:15 — "all will be complete."

I looked at my watch. It was ten before seven. What could we do so quickly?

Suddenly she stopped. "Wait!"

She returned to the room. Her gloves, I thought. She never goes out without her gloves. But I was wrong. When she reappeared, after closing the door with an audible click, it was her gold lighter she was carrying, not gloves. Joining me as the elevator arrived, she dropped it into her bag.

The elevator operator tended his machine as if we weren't there. The doors then opened onto the main lobby, the bustle of arriving guests, of porters handling luggage, of waiters sailing among the tables and chairs of the open lounge to one side, all spread against the yellow glow of twilight just showing itself through the far wall of floor-to-ceiling windows. I followed her into this complicated scene, aware that she was coolly striding toward the entryway with nary a glance to one side or the other. It fell to me to eye the strangers around us, especially the lone men — three of them, no, four — sitting at separate tables and on sofas in the lounge area.

And sure enough, as I followed Charlotte through the revolving door into the full soft light of evening, I looked back and one of those men was up and walking after us, fast.

I fell into step with Charlotte as she cut into the pedestrian flow, and like strollers around us, I linked arms with her. With a quick glance back I said, "Don't look, but we have company."

"Does not matter," she said.

"We should —"

"Paul!"

Whatever she proposed to do now, it would be known, if not prevented. Her behavior contradicted any plan I could imagine. In her carelessness, she had let the hotel room door close with a noise and waltzed through the lobby and out the front door.

She carried us along, offering no comment, no explanation, no acknowledgment that I was even with her, except for the crook of her left arm. Holding on to her had become my purpose.

Up the Kurfürstendamm, one block, another, and another, past the crush of sidewalk cafés that were nervously alive with high-toned theatergoers and club haunters; past the brass piping and awnings of deluxe hotels; past the light show of galleries and shops, now closed, but with their plate glass windows glittering. All around us were self-styled boulevardiers in pegged trousers and cravats, women in stiletto heels and seamed nylons, lace veils, and fur stoles. There were dandies carrying walking sticks.

The ghost of Isherwood was out, one Sally Bowles after another, on the hunt for parfait and crème de menthe. They were a legion, one could say, of impressionists, half taking in the scene, wanting only to *be* impressed, the other half defining it, happy to oblige. Yet to me and Charlotte, the twilight revelers were mere obstacles, even if, to the enemy across the city — or behind us — they were a decadent throng, cosmopolitanism itself, proof of the virtues of Socialist struggle.

We passed the bombed-out Kaiser Wilhelm Church, left standing as a memorial now, an accidentally ironic one, since the horrors it kept in mind had been inflicted by the heroes this half of the city wanted only to emulate. The wreckage rose from the bustling avenue like the charred, half-broken tooth of a monster giant. It might have warned against the surrounding sparkle, but the church was itself newly decked with Chartres-made glass, as if to proclaim that in the West even the ruins are beautiful. Sparkle is all.

At the street beyond the church, Charlotte led us left onto a narrower sidewalk where, because of the press of people, we had to slow down, then separate. Here, instead of boulevardiers, the crowd was made up of the vacant-eyed and lost, refugees from the East, and opportunists looking to exploit them, sharpies and hawkers. When I glanced back, I glimpsed the same man cutting across the street. I knew better by now than to warn Charlotte. I walked one step behind her. We went along the block and across the next street, approaching the mammoth central train station.

As we neared the entrance, beggars, including the aging war-wounded and one or two gypsy women holding infants, reached out, and, unseeing, Charlotte brushed by them as if their proffered hands were turnstiles. At the last moment, before entering the station proper, she stopped. She turned and looked back the way we'd come, and I sensed it as she spotted the man from the hotel. For a long moment she simply watched him, as if rules required that we not get too far ahead. Then, without a glance at me, she turned and walked into the train station.

Compared to what it must have been on weekday evenings, the cavernous waiting area was no doubt uncrowded now. The restrictions on travel between Berlin and its environs meant that this station was a terminal mainly for trains from distant West Germany. Most of the trains would normally have carried businessmen, few of whom were in evidence. Charlotte strode through the vast hall, heading for the overhead arrival board.

With its clacking letters and numbers, the display was designed around a large clock. It was 7:18. Charlotte barely slowed down as she took in whatever information she needed. She angled toward the wall of doorways and the train platforms beyond.

Beside track 11 was posted a permanent block-lettered sign reading "U.S. Army Duty Train," with times for two daily departures and two daily arrivals, one of which, I saw as we whipped past, was 1915 hours. Now.

This train had set the day's schedule, I realized. The afternoon had in effect been Charlotte's killing time. To my surprise, recognizing this changed nothing.

Track 11, alone of the track platforms, was bustling with people, a stream coming toward us in the dull smoky cavern. Evening light filtered gray through the massive glass roof above us, the light fading but bright enough to dominate the electric lights on columns along the platform. It was instantly apparent that the arrivals were Americans, mostly young soldiers in khaki, with duffels hoisted, but also dressed-up women holding the hands of toddlers and porters pushing luggage carts. There were middle-aged men in suits and ties — American suits with cuffed trousers and three-button jackets, not German ones with narrow legs and boxy coats. The men's ties, like my own, were narrow and clipped.

We breasted through the arriving travelers, walking beside the long line of train cars. Passengers were still disembarking, stepping gingerly down. This was an American train with English-language signs and the Stars and Stripes painted on the doors, but the cars had the characteristic rounded rooflines of the German railroad, windows that displayed not rows of seats but individual compartments, the small plush parlors that made European rail travel exotic.

As I followed Charlotte along the train, I noticed that every car — those upholstered sofa-like benches, brocade curtains framing shades, gleaming railings — was first class. No second-class travel for the occupying Army, or its women and children.

I assumed that Charlotte was there to meet someone, one of these arriving travelers. Then it hit me: Healy? She was clearly on the lookout. As she slowed at each new car, I realized she was eyeing its number. So she was searching for a particular car.

Two thirds of the way down the train, she found it. By then, the stream of passengers had thinned, and now only the odd straggler passed us. Charlotte swung up and onto the car. As I followed, I paused from the high step to glance back again. In the distance, yes, I saw the man from the hotel, just coming onto the platform, and then, closer, I saw another man, tall and bearded, heading for us. As he pushed past a laden luggage cart, he rudely bumped the porter. Behind him, obscured but evident from passengers making way, someone else was violating the traffic flow.

In the car, Charlotte moved quickly along the aisle, checking number plates at each compartment.

No one else seemed to be in the car. Near the far end, she read a compartment number, slid the door open, and went in. By the time I reached the door, she was bent over the seat in the corner by the window, like a woman looking for a dropped earring. Both her hands were plunged into the crevice of the upholstery where the seat joined the backrest.

My visceral alarm, I think, was that she had lost her mind.

"Charlotte!" I said, but she ignored me. What she was doing made no sense until, just then, she straightened and faced me, holding the thing she had found. She held it between her fingers, a 35-millimeter film canister.

"Now, Paul, I need you." She brushed by me, out into the aisle, down the short distance to the near exit. She leapt off the train. Quite deliberately, she peered down the length of the platform toward the terminal.

When I joined her, I saw two men running toward us, closing from perhaps thirty yards away. Behind them was another running man, and behind him, another.

I glanced the other way. A pair of exceptionally tall, white-helmeted black MPs were sauntering our way, as yet unaware of us.

"Here," Charlotte said. She had unscrewed the canister lid and was now calmly unfurling the roll it held. She pulled the gray film out into the light as if it were a streamer to throw at a departing ship.

I noticed how thin the film was — 8-millimeter at most, not 35-millimeter at all.

The day before, Healy's man in Alexanderplatz had said the missing film was tourist pictures with an edge of microfilm, but this, I guessed, was the microfilm itself.

Charlotte had the film unspooled. It was perhaps six feet long, draping her arm and shoulder.

With a quick glance at the men rushing us, she said, "Here, hold it. Hold it high."

I did, unsure exactly what I was doing or what she wanted. I gripped the film at its midpoint, letting it dangle over my hand in two roughly equal ribbons. I held it up like a starter raising his gun, and then I realized that what she wanted was for the thing to be seen.

"Hey!" A gruff voice from behind. I turned. One of the MPs, approaching fast, was pointing. "Hey!"

The MP was not calling to us, as I saw when I turned. The nearest man approaching from the other direction had a pistol in his outstretched hand. Not the man from the hotel, yet he was someone I had seen before. The MP was pointing at him.

Charlotte had bent to her bag, and as she came up from it, I saw the gold lighter in her hand. She made it flame and brought it to the bottom of the film strip I was holding, igniting first one end, then the other. The celluloid flared and the fire shot quickly up. I had to extend my arm away from my body. "They will not release Ulrich," she had said, "tomorrow or *ever* until the film is dealt with one way or another."

One way, exposing it to light, *and* another, burning it. The film with its state secrets — names of agents, plans for war, whatever the hell it was — gone.

The pair of flames met in the air to become one licking tongue of fire. It scaled the film, rising toward my hand. I held on to the thing as long as I could, displaying it for all. Once again I was her trained circus performer, happily so. Every ounce of my former unwillingness had drained from me as I joined in her defining choice. No to national security and state secrets. No to General Healy. Yes to Ulrich, pure and simple — to see the film removed as a factor from her son's future. I was a mere instrument of her choice, not an object of it, which was all right with me.

Amid the swirling commotion of which I was the momentary still point, my mind settled on the flame. Oddly, instead of turning to ash and blowing away, the film, as it burned, was melting, an ignited liquid. I think now of the sea afire around the still point of the sinking *Stephen Case*.

"Stop right there!"

To one side, the MP had gone into a marksman's crouch, his side-arm aimed at someone coming fast toward us. The prescribed posture, yet the MP was far from cool. His hand shook. "Drop that, goddammit!" His voice, high-pitched, cracking, carried an overpowering note of terror.

The man rushing at us, his gun just as ready, I recognized as the Russian, the black-clad KGB apparatchik. It was at him the MP was aiming. "Drop!" the MP cried again, and there were a pair of gunshots in succession, whose echoes bounced off the glass roof above.

It happened too quickly for me to take in intelligibly until later. The onrushing man whose drawn gun sparked the MP's panic was familiar to me because he had silently watched over our meeting with the kids the day before, clearly intimidating Colonel Erhardt. As I eventually understood, this Russian was the KGB imposing itself on the Stasi after the Schloss Pankow fire that had killed Erhardt's chief, Sohlmann. As Moscow had moved in on East Berlin, the KGB officer moved in on us — at just the wrong moment.

He was the one, obviously, who set it up for Ulrich to confide his secret in his mother's ear, and he was the one who then followed her. But the KGB strategy was one with which Charlotte had her own reasons to cooperate, and of which she needed no warning from the likes of me.

So this was the figure rushing toward us with his weapon drawn, hoping to prevent the destruction of the film, his only object. Beside him had been his comrade — the man I saw following from the hotel. And behind them had come Hal Cummings, in his false beard and dark turtleneck. His firearm, too, was drawn.

And with Cummings, finally, had come the hard-breathing Hans Krone, clutching not a weapon but binoculars — the binoculars I had glimpsed in the Lindenhof, across from the Kempinski. So Krone was not Stasi after all. He had been recruited through Cummings by General Healy, either yesterday or a long time before. Cummings's presence with Krone meant it had been Healy's men watching us at the hotel, Healy's men listening in on us.

As quickly as this knot of people had converged, at the sound of gunshots it dispersed. The KGB man and his partner, seeing the film destroyed — its agents' names? its war plans? — had simply turned and run back the way they'd come, disappearing. At first I assumed that they were the ones who had discharged their weapons.

One of the MPs ran after them, but he was crying, "Medic! Medic!"

The other MP had fallen to his knees beside me and Charlotte. He was crying over and over, "That bastard was going to shoot!" His explanation. His excuse. "That bastard was going to shoot."

This MP was the one who had fired, the only one. Whether because of his ineptness or because Charlotte had put herself between me and the KGB agent, one of the two shots had struck her in the head.

I think she was already dead by the time I lifted her from the cold cement into my lap, where I sat beside the last mercury-like beads of the burned celluloid. The film was destroyed, but so was Charlotte.

I remember trying to pull strands of her auburn hair free of the blood. I remember wiping her face with my sleeve, trying to dam the red flow away from her neck, as if she would have wanted me to protect the collar of her blouse.

What I do not remember is leaning down to her face and kissing her. But I must have, because the metallic taste of blood was on my lips for a long time. I can taste it now.

17

THE NEXT MORNING, Hans Krone rang my room at nine sharp, as he'd said he would. I was ready. I never slept that night. Instead, I had relived everything — pushing up through the blue water, lungs bursting, body stretching toward the light, coming at last to the surface. And breaking through the surface with a gasp, what had I found but more water. After rising from the bottom of one ocean, I found myself at the bottom of another.

First Edie, then Charlotte. One of my permanent regrets had been that I was not with Edie when she died. I always thought it would have mattered — to me if not to her. But being with Charlotte taught me that at such a moment, nothing matters.

Edie's death: Charlotte had wanted me to put aside the self-damning burden of it, with the obvious benefit that would be for Michael. In our two brief days together, she never said what the benefit might have been for her.

Edie's death: Charlotte had wanted me to accept the independence of Edie's own destiny by acknowledging at last that the accident on the road was no more my fault than hers.

Edie's death: I had stolen her wind in the Lightning race on that first day; years later, by making her death something of mine, I had stolen her wind at the last. Through that endless night in the hotel, I saw all of this, and the proof of my overdue honoring of Edie's quite separate integrity was that I honored Charlotte's — her freedom, the mystery of her choices, her life — by not taking the accident of her death as something I had caused.

Yet one day can mark a person forever. That day marked me.

I knew that night that its shock entailed a loss I would not recover from — not the loss of Charlotte, since she was never mine to lose. What I lost was the hope she gave me that the harsh and dreadful ache of loneliness was something of which I could, as she kept putting it to me, *let go*. She would not approve of this, I know, but as the weight of this story shows, it never happened.

After such a night, I was relieved to get Krone's call.

I walked out of the hotel into a bright, crisp morning. A breeze was blowing into the city from the unobstructed flatland stretching to the Urals, a great plain that had put Eastern Europe at the mercy of the Red Army and its tanks. Killer tanks. We *were* at war.

Krone's car was at the curb. A first clue of what was coming was that I saw Krone sitting in the passenger seat in front, as he so unwillingly had — was it only the day before? The rear windows had curtains drawn across the glass. A second clue was that the driver did not get out to open the rear door for me.

When I opened it myself, I saw General Healy sitting in the far corner, looking not quite the same as I remembered him. He was wrapped in a cloud of cigarette smoke. As he turned to look at me, the smoke and some undefined quality of his presence made it seem a movement in slow motion. He was in civvies, wearing aviator sunglasses. He had shaven his RAF mustache. But it was him.

I returned his stare for the stretch of time it took him to remove the sunglasses, so that his unfiltered, steely eyes could settle on me. "Get in," he said.

I did, closing the door behind.

At the wheel, now without the false beard, was Hal Cummings. He wore the black suit and cap of Krone's chauffeur. He put the car in gear and slowly pulled into the brisk traffic of a Monday morning.

Healy, now facing away from me, was looking out the window through a crack in the curtain. He wore a tan windbreaker with the collar up and a golfer's cap. When he put his cigarette to his mouth, I sensed a faint tremble in his fingers.

My impulse was to say I was sorry.

But I checked it because I did not want him to misunderstand. I was sorry beyond words that Charlotte was dead. And I was sorry for his suffering and his loss — which I could imagine. But I was in no way sorry that Charlotte's last hours were with me, were what they were, were what Healy knew they were.

"What's the drill?" I asked, as if this were merely a pre-op briefing.

Healy firmly snuffed his cigarette in the armrest ashtray, a simple gesture with which he claimed his authority. "Pro forma. They know what's happened." Now he turned to me with a fierce, cold gaze. "They want nothing further to do with it. They are terrified it will become an incident, one they don't control. So they want the kids out, now."

"Because the film is destroyed," I said. "And they know it."

"Film, Mr. Montgomery? What film?" His eyes were ball bearings.

I saw the pointlessness of getting into it with him.

He resumed the briefing. "Therefore, at the hearing the case will be dismissed. There is no way to screw it up. You will be permitted to see the kids just before the hearing, so you can reassure them and emphasize that they should say nothing, *nothing*. Then you wait. Only the lawyer from JAG will actually be allowed in the courtroom. He will be the only one from our side, but he'll have been briefed. It's all worked out. As I said, pro forma."

"And I am there —"

"Because I can't be. If it were possible for me to handle this, believe me, Mr. Montgomery, you would be back at your hotel."

"And you can't 'handle it' because — ?"

"You know damn well why."

"Not even now, General?"

"Especially not now. I don't suppose you can understand this, but the one thing that keeps this procedure pro forma is my distance from it."

"And my presence works because that is what they expect."

"Precisely. As was the case yesterday, you are there as your son's worried father. All three kids will be released into your custody. And facilitating your safe return to West Berlin will be Herr Krone, who is well known as your assistant and personal interpreter."

"As he was yesterday," I said. I faced forward. "Good morning, Hans."

Krone looked back at me, but he had the grace to say nothing.

"If it's pro forma," I asked, "why has Colonel Cummings drawn motor pool duty?"

"In case, Mr. Montgomery. In case."

"In case what?"

"In case of surprises. There have been surprises, wouldn't you say?"

"No one has been more surprised this weekend, General, than I have."

Again his stare. A restrained but efficient way of singeing me with the blast furnace of his rage.

The button controlling the glass partition was on my armrest, and I pushed it. Slowly the barrier rose from its slot. When Healy and I were sealed off, I faced him. "What does this have to do with Charlotte's dead husband?"

"My wife's history is none of your business, Montgomery."

"But if it's her late husband, General, that would be Ulrich's father, and for a time this morning Ulrich's history *is* my business, especially if it involves the possibility of surprise. What surprise do you have in mind?"

"If I had it in mind, it wouldn't be a surprise, now, would it?"

"I know that Wolf von Siedelheim was a Communist, and that he is honored as a martyr by the Stasi. And I know that someone killed his brother or cousin in Frankfurt last week." Healy registered my statement with an abrupt turn of his head, speaking of surprises. I pressed him. "Do they know that Ulrich is von Siedelheim's son?"

"No." Healy dropped his voice to a whisper. "And they must not know. Whatever you do, don't refer to it."

"Ulrich doesn't know?"

Healy shook his head.

"And how did this boy's family history become a matter of 'national security'? The spy caper, the microfilm, the border crisis, the fire at Schloss Pankow, the KGB — all this crap. How is it tied to Ulrich?"

Healy shook his head, suddenly at the mercy of what I recognized as grief. "A terrible coincidence," he said slowly. "Two worlds that should have had nothing to do with each other, and wouldn't have, except" — his hesitation was before a bitter self-reproach — "ex-

cept for my fucking bag, left where Rick could take it. Rick's goddamn rebelliousness, all leading to 'flashpoint Berlin.' All a terrible accident."

A terrible accident. The exact phrase a New York state trooper had
uttered to me on the phone that night at the lake. A terrible accident.
A woman's fate. A man's epitaph. Mine.

Without my being aware of it, the car had stopped. Cummings
rapped on the glass partition.

Healy peered through the curtain, then raised a hand to Cummings. *Right.*

Through the curtain on my side, I saw that the car was in a narrow
cobblestoned side street. I took in a row of warehouses. The street was
deserted.

Healy grasped the handle of his door. "This is where I get out," he
said, then added with his former chill, "This is not the Navy, Montgomery. But there *are* torpedoes."

Did he know? I found it possible to say, "Damn the torpedoes,
General."

"Full ahead then."

"Right."

"One other thing," he said.

"What?"

"Don't tell Rick."

"About his father?"

Healy had the skill of showing only what he wanted seen. That he
closed his eyes for a moment told me of his utter indifference to any
impression I might take. He let his head fall slightly back, then inhaled sharply. "No. About his mother," he said, and then opened his
eyes to look at me. "I want to tell the boy that Charlotte is dead. It is
important that he hear it from me." And in that unadorned statement,
I glimpsed the depth of Healy's love for Ulrich. *He brought the baby
milk!* It was a completion of his love for Ulrich's mother, an extension
of it. General Healy loved the boy, that was all.

"I understand, General," I said. "Of course."

Healy nodded. To my complete surprise, his eyes had filled. He put
his sunglasses on again.

I said, after all, the words "I am sorry," but he had already opened the door and leapt out of the car. I had no reason to think he heard me, or if he had, that he cared.

Less than five minutes later, we were at the sector checkpoint. Cummings exchanged a few words in German with the *Vopo,* who handed back our documents and waved us through.

I had assumed that we would be returning to Schloss Pankow, but the hearing was a matter of a petty currency violation, not state security, and Cummings brought the car to a stop in front of an innocuous two-story building a few doors from the corner of a street that opened into the vast, nearly deserted Alexanderplatz, the site of Saturday's festivities. We were across from the *Rathaus,* in front of which the rough lumber reviewing stand was being dismantled. Litter blew in small, circular bursts here and there in the plaza, and men in blue smocks pushed brooms beside wheelbarrows.

The vista evoked nothing of the May Day spectacle, and as I got out of the car, nothing anchored my eye to keep it from floating to the top of the *Fernsehturm.* From that perch, Charlotte and I had taken in the grim panorama of the past.

Cummings stayed with the car. Krone took my elbow. "This way, sir," he said, and I let him usher me into the building, past a sign with the Gothic lettering of German officialdom: "*Die Hauptverwaltung Aufklärung.*"

"What is this?" I asked Krone.

"Office of Border Security."

"I thought Berlin sector boundaries weren't borders. Isn't that the point?"

"They are prepared to yield the point, Paul. But first they want to *make* the point."

We passed an indifferent guard slouching in the vestibule and walked down a broad corridor with undulating uneven floorboards. At the corridor's end, through heavy double doors, we entered a bustling office. Behind a counter, perhaps a dozen people were at typewriters and adding machines.

A frumpish clerk approached from her side of the counter. Krone told her what we wanted. She nodded. She went through a side door and soon returned with a man in a shoddy blue uniform I did not recognize — People's Border Police or something. He looked like a passed-over train conductor. The Germans and their uniforms.

He led us back out through the doors, down the corridor once more, past the entrance we had come in by, to the opposite end of the building. The double doors there, apparently, opened into the hearing room to which, if Healy was right, we would not be admitted.

Indeed, the man stopped short of those doors to take us through another, smaller one. It led into a kind of waiting room lined with ten or twelve thick-legged wooden chairs. Where a window might have been was a stylized portrait of Walter Ulbricht — the spectacles, the chin beard, a double-breasted tan suit with a row of medals at the lapel. He wore the stern expression of a man wanting to be taken for Lenin.

Half a dozen people were seated in the room, separately. Our escort, at the door, spoke loudly — two sentences, three, and then the room's occupants sheepishly stood and filed past us, out into the hallway. At that point, the man gestured at the now vacated room — it was ours.

Departing, he closed the door behind himself, leaving me and Krone alone.

Several standup ashtrays were posted around the room. I took a chair near one, took out a cigarette, and lit up. Krone sat next to me. I offered the pack, but he shook his head.

"Paul, I —"

I raised my hand. "Don't say it, Hans. I have one question, only one question. I want the truth."

He nodded glumly.

"Was it Saturday or was it before? If you were working with them before, you're finished with Chase, and I'll finish you with every American bank."

"You threaten that and still expect the truth?"

"Yes."

"They gave me no choice. And we were still to be on the same side, you and I."

"Really?"

"It was Saturday. Colonel Cummings approached me after I left you."

"While Charlotte and I were in the restaurant in the tower?"

"He gave me no choice. He made it seem possible that Mrs. Healy had tricked you. It was you I was —"

"Never mind."

"But I never —"

"Enough, Hans. You've answered me."

"That is all?"

"Yes. Forget it."

"Paul, I am regretful —"

"Let's just do what we're doing, Hans. Let's get these kids home."

"In that case, I will have one of those cigarettes, if I may. *Danke-schön.*"

I was on my third cigarette when the door opened, the same German holding it.

An American Army major, the JAG attorney, walked in. His crisp tan uniform impressed, adorned as it was with a pale blue braid of rope at the shoulder, a ladder of ribbons on his chest, and unit patches on each sleeve. His shoes gleamed, but the overall effect of martial splendor was undercut somewhat by his crew-cut red hair, stiffened in front with goop, which made him seem far too young to trust.

His bright, eager expression as he approached us with hand extended reminded me of the uncomplicated, chipper boy I had always hoped to find in Michael. No more.

"Mr. Montgomery? Major Stahl. Glad to meet you, sir."

"Major, thanks for your help."

Krone and the major then shook hands, but the officer declined to sit, saying he had arranged for a prehearing session with the magistrate — "just to make sure we're all singing the same music." He winked and left the room, taking much of my confidence with him.

A few moments later, the door opened again and the young girl appeared, Katharine Carson, looking waif-like in her boyish black hair. The oversized field jacket made her seem even smaller than she was. She entered the room tentatively, her eyes darting, as if not convinced that Krone and I were the only ones there. She walked right over to me. "Mr. Montgomery, thank you for getting them to give me back my book." She held it up for me to see, a small accountant's ledger, the familiar green cloth cover.

314

"I'm glad they returned it to you, Kit," I said. "I hope you wrote some fabulous stuff."

"I did."

"I don't doubt it. How are you?"

"I'm okay."

"And the fellows?"

"Having a right good time." Her sarcasm was only friendly, and I laughed. I was relieved to have the signal that nothing terrible had happened here, at least.

Before I saw my son, I heard the faint click of his leg braces as he approached the door from its other side. My brain was keyed to that sound. When he appeared at the threshold, steadying himself in the doorframe, he grinned. "Hi, Dad."

I went to him with my arms open. He stepped free of the door into my embrace, which I made firm and lasting.

When I released him, he looked me in the eye with a clear, strong expression, which elicited from me an unplanned declaration. "I'm proud of you, Michael."

"You're not pissed? I thought yesterday you were pissed."

"I'm proud of you," I repeated.

Before he could respond, Rick came into the room, wide-eyed with expectation and, I saw, relief.

He glanced at me, but turned his gaze loose on the room itself. His eyes went from chair to chair, snagged briefly on the portrait of Walter Ulbricht, then came back to me. "Where is my mother?"

Michael stepped away from me as if he knew the secret I carried in my breast. He eased himself into a nearby chair.

"Your mother is not here, Rick," I said.

"I see that. Why not?"

It seemed that Rick had succeeded in stifling his nighttime agitation, but perhaps he had done so only by imagining the arrival of this moment, living for it. And it was wrong, essentially wrong, without her. Not waiting for me to answer, he glanced with hot suspicion at Krone.

"This is Mr. Krone," I said. "He is with me."

"But, I —"

I cut him off, trying to deflect him. "The hearing will go quickly. And then we will be out of here. And then —"

"Where is she?" he demanded.

"She is in West Berlin, Rick. With your father."

"My father?"

"I mean your stepfather."

"Why? What is *he* doing here?"

"He's not here. He's in West Berlin. We will see him later."

"He cannot be in Berlin! Nowhere in Berlin! Because of his job! Why is he in Berlin?"

"Because of — everything. Everything that has happened, and that is still happening."

"But his job —"

"The rule about his job does not apply anymore."

"Why?"

I could not think of what to say, how to answer. I wasn't going to lie to him. I said nothing.

But Rick pressed. "Did he stop my mother from being here? He kept her from being here, didn't he?"

"No, he didn't. Try to calm down, Rick."

"Dad," Michael put in, "his name is Ulrich. Ulrich, for God's sake."

I might have taken Michael's point, should have finally, but Rick was what Charlotte had called her son, and so it was how I had to think of him.

Rick was about to speak again, angrily, when Major Stahl came in behind him. "Excuse me," he said.

The boy stepped aside. The major entered, pulling the door after him, but the blue-uniformed German appeared suddenly, and he held the door open simply by standing there. The major looked at me, so I said, "This is Major Stahl from the U.S. judge advocate general's office at Berlin Command. He's here to make sure the proceedings are kosher. Right, Major?"

"Correct. Things should go smoothly. This is not a big deal, since the minister is ready to dismiss the case as BND mischief, which — who knows? — maybe it was." The officer grinned. I saw that his boyishness was at the service of a disarming technique. "I'm not authorized to speak for you in there, but they have agreed to let me serve as your interpreter."

"*Ich möchte keinen Dolmetscher haben!*" Rick said, a statement I recreate here using a dictionary. "No interpreter for me!"

Major Stahl did not hesitate. "*Nicht so schnell, Herr Healy.*" And then he barked another two sentences in German. Stahl sternly waited for Rick to reply. When he didn't, the major looked at the other two youngsters. "I am your insurance in there. For one and all. *All.*" He faced Rick again. "So when I put the questions to you in English, you will hear how I want you to answer, get it? Instead of saying, 'Did you have the currency in question?' I will say, 'You didn't have the currency in question, did you?' And you answer, 'No, sir, I did not.' Like that. At home we call it leading the witness. *Verstehen Sie?*"

"Yes, sir," Katharine said, and Michael nodded. Rick only stared back at him.

Major Stahl consulted a briefing sheet. "So you are Katharine Carson? Dependent daughter of Master Sergeant Earl Carson, USAF?"

"Yes, sir."

To Michael he said, "And you are Michael Montgomery, dependent son of USGS-19 Paul Montgomery?"

"Monty," Michael said, the name I thought he hated as much as I.

"And you are Rick Healy —"

"Ulrich," Michael put in.

"— dependent son of Major General David Healy, USAF."

"Not 'son.'"

Major Stahl's expression softened with a kind of willed sentimentality, a variation on that forced boyishness. The shift set off an instinctive alarm in me, but too late. The major said, "I'm sorry about your mother, son."

"What?"

"I'm sorry —" The major reddened and glanced at me helplessly.

"What about my mother?" Rick demanded. And he swung toward me like a fighter. "Did my stepfather — ?"

"Your stepfather had nothing to do with it," I said.

"With what?"

What could I do? Or not do? I wanted desperately to honor Healy's wish, but I was not going to lie to this boy. I could not keep from him — as once I had from my own son — news of his mother's death.

"Your mother is dead, Ulrich," I said. And I started to add "I'm sorry," but before I got those words out, he grabbed me by the coat.

"No!" he said. "No!"

I tried to hold him, but he pushed out of my embrace. "How?" His fierceness was overwhelming.

"It was an accident."

"What kind of accident?"

"Ulrich, we can do this later. The important —"

"Tell me now! What accident?"

"A gunshot."

"Because of the film? At the train?"

"Yes. At the train. Your mother destroyed the film. Agents wanted her not to. KGB agents, I think. There were weapons. There was gunfire."

Rick was backing away from me. He stumbled against a chair. Michael was at his side, trying to take his arm, but Rick shook him off. "Whose gunfire?"

"It doesn't matter."

"She died to destroy the fucking film?"

"Ulrich —"

"The Russians killed her?"

"No."

He stopped. I could see a terrible new question coming into his mind. "It was not the Russians?"

"It doesn't —"

"Then who?"

"An American MP. An accident, Ulrich."

"American?" He looked away, his glance happening to fall on Major Stahl, who had watched with horror all that followed from his callow, unthinking remark. A look of pure hatred crossed Rick's face then, and he turned and bolted from the room. Michael went after him.

As I started to follow, the German officer stopped me. I faced Major Stahl. "Can we get this thing over with? Let's get these kids out of here."

"Yes, sir," Stahl said. He gestured toward Kit, who was standing in a corner with her notebook pressed against her breast. She went by without looking at me, out into the hallway, with the major right behind. The German closed the door. When I faced Krone, he had the stunned expression of a man who had witnessed a terrible accident, yet another.

It was not until some thirteen weeks later that Walter Ulbricht, pressed by Nikita Khrushchev, ordered the overnight construction of the Berlin Wall — shutting down that refugee flow in an instant. Yet in my memory, that pivotal political event of August 13 has always come twinned with the intensely private catastrophe of May 3. Indeed, the one anticipated the other — my personal Berlin Wall, which, brick by brick, I have been dismantling here.

When the door to the room in which Krone and I were waiting was finally thrust open, it was Michael standing there with an expression of agonized dismay distorting his face. "Dad!" he said, a child again, turning to me to make it better.

I stood. "What?"

"It's Ulrich," Michael said. "Ulrich is defecting."

Such an odd word for my son to use, is the way it strikes me now, but it was very much a word of the time. There had been numerous high-profile defections from West to East — Burgess, Maclean, and Philby — that would be matched on the other side by the likes of Nureyev and Baryshnikov, not to mention a dozen political figures whose names we could never remember. The verb "defect" implied the noun "defect," and even we knew that the idea was a sign of a pervasive Cold War corruption — corruption of us all. But to this news of Rick's defection my son and I reacted the way Philby's intimates must have, or Nureyev's: this can't be so, not someone of ours, not Ulrich, not Rick.

"What do you mean?"

"The magistrate let us go. They said we can go. But Ulrich said he wants to stay. He wants to stay in East Germany. The major is in there arguing with them."

I pushed past Michael into the corridor just as Major Stahl was coming out of the hearing room. He had Katharine by the arm, and she was sobbing. Two *Vopos* accompanied them, one ahead, one behind.

"What happened?" I asked.

Major Stahl shook his head. "The Healy boy has requested asylum, formally requested political asylum. The magistrate ordered him held pending a ruling by the Ministry for State Security."

"He's an American citizen!" I said. "They can't —"

"He claims he was born in Leipzig. Is that true? Leipzig is GDR."

"Yes, it's true, but —"

"He speaks fluent German, *native* German. He *is* German. Why wasn't I told this?"

"Major, go back in there —"

"Forget it. If he's German, from Leipzig, then this is simple repatriation. There are no obstacles in any of the Four-Power Agreements to his returning to what legally counts as his native land."

"He's a minor child! He can't —"

"He's eighteen years old."

"Yes, but —"

"That's not a minor. Not here. I talked to the kid. In German. He refused to speak English. He says he is staying. I ordered him to come with me, and he said that would be *Kadavergehorsam.*"

"What the hell is that?"

"'Obedience of a corpse,'" the major said, shrugging. "He says his mind is made up."

"Do you understand what his father's position is?"

The major stared at me. "Not his father, Mr. Montgomery. The boy himself just said it in there: his father is dead. Now his mother is dead. From this point on, it will behoove us to be very clear about this particular fact: the general is not the boy's father. This boy is German. This is a German matter." The lawyer was speaking with an authority he had not displayed at first. His counterfeit callowness was completely gone. "The boy is acting freely. I saw that myself. The U.S. military has no stake in this. I am sure the general will agree."

And that was pretty much it. General Healy did whatever he did. I never knew. In fact, when we returned to West Berlin that day, I never saw him. Some days later, I requested an appointment with him in Wiesbaden, but he refused to meet me. I did not see him again for many years, and the sealing of the border guaranteed that we would not see Rick, either. I always assumed he went back to Leipzig, but who knew? If he had a change of heart about making his life in the

East once the Wall went up — when the Brandenburg Gate became the uncrossable border of what the Communists then called the "free city" — it no longer mattered. With thirty million other Germans in the East, Rick was stuck.

That day, I turned away from the major to find Michael and Katharine standing behind me. When they saw the defeat in me, the girl fell into Michael's arms, not quite knocking him off balance. She sobbed against him, and he held her. My son's depth of resolve was not news to me — he had survived the disease — but I had never imagined his strength in helping someone else. I saw him not as a boy with a girl, but as a man with a woman.

As we started to leave the building, I was on one side of Katharine, Michael on the other, each of us holding an arm. At the vestibule, I stopped her. "Kit," I said, "your notebook." It was gone.

She looked up at me. "I gave it to Ulrich. When he said he wasn't coming, I gave it to him. He said he would only borrow it."

Michael looked over at me. "We told him we would come back. We would see him again. We promised."

"And you keep your promises," I said.

"And Kit's book is a sign of it."

I put my arm around Katharine and squeezed. No one of us imagined at that moment how a wall would trump the pledge-token of a would-be writer's jottings. "That was good of you, Kit," I said.

Michael said, "I gave him my cigarettes. I wish I had something real to give him."

"But you did, Monty," I said. I guess I was fending off the air of presumption by using his chosen nickname. I stepped around Katharine to come between them, putting an arm around each one. I had come here to rescue my son, but even with this staggering outcome, I could see that he had done more rescuing than I. Yet only to a point. Rick, after all, was lost. Charlotte was dead. And the dream we'd had of ourselves was gone forever.

Given all that, it was a relief when Michael leaned into me, accepting my support as if I were one of his friends. A small thing. And didn't that prove, at last, how little he needed it?

Part Six

18

NEARLY TWO HUNDRED people were shot dead attempting to cross the Berlin Wall in the twenty-nine years that stand between us now, a year after the Wall's collapse, and the day not long after Kit and I bade Ulrich farewell, when the Wall went up. As we promised, we have returned here, with my father, and it is in the glorious context of the Wall's demise that we were drawn back into this story.

So much of that summer of 1961 was bent to the service of falsehood. In June, President Kennedy met with Khrushchev, who seemed ready for war over Berlin because of the border issue that had become so personal to us. In July, Kennedy warned Americans of the possibility of nuclear attack and advised families to build fallout shelters. What he did not tell us was that the real threat was coming from his own generals' pressing for a preemptive strike against Moscow. We came closer to nuclear war that summer, perhaps, than we would over Cuba a year later, but what we Americans didn't understand and still don't is that the nightmare would have begun, in the name of prevention, with us.

The Berlin Wall, which Kennedy and every U.S. president after him derided as a grotesque symbol of Soviet evil, was in fact what preserved the peace, which is why Kennedy did nothing to stop its erection. By ending the mass outflow of refugees from East to West, the Wall took the pressure off Berlin, and therefore Khrushchev, and therefore Kennedy. Our young president did not want to yield to his trigger-happy generals, although by August he showed every sign of preparing to do just that. The fallout shelters he wanted Americans to build were to protect against the radioactive cloud spawned by our bombs, not Moscow's. It may not be too much to say that the detested Wall saved the world.

But by sealing off its only outlet, the Wall made a vast prison of Soviet-occupied Europe. The conventional wisdom in the West was that the Wall would come down only as a consequence of ultimate war. The Soviet enemy, a reification of the intractable obstinacy of absolute tyranny, as the "totalitarian school" of U.S. Sovietologists defined it, was incapable of change from within, and would be undone only through force of arms. Moscow matched us all the way in accumulating those arms, until between us we had the power to destroy the earth a thousand times over. "Mutual assured destruction," an unironic Robert Strange McNamara called it. MAD.

And how did the madness end?

Unexpectedly, by the act of a Polish peasant nobody, an uneducated farmboy who'd made his way to the city — Gdansk — and become a shipyard electrician. When ordered back to work by an armed Communist apparatchik, he'd said simply, "No." His name was Lech Walesa, and when others quickly joined in that "no," Solidarity was born, and the stunningly nonviolent end of the most brutal regime in history was begun. The "no" ultimately of entire peoples was addressed to puppet regimes, the nomenklatura, the Politburo, the Comintern itself. Within a few years, on December 7, 1988, Mikhail Gorbachev stood before the United Nations and pledged a full withdrawal of Soviet troops from Europe, swearing to uphold "freedom of choice," as he put it, for the nations formerly known as satellites. What began on December 7 at Pearl Harbor ended on December 7 in New York.

And at last the truth of the old domino theory proved itself — but in reverse. Communism fell in Poland: in June 1989, its first free election gave every Polish senate seat save one to Solidarity. Then Hungary dismantled its barbed-wire border with Austria, a first literal breach in Churchill's Balkans-to-Trieste barrier, and then a river of East Germans, voting with their feet again, began flowing by the thousands through Hungary to the West. In October, Gorbachev came to East Berlin, and when hundreds of thousands called out to him, "Gorby, save us!" he ordered Soviet troops off the streets and out of sight. The minute the Soviet leader departed, a frenzied Erich Honecker ordered his army to shoot the demonstrators, and his army refused.

The rallies grew larger throughout East Germany, until November 9. On that night in 1989, as if to redeem the crimes of the same night in 1938, huge crowds gathered on the east side of the Wall in Berlin. East German soldiers and *Volkspolizei,* following orders, pushed the people back. But then one man scrambled up onto the narrow ledge of the Wall. The crowds fell silent as the man stood with his arms up-raised, presenting himself to be shot by the hundreds of fully armed soldiers and *Vopos.* Despite orders, not one of them fired.

The man leapt safely down into West Berlin, and the throng roared its approval. A rush of people followed him up and over, as hundreds, then thousands, then — with the *Vopos* opening gates — tens of thousands poured into West Berlin.

We Americans began at once to speak of having "won the Cold War," as President George H. W. Bush would put it in a State of the Union speech, showing how little we knew. In fact, for the first time in history an empire had dismantled itself before the watching eyes of the world, not in response to violent revolution but in response to moral vision — a vision vaguely glimpsed and then fiercely clung to not first by the various nomenklatura or politburos but by what had long been denounced as "antisocial elements." They were the empire's "unofficial" people, like the scientist Andrei Sakharov in Russia, the electrician Walesa in Poland, the playwright Václav Havel in Czechoslovakia, the musicologist Vytautas Landsbergis in Lithuania, the conductor Kurt Masur in Leipzig, a nameless legion of border soldiers who held their fire, and finally a throng in East Berlin, one of whose leaders, we soon discovered, was Ulrich von Neuhaus.

Ulrich, like Kit and me, was in his mid-forties now, in his prime as a professor of philosophy at Humboldt University. He had earned his doctorate at Leipzig, where his mother had studied. Beginning there, he would tell us, made him feel close to her.

At Humboldt, on Berlin's Unter den Linden, Ulrich had distinguished himself as an early theorist of what came to be called the

New Marxism, an intellectual complement to the slow evolving of what Alexander Dubček had called "socialism with a human face." In the mid-eighties, Ulrich was a founder of the Citizens' Committee, an East German equivalent of the Civic Forum in Czechoslovakia, an analogue of Solidarity in Poland. This democratic resistance movement implicitly, and then openly, challenged the ideological assumptions of DDR state socialism. I was not surprised when I learned of Ulrich's role: "Disobedience," I remembered him declaring, "is how I know I am not dead."

Overt challenges to the political structure were not possible until Gorbachev's influence began to be felt across the plains. Emulating Herbert Marcuse, perhaps, Ulrich emerged as a mentor of the student movement centered in Leipzig and Berlin, a movement that by 1989 had become the engine for nonviolent democratic change throughout East Germany.

From my perch as a political columnist at the *Atlanta Constitution,* I had observed most of this long before November 9. Nothing was going to keep me and Kit away from Berlin once the world knew that the Wall was breached. One advantage of marrying young was that our kids were both in their early twenties, and we could leave on a moment's notice. Kit got a colleague to cover her classes at Emory, and the *Constitution* dispatched me to join our man on the scene.

My father, flying from Manhattan, rendezvoused with us at the airport in Frankfurt, and for the obvious reason we took the train from there to Berlin. Now it was a German train, of course, with crews changing at the border — very different from the duty train Kit and I remembered. As they had once before, the sights of East Germany — rusted factories, chimneys rising from ruins, forlorn-looking livestock, dull-eyed farmers — imposed a somber air on the journey. But now the landscape evoked an interior wasteland, the place where Kit and I stopped being young. I could not begin to imagine what associations that train trip stimulated in my father. Suffice to say the three of us found ourselves sitting silently in a compartment beside two other mute passengers, staring out the window as if we were all five strangers.

It was the afternoon of November 11 when we arrived, and that date, too, underscores the difficulty throughout this story of getting

328

out from under the weight of the past — the nightmares of the dead, as Marx put it; *Vergangenheitsbewältigung,* as Germans put it. And I had thought the phrase applied only to children of the Third Reich.

Kit and I surely arrived at the Berlin *Hauptbahnhof* in a mood far different from my father's. For us the thrill of that first disembarking there, even the memory of the duplicitous Tramm, could still strike the spark of adventure that had brought us together. For Dad there could be only the image of Ulrich's mother dying on the platform, perhaps the very platform onto which we had just stepped.

We joined the exuberant crowd, aiming for the great city outside, which was still in the early throes of celebration. From all across Germany, and from elsewhere in Europe, pilgrims of the Velvet Revolution were coming to dance on the Wall — as, in a way, were we.

Our progress out onto the broad avenue was made simpler by the automatic courtesy of the crowd in making way for my wheelchair. I should explain that six years ago my left leg was amputated above the knee, because accumulated scar tissue caused clotting in its veins. My right leg is intact, but it has atrophied from the calf muscle down and probably won't be with me when I die.

The *Constitution*'s European bureau chief, Pete Raymond, was waiting for us with a van outside the station, as promised. Pete was based in Bonn, but he'd been in Berlin nonstop for weeks, and he welcomed us with the hearty ease of a man at home. Kit knew Pete from Atlanta, and liked him. When I introduced him to my father, Dad seemed distracted, too antsy to pay much attention to my friend. I began to feel a bit jittery myself — being driven in a van in Berlin again — which prompted me to ask, "Whatever happened to Herr Krone, Dad?"

"Hans died about seven years ago. Here, in a hospital. He had served with Willy Brandt, both here and in Bonn. He was much admired."

"I remember now. You went to the funeral."

We were headed for the hotel, but Pete abruptly asked, "Do you want to see the Wall?"

"Sure," I said.

Pete spoke to the driver in German. He then explained to us that Potsdamer Platz was as close as we would get to the Wall in a car at that point, such was the size of the crowds. At Potsdamer Platz, he explained, the Wall consisted of two barriers separated by a barren stretch of landscape several hundred feet wide — the death strip. As we drew within a block of it, we could see that the open space was jammed with people, milling around as if they'd just been released from prison but were unable actually to leave. Lost among them, Pete said, were the small pillboxes from which *Vopos* had, until only two days before, manned machine guns.

To the south, beyond the death strip, rose the majestic form of the Brandenburg Gate, on the top of which, in the fading light of that November afternoon, figures could be seen waving flags, generally cavorting, leaning down to haul other celebrants up to join the fun. We watched from the van for some moments, then Kit said, "Novemberfest." And she took my hand.

As we pulled away, Pete turned to face us. "Oh, by the way, I found your guy."

Kit jumped. "Ulrich?"

"Ulrich von Neuhaus?" I said.

"Never heard of the 'von' except from you," Pete said. "But there's an Ulrich Neuhaus, a professor named Ulrich Neuhaus."

Kit said, "Of course. 'Von' and socialism, Michael? Rick would have dropped the 'von.'" She said this with an old edge, a sudden reminder of the structure of our past. Reminders like this I had spent years deflecting.

"If it's the same guy," Pete was saying, "he spoke at the rally last night. He's a kind of Havel here. So far, anyway. His speech was a litany of tributes to other people. 'The secret heroes,' he called them — no longer secret. It was very moving. The 'Wall dancers' love Neuhaus."

"How did he look?" Kit asked. "What's he like?"

"You talked to him?" I asked.

"Yes. After the rally, for a couple of minutes. He didn't want to be interviewed. Not by me, anyway. If you can get an interview with him, you'll scoop the *Times*. I told him you were coming. He said to tell you he wants to see you."

"How do we arrange it?"

"I know one of his associates on the Citizens' Committee, and Neuhaus told me to call him. You tell me."

"Right away," Kit said. "We want to see him right away."

"Well, propose something," Pete said.

Before I could answer, my father said, "Tonight. Tell him tonight."

"There's another rally," Pete said. "Speeches, fireworks, rock music, vodka, dope. That gets cooking at nine or ten. He may have —"

"Tell him eight, then," my father said. His urgency surprised me. "We'll stand by at the hotel at eight. Will he have a problem crossing over?"

Pete laughed. "No, Mr. Montgomery. That's the point."

Kit had wrapped my hand with hers, squeezing my fingers together. Now she let out a long, slow breath, as if she had postponed exhalation for nearly thirty years. Ulrich was good. That was the relief. Ulrich was good.

Soon we were at the Kempinski, on the Ku'damm, still the city's best hotel. When I had first proposed staying there, on the phone to my father, his silence was so long and so complete that I thought the line had gone dead. Finally he'd said, "Yes. Good idea."

At the desk, as we checked in, Pete went off to find his contact and pass along our message. I had no idea if it would get to Ulrich, or when, or what would happen then. As I tried to imagine what was coming, a vast weariness overtook me. The sudden crushing fatigue was the one thing about my condition that I still hated.

Kit and I had a room on the fourth floor. For my father, I had booked a suite on the top floor, a standard of luxury he'd not have insisted upon but would take for granted.

As the elevator door opened, Kit rolled me over the bump of the threshold and, with a practiced swivel, turned my chair back toward my father. Standing in the elevator car alone, he seemed framed by the box of it. Seventy years old, but he'd retained his fine posture and trim figure. Though careful as ever of his appearance — well-cut blue suit, handkerchief folded just so, silk tie knotted to ride precisely in the notch of his Oxford button-down — the impression he created seemed as unselfconscious as ever. So entirely American. So fully in possession of himself.

But it was not true. He should have had less at stake in the possible reunion with Ulrich than either Kit or me, yet in the hours of our journey from Frankfurt, he had conveyed in subtle ways the depth of his anticipation and anxiety, and in the van he had all but declared it, as if what had happened on that May Day nearly three decades ago had been as much an interruption in the flow of his life as ours. Over the years, we had hardly spoken of it, and in truth he and I had grown apart. By now I had no idea what the events of that weekend meant to him. Ever the successful banker, yet he had lived a lonely, disappointed life, and being in his presence always made me sad.

"Will you be able to sleep, Dad?"

"A quick snooze," he said, winking. "What your generation calls transcendental meditation."

Our generation. Have two generations ever been more aware of each other *as* generations? Differences, disappointments, defeats. These years had sealed the distance between us. Social history and personal history — it amounted to the same thing. The sight of my father framed in the elevator made me wonder, not for the first time, what had happened to him.

"So we'll see you at quarter to eight," I said.

At ten past eight there was a knock on the door, and with a push of one wheel I swung my chair around. My father left his couch and started for the door, but Kit fairly ran there. She wore a flowing navy skirt and a white blouse that set off her long neck and head of gray-flecked short hair. She was one of those rare women who, pretty in youth, age into beauty, yet I knew she worried that Ulrich would think her old. Still, whatever of worry was in her had been overtaken by joy. She hopped slightly, an unconscious dance step, as she turned the doorknob. Her free hand went to her mouth as the door opened.

All these years, we had pictured Ulrich with that beard and long hair, our first hippie, and she no more than I could have anticipated the clean-shaven, lean-jawed, balding middle-aged man standing in the threshold. "The Most Unforgettable Character I've Met": the old *Reader's Digest* phrase popped into my mind, and I thought, Yes, still.

He wore a shapeless dark corduroy suit, a white shirt, and a black tie. He had a tan, which seemed odd. But with dark circles under his hollow eyes, he looked anything but rested. About the only thing that fit him for the role of heroic resisting professor were his wire-rim spectacles. More Lennon than Lenin, I thought. I remembered Ulrich's quip of years before: More Groucho than Karl.

When Kit threw herself on him, Ulrich was clearly ready for her, returning her embrace with every ounce of feeling she put into it. They held each other for a long time. When at last they pulled back to look at one another, Ulrich said, "*Du bist sehr schön, Kit. Immer noch.*"

Kit fell back against him, and I knew how relieved she was, not at the compliment, but at his use of *du*. It would have crushed her if he'd said *Sie*.

Ulrich looked across Kit's head to us, first to me, then to my father, who now stood next to me. I sensed each small quake in Ulrich as he took in how time had touched us — my wheelchair, my father's age. Kit released Ulrich and led him into the room by the hand. He leaned down to me and hugged me so gracefully it seemed impossible he didn't do it every day. Then he shook my father's hand with warmth and firmness. "You are *all* beautiful," he said, and broke into a broad smile. I heard a hint of his British accent, from his school days in England. Looking more closely at him, I realized that his elegant leanness was actually a shocking gauntness, and that the tan of his complexion was in fact the tinged pallor of illness.

My father offered drinks, and everyone sat. In this well-appointed room in prosperous West Berlin, it was inconceivable that only yesterday this spot had been on the very edge of the earth's abyss. And why shouldn't our conversation have begun slowly, with disjointed half-sentences, awkward laughs, unfinished thoughts? Ulrich had a bad cough, which cut into everything he tried to say.

We were on an edge of time's abyss, too. How much time Kit, Ulrich, and I had lost — that was the feeling as we each tossed up jagged memories of H. H. Arnold High School, as if only that could anchor our time together now. But, for all our reminiscences, we could not capture the essence of what we'd been and been through, a failure caught by Kit when she cracked, "Nostalgia — it's not what it used to be."

I turned the conversation to the Wall. Ulrich summarized the exhilarating events in Berlin over the past weeks, "our return from the cave of shadows," he called it. That remark led to talk about his own career, and he settled into the self-effacing mode of a man telling a story he finds less than interesting. He had published work on Plato's critique of tyranny in *The Republic,* which, he said, the dull-witted despots of "free Berlin" had regarded as harmless because the subject predated the glorious revolution. But in lecture halls, he said with a smile, he brought Plato up to date.

After a century of intellectual passivity in the face of the various totalitarianisms, he said, there had come the great Solzhenitsyn, whose challenge to the right and left both had lodged like a virus in the minds of the young. "I have been racing to stay even with the ones I have been teaching," he said. A modest statement, yet I could see through it, because I recalled the thrill it had been to listen to him think out loud — Marcuse, Sartre, Camus. When had ideas ever been more exciting to me?

Still speaking of his students, he added, "And we made each other pregnant." Ulrich smiled at this metaphorical jump from virus to seed. He looked at Kit. "In a world of ugliness, we have been waiting to beget what is beautiful, and now we have."

Kit nodded. "And literally? Do you have your own children?"

"Yes. A son. Isaiah. He is three. He is Jewish, like his mother. I, too, am Jewish."

That statement brought a moment's hesitation, then Kit moved on to tell of our children. It fell to me to explain how Kit and I had stayed in touch through college, finding it impossible to let go of each other and of what we had been through together — with him.

At one point, Ulrich reached into his coat and pulled out a pack of cigarettes, coughing as he did so. "With permission?" he said. As my father went to find an ashtray, Ulrich offered his pack to me and Kit. When we declined, we all laughed. "In the East," he said, lighting up, "lung cancer is the last thing we worry about." The shock of his statement was in its revelation: he himself had the disease.

Ulrich turned to me with a nod at my chair. "And you, Monty?"

No one had called me that in years, and it brought me right back to what I had found irresistible in him. Also, I welcomed the deflection from the subject of his own illness. I recited the short-form saga of my amputation. I remembered that he was the first friend I ever had for whom the polio had registered as something other than the primary fact of my existence. And was that how he felt now about his cancer?

As often happened, the discussion of my infirmity led to an interlude of silence. In that silence I became aware that so far my father had said almost nothing. Ulrich shifted in his seat, just enough to draw him in.

And what my father said was "We came to Berlin today by train."

Ulrich waited.

"And it put me very much in mind of your mother. I have never forgotten her, Ulrich."

Ulrich nodded, sensing, perhaps, as Kit and I did, what an understatement that was.

"And I think she would have wanted me to tell you something." My father leaned forward, his forearms falling onto his knees. "Does the name von Siedelheim mean anything to you?"

"No," Ulrich said.

My father sat back. "Then there is something I want to explain. It has to do with what happened to your mother."

"I know what happened to my mother."

"Perhaps not everything, Ulrich. I thought I knew, too. But I did not. Not until several years ago. In the fall of 1983, I received a phone call at my office in New York from a woman who said she was calling from the hospital at Andrews Air Force Base in Maryland, just outside of Washington. She told me to come. General Healy, by then long retired, was dying. He died of lung cancer."

My father stopped. The words hung in the air. Lung cancer. I had not heard my father speak of this telephone call, and I sensed, from exchanging a look with Kit, that neither had she. We waited for him to resume.

Finally, he did. "General Healy wanted to speak to me, the woman said. So, just before he died, I went to see him."

"You *saw* General Healy?" I asked.

My father glanced at me, but his business here was with Ulrich. "And the first thing the general said was that someday I might find it possible to talk to you, and he wanted you to know —" My father stopped, visibly having to deflect an inrush of emotion. Then he went on, "General Healy told me this only because he hoped that someday I could tell you."

Ulrich exchanged glances with Kit, then me. Each of us conveyed that this was stunning, astonishing news. I knew my father, I thought, and I didn't know this?

Ulrich said, "Tell me what, Mr. Montgomery?"

My father leaned forward. "In 1945, Wolf von Siedelheim was a Wehrmacht major in command of Moabit prison, on Lehrter Strasse here in Berlin."

"I know Lehrter Strasse," Ulrich said. "I have heard of the prison."

"Then you know it is long gone," my father said, and with a firm but neutral voice, he recited a narrative as if he had rehearsed it. "Moabit was where the Nazis kept political prisoners, which meant mainly Communists, KPD. On the first of May 1945, with the Russians closing in on the city, and with the Nazi high command having collapsed, Major von Siedelheim had to decide on his own authority what to do with his prisoners. There were thirty-one of them. He could have opened the doors and let everyone walk away, but he did not. He ordered them executed, each one shot in the nape of the neck, which was how the Nazis put Communists to death — each enemy group its signature execution."

I felt as if I were hearing the voice-over of a Cold War documentary. How to square what was being said with the solemn narrator's being my father?

"One man survived," he was saying. "A man named Friedrich Sohlmann. His bullet went through his neck and jawbone, but it did not kill him. Pretending to be dead, lying on the ground of the prison courtyard, he witnessed the massacre. I say massacre, because it wasn't just KPD members who were killed. Apparently von Siedelheim was a man devoted to the exact fulfillment of procedure, and by that late in the war, Nazi policies aimed at rooting out Communist traitors included the so-called *V und V* tradition. Do you know that?"

"No."

"Forgive my German — something like '*Verhältnis und Verwandten.*'"

"What, 'relatives and family'?"

"'Kith and kin,' we say in English. It meant that not only KPD members were to be executed; their families were too. It was a function of brutal Nazi enforcement, but also, apparently, an extension of the Nazi racial myth, the belief that evil had biological sources. Eliminate the evil by eliminating the biological strain — the families of the undesirables. Von Siedelheim, left in charge of his Communist prisoners and the family members in his custody, carried out the 'kith and kin' executions. *V und V.* Perhaps he was an SS fanatic. Perhaps he was only an order-following martinet . . ."

Kadavergehorsam, I thought.

"But he did it. One hundred and twenty-seven relatives of the already executed thirty-one — their wives, children, siblings, parents — were murdered on the same day. These relatives were kept in a large converted warehouse adjoining the prison. They were herded into the courtyard, where already corpses were piled. They were forced into the back of a large truck, which was then shut tight, and the truck's own exhaust was piped into it. They were gassed."

My father's voice had become devoid of affect, except for the way he paused now and then, as if unable to remember what words to use.

"Among those killed in this way," he said, "were Sohlmann's wife and two small children." Another pause.

"Once the Russians took over Berlin, von Siedelheim was captured. He was quickly tried by a Soviet military tribunal — one of the show trials, to make the political point. Sohlmann testified against him. Von Siedelheim was found guilty and executed by firing squad. But that was not enough for Sohlmann. Not nearly enough.

"He swore his own 'kith and kin' revenge. As a KPD leader who had survived in resistance, he immediately became an East German hero and a man with power. He was a founder of what would become the Stasi. He recovered from his wounds, but was apparently terribly disfigured. As soon as he could, with a small, trusted group of henchmen, he launched a search for von Siedelheim's kith and kin. The von Siedelheims were a prominent Leipzig family who mostly had little knowledge of the major's wartime function. They were taken by surprise, his father and mother first. Sohlmann's personal death squad, established as a Stasi unit, systematically tracked them down. Seventeen family members were murdered in Leipzig, Berlin, even in Brussels, between 1946 and 1950 — all with a bullet to the neck. Relatives who escaped Sohlmann's campaign went into hiding. One of them, fleeing Leipzig, was your mother, who knew nothing of what her husband had become during the war, or what he had done."

"Her husband?"

"Your father."

Ulrich had moved forward in his chair, was leaning most of the way out of it. Now, like an air toy deflating, he sat back. His eyes never left my father. He said quietly, "Continue, please."

"Your mother brought you here when the danger in Leipzig became apparent. Von Siedelheim's sister had been shot dead in front of her, and Charlotte narrowly escaped with you. For obvious reasons, she and you were at the top of Sohlmann's list. Your mother went into hiding, first in the mass of displaced refugees, and then here, as a rubble woman. She was determined to find out why von Siedelheims were being murdered, and it was General Healy — Colonel Healy — who helped her. He learned from Soviet files about the Moabit prison, and eventually he discovered what Sohlmann was doing.

"Colonel Healy went secretly to Leipzig, burglarized the *Rathaus,* and destroyed the records of your parents' marriage. He also wanted to destroy any record of your birth, but that, it appeared, had already been taken. He went to the church where you were christened and destroyed the baptismal records. But your missing birth certificate gnawed at him.

"With Healy's help, your mother invented a new past — the story you were brought into. That she had been raped, a wartime victim; that your biological father was someone she never knew — a shameful past, but not as shameful as the truth. Healy married your mother and adopted you to seal your new identities. He brought milk to you, she told me once, and I think this is what she meant: he gave you a way to live when she, by herself, could not.

"It was clear to me, Rick, when the old general was telling me this, how very much he loved your mother. And he told me that he always knew she married him because of the protection he offered, not because of love. Which was enough for him. And I was able to tell him what she had said once, a line of Dostoyevsky's — that love, compared to fantasy . . ." My father had to stop here, overcome by feeling.

338

Then he continued, ". . . can be harsh, dreadful, while being love nonetheless.

"All of this might have been safely in the past, but then, even before you, Michael, and Kit chose to go to Berlin that day in 1961, something happened to make it all terribly, dangerously fresh. On April 26, early in the week of that May Day, a man named Markus von Siedelheim was shot in the back of the neck in Frankfurt. As it happened, I was there, a meeting of bankers and financiers and government ministers. This von Siedelheim, having left Germany in 1947, had made a career in Third World development, based in Liberia. People assumed that he had fled a Nazi past. This meeting was his first high-profile return to Germany. By then Sohlmann was director of *Arbeitsgruppe Aüslander*. Did I say that right? I gather he was in charge of running spies in Bonn, but his personal 'kith and kin' vendetta remained unfinished. That day it resumed, as I saw with my own eyes, although not understanding at all.

"When this von Siedelheim was murdered in that particular way in Frankfurt, General Healy realized that he himself had grown careless, especially in allowing you to come back from England. You were in the gravest danger because you were the son of Sohlmann's nemesis — the heart of 'kith and kin' revenge. And yours was the one set of records Healy had never succeeded in destroying. By killing Markus von Siedelheim, even in 1961, Sohlmann was saying he still wanted you dead."

As I listened to this narrative, watching a stunned Ulrich take it in, I had to fend off a disorienting sense of unreality. My investment banker father, always the most fastidious of men, now elderly, rheumy-eyed with age — how could he be recounting such a melodrama of moral anarchy? And how could I myself, and Kit, have once stumbled onto the stage where it played out? *Don't be the thing that brings a hair-triggered weapon out of its holster.* The MP's words had come back to me again and again, in guilt. But how little I knew, thinking the hair trigger had only been that soldier's. Now I was learning that the trigger was Ulrich's own life.

"And so the day after the murder in Frankfurt," my father was saying, "General Healy sent his agents into East Berlin — one of them was Colonel Cummings. The run-up to the border crisis of that summer became, in effect, Healy's cover. Only Cummings knew what the real mission was, a mission for you. Cummings and his accomplices, including one Stasi double agent, entered Schloss Pankow at night. They broke into Sohlmann's office and, as expected, found him sleeping there, as he often did. The agents did three things, acting on Healy's orders. They killed Sohlmann, suffocating him. They rifled a particular Stasi file, the Bonn spy network. And, acting apart, Cummings found Sohlmann's personal file, the von Siedelheim file, which amounted to an elaborate family tree, with careful notations indicating almost all the members were dead. The file included prewar pictures of your mother, and your missing birth documents. While Healy's other agents photographed the Bonn spy file, Cummings took film of the von Siedelheim material expressly to bring to Healy, so that he would see that Sohlmann's 'kith and kin' records had been destroyed. After photographing it, Cummings used that file to start a fire — the fire that gutted Sohlmann's office, which we could still taste in the air the day you were brought there.

"Sohlmann was made to appear to have been drunk, but no one was going to take the fire as an accident. Healy wanted Stasi and the KGB to see the burglary and murder as a mere espionage operation ahead of the border sealing, and it worked. Sohlmann was dead, but it wasn't certain that his 'kith and kin' vendetta would die with him, which was why destroying the last link between you and von Siedelheim was still important. That was the film, which your stepfather had not had a chance to develop, view, and burn before you took it.

"Stasi and the KGB thought the film was something else — the usual espionage — but your mother knew it concerned only you, the last link. Destroying it was all she cared about at the end, and your stepfather was her partner in that. Neither of them gave a damn about national security, which was one of many things I misunderstood. I saw all of this in pieces at the time, but I never put it together. Because my German is nil, I misread the tablet at Schloss Pankow that identified von Siedelheim as the Nazi murderer. I thought he was listed as one of the martyrs. After General Healy told me all of this, I had Hans Krone check that tablet, and it even included the phrase *Verhältnis und Verwandten,* but I had missed that, too."

Ulrich's lips were pressed into a tight line. His hands were clasped, a shelf below his chin, his knuckles white. His eyes were sunk even further into the dark caves of their sockets. He looked very tired, and his formerly sure voice, but for that cough, was weak now as he asked, "This was my father?"

"Your father, as Charlotte told me once, was destroyed by the war — morally, then physically. He began as a brilliant philosophy professor at Leipzig, where she knew him. They married as he was shipping out. They conceived you when he was home on leave, which I believe was in 1942. She never saw him again. A lot of things changed for the worse after 1942, Rick."

"Everything."

My father fell silent, eased back into his chair. He reached for his scotch, swirled the ice, took a hefty swallow.

"When General Healy told you all of this —"

My father interrupted. "General Healy told me one last thing. He wanted me to say to you that you were his only son. And he loved you. 'Always loved Rick. Always' were his words."

Ulrich said, "I misjudged him."

"So did I," my father said.

"And my mother?"

"She knew his goodness. She —" My father brought the fingers of his left hand to his brow, where they trembled slightly. He closed his eyes. A man of my generation would, I know, have wept. Indeed, instead of tears overflowing my father's eyes, they overflowed mine. Now I understood what had happened to him. Recovering from the death of my mother with Ulrich's, he had never recovered, then, from the death of Charlotte Healy. I had never seen this in him, which made me realize I had never seen anything that mattered.

The day after our meeting at the Kempinski, Kit, my father, and I went to Ulrich's flat in a sprawling university housing complex on the far edge of East Berlin. Humboldt had been a center of Weimar intellectual ferment, and for all I knew, it had recovered that status under communism. But all of the university buildings there had the lumpish impersonality of postwar Socialist style. That section of the city had been leveled by the war, and not much thought or money had gone into the reconstruction. So Humboldt housing hardly impressed the eye. Or was the gray monotony the point? Was the shoddiness an assertion of Socialist principle?

Ulrich's apartment was in a barracks-like building three stories high, but luckily for me it was on the first level — an easy lift of me and my wheelchair. We met Ulrich's wife, Naomi, a plain woman who he said was ten years younger than we were. But if anything, she looked older. She, too, was on the faculty at Humboldt, a professor of mathematics. She served us tea and cake that she had baked herself, but she was otherwise at a loss. She spoke English, but had little to say. She seemed afraid.

Ulrich opened a bottle of vodka, and there was something greedy in the way he threw down his first glass. He lit one cigarette after another, between coughs. He and his wife looked like casualties of a long and terrible war. Fighting its battles had clearly wounded him, and not even the thrill of victory was going to reverse that.

But then we met Isaiah, a bright three-year-old who woke up from a nap with a raucous, happy cry. As Naomi brought him in from the bedroom and handed him over to a delighted Ulrich, Isaiah seemed the one source of uncomplicated joy in their lives. When Ulrich called him one of his *Edelweisspiraten,* Kit and I laughed out loud.

We were leaving the flat when, apparently as an afterthought, standing by the door, Ulrich addressed my father. "My mother," he said.

"Yes."

"Where is she buried?"

"Wiesbaden. The Russian Chapel."

Ulrich took this in with an almost imperceptible nod. A moment passed, and then another. He did not move. He was still holding his son in his arms, as if drawing strength from the child. Charlotte's absence appeared to overcome Ulrich all at once, and he seemed paralyzed by grief. My father must have read this in him, too, because he said, "What happened to your mother, Ulrich — it was not your fault."

Ulrich turned away to stare at the flaking doorjamb.

"If I had not —"

He stopped, but in my mind I finished the thought: If we had not caused that weapon to come out of its holster.

My father touched his arm. "You did what you did, Ulrich. So did I. But Charlotte showed me how to honor what *she* did."

"Then why have you not recovered from it?" Ulrich asked.

"From the grief, the guilt — long recovered. My love for her is what remains with me. And I know it always will."

"Did you speak of that to General Healy?"

"Yes. It was what we had in common, as he already knew."

"And his burial place?"

"Arlington."

And then, adjusting his son in his arms and bringing himself to his full height, like a man about to scale a wall, Ulrich said, "I will bring my boy to Wiesbaden, but someday you could perhaps bring him to Arlington? To explain about David Healy? To explain about all these things?"

"I will take you *all* to Arlington," my father said.

Ulrich shook his head. "I will not be going to America."

We heard the finality of that simple statement. There was too little time.

"I am thinking of my son," Ulrich said, addressing us all. "How the past we give our children can be such a burden, but perhaps should not be. I wish that my son could know more of me. What I come from, who I come from — the things I myself can make known to him only indirectly." Ulrich looked at me. "Such knowledge is what we sons all want, no?"

And I realized that, knowing too little of what my father had been through here, I also had a stake in learning of this past. Kit took my hand and said, "And daughters also."

And then, perhaps showing the effect of the vodka, Ulrich made a spontaneous, outlandish request of us. "Would you put our story down on paper? Our May Day story. So that Isaiah will have it." His eyes were wet. There was no question of his referring to his illness, but we knew that was what he was speaking of. Yet another son growing up without a father. Here was the grief in Ulrich's life. "My son must have the story of his father from you." Now Ulrich turned directly to my father. "All of it," he said. "Including my mother's story, Mr. Montgomery, as you came to know it."

"Her story became my story, Rick." When Ulrich said nothing in reply, my father nodded. "I would be honored to do that, to try."

I, too, agreed to try to write something, realizing already how my need was as tied to this as Ulrich's.

Kit said, "I'm a professor of English, Rick. Other people's writing, not mine." She smiled. "'To have great poets, there must be great audiences, too.' That's me. I'll be Michael's first reader."

"You once wrote a story."

"Everyone writes stories before the age of twenty."

Ulrich held his hand up. "Wait a moment." He gave Naomi the child, then went quickly back into the apartment. He returned carrying a small green clothbound book. He held it before Kit. *Accounts.*

"Did Faulkner take you on?" he asked. "What did you call it, what you were going to be?"

"His page." She laughed that small, self-deprecating laugh of hers, even as her eyes filled at the sight of the old book. "Yes, he did."

"A man of genius, how could he not?" Now, formally, Ulrich held Kit's book out to her. "Actually, you have already written the account I needed. This work of yours sustained me. It made me know that our friendship was not a dream, that where there is such a past, there is a future."

Rick handed Kit's book to her, and all at once she gasped aloud and fell against him, racked with sobbing. Rick's arms went around her easily. His face went down to hers. Their intimacy was total, and private.

As I had seen the evening before, my father's deepest love, his deepest wound, was unknown to me, and now I saw that my wife's heart had belonged all these years to this other man. She had married me to keep this feeling — her one love — alive. That I loved Rick too did nothing to soften the blow of recognition. I had to look away.